The Touch of Her Voice

Sara Scott

ISBN: 979-8-9858536-0-5

Cover design and book layout by: BLCgraphics.com
Photo licensed from Shutterstock.com
Printed in the United States of America

Acknowledgments

No list of acknowledgments could begin without a nod to the junior and senior high school teachers who nurtured my writer's soul — a soul that laid dormant until it came roaring to life three years ago with a plot that I couldn't NOT write.

To Bonnie C., thank you for your creativity and technical skills. It was a joy to collaborate with you. Sherri H., thank you for agreeing to edit your former teacher's book. Your suggestions were always worthwhile and on point. But most of all, thank you for telling me in your professional opinion, that my book not only could be published, but that it *should* be published.

To Zoe S., thank you for going through several drafts of the book, not only scouting for spelling errors and grammatical mistakes, but also highlighting the sentences you thought were "WOW" worthy. You are a champion.

And to Donna D., Gale D., Nancy T., Shannon A., Joan A., Stella G., Marty M., and Tammy S. — my "readers." Your opinions, insights and suggestions were always taken to heart, and more often than not implemented in a heartbeat. Thank you for accompanying me on my journey of a lifetime.

The Touch of
Her Voice

Prologue

I was done being elbowed, pushed, slapped at, and stomped on. When the final buzzer sounded for my last game at State, it could just as easily have been the starting buzzer to a new chapter in my life.

Sure, I'd miss the camaraderie and irreverent chatter of my teammates: the complaints about long, hard practices and the elation over hard-won victories. I'd dearly miss the thrill of playing the game I had loved all my life. But I was a graduating senior and now had a new path, on which graduate school would substitute for basketball.

A graduate degree would add another chapter to my accomplishments: an undergraduate degree and a university basketball career. My life had been filled with successful chapters — except when it came to romantic relationships.

During my undergraduate years I had often found dates in the hangers-on who stood outside the arena after my games. There were numerous dates but few with staying power. Most of the blame rested squarely on me and the unrequited love I harbored for my high school basketball coach, Lisa Fitzhugh. My feelings for Fitz had turned me upside down and changed the course of my relationships in the years that had followed her exit from my life. My heart was so filled with her, there wasn't room for anyone else. Even when I entered into other relationships, the torch I carried for

Fitz was the major contributor to their demise.

My passion for Fitz had burned so hot, I didn't believe I could ever love that deeply again. My junior year in high school I impulsively told Fitz I loved her, then initiated a kiss whose passion, I was certain, she had returned. I had been so obsessed with her that I couldn't think of anything or anyone else. Unable to leave things alone, I continued to pressure her, but Fitz never admitted to sharing my feelings. When she hurriedly left Tolliver after the end of my junior year, I was grief-stricken. I doggedly clung to that unrequited love, whose embers could be stirred to a flaming intensity that left me both breathless and heartbroken.

My first post-Fitz relationship was my sophomore year at State. Karen was a graduate student, hired to tutor some of my teammates. She was kind, soft spoken, and listened to my ramblings about Fitz. Despite that we eventually began to date, and at the end of the season I moved in with her. But my obsession with Fitz and my constant references to her took a toll.

That summer, Karen told me I needed to leave. "You're a good person, Jensy, and I know I love you more than I should," she told me tearfully, "but there are three of us in this relationship. And I don't want to share you."

I felt guilty, sorry, and flooded with failure, but I understood. It wasn't fair to Karen, who deserved so much better than what she got from me.

Not long after that, I met the wild, brash and brazen Tracy. For my part, I was hurting and on the rebound from both Fitz and Karen. Without giving the situation much thought, I moved in with Tracy. We partied and drank. It was during those maudlin drunks that I blubbered endlessly about Fitz. Heated arguments ensued; about Fitz — about me — about Tracy. The first time we ended it, I was the one who left.

The second time I went back to her I knew Tracy wasn't the right one, though she seemed better than nothing. But it was the same pattern as the first time, and I returned home one day to find Tracy piling my few belongings on the front sidewalk. "Take your things and go," she told me, her tone snide and disparaging. "And take Fitz with you."

I promised myself I would never mention Fitz's name in any future relationships. I took those memories and locked them in a far corner of my mind. In place of romance, I turned to graduate school and focused on pursuing a master's degree in school guidance counseling. I was excited about my new adventure; comfortable being on my own.

Then, suddenly, there was Sophie.

Part One

One

Don't look now, but there's a young woman who's been watching you ever since we sat down." Jane Corman glanced over my left shoulder, and I instinctively twisted my neck to take a peek.

"I said, *don't* look," she hissed, and I obediently swung back. "I'll tell you when. She has short, dark hair. She's pretty."

"How do you know she's looking at me?"

Jane and I were sharing a table at the Ground Up coffee shop, where we were working on a project for our "Strategies in School-Based Counseling" class. A tall, large-boned woman in her mid-thirties, with wild, flaming red hair and an infectious laugh, Jane raised her eyebrows and snorted a laugh. "Well, she's certainly not looking at me."

Jane looked away from the woman and rubbed her eyes.

"Are you okay?" I asked.

She sighed loudly. "Just tired … too much school, too much motherhood … too little time … I —" she glanced over my shoulder again.

"Jane?"

"NOW!"

I turned my head and immediately zeroed in on a dark-haired young woman seated on the other side of the coffee shop. She was conversing with a young man, tapping her finger on a book that lay open between them. As soon as she glanced my way, I turned back to Jane.

"The one with the blue scarf?"

"Is there any other dark-haired, pretty woman in that area?" Jane demanded.

"She's not pretty —" I began, but Jane cut me off.

"She most certainly is."

"— she's stunning," I finished. "Do you think she's a ... I mean ..."

"A lesbian?" Jane asked. "Jensy, just say it."

"But she's sitting with a guy."

Jane rolled her eyes. "You're a lesbian, and you're sitting with me."

"True." I didn't want to get my hopes up. I quickly reminded myself how satisfied I was with my life as a graduate student. *I am not interested,* I chided myself.

I turned again and caught the young woman staring at me. She ducked her head, then slowly raised her eyes to mine. Her eyes focused on me and left me lightheaded. Their lure was more powerful than a magnet. I burned hot and cold at the same time and drummed my fingers on the tabletop to stop the pinpricks and tingles. My heart skipped erratically and the pulse in my throat beat so wildly, I wondered if she could see it from where she sat. Across the room, I could see color creep up her throat and burst into flame across her cheeks. Embarrassed to be caught looking, she glanced away.

"You're right. She *is* looking at me."

I shoved back my chair, its legs scraping loudly along the concrete floor.

Jane arched her eyebrows in startled surprise. "Where are you going?"

"To introduce myself." I had no choice. Pushed by my desire — pulled by her magnetism — I had to meet her.

I lurched erect and gave myself a five second inspection in the window's reflection, while I watched her watch me. My tousled, short, sandy brown hair was a bit too long over my ears. I quickly finger combed unruly strands out of my blue eyes and away from my face. I should have cut it last week.

I cringed at my thin, old T-shirt; topped by an even older flannel shirt. The threadbare jeans that covered my lanky frame made me flinch. I wished for a brief second that I cared more about my appearance. Too late ... a slight shrug ... I was who I was.

I was a sought-after basketball jock who didn't need to approach women. The tingling limbs, the pounding heart, and the magnetic pull were new feelings for me. I wanted to meet her. No, I *needed* to meet her. I was *going* to meet her. Now. Today. Right this minute.

The world had changed to shades of grey as I squared my shoulders and turned around. The woman with the short, dark hair and the blue scarf was the only source of color in the coffee shop. Never taking my eyes off her, I seemed to glide above the floor until I stood beside her table. Start to finish, her eyes didn't leave mine. Those amazingly large, blue-grey eyes held me spellbound with a current so intense I believed I could see it. Her smile revealed a dimple on her left cheek. Her short, dark hair was perfectly in place, shiny and full. She had been stunning from across the room; up close, she dazzled.

My mind and body were out of sync, each acting of its own accord. My legs were jelly, and my mind couldn't formulate a rational thought. The only thing that ran through my mind was *"Now what?"* I watched in amazement as my hand moved and extended itself to her.

"Jensy Willett," I rasped.

"I know." Her voice was soft and low — musical.

The electricity when she took my hand was so intense my stomach dropped to my knees. Current rushed through me and the hairs on my arm stood on end. My skin was hot. Sweat gathered under my arms. Our hands were locked together; I couldn't let go. The moment was so charged I grabbed the edge of the table with my free hand to keep my shaking legs from buckling. The young man looked back and forth between us and quickly began to pack up his books. Still, I held her hand.

"Nice job on the mock trial today. We'll finish this later." He indicated the papers scattered on the table. "Call me."

I reluctantly pulled my hand away and sank onto his vacated chair.

"Do I know you from somewhere?" I found my voice and the words rushed out, though I already knew the answer. I would have remembered. I could not have forgotten those eyes, that smile, the slender fingers ... any of it ... all of it.

"No." She shook her head. "I know *you*. From basketball."

"Really? You're kidding." I looked at her in surprise. She was not the typical women's basketball fan I saw in the stands or waiting outside the arena. I couldn't imagine those fans dressed the way she was dressed: A black blazer covered her collarless white blouse and opened to reveal a pearl necklace resting just below the hollow of her throat.

"Last winter, a friend of mine had an extra ticket and asked me if I wanted to go. It was that dreary time of winter and I'd never seen a game. So, I said sure." She lifted her shoulders in a slight shrug. "I ended up going to the rest of the home games."

"And you either decided basketball was a great sport, or that women's sweaty, athletic bodies were appealing." My unthinking, flippant remarks had served me well in the past; but this flippant remark with its added element of sexual joust made me want to stuff the words right back into my mouth. I had embarrassed myself in front of this woman who already seemed so out of my league.

Though color rose again and covered her throat and cheeks,

she surprised me and jousted back.

"Just one sweaty female body." Her soft-spoken words, so matter of fact, caused me to blush furiously. The electricity, the innuendos, the physical attraction were intense. I'd never met anyone like this. Never. Not even Fitz. *What's happening?* I asked myself as my heart raced.

Jane Cameron approached, dropped my backpack onto a vacant chair, and broke the tension. "I'm Jensy's study-buddy. On my way home to my husband and two-year-old son." But Jane remained where she was and didn't make any effort to move.

"And I'm a would-be lawyer who very much enjoyed watching Jensy's sweaty body play basketball." The woman's eyes sparkled mischievously. I was flustered, embarrassed, and impressed by her boldness. I was more than willing to hear her say more.

"An excellent start," Jane acknowledged, and turned her gaze to me. "Jensy, I'll see you in class next week." A pause. "I hope." With a quick wave and a knowing smile, she headed out the door.

My fingers lightly tapped a restless staccato on the table, much the same way they had done before a big game when I feared I might be outmatched: Anxious to get started, but afraid to be blown off the court. I stole a quick glance at the flawless young woman and wondered why I was sitting there. I couldn't imagine why she seemed interested in me.

She looked away — rubbing her thumb repeatedly over her folded hands, and I realized she was nervous, too.

"There were other things I admired: how hard you played, your leadership, the respectful way you treated everyone ..." Her voice faded but the look on her face was almost ... contrite. Her attempt to undo what she had said before.

She sighed. "I apologize. I was too forward about watching you play. I shouldn't have been so blunt."

"Don't apologize. You can say whatever you want — about anything." I finished lamely. I shivered with the knowledge of how she had studied the way I played. My nerves fluttered like anxious butterflies trapped inside my chest. I was off-kilter and out-of-sync. I gulped in a lungful of air to help me calm down.

The conversation lapsed into silence. The jitters had dried up my normal pool of repartee. I was tongue-tied and my thoughts were muddled. Not knowing where to begin, I searched for words. I wanted to impress her, to show her I belonged in her sphere. I was afraid I had done neither. I searched for possible topics of conversation, as empty space stretched between us.

She looked at her watch, sighed, and began to put books and papers into her backpack. "It's late and I should be going. I have a lot of work to finish and an early class tomorrow. I'm sorry." She sighed again and stood up, pulling on her coat.

Questions raced through my mind. Was that the real reason she was leaving? Or was she looking for a way out by using a convenient, timeworn excuse? I was scared that her abrupt departure meant I hadn't measured up. Scared that she would leave, and I would never see her again. And I wanted to see her again. *Dammit, you need to tell her*, I scolded myself. *Don't just let her walk out the door!*

I swallowed noisily over the lump that blocked my throat. "Can we get together sometime? To talk ...?" I knew my voice sounded raw and desperate.

"I'd like that." She stopped buttoning, looked into my eyes, and then down at my hand. As if in slow motion, she reached out and brushed the back of my wrist with her fingertips.

In quick succession I felt relief and then — like the first time — the jolt. The electricity shot from her hand to mine and locked us together. I looked up at her, then back to our hands. A flood of intense, physical sensations washed through me. I bit back a moan.

"I can't concentrate when you do that," I choked as I looked at her fingers.

"Do what?" She asked. But she already knew.

"Touch my hand. Look at me. Whatever ..." I stammered lamely. "Now, *I'm* being too candid." I blushed again.

"On the contrary, I would love to hear you say more." Her voice washed over me like a touch.

Coat buttoned, she cinched her belt and hoisted her backpack over her shoulder. Her smile reached her eyes. "Next week. Here. Same time. I promise; no homework — no Phil."

"No homework," I repeated, in a trance. "No Jane." She was clearly too lady-like, too sophisticated, too classy and refined for the likes of me. But I was ecstatic she was willing to see me again. I wasn't sure I was worthy — but I was positively sure I was interested.

She moved gracefully toward the door. My heart raced up my throat. Slim and erect in her skirt and high, fashion boots. My elation quickly turned to panic when I realized I didn't know her name. I jerked out of my chair and knocked it backward, catching it just before it clattered to the floor. I opened my mouth to call after her. At the same time, she turned to face me, laughing, as if she had read my mind.

"Sophie Barnes." Her name floated across the coffee shop. Still watching me, Sophie Barnes reached behind her and opened the door. "Good night," she mouthed and disappeared into the cold November evening.

I sank down onto the chair. I felt like I had just run wind sprints: winded, tired, and gasping to catch my breath. I hadn't taken a normal breath since I saw her.

Sophie Barnes.

I couldn't believe someone who exuded such class, would be interested in me. I glanced down at my old clothes and scuffed hiking boots. I looked at my reflection again. What could Sophie Barnes possibly see in me? Did she see some worthwhile qualities that Fitz had missed? Or did she fail to see the inadequacies Fitz had seen all along? Would the ghost of Fitz appear once again to upset my life? Despite my questions, my heart raced forward.

For the next week I thought of little but Sophie Barnes. When I closed my eyes I saw the dark brown hair, the blue-grey eyes, and the dimpled smile. I heard her soft, melodic voice. I felt the electric current when our fingers touched. I pictured her walk to the door of the Ground Up: slender, erect, flawless. What I felt was more than just a spark, it was an electric current that coursed through me. Though she wasn't the athletic type I was typically attracted to, my racing pulse knew there was nothing typical about Sophie Barnes. More than once, I shook my head and wondered if I had imagined everything.

Sophie was casual this time: jeans, turtleneck sweater, pea coat, the blue scarf, and a hat. Her cheeks, red with cold, made her eyes more startlingly blue. I stared at her long, slender fingers as she pulled off her hat and fluffed her hair. I forced myself to close my mouth and stop gawking. It didn't matter what she wore, to me she was the most attractive woman in the room — in any room. We ordered our drinks, silently grinning at each other, then made our way to a table near a window, away from counter traffic.

"Sophie Barnes," I said, apropos of nothing, and she looked at me questioningly. I had been saying her name all week, practicing for the moment I would see her again. "I didn't get to say it when we met, so I thought I'd say it now." She smiled.

Conversation came more easily than I thought it would, and my nervous leg finally stopped bouncing and my fingers were still. I found my voice and sense of humor, and we talked comfortably, moving smoothly from topic to topic, sharing volumes of information and asking a myriad of questions.

Sophie had three younger brothers. She was close in age to two of them, but nine years older than the youngest. In my family, I was the only girl and the youngest of three by eight years. Sophie grew up on a dairy farm where she learned to milk by hand and named her favorite cows. I grew up on a hobby farm where we raised a couple cows and pigs for meat. I learned early on that naming them was not a good idea for such a short-term attachment.

We were both driven to have meaningful, satisfying careers. Sophie's passion had always been the law: it was the only career path she had ever considered. I, on the other hand, had drifted through possibilities that ranged from teacher to coach to photographer. My goal had been to *find* the career I would be most passionate about.

Sophie was more athletic than I initially thought. We simply thrived on different types of activities. Sophie preferred individual exercise like running and swimming; she loved the introspection and quiet time they gave her. But she did enjoy watching most team sports. I, on the other hand, gravitated to team sports and loved the competition and camaraderie of basketball and softball.

It was after 10 p.m. when a barista approached us. "I hate to break this to you ladies, but we've been closed for twenty minutes. We're ready to stack the chairs and lock the doors."

We stepped out into the winter night, and as if I had done it a hundred times before, I began to walk Sophie to her car. When Sophie slipped on a patch of ice, she linked her arm through mine and left it there. Her touch seemed to burn a hole through my thick jacket. "Just a precaution," she told me, but the look in her eyes told me the lingering contact was more than that.

"Car keys?" I held out my hand. Puzzled, Sophie placed them in my outstretched hand. I unlocked the door and held it open for her. When she had settled inside, I handed the keys back to her.

"Will I hear from you?" she asked.

I leaned down into the open door, and my words tumbled on top of each other. "There's a women's basketball game on

Wednesday night. Would you like to go? Maybe we could get a bite to eat before?"

"I'd like that."

"I'll call," I promised and closed her door.

Sophie started to pull away, then stopped and lowered her window. "I had a really nice time tonight. Thank you."

"Me, too."

"I'm already looking forward to Wednesday."

"Me, too." *Sparkling conversation, Jensy,* I chided myself.

"Well …" Sophie seemed reluctant to leave. "Good night."

"Good night." I thought about kissing her but hesitated a fraction of a second too long, and her car pulled away.

I grinned. Filled with boundless energy, I ran back toward my car. My intention not to become involved had evaporated at the prospect of seeing her again. My failure with Fitz was, for that moment, a thing of the past. I laughed out loud and skimmed along the icy sidewalk, barely touching the ground. I thought I might fly.

That weekend, on my monthly trip home to see family and friends, my happiness came to a screeching halt.

My visits often included spending time with Alyssa, my best friend from my high school days. For years, we had shared everything: basketball, classes, gossip, and our deepest secrets. I trusted her with everything about me, good and bad. "Everything" included my love for Fitz, my disastrous relationship with Karen, and my tumultuous affiliation with Tracy. Alyssa always listened carefully, then followed up with her "take-no-prisoners" advice. Though it was often difficult to hear, I trusted Alyssa to give advice with my best interests at heart.

We sat at Kiddie Land Pizza and watched as two- and four-year-old Caleb and Emma romped in the play area. "Well, you can see what I've been doing," Alyssa shared as she patted her swollen, pregnant belly. Marriage and kids were all Alyssa had ever wanted, and she had achieved her goal and more: her husband, kids and farm made Alyssa as happy as I had ever seen her.

Alyssa leaned across the table and picked a piece of pepperoni off Emma's unfinished pizza slice. "What about you? What have you been up to?"

"I met someone." I hadn't planned on saying anything, but with Alyssa I could never hold back.

"Really?" Alyssa raised a skeptical eyebrow.

"She's smart and funny and charming and genuine and absolutely stunning." Adjectives spilled from my mouth.

"Does she have a name?"

"Sophie. Sophie Barnes."

"Hmmm …" Alyssa's thoughtful silence sent a chill through me. I knew her too well.

"Jensy, I don't mean to dampen your enthusiasm —"

"But you're going to anyway." I finished for her. My lungs deflated, and my throat went dry. My excitement drained to the floor.

Alyssa shrugged, "I've seen you jump into things too many times. You leap in … you get hurt …"

"This isn't like that," I replied stubbornly. "It feels different."

"Jensy, all relationships feel different at the beginning." She locked her eyes onto mine.

I didn't want to hear this right now. I rocked back and forth; my stomach knotted and my head spun. But eventually, I nodded for her to continue.

She checked on Caleb and Emma before she turned back to me. "How many months ago did Tracy end things?"

I counted back. "Six."

"And before that there was Karen. Two relationships that went nowhere but bad." Then Alyssa marched through the litany of my other short-term dating situations.

"But there were only two *real* relationships," I countered defensively. "I have several friends who've had more."

"I'm not talking about your friends, Jensy, I'm talking about you." Alyssa brushed my comment aside. "Not to mention — Fitz. You've never gotten over her." Her voice, though not unkind, was definite. "Your feelings for her have made new relationships impossible." She sighed. "Now you're gonna do it again? I worry about you, Jensy. It's a sad pattern."

My eyes started to tear. The seeds of doubt had been planted. Alyssa was right. There was a pattern, as well as a huge flaw in my personality: feelings for Fitz that wouldn't allow anyone else to measure up. But I wouldn't give in so easily and made a last attempt. "You don't know Sophie," I argued.

"Neither do you," Alyssa challenged. "But I do know *you*, Jensy Willett. Why can't you just relax and think about graduate school? Do you really need someone right now? Is it that important? Can't you just take a break?"

I held up my hands and helplessly shook my head.

"I'm worried there'll be another episode of picking up the pieces of Jensy Willett," Alyssa said, touching my arm sympathetically. "I don't want either of us to go through that again."

Two-year-old Caleb toddled over to his mother. Alyssa picked him up and indelicately sniffed the air. "Someone needs a change." She hoisted her huge tote onto one shoulder and scooped up Caleb with her other arm. "Keep an eye on Emma, would ya?" Carrying her precious cargo, Alyssa waddled to the restroom.

For the next two days I was upset, and my thoughts were spinning. I relived my past failures and forced myself to search my soul. Was I ready to move on from Fitz? I wasn't sure. Over and over, I replayed my conversation with Alyssa. She was right — I didn't really know Sophie. And I did have a history of leaping into involvements before I stopped to think. Maybe it would be easier to simply step away from Sophie before anything started. I tried to dispassionately examine my situation from all the angles.

Edgy and tense, I grabbed my jacket and headed out into the bitter, early November cold. My ears stung and my bare hands smarted after only a block, but my mind ran hot. I strode by the Ground Up but kept myself from looking in the window. *How can she possibly be interested in me?* I asked myself out loud. Not paying attention to anything but my thoughts, I had to dodge a car barreling toward me when I crossed the street. *Foolish, to even think of her with my relationship track record,* I continued to bitterly admonish myself, as I plowed through the coating of snow. *It doesn't really matter if this feels different. "Am I different" is the question I should be asking. Have I changed?* I knew the dismal truth about myself: as far as relationship material, I wasn't anyone special. I was a three-time loser, with an excellent chance to make it four. I exhaled in cold, little puffs and I stuffed my hands into my jacket pockets. When I returned to my apartment, I was no further along than before.

By Monday evening I had made up my mind. I had repeatedly weighed the pros and cons and unhappily decided to cast my line into the sea of caution. I would wait before I rushed into something new. I would back away from Sophie to save her from an unfair comparison to Fitz.

I stood in my apartment with the phone to my ear. From the window, I watched as people slipped on the icy sidewalk, much like the ice I was slipping on in my mind. I relived moments: walking Sophie to her car, hearing her laugh, looking into her blue-grey eyes, listening to her voice ... and yet ... I rubbed my hand over my forehead. It was a risk I couldn't take. I didn't want to fail again — myself or Sophie.

"Listen, Sophie … about Wednesday …" My voice was clipped and distracted.

"Yes?" Hearing my tone, her voice became wary.

"Well … the truth is, this may not be the right time for me … for me to …" I took a deep breath and swallowed hard. I started again. "You know … school and my job … and things are really busy. And I not all that long ago, I was in a relationship …" Words failed me, and I trailed off into the silence at the other end of the line.

Even in my cold apartment, I was sweating. I felt sick to my stomach. *It shouldn't be so hard to do the right thing,* I told myself miserably.

It felt like an hour as I waited for Sophie to fill the void and respond. "Okay. Thanks for calling, Jensy. Take care." Her voice was distant, filled with confusion and hurt.

There was a click followed by dead air. Our connection was broken, and so was I. If this was the right thing to do, why did it feel so wrong? *Work on yourself first,* I chastised myself. *Figure out who you are and what you want.* And yet, I was afraid I had just blown the answer to what I was looking for. I was devastated. I swallowed back the bile that rose in my throat.

Thursday evening Jane and I trudged through newly fallen snow. We were headed to the Ground Up for a dose of caffeine after a particularly boring class. Earlier, when I had shared a summary of what had happened with Sophie, Jane had stared at me in disbelief. I knew she would have plenty to say once we got inside.

I pounded my boots free of snow and followed Jane up the steps. I didn't notice that she had stopped abruptly just inside the door and bumped squarely into her back.

"Sophie's here," Jane whispered over her shoulder. "With

that guy."

I stood on tiptoes and peered over Jane's shoulder. Blood drained from my face. "Phil." I responded inanely.

"Whoever," Jane said impatiently.

I grabbed the back of her coat. "Let's go," I begged.

When she turned to face me, Jane blocked out Sophie, Phil and half the room. "Jensy," she admonished me, "I know your hometown friend has your best interests at heart. She probably knows you like a book and really believes she gave you the best advice." Jane waved her hand as if to dismiss what Alyssa had said. "And I know you said your other relationships were failures. I get that. But your friend wasn't here the first time you met Sophie." She peered at me intently. "I was."

She glanced over her shoulder in Sophie's direction, then back to me. "What I saw was the Sophie Barnes Syndrome: more intoxicating than alcohol — more addicting than drugs. I saw 'chemistry.'" She fixed me with a hard stare. "Jesus, Jensy, don't be a fool."

Jane pretended to dust snow off my shoulders. "I am going to get a cup of coffee and go home. You are going to get a cup of coffee and wait as long as it takes to talk to her. Understood?"

Jane's departure left me uncomfortably alone, standing by Sophie's table waiting for her to notice me. It took several excruciating minutes before Sophie allowed herself to break away from Phil and acknowledge me.

"Jensy." Her tone was flat and distant. "Phil and I are working on a project."

I had been dismissed. I was shattered, though I had no right expect anything else. I nodded, got my coffee, shuffled to a chair by the window, and watched Sophie and Phil in the reflection. My stomach lurched. What a terrible mistake. I had listened to others, thought too much, and messed up everything. I should have trusted my feelings.

Eventually, I dug in my backpack, pulled out a highlighter and opened a random textbook. The pages remained unturned, and my highlighter hovered over blurry words. I rested my forehead on my fingers and blinked rapidly. I couldn't focus on anything except the woman four tables away in a scarf that matched the color of her eyes.

The next time I glanced at the reflection, Sophie was gone, and Phil was headed my way. He loomed over me, his hands on his hips.

"In case you're wondering, she's still here." He didn't wait for me to respond. "I don't pretend to know what's going on. But I do know *Sophie* wonders what she did wrong. She can't focus — can't concentrate. I'm not exactly sure why, but she thinks you're special. So, I would really appreciate it if you could work this out. I need *my* study partner back." His voiced was tinged with irritation.

Phil took several steps back toward his table, hesitated, then returned to me. "Just an unsolicited observation." His voice was terse. "Sophie is the one of the finest people I have ever met. She's kind, funny, intelligent, and beautiful. And she's interested in you. Anyone in their right mind would be thrilled. I can assure you, if she wasn't gay, I'd be working overtime to put a ring on her finger."

His words stung. For the second time that night, I had been taken to task. And that didn't begin to count all the self-berating I had done.

When Sophie returned to her table, Phil was putting on his jacket. I expected her to leave with him, but she didn't. I watched, instead, as Sophie gathered her things and crossed the floor toward me. She pulled a chair from the neighboring table, clutched her jacket to her chest and sat down.

"I have a few things I need to say," she began softly.

"Take a number. It's been that kind of evening." It was a flippant, impulsive remark made to hide my nerves. I blanched as soon as I uttered it.

"Please, don't make light of this."

I closed my book and turned toward Sophie. "I'm sorry. I didn't mean to make light of anything."

Sophie bit her lip and looked at the ceiling before returning her eyes to me. "I'm not sure what happened. I don't know. I do know that I was looking forward to that basketball game, and spending time getting to know you."

I started to reply, but she cut me off. "You talked Monday night. Tonight's my turn." She closed her eyes briefly. "You said it was too soon. That the timing wasn't great. For what, Jensy? For us to get to know each other? To see what's there? Because there is something there. It was there from the moment our eyes met. You know that."

She stood up. "You said you'd just been through a breakup. I know that can be hard. But I am *not* her. Don't confuse me with someone else. I understand if you want to be cautious, if you want to move slowly. That's okay. But I know what I want: I want to get to know you."

Sophie resolutely pulled on her jacket, scarf, and hat, then hoisted her backpack over her shoulder. "I need you to give me a simple yes or no. Yes, if you're interested in moving forward. No, if you're not. *I* need to move forward, or I need to move on. I am too interested in you to stand still." She paused to let her words sink in. "Call me when you know what you want."

Incapable of speech, all I could do was stare at her. I was stunned. The intensity of Sophie's words caught me off guard. Consumed by my selfish thoughts the last several days, I had forgotten that she might feel as deeply as I did.

Before I could even begin to formulate a response, Sophie was out the door and swallowed by the night.

Two

Beaten and discouraged, I trudged slowly back to my car. I was overwhelmed by the advice, admonitions and ultimatums coming from all directions. Alyssa reminded me of all my past patterns and failures. Jane warned me not to be a fool. Phil told me he couldn't imagine what I was thinking. Then there was Sophie, who told me to move forward or she would move on. And finally, there was my own emotional turmoil. I wondered if my heart was ready for any of this

Once again, I found myself in my darkened apartment looking out on the winter evening. Voices swirled inside me. My mind spun through my *past*, considered my *present* and evaluated my *future*. I weighed everyone's words, replaying them repeatedly.

Then, it hit me like a wake-up call. No one else could figure this out for me. Nor could I try to please everyone else. *I* had to make a decision. For *me*. *I* needed to do what *I* needed to do. It was after midnight when, with shaking hands, I picked up the phone and dialed her number. I wouldn't be able to sleep if I didn't — I had to do it now.

"Jensy?" Sophie answered on the first ring, knowing it was me before I said a word. She sounded wide awake and, maybe, hopeful.

I cleared my throat, "Are you willing to try this again? There's another basketball game this Saturday night. Will you go with me?" My words tumbled hurriedly on top of each other.

"We're moving forward?" Checking her reality.

I sighed with relief. "Yes. Please, come with me."

"Yes. Yes, I'll go with you." I pictured her smile, and her voice washed over me like a touch.

After we hung up, I ran up and down the steps to my apartment until I felt the adrenaline subside. I leaned my sweaty face against the door frame and sighed with relief.

For someone who wasn't "particularly interested" in basketball, Sophie surprised me with her knowledge. She recognized defenses, knew the rules and was familiar with game strategies. When I accused her of holding out on me, she simply smiled and shrugged.

After the game I picked up a basketball and led a surprised Sophie onto the court. "Now you'll be able to say that you shot hoops on State's basketball court."

"A life-long dream," she chuckled. I watched as she positioned herself ten feet from the basket, banked her shot off the backboard, and faced me triumphantly when it fell through the net. Sophie blew on her fingers and swiped them across her jacket.

"Your turn, hot stuff." She casually tossed me the ball.

I felt the familiar pebbled texture against my fingertips and smelled the leather as I rolled the ball between my hands. Sensations of a game that would always hold me in its thrall. I shot where Sophie indicated: free throw line, top of the free throw circle, and the corner of the baseline. Finally, I reluctantly handed the ball back to the manager.

"I have another surprise for you," I told Sophie as I guided her down a back hallway, to a door that opened into a small room.

"Only for you, Jensy," I was told by Patrick, the maintenance man, as we followed him through a maze of hallways and steep stairs. "This never happened." He winked at me and opened the door with a flourish. "Welcome to the catwalk."

High above the court, we walked gingerly onto the see-through metal grate. "I don't know about this," Sophie's voice was uncertain, and I detected a tremor. She took a deep breath and we moved forward.

"Don't worry. I've got you," I assured her as we slowly made our way above the center of the court. I rested my hands lightly on her waist, but that wasn't enough. Sophie pulled my arms around her and leaned back against me. My arms easily encircled her slender frame, and I protectively held her. We stood motionless, and our breathing slowed to the same rhythm. I closed my eyes and inhaled the scent of shampoo that mingled with her cologne. I sighed with happiness.

"It's huge. So much bigger than it looks from down below," she observed in a hushed voice, seeming to forget her insecurity.

I opened my eyes and returned to reality. "A bird's eye view of four years of my life."

Sophie squeezed my hand. "Thank you — for this — for the game — for everything."

As we braved the cold and walked slowly back to her car, she turned to me. "It was a wonderful evening." Her shining eyes searched my face to see if I agreed. "Will I see you again?"

I smiled and nodded. "Sophie, we're still moving forward."

She took a deep breath and returned my smile. In what already felt like our routine, she took her car keys from her pocket and placed them in my hand. When she was seated, I handed her the keys, and my fingers grazed her palm. She looked at me expectantly, but I was already backing away and closing the door.

"I'll call you. Soon." I knew I had just passed on another opportunity to initiate a kiss. To keep from repeating previous mistakes, I was making myself take things slowly. My past failures still haunted me. This time, I wanted to make sure I did things right. I took a deep breath. I was so absolutely taken and captivated by Sophie, that I wanted everything to be perfect.

The next three weeks we saw each other as often as possible. In addition to classes and studying, we both worked part-time jobs. Free time was scarce, but we did our best to juggle our schedules and maximize the time we spent together.

I enjoyed Sophie's company more than anyone I had ever met. She had an unusual effect on my emotions. On one hand, she made my heart race and my head spin; on the other, she calmed and grounded me. I was both wonderfully happy and happily content.

We shared conversation and laughter at the Ground Up. We spent hours at the law library — though I wasn't certain how much studying we accomplished. We had dinner and one evening we saw a movie. On a mild day we strolled along a path overlooking the river. I didn't care what we did as long as I was with Sophie.

Yet, I made no move toward the romantic. I had not kissed her, nor had she made a move to kiss me, though every look, glance, and touch said there was more than just friendship. Physically, I was ready — I wanted Sophie. Emotionally, I lagged behind. I blocked any thoughts of Fitz and focused my energy on Sophie. I was cautious to the extreme because I didn't want this to fail. But I was also perceptive enough to know that we were approaching another turning point. I needed to allow myself to take *another* step forward or once again risk Sophie's challenge: move forward … or she would move on.

In the fourth week of our "non-romantic" courtship, Sophie suggested we go to see the play, *The Great Gatsby*. She proposed we meet for an early dinner then head to the theater to purchase rush tickets, discounted seats for graduate students on a budget.

The theater was an upscale venue, so I dressed up — at least as much as I ever dressed up. I hunted through my closet and found a pair of gabardine wool slacks, a white button-down shirt, and a navy-blue crew neck sweater. Instead of my old, worn bomber jacket, I wore a thigh-length, black wool coat. I wasn't particularly chic, but I was passable.

Sophie was late getting to The Brew Pub for dinner, slipping into the booth just as I felt a twinge of concern. "I'm sorry. Car trouble." She'd called AAA and eventually asked the tow truck driver to give her a ride to the restaurant. I chuckled at the image of Sophie in her skirt, dress boots and trench coat clambering into the cab of the tow truck.

"Long story short, can I bother you for a ride home tonight?"

"You can bother me for anything." I was delighted to comply; thrilled to be needed.

After dinner, I drove to the Cobblestone Bridge, a pedestrian bridge that spanned the river and connected the river road parkway to the theater district. The waterfall just north of the bridge made it one of my favorite places. From that vantage point I often admired the falls, inspected the city's skyline, or marveled at the buildings in the theater district. I went there when I needed to think or wanted time to myself. It was my special, magical place. After the play, I wanted us to stop and admire the setting.

My undergrad degree was in English, and I loved *The Great Gatsby*. I was so familiar with the book, that I could often recite the play's dialogue. During the second act, Sophie put her hand on my arm, and rested it there until the final curtain. My arm burned beneath the fabric where her fingers touched me. I hardly breathed for fear of her breaking the contact.

As we left the theater huge, snowflakes began to lightly dot our coats and hair. But the temperature remained mild, and we savored the evening as we began our stroll across the bridge. We discussed the merits of the book versus the play, and Sophie asked which I preferred.

"Definitely the book." Sophie looked at me for an explanation. "The book allows me to linger over Fitzgerald's use of words. I love his imagery and symbolism. I love the way the words sound ... the way they feel on my tongue. They taste like good wine."

Sophie stopped for a moment and studied me. "Is this the deeper side you hide behind your flippant remarks?" she asked curiously.

Sophie was right. That was exactly what I did. Flippant remarks were an excellent way to hide my thoughts and emotions. I laughed as I deflected her question. "I don't know about a deeper side. I think you may be giving me too much credit."

"I disagree. I haven't given you enough credit."

The streetlights that dotted the Cobblestone Bridge provided patches of hazy, yellow light that caught the snow as it sparkled on its way to the bridge's surface. We walked silently until we reached the center of the bridge; the place I often sought during my late-night walks.

"Look." I turned Sophie to face the waterfall. The ice-free portion of the river, just above the falls, reflected the lights of the downtown buildings in a profusion of colors. The rainbow-colored water continued its journey and plunged over the edge, cascading into the churning foam below. I watched the colorful show with a mixture of awe and delight.

"You're full of surprises tonight," Sophie told me softly.

"Why do you say that?" My eyes left the falls to look at her.

"You linger over words and drink them like wine. You look at the world and find magical places." She gestured at the falls and the lights.

"No." I whispered. "The magic is standing right in front of me." That night, on the Cobblestone Bridge, I finally allowed myself to admit I had fallen in love with Sophie Barnes.

Sophie linked her arm through mine and pressed herself tightly against me. We stood a bit longer, caught in the spell of the moment. Then she gently nudged me. "Come on, Jensy. Let's go home."

We drove north on the river road, past the campus, under a

couple bridges and arrived at a newly paved section. The river continued its border on one side, and the other side contained a new development of beautiful and unusual two-story townhouses.

"There! Grab that space." Sophie pointed to the only parking space on the block.

I nimbly pulled in and sat with the engine idling. I wondered what we were doing stopping in this well-to-do neighborhood.

"This is it, Jensy," she pointed. "The one with the front light on."

I scrunched down in my seat, peered up at the townhouse and whistled. "You must be rich."

She laughed. "Far from it. It's a long story. You should come in to hear it."

I heard the suggestive tone in her voice and quickly got out of the car. I followed her up the steps to the front door, expecting her to unlock it. Instead, she turned, took my coat in her hands, and pulled me to her. "Am I going to grow old waiting for you to kiss me?" She breathed and brushed her lips against mine.

Wordlessly, I tilted my head and gently kissed her. Afraid that my shaking legs would buckle, I backed Sophie against the front door. The sound of Sophie's gasp for breath when I ran the tip of my tongue over her parted lips made me weak. Her hands were in my hair. My hands circled behind her, grabbed below her waist, and pulled her hard against me.

"I should leave before I can't stop," I groaned, every inch of me on fire.

"Who said you should stop?" She breathed against my mouth.

Sophie fumbled to fit the key into the lock; until I took it from her shaking fingers and opened the door. We almost fell into her living room as the door swung open. I reached backward with my foot and impatiently kicked the door shut.

I threw off my jacket and stepped out of my boots. Sophie sat on the stairs to remove her tall dress boots. I knelt and unzipped them for her, willing myself to slow down and take them off slowly. I breathed unevenly while Sophie ran her hands over my shoulders and up through my hair.

Sophie led me upstairs to the top of the landing where she kissed me again. Her hands moved up my sides and pulled my sweater up over my head. She unbuttoned my shirt and removed it slowly, her hands dancing across the skin of my shoulders and gliding down my arms as she pushed my shirt onto the floor. She removed my bra with the same slow, sensuous movements. I couldn't seem to catch my breath. I was light-headed, almost dizzy, with anticipation.

My fingers trembled uncontrollably as I began to undress her. I fumbled at the zipper of her skirt, breathing deeply to stem my impatience. I slid the skirt over her hips, my hands grazing her thighs. It seemed to take forever to unbutton her blouse and remove her bra, but when I did an involuntary gasp escaped my lips. Her skin, her breasts, her abdomen ... Sophie was perfect ... every inch of her. I tried to catch my breath, but she took it away.

I watched my fingers touch her cheek, outline her lips, glide down her throat, and trace the mound of her breast. Sophie's breathing deepened and she shuddered at my touch.

"I ..." Hopelessly tongue-tied, I found her so breathtakingly beautiful that words failed me.

"... want you," she breathed.

Sophie led me to the bed. I was all desire, want and need; feelings more powerful than anything I had ever experienced. There was the fever of skin against skin ... kissing, touching, stroking ... Our mouths and hands were everywhere on each other. Sophie rolled me onto my back and pinned me there. She kissed my forehead, my eyes, and the tip of my nose before her tongue entered my mouth. My hands ran up and down the velvety skin of her back.My hips moved beneath her; my arousal was intense. My body was on fire with an urgency like no other.

"I've got this," she whispered. Her fingertips brushed against my lips, traveled down my body … neck … breasts … followed by her lips. My back arched involuntarily when her mouth touched my breast. Her tongue swirled on my nipple, and I couldn't suppress a moan. She continued to move downward: first her fingers, followed by her mouth and tongue. My legs parted. I grabbed the sheets as her tongue swirled and thrust inside me. My breath came in shuddering pants and jagged gasps. My body arched and pushed itself against her. Then her fingers entered me, and wave after wave of release followed.

"Dear God," I moaned, when my breathing finally returned to normal. It had been so long since my last time, but no time had *ever* been like this. Never this emotional, never this passionate, never the waves of pleasure, never the explosion of sexual release. *This is what love feels like*, I told myself. All my fantasies had just come true.

Sophie raised up on an elbow and gazed at me. Her fingers traced a line from my shoulder down the inside of my arm, glided over my palm and entwined with my fingers. She brought my hand to her lips and gently kissed each fingertip. "You are so lovely."

No one else had ever made me feel so desirable or so beautiful. I swallowed the lump in my throat. I put my hand behind her head and ran my fingers up her neck into her hair. "I never want to wake up from the dream I've been living since I met you." I was overwhelmed with emotion. "I'm so afraid I'll blow it, like I've done before." I shook my head in disbelief. "I can't imagine what you see in me."

"Oh, Jensy," Sophie ran her fingers over my cheek. "I see my world in you."

She pressed her lips against my chest and let them linger. I ran my hand over her shoulder. Minutes passed.

"Tonight was perfect," I whispered into her hair.

"Do you think it can ever be duplicated?" She raised her head and gave me a coy, seductive smile. Her radiant eyes studied mine.

"I think we should find out." My hand moved to her hip, and I gently rolled her onto her back.

The morning light woke me. I tenderly moved Sophie's hand from my hip and slipped out of bed. I pulled on my slacks and sweater and padded downstairs in search of coffee. The coffee maker was on the counter, and after a bit of scrounging I found some dark roast. After I started the coffee, I explored the townhouse.

Across from the kitchen a door was halfway open. That room contained a small law library. A floor-to-ceiling bookshelf, with an attached rolling ladder, covered one wall. It was filled with impressively bound, legal tomes: casebooks, legal citation guides, law dictionaries, and legal history books. I ran my fingers over them: eight rows at ten feet long, and at least eight feet tall. Opposite was a much smaller bookcase. One shelf contained textbooks: law, economics, and social justice. The second row contained fiction: *The Great Gatsby, To Kill a Mockingbird*, and *Watership Down* among them. A few books of poetry also lined the shelves: Emily Dickinson, Robert Frost, and a slim volume of haiku.

I picked up a Barnes family photograph from the top of the small bookcase. The high school Sophie was the image of her mother. Sophie's mother, brothers and Sophie were all smiling. Only her father stood firm and unyielding; emotionally removed and distant. I thoughtfully returned the picture to its place.

I started to turn away, but two books at the end of a row caught my eye. One was *The Fundamentals of Basketball*, and the other was a volume on coaching basketball. I took one off the shelf, flipped it open, and saw several highlighted passages. I was placing it back in its place when, out of the corner of my eye, I detected movement. Sophie stood leaning against the doorframe, arms folded over her chest, wearing my white shirt and nothing else. Her hair was tousled, and her eyes still sleep-filled. She smiled sheepishly.

"Caught me." Sophie smiled and shrugged. "You're looking at my sources of basketball wisdom."

I chuckled. "I was right, you were holding out on me."

"I bought them while you were playing. I thought I should know something about basketball since I was going to all your games. Then when you were done, I kept them as a connection. I never, ever thought *this* would happen." She looked down at my white shirt and blushed self-consciously.

Her simple words touched and overwhelmed me. My heart filled.

Sophie finally broke the silence. "As long as I'm confessing, I have one more item." This time her eyes were twinkling.

"Let me guess." I grinned at her. "You were less than honest about your car trouble."

Her eyes widened. "Yes ... well, no ... There was actually some trouble." She hastened to explain. "I needed a battery. And the truck driver did drive me to the restaurant. I wasn't sure about the battery, so most of the story ... well, some of it ..." Sophie's voiced trailed away as she realized how ridiculous it sounded that she wouldn't drive a car with a new battery. "Okay, some of it is true. But I did use it to my advantage."

"So, you plotted the entire evening to bring me here and take me to bed."

"It wasn't plotted. I was just inspired." Embarrassed again. "Are you upset?"

"No! How could I be upset?" I laughed. "It's the most flattering thing anyone has ever done to have their way with me." I closed the distance between us, and her arms went around my neck. "It's the most flattering thing period." I babbled on. "You make me happy and excited and —" I shrugged. "And everything."

She sighed in relief. "That's good, because I thought about

doing some hands-on research and exploration today." Her eyes sparkled, and her tone was suggestive. "Do you have to work?"

"I'm supposed to, this afternoon." But there was that seductive look in her eyes. "I think I can get out of it." I hastily amended.

"Get out of it." Sophie whispered. Captivating, enticing … irresistible.

I did.

✦

We balanced lovemaking with learning more about each other. I talked about my failed relationships with Karen and Tracy. I was honest as far as I went. But to stay true to the vow I had made, I didn't mention Fitz. I was superstitious and wasn't about to let anything get in the way of my feelings for Sophie. Especially Fitz.

I was more than curious about Sophie's dating history and couldn't imagine she hadn't had at least one significant relationship. I didn't think anyone as smart, nice, and attractive as Sophie could have come this far without being seriously involved.

"I bet guys in high school asked you out," I speculated, and steered the conversation to her life. "I can't imagine they didn't."

Sophie laughed, "Several asked. None were chosen."

"High school girls?"

"Heavens, no. None of us in high school would have admitted we were lesbians. Things changed when I came out at State."

I had no doubt when I looked at the whole attractive package that was Sophie Barnes "So, were any chosen?" I was unashamedly fishing for information.

"You."

I blushed. "Before you met me, certainly there were others. Or someone —"

Sophie blushed as well. "No. Not really. I was so committed to my career path. I didn't take the time to look for anyone."

"So, I'm the first?" As I said it, I knew it wasn't fair of me to ask or even to want that.

"I wish." Sophie touched my hand. "Did I have any long-term relationships? No. Did I have sex?" There was a long pause, as Sophie bit her lip and crafted her response. "Yes. Though, rarely." Her face reddened. "But if you ask me if I made love, the answer would be 'no.' I was never in love when I had sex. Even when it was good, I never was 'in love.'" She lifted her shoulders slightly. "The more I thought about it, the more it seemed like a lie to have sex without being in love. I decided I really didn't want sex without love. Does that make sense?"

It was so different from my experience, but it made sense. My eyes opened wide with a thought so startling it caught me totally by surprise. A thought that struck my heart and soul. Without saying the word, Sophie had just told me that she loved me.

We were on the couch in the early evening of our first full day together. A fire was going in the fireplace and two mugs of hot chocolate were on the coffee table. *We look like the picture of domestic bliss,* I thought lazily. Sophie stretched out and rested her feet in my lap. Just so I could touch her, I began a massage.

"Oh, God," Sophie sighed, "Have I died and gone to heaven?"

"I'm sure *I* have." I winked at her. "An opportunity to massage such beautiful feet doesn't come along every day."

Sophie groaned, "Harder on the arch."

"Any harder and it could be considered torture."

Ummmm ... but such exquisite torture." She rested her head against the arm of the couch, eyes closed, and allowed her breathing to deepen.

"Do you remember your ploy last night? The one you used to get me to come into the house?"

"Ploy?" Eyes still closed; Sophie chuckled. "Ah, yes ..."

"So, what's the story on the townhouse? It's yours through

ill-gotten gain? You're a kept woman? Running drugs? Independently wealthy? This certainly isn't typical student housing," I remarked, while thinking about my small apartment over an Italian restaurant where it always smelled like garlic and tomato sauce.

"None of the above. You make me sound far more interesting than I am." She laughed, a light, happy sound that made me smile.

"But, if you're interested, here is the complete, unvarnished truth about how Sophie Barnes, a modest, small-town farm girl, came to be living in a gorgeous townhome overlooking the river — but you'll have to keep massaging to get it."

"I'm interested." I confirmed and kept my hands busy massaging her feet.

"Have you heard of Baxter, Cragen and Reed?"

I thought for a moment, then retrieved the information. "High-powered corporate law firm."

Sophie nodded. "Two years ago, the Baxter firm came to campus to recruit two or three law students to be summer associates. I was fortunate to be offered one of the jobs. That summer I worked at least fifty hours a week in the office, took work home, and spent my weekends at State's law library. I had no other life. I didn't want one. I loved every minute of the job." Sophie sighed again as I worked on her arch.

"And then …" I prodded.

"And then Henry Baxter appeared at my desk one day in the late summer and told me we were going to lunch. Didn't ask — just told. He told me to order anything I wanted. 'Eat it all, for God's sake,' he told me." Sophie smiled at the memory.

"Henry told me I looked thinner than the first time he had met me. Probably accurate. He was worried that I wasn't eating enough, often enough. Probably true. He told me that he needed to protect his firm's investment, because I would be spending the rest of the summer reporting directly to him and Alex Reed. To say the least, I was taken aback. All of a sudden I felt I like a potential hire who was being groomed by the bosses.

"The next summer I again reported directly to Henry and Alex. But that summer was different. I was invited to dinner several times at Henry and Clarisse's townhouse." Sophie made a sweeping gesture of the room. "They made me feel like a member of their family. I was also assigned a desk in the partners' law library. Everything was going well until ..."

Sophie paused. "Until one of my co-workers informed me there was gossip floating around the office. Some of the associates were wondering if I was 'doing' Henry and Alex — separately or together. Shortly after that, I overheard one employee asking another if he thought I was a good lay. Not that I specifically heard my name, but I could tell by their guilty reactions when they saw me that I had been their topic of conversation.

"Nothing was ever said directly to me, just bits of overheard conversation, some gossip from a couple friends, and some speculative looks by some of the males on staff." She paused again for several moments before continuing. "It was an unsettling introduction to a darker aspect of the business world and corporate culture."

I stopped the massage and looked at Sophie closely. There was no trace of anger in her tone or on her face. Maybe sadness, but not anger. I, however, was seething. I took her hand and rubbed it with my thumb. "I hope you went after them."

"On gossip and a bit of conversation with no specific names? No. But I worked hard to grow a thicker skin. I ignored the gossip. I kept my chin up and did my job.

"At the end of my second summer, Henry and Clarisse invited me to dinner at one of those restaurants that most of us don't mention because we can't afford to eat there. That night I was offered a job contingent on my finishing school and passing the bar exam. Henry told me he thought my intelligence and drive would put me on the fast track to a partnership. I couldn't believe it. I was so flattered and excited.

"But he also informed me that he was having some heart issues. He and Clarisse had decided a warmer climate might help, so they were moving temporarily to Florida. Henry would still oversee the business and be actively involved, but for a while it would be from afar. They weren't going to sell the townhouse, but they didn't want it to sit vacant. So, they asked me if I would be willing to house sit.

"I told them it was a generous offer, but I felt I would be taking advantage. We discussed rent, and with that understanding, I told them I would accept. When we talked about the job offer, Henry and Clarisse were stunned when I told them I wasn't sure."

I stopped rubbing Sophie's foot and stared at her. I was stunned, as well.

"When Henry asked why, I told him there were several reasons. I wasn't sure that those left running the company would feel the need to hire me if Henry wasn't there. I didn't want to commit if it would put me at a disadvantage in seeking other employment. Henry told me the firm would put something in writing. He also assured me that Alex Reed and Daniel Cragen were on board with my hire. He repeated that my only responsibility was to finish school and pass the bar.

"Then I mentioned the gossip that had been circulating around the office. Clarisse was horrified, and Henry was appalled. Henry promised it would be addressed and dealt with before he left in October. He warned me that great talent can be a great target. I knew the issue wouldn't go away overnight, but at least I felt it would be addressed.

"Henry said he hoped he had put an end to my reservations. So, I took a deep breath and told him there was one more thing. I told them I was a lesbian. Clarisse put her hand on my shoulder and said, 'Why on earth would that matter? We love you like our own.'"

I rubbed Sophie's leg.

She looked at me thoughtfully, "You know, Jens, it's ironic. All I ever wanted was to please my father. I worked harder on the farm than my brothers. I studied harder in school. I worked as hard as I could, but it was never enough. No matter what I did, I never seemed to meet his standards, although I'm not sure either of us ever knew what his standards were. Even before I told my family I was a lesbian, I was perceptive enough to know I was a disappointment. I think, somewhere inside of him, my father loves me. But I've been hard-pressed to find that." Her smile was sad. "Then there are Henry and Clarisse Baxter. They believe in me, accept me, and treat me like a daughter. They think I'm someone special."

I felt profoundly sad for Sophie and her plight with her father. I thought about my family: the closeness and understanding that was so typical of our interactions. The unconditional support I received. I bent over and rested my cheek on Sophie's thigh. Her fingers combed through my hair.

"Life is funny, isn't it?" Sophie asked. Her question was rhetorical, but we both knew the answer.

Later, when I walked through the door to my empty apartment, my life suddenly felt empty. Even with all the lights on, the room was missing the glow of Sophie's presence. With a sigh, I turned out the lights and sat in my overstuffed chair, watching the snow-covered cars in the parking lot.

I briefly thought about Fitz and the decision I had made to not talk about her; to keep that part of my life safely hidden in the past. There was no reason for me tell Sophie about Fitz. No reason to take any chances that might ruin what I had with Sophie. I didn't want to give Sophie any reason to reconsider. I was beginning to believe that things with Sophie might work out. If

I kept that piece of the past to myself, I wouldn't make a mess of our future.

I had been home twenty minutes when my phone rang.

"Please, come back."

That was all I needed to hear.

Three

Four months after meeting Sophie I could hardly remember what my life had been like before her; nor could I imagine life without her. My world had tilted on its axis, and that axis tilted toward Sophie. She chipped away at the self-protective and wary part of me. I found myself able to enjoy the present and not borrow trouble from my past. I was throwing away my personal caution and replacing it with the heady rush of being in love.

Though she was practical about many things, Sophie was also deeply romantic. She'd leave whimsical notes in my textbooks, or she'd call me just so she could hear my voice. On winter evenings she would often bring me a mug of hot chocolate while we sat in front of a roaring fire. The romantic Sophie believed the very first time she saw me that she had found her perfect fit. Though one part of her life was firmly planted in the "real world," in her other world she saved her romantic soul for me.

On Sundays I worked an afternoon shift at the Italian restaurant beneath my apartment. Since meeting Sophie, it had become much more difficult to force myself to go to work; however, the lure of a few extra dollars in my pocket usually won the day. After my shift, I would trudge up the stairs to my apartment for an evening of studying. But one Sunday, Sophie asked me to return to the townhouse after my shift.

"Don't eat at work. I'll feed you when you get here," Sophie instructed when she phoned me. "Call me when you're on your way."

I arrived at the townhouse wearing my appetite and my work uniform: black slacks, white shirt, and a multi-colored, Windsor-knotted tie. I had been instructed to go directly to Sophie's, and I was proud that I would arrive free of Italian restaurant tomato stains.

The townhouse looked dark, although the front light was on. I knocked. For several long seconds, nothing happened, and I thought Sophie might have run a quick errand. I was just turning back toward my car when Sophie opened the door. She was dressed in cream-colored slacks, and a soft blue, scooped-neck blouse. Her heels bridged our three-inch height difference and she looked directly into my eyes. Behind her the townhouse was dark except for a fire burning in the fireplace and three tapered candles on the small dining table.

"Are you expecting someone special?" I quipped, looking over her shoulder.

"Not anymore. She just arrived." Sophie helped me out of my jacket, took my hand and led me to the table. She had carefully set it with linens and china. An ice bucket holding a bottle of champagne waited next to the table. "Would you do the honors?"

I pulled the bottle from the ice: Billecart-Salmon Brut Rose. The champagne I had once mentioned was the most expensive bottle we served at the restaurant. I had told Sophie that the taste of that champagne reminded me of kissing her: heady and intoxicating. I looked at her in surprise.

"What's the occasion?"

"You."

"Really?" Embarrassed, flattered and perhaps a little dubious. "Am I really worth the price of that bottle of champagne?" We laughed. I stripped the foil, twisted off the wire, placed a towel over the top, and gently worked the cork until it popped. Then, I carefully poured the beautiful, liquid bubbles into two champagne flutes and handed one to Sophie.

"To you. To us." Sophie raised her glass. In the soft light Sophie looked lovely. The blue blouse highlighted her eyes, and her smile showcased her dimple. Her slender fingers gently caressed the champagne flute. I couldn't take my eyes off her. My heart raced.

"To us. To you," I whispered as we raised our glasses a second time. Something was different about Sophie, and I sensed it was more than just the clothes. She was on a mission. Her sparkling eyes radiated conviction and confidence. We stared at each other while we finished our first glass.

When I asked if I could help with dinner, Sophie touched the back of a chair. "Just sit. You served others all afternoon. Now it's my turn to serve you." The meal she served was wonderful: fresh-baked bread, glazed salmon on a bed of mushrooms, sautéed asparagus, and scalloped potatoes made from scratch.

"Good lord, Sophie." I sighed as I pushed back from the table, feeling pampered and full. I knew she liked to cook but had no idea she was such a gourmet. "Is there anything you can't do?"

Her laugh was infectious. "Well, I can't play team sports. I can't jump rope. I can't drive a stick shift, and I certainly can't pat my head and rub my stomach at the same time —"

"Enough!" I laughed.

Though her eyes still smiled, her tone became serious, "And I can't hide my feelings for you."

She pushed back her chair, came to me, and sat on my lap. Slowly, she unknotted my tie and pulled it free from the button-down collar. Her lips tasted like champagne when she brushed them over mine. I pulled her closer and her kiss ignited a fire that raced through my body.

"I have two desserts," she whispered after her tongue had traced my jaw line and swirled inside my ear. "Which would you like first?"

Much later, Sophie got up from the couch, put on my shirt and made her way to the kitchen. "I'll start clearing the table. We still have another dessert." Sophie looked over her shoulder and winked.

"I'll help."

"No. Really. If you are looking for something to wear, there's an old sweatshirt upstairs in my bottom dresser drawer."

Mellow and relaxed, I floated upstairs and located the big, old State sweatshirt. When I strolled back downstairs, Sophie had reset the table with fresh napkins and clean utensils, refilled the champagne flutes and relit the candles. She set a slice of chocolate chip cheesecake with a raspberry drizzle in front of each of us.

"I suppose you made this, too?" I asked.

"I did."

I took my napkin and tried to pull it through the tight fit of the napkin holder. It was taking more effort than I would have thought, and I looked down to examine it further. Something dangled on the underside of the holder and clanged against my plate. To my surprise, the napkin holder was a key ring, and the item that had knocked against my plate was a key. I held it up and looked at Sophie.

"The key to the townhouse?"

"Yes. *Your* key to the townhouse." Sophie reached across the table and took my hand in hers. "I'd really like … what I really want … what I'd really love is for you to move in with me. I want us to live together. Here in the townhouse. I want you for as much of each day as I can have you."

I put my hand on my heart and gasped to catch my breath. I was surprised, elated and speechless. I couldn't find the right words to say what I felt. I turned the key over in my hand, feeling its smoothness and ridges. One second, I was giddy — the next, the nagging fear of failure rose in me and my doubts surfaced.

I wanted to share Sophie's unlimited confidence and unbridled optimism. But thoughts of Fitz and my past failures continued to haunt me. *Will I always have these self-doubts?* I questioned. My hands rolled into fists, and I could feel my fingernails dig into my palms. *Stop it!* I angrily berated myself. The best thing that had ever happened to me was sitting right across the table. It was time to stop being afraid. There was no way I was going to let this fail.

"Jensy." Sophie broke into my thoughts and shook her head. "One last time — I don't know what happened in your old relationships. What someone else may have done to you, or what you may have done to someone else. And frankly, I don't care. Don't let the baggage from your past define who you are now." Her words washed over me like a gentle touch. I breathed deeply.

"All I know is right now. I know we are the right fit. I love you. I know you love me. That should be the only thing that defines our relationship. Trust our love. Trust me. And most of all, trust yourself. We'll be fine. Better than fine." Her eyes drew me in, and her voice radiated strength and confidence.

I swallowed hard and with one last push, banished the negative thoughts from my mind. Her hand closed over mine, and I began to relax. My mind slowed down and the pounding in my heart subsided. When I spoke, it was from my heart. "I do want to live with you." Tears stung my eyes. "I love you," I whispered.

Sophie met me when I stood up from the table. My arms circled her, and my hand found its resting place at the nape of her neck. "I want to be the person you can't wait to come home to, because that's who you are for me. My heart knew that the first time I saw you. Sophie Barnes, I can see my world in you." I repeated what Sophie had told me months ago; words that had touched my soul.

✦

I had been in and out of a light doze most of the night, thinking about the evening. Occasionally, I would look over at Sophie and smile. The idea of our living together was taking root. I marveled at how good we were together — our "rightness of fit," as Sophie called it. I watched in the semi-darkness as Sophie's eyes slowly opened.

"I know you're watching me." Her voice low and slow.

"I can't get enough of watching you. So, get used to it."

A half-smile formed on her lips, "I'll never get used to it. I'll savor it each time."

A couple minutes elapsed.

Sophie was more awake when she began to talk again, and her sleep-deprived voice sounded almost embarrassed. "There is one more thing I'd like us to do before we officially move in together."

I stroked her hair. "What would that be?"

In the semi-darkness I could see Sophie's eyes dart from me to the ceiling and back again. *She has just asked me to live with her and trust our future, maybe she feels a bit sheepish asking for something else.*

"It's really important to me that we meet both sets of parents before we move in together." She was wide awake now, her words coming in a rush.

"A modern, old-fashioned girl." I smiled. I pulled her to me so that she rested her head on my shoulder. "So, we're going to ask their permission?" Sophie raised her head and gave me an *I'm serious* look.

"I think we should," I hastily amended.

She sighed. "In an ideal world I'd love their approval. But I'm afraid my parents will be a test. Almost everything about me is an issue with my father, but this especially. *You* will be the physical embodiment of his worst nightmare. My father doesn't accept anything about my orientation.

"It's hard to know what my mother thinks. She cried when she found out, but I think she is more accepting now. Rick and Steven will be okay; they've always supported me. But I'm not so sure about Kevin." Sophie stared at the ceiling. "I'm asking you to do something that won't be easy. But I need them to see that I'm happy; no matter what they think of how I live my life."

She returned her gaze to me. "I hope your parents are more accepting."

"I'm sure they'll be fine. They'll love you, Sophie. They'll probably think you're too good for me." I laughed, but there was an element of truth in my words.

"No, they won't."

"Don't be too sure."

We chuckled softly as we left behind the topic of parents and acceptance. At least Sophie was laughing, and making Sophie laugh was one of my favorite things.

Four

We decided to visit my parents first. "You've never brought anyone home before. This sounds serious," Dad remarked when I told him I wanted Sophie to meet them.

Dad called Mom to pick up the extension, "Mary! Jensy has something important she wants to share!" I heard the click of the receiver being picked up, then Dad said, "Tell us all about this special someone."

I shared how we met, law school and her goals, her background, our similarities and differences, how we laughed and how happy she made me. When I finally paused to breathe, Dad chuckled softly. "We look forward to meeting her." Mom agreed.

My mother had known about my sexual orientation for years. I was in high school when I tearfully admitted it to her. She told me she thought she had known before I did, and that it didn't matter to her. "You're my daughter and I'll always love and support you. The only thing I want is your happiness."

Telling my father was harder. Not because I was afraid he would reject me. I just wanted the easier route; wanted him to know, like my mother had known. Mom had never told him, letting me choose my own time and place. That time had come after my sophomore year when Karen broke off our relationship. I had headed home to the comfort of my family.

As I had done so many times before, I climbed out my bedroom window and onto the porch roof. The sight of our land always brought me an inexplicable feeling of peace and security. From that peace-filled vantage point I sat and contemplated what had happened to my relationship. I hadn't been sitting very long when there was a knock on my bedroom door. It wasn't Mom's light, almost hesitant rap; it was Dad.

"Come in!" I called out.

Dad came to the open window. "I suspected I might find you out here. May I join you in your office?"

I laughed and scooted over to make room. "Sure. But it's your office … I just occupy the space."

Dad hoisted himself through the window, stretched out his long legs and got himself situated. He filled his ever-present pipe, tamped down the tobacco and lit it. Soon the pleasant aroma of pipe tobacco filled the evening air. With the pipe lit, Dad turned to me. "So, what brings you home?"

"Does there have to be a reason? Can't I just come home to visit you and Mom?" I attempted the light, but slightly injured tone of one whose motives are questioned.

"Of course. But your mother thought you might need to talk."

I drew my legs up and circled them with my arms. "I had a relationship end."

"I didn't know you were in a relationship." I knew he was looking at me. I could feel his eyes on my face, and my cheeks burned crimson.

I knew it was time to tell him. I took a huge breath, "A relationship with a woman." It was finally out. I couldn't look at him. Instead, I stared down at the basketball court he had made for me. For a moment I felt my dinner rise in my throat. It was harder than I thought it would be. The seconds of our silence ticked off like eternity.

I looked at Dad and watched as his eyes swept across our land and finally rested on the basketball court. He drew thoughtfully on his pipe and silently mulled over what I had told him. I waited.

"I've wondered," he finally said. "Everybody's different, Jensy. I just hope it doesn't make your life too difficult." He raised my hand, kissed it, and placed it over his heart. "I love you, Jensy. No matter what."

I sighed and wiped at tears that hadn't yet spilled. I leaned my head against his shoulder, and we sat like that until night fell.

On a bright, late winter morning Sophie and I headed out for our first round of "Meet the Parents." Sophie spent the better part of the early morning making very deliberate wardrobe choices. Though I insisted that casual was just fine, Sophie had her own ideas and finally settled on khaki slacks, a blue silk blouse and loafers. Clearly, she wanted to impress my parents, and I loved her for that.

"Don't worry. My parents would love you if you showed up in a burlap sack."

"They're your parents, Jensy," she said with a shy smile. "I want it to be right."

"It will be," I promised as we headed down the highway.

Just outside of Tolliver, we went by the diner where I had kissed Fitz. My heart froze.

"That looks like a really cute place. Maybe we should stop there sometime," Sophie remarked.

I had never returned to the diner after the incident with Fitz. I could picture myself in the parking lot, pushing myself against Fitz and kissing her. My hands gripped the stirring wheel and I looked straight ahead. "The food is awful," I lied as we traveled by. I didn't want to lie to Sophie, but I was determined to keep my vow of silence.

"What a shame. It's so cute."

A short time later, we turned into the Tolliver city limits. I pointed out the park where my friends and I had spent so many hours. I drove down Main Street past our family's drug store. We cruised by Tolliver High School, site of some of the best and worst times of my life. At last, we turned down the road to my childhood home.

Sophie opened the visor mirror for a final inspection. "Are you sure I look all right?"

I suppressed a smile. "I think your insecurities are showing."

Sophie immediately looked down the front of her blouse. When my comment fully registered, she chuckled an embarrassed laugh. It was the first time I had seen her look nervous and insecure. I briefly rubbed her back, trying to let her know that she had nothing to worry about. I put my arm around her and felt some of her tension ease. By the time we arrived at the front door, she had transformed into the confident and controlled Sophie I knew.

Mom opened the door and Dad towered behind her. She approached Sophie and immediately drew her into a warm hug. "I'm so happy to meet you," Mom told Sophie, then turned to me and said, "Shame on you, Jensy. You didn't do Sophie justice — she's even prettier than you said."

The ice was broken. "Jensy's in trouble." Sophie gave me an admonishing look, blushing and laughing at the same time.

Dad enveloped Sophie's hand in his big paw. "Welcome, Sophie."

He relieved me of our gift, a homemade red velvet cake. Prior to dinner, over glasses of wine, my parents peppered us with questions. They probed Sophie's interests and opinions and discussed her career choice and job prospects. Dad even asked Sophie a few legal questions. I was touched by my parent's efforts to make Sophie feel comfortable.

There was a flurry of activity as Sophie and I helped Mom serve the meal. Then we were seated, grace was said, and plates were filled. During dinner the conversation continued in an easy, relaxed give-and-take. Sophie mentioned growing up on her family's farm. Dad talked about the family business and his position on the school board, and Mom talked about her community and church work.

Sophie's red velvet cake was served, and my dad easily polished off two large pieces of the rich, buttery delicacy. "Oh, my," Dad sighed as he patted his stomach. "What a fabulous meal and dessert."

"So, we've talked a lot about you two as individuals." Mom began as we sat surrounded by empty dessert plates and cups of hot coffee. "What about the two of you? As a couple."

I placed my hand over Sophie's and gave it a quick squeeze. "As a matter of fact, that's part of why we're here. We're planning to move in together, but we wanted to tell you before we did." I looked solemnly at my parents. "We'd like your blessing."

"I'll take good care of Jensy." Sophie was so earnest, her words so heartfelt that she further cemented her place in my parents' hearts. "I love her." She looked at me, then at Mom and Dad. "We've talked about this over and over. We've discussed the benefits and possible drawbacks. We understand there will be both. But we know it's right for us."

Dad spoke for my parents, "Of course, you have our blessing. Welcome to our family, Sophie."

Mom rejected my offer to help with the dishes, enlisting Sophie's assistance instead. After they headed to the kitchen, Dad stood up.

"Let's head to my office," he suggested.

Cup of coffee and jacket in hand, I headed toward the stairs on my way to the window in my room.

"I no longer use that office," Dad laughed. "I'm too old to crawl through the window." He headed to the front porch and the large, suspended swing. He patted the space beside him, and I dutifully sat down. The temperature was warm, and the snow glistened and melted as we sat in the sun. When his familiar pipe-filling ritual was complete, Dad turned to me.

"When your brothers brought their chosen partners home, I brought them out here to have a conversation." I noted his careful use of the word "partners."

"And Mom took the girls into the kitchen for similar conversations," I added.

"I suspect that's the case. Although, for all I know, they were just doing dishes." Dad drew thoughtfully on his pipe.

I doubted that. There was a long silence and I guessed that our conversation would be somewhat different from those he had with my brothers. I sipped my coffee.

Dad had always wanted to be a psychologist, and though he had never finished his degree, that didn't stop him from studying and analyzing people — including his family. My brothers and I chuckled when we shared "Doctor Tom" anecdotes. However, we were often surprised by Dad's uncanny ability to see into the hearts and minds of those around us.

My brothers had forewarned me about "The Talk" with Dad, telling me I would probably suffer a similar fate. They painted a picture of Dad giving his advice about what constituted a good and happy marriage. I now awaited my version of "The Talk."

"Jensy, from the time you were little, you always tended to keep your deepest emotions bottled inside. You tried to hide your biggest disappointments, preferring to handle things yourself. The older you got, the more private you became. You always kept your deepest feelings inside."

Dad held up a hand before I could say anything. "There's a

reason I'm saying this, Jensy. Bear with me." Reluctantly, I nodded. "Instead, you showed your mother and me that you loved us. You helped your mother without being asked. You showed up at the drugstore because you thought I might need the help. Mom and I always felt your love, and believed you loved us deeply. You just didn't say it very often. And that was okay because we understood you."

I took a sip of my rapidly cooling coffee. My mind turned immediately to Fitz. *And when I finally did share my feelings, look where that got me.* I buried my wounded feelings and built my defenses higher to shield myself from further hurt and disappointment. Those three words — I love you — had all but disappeared from my vocabulary.

"Do you love this young woman, Jensy?" Dad broke into my reverie.

"Yes." I surprised myself with how easily this answer came. Surprised at how far my wall had come down.

Dad looked closely at me. Perhaps he, too, was surprised by the readiness of my answer. "Are you able to tell her you love her? Because it's obvious that Sophie loves you."

"Probably not as often as I should," I admitted guiltily.

"Does Sophie tell you? Often?"

I nodded, and Dad nodded, too. I think he guessed that she would tell me often.

"I think you need to tell Sophie you love her — often. Be the first one to say it." He relit his pipe and took another long draw. "From what little I've observed, I believe there are two sides to Sophie. One side of her is a driven, career-focused young woman. That Sophie is tough and determined. Driven to succeed. But your Sophie ... the Sophie who has given her heart to you ... that Sophie is fragile. You hold her heart in your hands, Jensy. Be careful with it. Leave your past in the past and move into the future with Sophie. Leave any other memories behind."

I glanced at him, then quickly looked away. My heart stopped as I realized that he might have known about my feelings for Fitz. It occurred to me that he had, once again, been able to see into my heart and mind. I drained the last of the coffee from my cup.

Dad tapped tobacco into the coffee can he kept by the swing. He stood and patted my hand. "I bet your mother is finished with Sophie by now." He winked at me, put his arm around my shoulders, and we headed into the house.

Mom squeezed Sophie's arm affectionately as they exited the kitchen. "Sophie mentioned that she would like to see your room, Jensy. She wants to see that window you crawled out of so often."

I laughed. "Okay. A glimpse into my childhood, coming up."

I led Sophie up the stairs and down the hallway. Once inside the bedroom I quietly closed the door. It was virtually the same as it had been the day I left for college. The same awards on the wall and books in the bookcase. The same desk, chair, dresser, and bed. I knew the closet and dresser still held clothing I hadn't worn in years. My bed was still covered by the same blue comforter, and the rug on the floor hadn't moved. In more than five years, my parents hadn't changed a thing.

Sophie crossed to the window and looked out. I opened it, but it was too wet to crawl outside to sit.

"I can see why you like this slice of the world." Sophie scanned the countryside, her eyes finally coming to rest of the basketball court. "I can picture you as a young girl shooting baskets day and night in all kinds of weather." I had told her my story of shooting baskets in the middle of winter, a glove on one hand and my shooting hand bare and swollen with cold.

"When I was too small for a regulation backboard and basketball, Dad made me a junior-sized board and gave me a smaller basketball."

"What a nice memory." Sophie moved to my desk and pensively read the framed certificates on my wall. "Mid-East Valley

All-Conference. All-State First Team. Ms. State Basketball —
third place. Tolliver High School Athlete of the Year."

She looked down at the top of my desk, where a scrapbook
rested. I was certain my mother had placed it there on purpose.
I stood with my hands in my pockets, rocking back and forth on
my heels watching silently as Sophie turned the pages. I knew
what was in it: college basketball awards, newspaper clippings,
programs, additional certificates ... .

Sophie slowly closed the book and turned to look at me. "I had
no idea there was so much."

I blushed and muttered, "An embarrassment of riches."

Sophie looked at my wall again and noticed the framed picture of a single magazine page; the Honorable Mention award for
the statewide "Scholastic Eye" short story contest. "You write?"

"Used to."

"You should again."

"Maybe someday," I shrugged. "If I find a story to tell." I
thought about the scraps of paper and notes still hidden under the
desk blotter. Notes for the story about Fitz; the story I doubted I
would ever write.

I turned and followed Sophie as she sat down on my bed. She
ran her hand slowly over the comforter. "Did you ever bring a girl
up here and make out on your bed?"

I snorted. "I never kissed a girl in high school — alone made
out on my bed."

"I think we should correct that oversight right now." There was
a mischievous glow in Sophie's eyes. She stretched out on my bed
and beckoned me with her finger.

"Here? Now?"

Her finger continued to beckon me. Her smile widened.
"Here. Now."

"Like two horny teenagers?"

"Just like."

I lowered myself on top of her, propped up by my elbows on either side. Sophie put her arms around my neck and pulled me to her. We made out like two horny teens, rubbing and feeling each other through our layers of clothing. We laughed.

Sophie stared into my eyes. "Oh, Jensy, I love —"

I put my finger on her lips. "Shhh." I heard my father's advice. "I've got this." I echoed Sophie's words from our first night together. I moved my head, so my lips barely touched her ear. "I love you."

I kissed her neck. "I love you."

I kissed her lips. "I love you."

We decided to go back downstairs before my parents began to wonder whatever they would wonder. I swung my legs over the side of the bed and watched while Sophie fluffed up the hair on the back of her head and ran her hands down her blouse to smooth out some of the wrinkles. She surveyed herself in my old floor-length mirror. "There, as good as new."

I kissed the back of her neck. "Well, maybe slightly used."

Sophie winked at my reflection in the mirror as she elbowed me in the stomach. "Maybe so," she admitted.

We headed toward the stairs, but I turned around one last time to look at my old bedroom. "Thank God we can cross that off our bucket list." I said to myself as I smiled at my bed.

Five

If Sophie had been nervous about meeting my parents, she was much more apprehensive about taking me to meet hers. We discussed Sophie's family as we prepared for our two-hour journey to her parents' farm. Sophie's father had been thirty when she was born, an older start to parenthood, especially in their farming community. To Sophie he had always seemed much older than his years: stern, set in his ways and intractable in his attitudes.

"Dad was never the doting father of an only daughter," Sophie remarked wistfully as we neared the farm. "He was always inflexible and strict. He never changed his mind about anything." His detachment had become more pronounced after Sophie disclosed her sexual orientation. "I still try to please him. But —" She sighed and shrugged her shoulders.

Sophie's mother was twelve years younger than her husband. "I think she molded herself to reflect his attitudes. At least enough to keep peace in the family. I think she's proud of me, just reluctant to say it out loud. Especially with Dad always being so negative."

Sophie's hands gripped and released the steering wheel in a nearly constant rhythm. She fidgeted in her seat as the farmland rolled by. I reached out and put a sympathetic hand on her leg. "I'm afraid I'm making it sound like my parents are terrible people," Sophie sighed. "They're not."

"I'm sure they're not, Sophie." But briefly, I wondered.

"They're set in their ways. Daddy doesn't understand me. Nor does he want to. He thinks I *chose* to be gay. He doesn't understand why I *chose* to be a lawyer. Or why I *chose* not to move back here." Sophie put her hand on mine. "I'm putting you in a difficult position. It's not going to be like going to see your parents. We could just turn around and go home," she offered. "I just hoped, if they could see how happy we are …"

"Then let's go show them." I attempted to sound reassuring, but in truth, I was feeling more and more anxious. Sophie's anxiety was rubbing off on me. Her parents' attitudes seemed to be stacked against us. I wondered why it was so important to Sophie that I meet them — except that it was. And my role was to be supportive and protect Sophie.

It was another warm, sunshine-filled, late winter day. The highways and back roads were snow free, and even the dirt road to the Barnes' farmhouse was clear and hard-packed. From what Sophie had told me — "Don't be surprised if Daddy is wearing overalls" — I had formed a mental picture of a struggling farm run by farmers like the husband and wife depicted in the painting "American Gothic."

But when we turned down the long driveway, I saw that my pre-conceived notion was wrong. The huge farmhouse had a large porch on three sides. Just north of the house stood an enormous barn flanked by four towering silos. A massive garage peeked out from behind the main house.

"It's huge, Sophie!" I exclaimed. Then all at once it was as clear as if I had read it on a sign. "Barnes Creamery?" An exclusive creamery that sold milk and dairy products to upscale grocery stores in the city. "Are you *that* Barnes?" I was astonished. "You never said anything." My eyebrows raised in a question mark.

Sophie shrugged. "It's not important to who I am. I was never more than the daughter who was just passing through." Sophie's sad smile was unreadable and her comment enigmatic. "Yes, my family is that *Barnes*. Dad, Mom and Rick; to eventually be joined by Steven."

"You're the outlier?" I was still shocked as I looked at the mammoth operation.

"I am. With Kevin it's probably too early to tell. If a baseball career calls someday, he'll leave and become the other outlier." She stopped the car, looked at me, and smiled a cheerless smile. "Let it begin."

We entered the front door carrying our "peace offerings," as Sophie called them: apple pie (her father's favorite) and yellow roses (her mother's favorites). Sophie's father awkwardly patted her arm and proffered his hand to me for a very brief handshake. Sophie's mother kissed her and said she was pleased to meet me. Kevin appeared uncomfortable and only nodded in Sophie's direction.

I was standing close to Kevin and offered my hand. He looked at it, then looked away. Sophie started to say something, but I touched her arm, vividly remembering a time years ago when I had denied Fitz the opportunity to shake my hand. Instead, I smiled and put my hand in my pocket.

There was no social time prior to the meal; we immediately sat to eat. Christine Barnes politely asked me about school and possible jobs in school counseling. Sophie's father disinterestedly questioned Sophie about job prospects, and Sophie responded with short, minimal answers. The tension between Sophie and her father was palpable. Under the table, I put my hand on Sophie's thigh and squeezed lightly.

As I looked away from Sophie, I caught Kevin watching me. He briefly looked away, then seemed to make up his mind and pointedly stared at me again.

"Do you play baseball?" It was the first thing he had said to me since our arrival, and I knew my surprise showed in my uplifted eyebrows.

"Softball," I acknowledged. "Sophie tells me you're a very good ball player."

"After we eat, want to play a little catch? Sophie said you used to shoot baskets outside in the winter, so I thought maybe —"

"Sure." I thought about the warm sunshine and the hard-packed driveway. A few minutes of attempted bonding wouldn't hurt, if that's what it took to win him over. "But I didn't bring a glove."

"I have an extra."

After the meal Kevin disappeared and returned with a base-ball and two gloves. I picked up my jacket and we headed toward the driveway.

We spread out and easily tossed the ball back and forth. The activity felt good, and I was confident I was making inroads with Kevin, despite his initial chilly reception. The warm sun beat down, and I paused to remove my jacket and place it on the hood of Sophie's car. Kevin did the same.

The wordless toss continued until Kevin threw me a verbal curveball. "You and Sophie — it's not natural." I was alarmed by the hostile shift in his tone.

The ball came hurtling through the air, hitting my glove with remarkable force. I winced as it struck the thin leather on the palm of the old glove. The glove Kevin loaned me had virtually no padding to protect my hand from the rocket that exploded into it. Our little outing had been a set-up — a way for Kevin to show his disapproval.

"Like it or not, Kevin, it's who we are." I kept my temper in check and tossed the ball back to him.

"Sophie should be getting married to a man. Not shacking up with someone like you." The venom in his voice matched the force of his throw; his words meant to hurt as much as the baseball he threw. The ball again burst toward me, racing toward my head.

I gloved it and winced — my hand throbbed. I was startled by his vengeance.

"It doesn't work that way." Still startled, I gently returned his throw. I knew he was spewing the sentiments of his father.

The blazing fastball found its way to my glove one last time. Tears of pain, anger and frustration filled my eyes. This time I reared back and threw the ball as hard as I could. It sailed over Kevin's head and bounced erratically down the long driveway.

"I'm done with this conversation, Kevin." I gingerly removed the glove from my hand. I didn't want to give him the satisfaction of seeing me examine my palm and thumb. "Whether you like it or not ... whether you think it's 'natural' or not ... I love your sister. No fastballs thrown in my direction are going to change that." I walked to the car and picked up my jacket before I headed over to Kevin. "Sophie would love your support." I pushed the glove into his chest. "As for me, I could care less." I carefully pulled on my jacket and left Kevin standing in the driveway.

I rounded the barn, out of Kevin's sight, and looked for a place to assess the damage. My hand was already bruised and swollen. Resting my right hand against the wall, I reached down and put my injured left hand in a melting snowbank. I took a deep, jagged breath as the sting of the cold snow offset the throbbing pain.

"Damn." I swore and wiped away a trickle of tears. I closed my eyes and stood for a few moments, letting the snow numb my hand.

"He makes a powerful point, doesn't he?" An adversarial tone came from behind me.

Keeping my hand in the snow, I turned to face Sophie's father. "Is that how he handles anyone he doesn't like?" I had had enough. "Classy." Anger fanned my voice: abrasive and heated.

William Barnes stared through me. "You'll probably have quite a bruise, if it's not broken. He has quite a fastball." I could hear the smile in his voice.

"And quite the anger issue. Or maybe he's just repeating things you say," I retorted, quickly tired of the effort this confrontation was taking. "You know, all we wanted was to come here and share our happiness. That's all. It's so important to Sophie." I pulled my hand from the snowbank and carefully wiped it on the bottom of my sweater. I passed by Sophie's father and began the walk back to the house.

"I don't understand why Sophie chose to live your kind of life," William Barnes called after my retreating back.

My hand throbbed, and my patience had ebbed long ago. Nothing I said was going to change his mind, yet I couldn't let his statement go unchallenged. I turned around to face him.

"She didn't choose it. I didn't choose it. It chose us. It's nothing we did, nothing our families did. It's the way we were from day one."

"It's not natural."

"So Kevin already mentioned." I pinched the bridge of my nose and counted to ten.

"She could have gone to school and come back here as a teacher or a nurse. Something useful. This town needs people like that. Could have found herself a nice young man. Had a big family."

I sighed. "That's your dream. Not Sophie's. She loves being in the city. She loves the law. And she loves me. Would you rather have her live your dream and be miserable because she's living a lie? Don't you want your daughter to be happy?" I looked into his stern eyes. "Don't answer that," I ordered him, because I already knew. He would only be happy if his daughter did what he wanted. William Barnes didn't care about Sophie's dreams.

I tried one more time, while he watched me closely. Anger took over my voice. "We came here to tell you that we want to live together in a committed relationship, and that we're happy. And *I* wanted to let you know that *I'll* be good to Sophie. I'll treasure her."

I took a deep breath and tried one last time. My uninjured hand closed into a fist and my voice sounded hoarse and raspy.

"Just because you want things to be different won't make it so." I took a deep breath. "I'd like you to accept us, for Sophie's sake. I'm going to make a life with Sophie, and I hope I'll make her as happy as she deserves to be." One last attempt to state our case. "We'd just like you to be happy for us." My shoulders raised and I could feel the muscles in my neck shorten and tense. Unblinking, I stared at him until he looked away. I finally made myself head back to the house.

"I can't accept anything about the two of you." He called after me, determined to keep the confrontation alive. "I won't."

I turned so abruptly he almost ran into me. "I didn't think so. But I also know that Sophie will keep trying to win your love and acceptance. It's a pity she'll never have either. But it's an even bigger pity that you'll never know what a wonderful daughter you have." I sadly shook my head. It was time to be finished, all my words were spent. I left him standing there.

Back inside the house Sophie's smile turned into a look of concern as she saw me favoring my hand.

"What happened?" Sophie looked from me to Kevin, who was just heading down the stairs. She took my hand and gently touched the bruise. "Did Kevin do this?" she whispered.

I winced and looked up at Kevin. Our eyes locked.

"He's going to be a great varsity pitcher," I answered Sophie, while staring at Kevin. "He has quite the fastball." Kevin's shoulders relaxed as he broke my stare and continued down the stairs.

After an awkward goodbye, Sophie and I headed quickly to the car. We were glad to get out of that big, cold house and leave for home. Her father had not looked me in the eye since our discussion. His goodbye consisted of patting Sophie on the arm then settling into his easy chair. *You bastard*, I seethed, *Sophie deserves so much better.*

Sophie drew a deep breath and tightly gripped the steering wheel. "Well, so much for family support," she said bitterly and closed her eyes. "Even though we never really did ask for their approval or support."

"I did," I told her. "I asked for your father's approval."

"He didn't give it." She knew without being told.

Just as Sophie turned the key, I saw Kevin and Christine emerge from the front door. Kevin jogged toward us, making sure we didn't pull out before they arrived. "Maybe all isn't lost," I remarked hopefully.

"I brought this for you," Kevin told me when I lowered the window. He handed me a dishtowel, an ice pack, and an ace bandage.

His mother moved him out of the way. "Open the car door and I'll bandage that for you, Jensy." It was the only time that afternoon that anyone in Sophie's family had called me by name.

I watched as Sophie's mother wrapped my swollen hand. The blue-grey eyes, the dark brown hair, the long fingers, the focused concentration as she applied the ice pack and secured it in place. It was almost like looking at Sophie twenty years into the future. Sophie was her mother's daughter.

"I'm sorry," Sophie's mother told me softly. "You're welcome to come back here."

The car door shut, and we started down the driveway. "I'm sorry it was such a wretched day," Sophie said miserably.

"Oh, I wouldn't say it was totally wretched." I shrugged off the top part of my seat belt and leaned over the center console. I placed my head on Sophie's shoulder. My bandaged hand rested palm-up on her thigh, while my right hand rested gently on her arm. "Progress, Sophie. We made some progress. Your mother and Kevin."

Sophie kissed the top of my head. I smiled and closed my eyes as we sped down the road into the dwindling light.

Six

L ess than a week later I stood in my tiny apartment with the not too daunting task of packing my meager belongings. My life had been scantily furnished when I moved in and nothing had changed. I wasn't a person who became attached to things, and it showed. A few books, some camera equipment, sports equipment, toiletries, and a minimal amount of clothing: my tangible life was contained in two suitcases, two boxes, a backpack and a couple of plastic bags. My personality took up more space than my belongings.

Sophie offered to help, but I declined. My tiny, dark, and dingy apartment was so small I feared we would just get in one another's way. Sophie had spent one night in the cramped quarters, and we decided we preferred the townhouse — large and light in a picturesque location with easy access to wherever we wanted to go. Sophie graciously called my apartment — which always smelled of Italian food — quaint. I called it expedient: convenient, practical, and cheap.

The landlord inspected the apartment, shook my hand, and handed back my damage deposit. The month-to-month rent made it easy to move out. "I'll help you move things to your car." We easily moved everything in one trip. "Travel light, huh?"

"Only what I need."

"I'll let you know if I find anything you left behind," he

offered helpfully.

"Keep it or toss it," I told him as I opened the car door. "I have everything I need."

I was floating on a natural high as I drove to the townhouse. My heart was beating so hard I could feel it thump against my rib cage. My fingers pounded a restless drumbeat on the steering wheel, as I whistled a meaningless tune.

It was almost impossible for me to believe I was moving in with Sophie. I had never imagined that someone like Sophie would come into my life, let alone fall in love with me. My thoughts raced forward, happily imagining our life together. Joyful, happy laughter burbled out of me and filled the car.

I found a parking space less than a block from the house. Carrying two suitcases, camera bag, backpack, trash bag and grocery bag, I made my way down the icy sidewalk and up the front steps. At the top of the steps, just as I began to feel my heavy load tip me backward, Sophie opened the front door and pulled me inside.

She took in my plight in a quick glance and began to remove items from my hands. "I heard you banging up the steps. Couldn't you carry anything else?" she needled.

"I tried to balance a box on my head, but it wasn't comfortable."

"You don't look very comfortable anyway." She grabbed my jacket and brought me close for a brief kiss. "I thought you'd never get here. But you are definitely worth the wait." Sophie kissed me again. "So glad —" Another kiss. "— you're here."

I refused Sophie's help when I told her I was going to get the rest of my things. I thought of the two small cardboard boxes still in the car and knew that two of us would be more than the job required. By the time I returned, Sophie had taken my other possessions upstairs.

"Is that it?" She asked, hands on hips.

I sheepishly shrugged, "Stuff isn't really my thing."

"Then it'll be easy to get settled." Sophie's eyes turned from teasing to serious. "I only care about what you have here," her fingertip touched my forehead, "and here." She placed her hand on my heart. "Welcome home."

That night I slept hard for several hours, then woke, suddenly thirsty. I slipped from bed and raided the refrigerator to pour myself half a glass of milk. I looked out the kitchen window into the dark backyard and thought about "home." I hadn't experienced a feeling of "home" since leaving Tolliver five years ago. I hadn't really felt content anywhere. Wherever I lived had simply been an address — a place.

Until now.

My peace and contentment seemed real enough to hold in my hands. It was Sophie who was responsible for that feeling. Sophie, with her romantic spirit and optimistic belief in us. She was my "home."

Later that morning as I slowly woke up, Sophie gently kissed my shoulder. I rolled onto my back and gazed at her. Tears glistened in her yes. "I may not have been your first," she whispered, "but, God, how I want to be your last."

My Sophie. My always.

Seven

Every day of our first winter together was fresh and exciting. We settled into a comfortable routine. I had never experienced anything like it before. Not with Karen or Tracy and certainly not with Fitz, who had been the constant, unattainable desire of my seventeen-year-old self. Sophie captured my heart and soul. I felt like I had awakened after years of struggle and confusion, of longing and wishing for something I would never find. My sense of humor returned. I was more relaxed. And I began to believe that I might be good enough. I finally had what I wanted. Sophie.

The ease with which our lives fit together astonished me. Sophie called it our "rightness of fit." We began to complete each other's sentences. We communicated volumes with just a look or a glance. We couldn't wait to be together at the end of the day; and when we were together, we couldn't keep our hands off each other. Because of our busy schedules, we jealously guarded the time we shared.

In the time we did have, we took turns sharing new experiences with each other. Sophie took me to art museums or to the symphony for an evening of classical music or old standards. Sophie introduced me to ballet (which I enjoyed) and opera (which I did not). She showed me a world of cultural experiences.

I, in turn, introduced Sophie to physical activities both common and off-beat. I had a variety of interests and passions that spurred me to try different things, and I wanted Sophie to experience the joy I found in these activities. Sophie called these activities "Jensyventures" — a one-word description of things that often rattled her comfort zone and caused her to be an agreeable, but reluctant, participant.

My demeanor leading up to a Jensyventure would be sweetly innocent. I wanted it to sound like fun so Sophie would be excited to take part. "What's on your agenda tonight? Do you have any studying to do?" I'd ask, and if her answer was "nothing" or "no," it was time for a Jensyventure.

Our first Jensyventure took place on a lazy Sunday morning. I received an early phone call from our friends Mary and Viv. Their ice fishing house was going to be available all day. Would we be interested?

"I don't have to bait the hook, do I?" Sophie shuddered when I told her. "Fish are so slimy and so is the bait."

I laughed. "We probably won't catch anything, anyway."

"Then why go?" Sophie's response was practical.

"Because —" I tried to topple the objection that was growing. "It's a Jensyventure! A grand opportunity. How can you turn it down? They have a warm, toasty ice fishing house. Furnished and everything. The lap of luxury. It's a perfect slice of frozen northland life. It's —"

"Foolish."

And that's when I knew I had her. Sophie would always try something she initially deemed as unworthy, if only to cement her original opinion.

"It's an introspective and meditative sport." I attempted to redirect her.

"So, we sit in this fishing house with our lines in a hole and guzzle beer."

"You can bring wine, if you prefer," I offered.

We drove half an hour to get there. Fishing houses and pick-up trucks dotted the lake.

"That's their house," I told Sophie, pointing out a large, blue rectangle less than a quarter mile away. "Here we go!" I began to ease my car into the existing tire tracks that led onto the ice.

"Oh, no. No. No. No. Jensy, NO!" Sophie grabbed my arm. "You are not driving out on that ice! We walk or we go home."

It wasn't a battle I was going to win. I reasoned it was better to walk than go home before we even started. We trekked slowly over the ice, toting the afternoon's lunch and drinks in our backpacks. The fish house contained a small heater, a table and chairs, large couch, small refrigerator, and some fishing equipment.

"See? What did I tell you? A slice of heaven." I gestured around the room.

I gave Sophie instructions on how to augur the fishing holes, while I supported her efforts by massaging her shoulders.

"Umm … this may have some possibilities after all." Sophie decided as she leaned back against me. We dropped our lines into the holes, and then we waited.

The small heater warmed the fish house, and we were able to shed our jackets. We opened our backpacks and took out lunch: sandwiches, chips, veggies, beer, and wine. Once we were finished, we sat back and looked at each other. The lines had not moved.

"So much for the word 'sport,'" Sophie teased.

We looked around the room and our eyes fixed on the couch. We both smiled.

"Well, there could be another sport," I shrugged.

"While we wait for the fish to make up their minds." Sophie agreed.

We moved to the couch. After about fifteen minutes we were interrupted by a knock on the door.

"Shit and damn," I muttered.

I hastily pulled on my flannel shirt, buttoned it, and was tucking it into my jeans when I opened the door. Sophie just finished pulling her sweater over her head. We were both blushing a deep shade of crimson.

"Hi!" Viv greeted me. She saw my mismatched buttons and looked over at Sophie who was attempting to hide my bra behind her. "Oh, my ... looks like our timing couldn't have been worse," she said over her shoulder to Mary.

"Oh no, it could have been a lot worse," Sophie ventured.

"Or a lot better," Viv smirked.

Mary popped her head around the corner. "Using a lure has just taken on a whole new meaning." She slipped into the room. "We're sorry. We brought you some fish we caught yesterday. All cleaned and ready to go. And Sophie, I brought you a couple fantastic recipes." Mary knew how much Sophie liked to cook. She set down the packages and backed up. "We'll just be on our way."

"Stay," we told them.

Viv and I sat by the fishing lines and had beer. While Viv talked about her passion for fishing, Mary told Sophie she went ice fishing with Viv just in case she had to rescue Viv if the truck went through the ice.

"Faulty logic, Mary. We'd probably both be in the truck."

"I'd still try to rescue you," Mary's voice was full of sarcastic sugar.

Viv smiled wryly and mentioned that she had noticed our vehicle's location. "Sophie's idea?" Viv asked.

I simply smiled. We looked over at Mary and Sophie quietly talking and drinking their wine.

"If you ever want to fish, just let me know." Viv put her hand on my arm.

"And Mary and Sophie can do whatever," I said as my line took a hit; followed quickly by a hit on Sophie's line. "We have fish!" The fresh catch was given to Viv and Mary in exchange for the fish they had brought us.

We were ready to call it quits for the afternoon, and though it took some convincing, Sophie finally agreed to take the short ride back to shore in Viv's pickup truck. When we got out, Viv lowered her window. "Jensy, you might miss this." She dangled my bra out the window.

Back in my car Sophie hung the bra over the rearview mirror. "Looks like we caught more than our limit today," she laughed.

I shook my head but did not remove it. A truck filled with guys went by and gave us the thumbs up. We blushed … but the bra remained.

"Did you have a good time today?" I asked.

Sophie smiled. "Any time with you is a good time."

"Is it a do-over?"

She laughed, her light, happy laugh. "Keep trying."

"Are you tired?" I asked nonchalantly when Sophie arrived home late one evening.

"Not particularly. Why?"

"Great!" I attempted to make my enthusiasm contagious. The last gasp of cold weather would provide my final Jensyventure of the winter. "Keep your boots and jacket on. And while you're at it, grab your hat and mittens." I pulled out two long, red plastic rectangles with a small rectangular hole cut into the ends. "Look!"

"What are they?"

"The tickets to tonight's Jensyventure." I pulled on my boots, jacket, mittens, and hat.

"It's after ten, Jensy."

Before she could think of other objections, I said hurriedly. "I know."

"I could think of an adventure we could have at home. Right now." Her voice was full of sexy promise.

"Later." I winked.

I ushered a reluctant Sophie into the car, drove to the State campus and parked at the Old Main building.

"Grab your sled."

"Sled?" But she followed my lead, grabbed a red rectangle, and followed me.

We rounded the Old Main building and stood at the top of the huge hill that glittered like ice in the moonlight. "Should we be here at this time of night? We might be trespassing." Sophie looked down the hill and back to me.

I raised my shoulders, "Maybe, but I have my lawyer with me."

"That's not very comforting."

"Maybe not for you, but it is for me, Counselor." I settled cross-legged on the red plastic, reached through the cut-out, and pulled up the front like a toboggan. "Come on!"

"Wait!" Sophie stopped me. "We're the only people here. We could get hurt. No one would find us until tomorrow — we'd freeze to death." Her breath exhaled in white, icy puffs.

"No guts, no glory." I pushed off and flew down the hill. The wind bit at my cheeks leaving sharp, stinging sensations. It was a fast, bumpy, exhilarating ride. At the bottom of the hill, I stood up and waved my arms at Sophie. "Come on!" I called.

Sophie climbed on and shot down the hill, her laughter cutting through the still night air. She came to rest beside me. "Let's go again!" Her cheeks were red, and her eyes were shining.

Up we went, slipping and lurching our way to the top. We jumped on again and rode down the hill side-by-side, tumbling off the sleds and laying in the snow at the bottom of the hill. Sophie laughed and I laughed at her laughter.

"One more time?" I suggested. "Tandem?"

Once again, we staggered up the hill. Sophie climbed behind me and gripped my waist. I pulled up the cutout. We flew! Halfway down the hill my hands began to slide under the sled. The added pressure of Sophie's body forced me forward and onto my hands.

I couldn't yell and I couldn't stop. My hands bent further and further under the sled until, finally, ass-over-teakettle we went. Sophie's hands let go of my waist and she sailed over me, knocking off my hat when her leg clipped the top of my head. We rolled down the hill and finally came to rest about ten feet from each other. The sled continued on without us.

I got up and stumbled over to Sophie. She was on her back, eyes closed — unmoving. I dropped to my knees. "Sophe? Sophie?" My voice was strangled with worry, and my stomach rumbled toward my throat. If my Jensyventure hurt Sophie, I would never forgive myself.

Her eyes slowly opened to slits. "Best — Jensyventure — ever," she breathed.

"Are you okay?" My relief was visible through my long stream of expelled air. "You're sure??"

Sophie nodded.

"You'd do it again?"

"Maybe. A definite maybe. I think I could be persuaded." She sat up. "But right now, let's go home for a Sophieventure."

"Ummm …."

"I think you'll like it, Tiger." She gave me a long, slow wink. "More than sledding. I promise it'll be exciting. And it will be warm — hot, even."

I started to go after the sled, but Sophie took my arm and turned me up the hill. "Leave it for some other happy couple," she said.

Eight

In late April the weekly phone call from Sophie's mother didn't follow the usual pattern. The first few minutes contained their typical mundane chatter and updates. I typically didn't listen, but a change in the speaker caught my attention that night.

Hey, Kev!" Sophie listened intently. "That's great! Congratulations!" She grinned at me and held up her hand to hold me in place. Then, "Oh, no, Kevin, I can't. I have a workshop on Friday. I know — but I paid for it. I can't afford to miss it." A pause. "Uh huh, not refundable."

She listened intently. "Jensy, it's Kevin. He'd like to talk to you." Sophie gave me an "I don't know" shrug and held out the phone.

I raised my eyebrows. I had not seen or spoken to Kevin for a couple months, not since his fastball had left bruises on my hand for the better part of two weeks. I hesitantly took the phone from Sophie. "Kevin?"

"Hi, Jensy." He sounded nervous, and I knew we were both thinking about our game of catch. There was a rather prolonged silence as I waited for him to speak. "I made the varsity baseball team." He sounded young and shy. "I have my first game on Friday. I'm the starting pitcher," he continued.

"Good for you, Kevin." I tried to sound warm and encouraging, though I flexed my left hand remembering the force of his angry fastball. "Congratulations. I'm sure you deserve it." It was a huge accomplishment for a freshman. Some of my wariness began to melt, and my excitement began to grow.

"Thanks." Kevin cleared his throat. "I was just wondering … I know Sophie can't come to the game on Friday. But I was wondering if you would come. I mean … you don't have to … I was just wondering." His words were halting and unsure, hesitantly offering me an olive branch.

I covered the mouthpiece with my hand. "Kevin asked me to go to his game on Friday. Are you okay with that?"

"You'd go?" Sophie whispered. "Even after what happened?"

"Yes." I uncovered the phone. "Kevin? I just checked my schedule, and I can come. Tell me where and what time, and I'll be there."

I handed the phone back to Sophie and left the kitchen while they said their goodbyes. A short time later, Sophie sat down beside me on the couch. She traced the base of my thumb where the fastball had done its worst damage. She said nothing, but I knew she was touched by my decision.

"I'm flattered that Kevin asked me. I think he's trying to make amends. Maybe it's a turning point, or at least a starting point." I smiled. "But whatever it is, it's about us, and I want to go. I *really* want to go."

She raised my hand to her lips. "Thank you." She placed my hand over her heart. "You continue to surprise me, Jensy Willett."

I arrived at the field shortly before the first pitch. Christine Barnes had saved a seat next to her. William Barnes was on the other side, and I was happy to let Christine serve as the buffer between us.

"Sophie's really sorry she couldn't make it," I told Christine. "The bar exam workshop she's at today was pretty costly and nonrefundable. If there had been any way she could have been here, she would have."

Christine nodded and looked at Kevin warming up on the field. "Kevin was so excited when you said you'd come. Thank you." Our eyes met and held for several seconds, and I wished I had more insight into Christine Barnes. I wondered why Kevin seemed to have changed his mind about me. Maybe because I hadn't "outed" his intent to hurt me with his repeated fastballs. Or … I glanced at Christine and speculated that perhaps she had influenced him.

"I'm glad I'm here."

William, on the other hand, was distant and only acknowledged me with a brief nod. Though I had anticipated his reception, it still irritated and prickled beneath my skin.

Christine and I cheered wildly when fifteen-year-old Kevin took the field and threw his first varsity pitch. He didn't disappoint. When the game was over, Kevin had completed a remarkable performance: only three hits, no runs, and seven strikeouts over six innings. At bat, he hit a homerun, a double and a single. Kevin was talented, focused and determined. I felt I had just watched a rising star.

Kevin's father clapped him on the back and his mother, eyes shining with pride, kissed him. Then Kevin turned his eager smile to me. "Thanks for coming, Jensy."

"You were terrific! I'm so glad I came." Kevin beamed at my words.

"Let's go to dinner," William Barnes interrupted gruffly.

I knew his statement didn't include me, and I drifted toward my car. But Kevin's voice stopped me, "You'll come, won't you, Jensy?"

His request seemed so earnest and sincere that I stopped walking, turned, and smiled. I briefly thought I should just go home, but instead I answered, "Of course."

Dinner was filled with baseball talk. We discussed the upcoming season during which Kevin would start at third base when he wasn't pitching. He talked about his dreams of playing either college baseball or being drafted into the major leagues right out of high school. Though they were dreams, I believed that with enough hard work and determination, his dreams might be possible. Throughout the discussion William sat stone-faced and I thought about Sophie saying that Kevin might also be an *outlier*, who would never make his father happy. A baseball career would take him away from home and the family business, and that would be a bitter pill for his father to swallow.

When Christine asked me about Sophie, William looked away while I answered. "She's working really hard, putting in a tremendous number of hours. Graduation is coming up soon. There's a lot to be done. I'm just trying to make sure she eats, sleeps and does something other than study — at least occasionally."

I proudly gushed on. "She's second in her class. That's a huge accomplishment. I'd say she's doing very well. She's proud, and she should be."

My last statement got William Barnes' attention. He momentarily paused in lifting his fork to his mouth. He continued to look at his plate, but his comment was directed to me. "All that work for second. Seems to me she doesn't want to work hard enough to be first."

There was silence at the table as he studied his fork. "Yes. It seems to me if Sophie had some God-given common sense, she would have made better choices with her life. Could have a fine job here and a fine life in her own community with people who know her." With that he raised his eyes and stared at me.

William Barnes and I had already been through this. The issue hadn't been resolved then, and I knew it wouldn't be resolved now. I ground my teeth; my jaw muscles worked furiously. My hands involuntarily clenched and unclenched. Unblinking, I stared back at him.

"William —" Christine started, but I put my hand on her arm. Christine Barnes had to live with him — I didn't. I wouldn't be silenced by his cold tone, harsh words, or icy stare. I would not let this go. Sophie was mine to defend. She was my family. I couldn't let his comments go unanswered. I leaned over the table.

"Come back here? To what? To you? She can't do anything right for you as it is. Is coming back here going to change that? Are you going to appreciate her?" I scoffed. "Second in her law school class — that's a huge success, not a failure. Putting herself through law school — that's a huge success, not a failure. Being offered a job at the most prestigious law firm in the city — that's a huge success." I pointed at him. "You, William, have no idea how lucky you are. You have no idea what a fine person your daughter is because you never even bothered to find out."

I gasped for breath. I felt light-headed and dizzy, but I wasn't done. "There's nothing wrong with the choices Sophie's made. Every choice was planned and thoughtful. You should be proud and grateful every day." I angrily swiped at the tears forming in my eyes. "Proud of the choices she's made and grateful that, in spite of everything, she still loves you." My voice trembled and the veins on my neck pulsed.

I abruptly pushed my chair back, took a twenty-dollar bill out of my wallet and placed it on top of his mashed potatoes. "My contribution."

I turned to Kevin. "I'm sorry to end your night like this, Kevin, because it is your night, and you deserve better. It was rude of me, but I won't apologize for what I just said." I nodded at him. "You're a wonderful ball player with unlimited potential. If you work hard, and I know you will, you'll only get better. I'm honored I had the opportunity to see you play."

"Christine." I acknowledged Sophie's mom, then left the table.

"Jensy!" Kevin breathlessly chased me to the restaurant's front door. "I've never heard anyone stand up to Dad like that before."

"I'm sure you haven't." I was emotionally exhausted.

Kevin looked back to where his parents were still sitting. "What I mean is, thank you for sticking up for my sister." Without waiting for a response Kevin returned to the table. My exhaustion lifted and I allowed myself a small smile. I felt like I had after a hard-won basketball victory: satisfied and exhausted.

I replayed the dinner scene as I drove home. I breathed out a long stream of relief. I knew how much Sophie loved Kevin and how much it would mean to her that her precious younger brother was an ally.

But the specter of William Barnes intruded into my drive home. I gradually talked myself into believing I couldn't have handled him any other way. But I wasn't sure what Sophie would think about my performance. I wasn't certain whether Sophie would welcome or vilify my actions, and I felt a cold sweat engulf me. It certainly wasn't the first time I had crossed the line into her family's business, and it might not be the last.

I arrived home to find Sophie on the couch reading a novel. Reading a work of fiction usually indicated Sophie was having a difficult time concentrating on anything else. She looked deceptively casual in jeans, and a big, old t-shirt of mine. I kicked off my shoes, crossed to the sofa, removed her glasses, and put her book on the table. I gently stretched out on top of her, my head on her chest.

She rubbed my back, "My mother called about an hour ago."

"I thought she might. She probably didn't think it was my best moment," I sighed into her chest. "I'm sorry."

Sophie's hands gripped the back of my shirt. "Sorry for what? Defending my honor? Believing in me? Extolling my virtues? Loving me? Don't you dare say you're sorry." She exhaled a long breath. "*My mother* said you were like a knight in shining armor, riding to my rescue. I should be thanking you."

"I don't know about that. But I do know your father probably won't want to see me again. And he might not want to see you, either."

"He hasn't really seen me for years, Jens. I think I'll survive."

Nine

My life finally slowed down. I graduated with my master's in guidance counseling and, at the insistence of Sophie and my family, participated in commencement exercises. My parents, brothers and their spouses attended. After, we went out to eat and the group regaled Sophie with stories about me. I was alternately embarrassed and pleased; embarrassed that they'd tell the stories and pleased that they loved me enough to share them.

"I love your family," Sophie remarked when we got home that night.

"And they love you." I told her. Because they did.

A week later Sophie graduated second in her law school class. Sophie's mother and three brothers attended the event, as did my parents. William Barnes did not attend. Christine had told Sophie in an earlier phone call that William wouldn't be able to come.

"I understand that things happen." Sophie alluded to the creamery emergency in a tone that attempted to be philosophical and forgiving. I was much less philosophical and not at all forgiving. I was angry and hurt for Sophie. In my heart, I knew William had done this to hurt Sophie and make his point.

After Sophie's graduation both families came to the townhouse to celebrate. We grilled hamburgers and chicken, and drank wine, champagne, and beer. It was the first meeting of our families, and everyone appeared to enjoy each other's company. At one point, Sophie and I exchanged relieved glances when we made eye contact across the room.

Sophie's brothers, Rick and Steven were cordial and treated Sophie with pride and affection. Kevin delighted both families with tales of his baseball season. His pride, determination and motivation were a mirror image of Sophie's approach to life. In so many ways they were so alike.

Christine was not as reserved as she was around William. She surprised me by greeting me with a hug and kiss. I watched as she easily conversed with my mother and father about the latest expansion of the creamery. Most important, Christine radiated an obvious pride in Sophie's accomplishments, seeking her out and showing her affection. But I still detected a modicum of remoteness and sadness that lurked just beneath the surface.

The Barnes family departed early in the evening. We sent them home with leftovers and waved them on their way. My parents were going to spend the night with us. Dishes done, food packed and stored, and vacuuming accomplished, Dad and I adjourned to the bench across the street. We needed some father-daughter time. He lit his pipe as we watched the boats cruising the river. The sun was setting, turning the sky from orange to pink to blue and finally, navy.

"I'm so proud of you, Jensy." He took a deep draw on his pipe and the aroma of cherry tobacco filled the air. "You'll be a wonderful teacher and Counselor. *And* you'll be a great basketball coach. Your life is falling into place."

In the gathering dusk, I put my head on his shoulder.

He relit his pipe. "That young woman in there," he motioned to the house, "has been so good for you. Sophie is everything your mother and I could wish for you. We're proud of her. She's a treasure."

"She is." I swelled with pride and love. To have my parents' love and support meant the world to me. That they thought so highly of Sophie meant even more.

Dad patted my knee. We watched as the boats turned on their lights and continued their progressions up and down the river.

"Where was Sophie's father?" he asked, concern and curiosity evident in his tone.

"At the creamery." I explained the supposed reason for his absence, as well as the strained and tense family dynamics. When I told him about what had happened at the restaurant — what I had done — he raised his eyebrows but remained silent. In the next breath I mentioned Kevin's change of attitude and Christine's warm greeting.

"Even so, I think she's an unhappy lady," Dad observed.

"I think so, too." I recognized part of myself in Christine; the part that guarded my emotions and built a wall of protection. Christine Barnes protected herself at all costs; it was her means of survival. I believed William dominated Christine's personality, something he had been unable to do with Sophie.

Dad thought for a moment. "Maybe 'stifled' is a more accurate word. Anyway, it's too bad that she's such a lonely woman. Today she was genuinely proud of Sophie. But underneath there's an underlying sense of sadness."

We sat silently, lost in our own thoughts. When dusk turned to dark, Dad put away his pipe and rose from the bench. "Think I'll go in and say goodnight to your lovely partner."

"Dad, thanks for coming to both of our graduations. It means a lot to both of us."

"Wouldn't have missed either of them, kiddo." He leaned over and kissed the top of my head.

"Think I'll sit for a while."

When he was gone, I sat and stared out into the darkness. I thought about Sophie and me, and how life was just beginning for us. Our futures were exciting and filled with opportunities

— our prospects seemed limitless. Then I thought about Christine Barnes, sad and lonely, going back home to William.

As we often did on weekend afternoons, Sophie and I walked along the path next to the river. It was a lovely late spring day, and the walking and biking paths were alive with people. Spring mud had dried up, everything was in bloom, and there were boats on the river. It was glorious.

We walked a mile to where the grade of the path rose and overlooked the river from the bluff. At the top there were two rows of trees on either side of the biking and walking paths. The trees were in full bloom, their white blossoms forming a pillowy canopy over the blacktopped paths. There was an unoccupied bench midway through the arched pathway.

"Let's sit," Sophie suggested.

Normally when we went for a walk we didn't rest. Sophie was always motivated to get some exercise. When we had settled on the bench, I turned to her and watched as she inhaled the fragrant scent of the blossoms.

"Let's enjoy the blossoms before they're gone." She arched her back and looked up at the canopy.

"You've been tired this week." I observed as she closed her eyes and sat quietly.

"I have," she admitted.

Sophie was rarely tired, and I often thought of her as indefatigable. But lately there had been several nights when I found her sleeping while sitting up in bed with books and papers scattered around her. Because Sophie was so driven to succeed, she would sacrifice food and sleep without a second thought. I wasn't as driven about work, grades, or a job, but I was totally driven to take care of Sophie and be the best part in her life.

"In fact, I think you're exhausted. You just finished finals, went through graduation, and hosted a graduation party at our house for both our families. You're about to begin some rigorous preparation for the bar exam, after three years of all-consuming study. Then on Monday you'll be going to work at Baxter again. And, not to mention — but I will anyway — you're living and dealing with me 24/7. It's no wonder you're exhausted."

Sophie rubbed her hand up and down my arm, "Dealing with you 24/7 is my joy. Besides, you're working, applying for jobs, interviewing … ."

"Not the same. I'm painting houses this summer. I can listen to music and chat with co-workers or clients. I'm outside enjoying the weather. I'm not studying for an exam that is going to determine my job. I have applications out and a couple interviews lined up. I'm confident I'll get an offer. Sure, there's some stress, but not all stress is the same."

Sophie took a breath and nodded.

"By the way, one of those interviews is at Washington Heights. Girls' varsity basketball coach, half-time school Counselor, and half-time English teacher." My eyes lit up, just thinking about it.

Sophie's eyes sparkled as she thought about the possibility. "That's a match made in heaven! Did you get an interview?"

"I did." My smile spread across my face. "On Tuesday."

"That's great!" She paused for a moment. "Washington Heights. Isn't that the school in the neighborhood we like?"

"It is. Let's drive over there after we get back home. We can look at the school, check out the neighborhood and dream a little. Then we can eat and have a margarita or two at Eduardo's restaurant, dream a little more, and float back to reality."

"Let's." Sophie took my hand and looked at me earnestly. "There is one other thing I'd like."

"Name it."

"Do you think you could come up with a new Jensyventure? Don't even worry about whether I'll like it. I just need to do something crazy-different with you. It's been such a long month and I need us to connect that way."

"Done!" Delighted, I immediately began running through a list of options, rejecting things outright or placing them in the "maybe" column.

We sat in silence and enjoyed the dappled sunlight and the heavy scent of the blossoms. A helmet-less bicyclist went sprinting by. Our eyes met briefly, then she raced beyond. My head swiveled to mark her progress.

"Do you know her?" Sophie asked, noticing my reaction.

"I think so …. Yes …" It had happened so fast.

Then I saw the cyclist coming back in our direction. Tracy. My ex. The last time I had seen her was about a year ago when she had been moving my belongings onto the front sidewalk. It had graphically signaled the end of our second attempt to make things work. I think I had always known our relationship was never going to work, but I had been stuck on the notion that it was better to have something bad than to have nothing at all. Together we had been a mess, attracted and repelled at the same time. We were a disaster that had ended badly … twice.

"Jensy Willett!" Tracy called as she applied the brakes and came to a screeching halt just inches from us. "It's been a while." She addressed me but was looking at Sophie.

Tracy was too quick to let me get a word in, and too blunt to be tactful. "Tracy Jordan. Jensy's ex." She extended a gloved hand to Sophie.

Sophie took her hand. "Sophie Barnes. Jensy's current."

I tried to hide my smirk at Sophie's pointed and possessive response. But I also noticed curiosity and wariness pass over Sophie's face as she extricated her hand from Tracy's. Sophie was not impressed.

"Yah, nice to meet you." I tensed as I watched Tracy's eyes look Sophie up and down. "Jensy and I were together over a year.

On again — off again. More off than on. But life was never dull, was it, Jensy?"

"That's one way to describe it." I mumbled, distrustful of anything Tracy might say or do. She had always been able to put me on the defensive, and waiting for that to happen left me nervous and edgy.

"Maybe we can get together, and I can tell you all about Jensy." Tracy winked at Sophie.

Suddenly my heart thumped wildly against my ribs. Fitz. *Dear God, don't let her mention Fitz*, I prayed. I knew Tracy would tell Sophie that my longing and love for Fitz were the reasons we broke up. My hands involuntarily clenched into fists. I felt the beginning of sweat under my arms, and my head pounded.

I exhaled in relief when Tracy, in her typical disjointed way, abruptly changed the subject.

"You used to like biking, Jensy. What do you think of this? Carbon fiber: lighter than air. And the twenty-eight-gear derailleur. Look." Tracy grabbed me by the arm and forced me to bend down to look at the gears. It was her excuse to whisper, "Impressive, Jensy. She's a looker. You don't waste any time, do you?"

I righted myself. "Thanks for coming back to say hello," indicating it was time for Tracy to leave.

She shrugged, then ogled Sophie one more time, as if imagining her without clothes. "Let's get together." Tracy winked.

My heartbeat leveled as we watched her ride away. Sophie turned to me, a slight smile played on her lips, but distaste showed clearly in her eyes. "You were with her? Really?" I blushed and looked away. "She certainly has an effect on you. You were nervous as a cat."

"The memories aren't pleasant." I didn't want to offer anything more. I didn't want to think about Tracy and all the things she could have said or done.

"Could I just ask what she whispered to you?"

"She said I hadn't wasted any time pursuing someone." I told Sophie sheepishly.

Sophie surprised me with a delighted laugh. "So, the joke's on her."

"Why?"

"Because I pursued you." She ruffled my hair. "I am *still* pursuing you, Tiger. I will *always* pursue you."

"Indeed?"

"Indeed." Glancing up at her, those wide blue-grey eyes ogled me. Tiredness forgotten, Sophie began to stride toward home.

This time, I pursued her.

Ten

The drive to Washington Heights High School took about fifteen minutes. I decided to let the universe know what I wanted and parked in the empty faculty parking lot. *Act like you belong here and maybe you will*, I reasoned. We got out and began to walk along the outside of the building. We peered in the windows of the large, double front doors and down a long corridor with lockers on each side.

"It reminds me of Tolliver High School. Of course, that was just a quick drive-by," Sophie teased.

I pulled away from the window. "We had more important things to do that day, as I recall," referring to Sophie's initial meeting with my parents.

But Sophie was right; Tolliver High was a similar, but much smaller structure. By contrast, Washington Heights was a three-story, brick and mortar monster. We continued around the far side where we saw a large, windowless, newer addition. "Must be the gymnasium."

"Ah, your home away from home."

Our walk around the gymnasium found us at the football field. It was a sea of green turf surrounded by a brick-red, all-weather track. Sophie and I slipped inside the fence, climbed up the bleachers and sat facing the field and the back of the school. My initial impression of Washington Heights was that it was a well-cared-for school and grounds. The wooden trim around the windows looked freshly and impeccably painted. The grounds and flowers were meticulously manicured. There was no graffiti anywhere, nor was there any sign that graffiti had been scrubbed or covered. A large sign told teachers and students to "Enjoy your summer. Be safe." It was a campus that exuded pride.

"I think you could find a home here." Sophie squeezed my hand. "The job was made for you, Jens. If you want it — it's yours. I can feel it."

Sophie's confidence was infectious. I began to visualize myself at Washington Heights. In quick succession I saw myself coaching, instructing an English class, and counseling students to work through difficult issues. I was excited. It would be a great step for me. The job was something I was confident I could do well. I believed Sophie was right: it was mine if I wanted it. I nodded.

"It's —"

"Hey!" A loud voice interrupted our conversation. "You need to leave!" A middle-aged man wearing a maroon and gold Washington Heights polo shirt and ball cap climbed the bleachers toward us.

"Sorry. We didn't see any signs."

"We were just admiring the grounds," Sophie added. "They're lovely."

"Liability issues," he offered as explanation.

"Jensy," Sophie inclined her head toward me, "has a job interview here on Tuesday. She was just getting a feel for the school."

When he shifted his gaze to me, there was a quizzical expression on his face. Then recognition dawned. "Jensy? Jensy Willett? The basketball player from State a couple years back? I thought you looked familiar."

I nodded. "That's me." I answered somewhat sheepishly.

"Ben Cutler." He introduced himself and we all shook hands. "I'm head of building and grounds at the Heights."

"I used to take my daughter to your games when she was in middle school. She loved watching you play. For an entire season it was 'Jensy-this and Jensy-that.' Am I shooting like Jensy? Dribbling like Jensy?" He laughed at the memory. "She wanted to be just like you."

I blushed, uncomfortable with any kind of compliment. But regardless of my comfort level, I had always tried to be a role model. I believed it was my responsibility to exhibit exemplary behavior on and off the court. Basketball had taught me such important life lessons, and I was determined to have a positive impact on others. However, acclaim and awards had always embarrassed me. I had never liked being singled out over the efforts of the team.

"Does she go to Washington Heights? Does she still play basketball?" I deflected the conversation from me.

He nodded. "Molly will be a sophomore at the Heights. She decided not to play basketball last year, even though I think she's really good." Ben Cutler laughed, "Of course, what do I know? I'm just her dad. Anyway, she didn't like the coach or the program."

He paused. "The last three years have been really bad. They haven't won a game. Molly lost interest when the team was losing by thirty or forty points almost every game." He shook his head. "I told her I thought that was a real shame. With all her talent I thought she should be playing, anyway."

We started down the bleachers.

"Hey, I'll tell Molly I met you. She'll be impressed."

"Ben, tell Molly, if I get the job, I'll expect to see her at practice."

"If you get the job, I'll escort her there myself."

We explored the six-block radius, fanning out from the school. The streets were wide, clean, and often canopied by a profusion of trees. The houses were well-maintained, and the lawns were green and lush. The neighborhood boasted several architectural styles: Tudor, colonial, bungalow, and Craftsman. Maple, oak, and river birch trees graced the yards, along with an abundance of flowers and shrubs.

"Ben Cutler's comments about his daughter were nice," Sophie mentioned in an offhandedly casual way as she looked out the side window.

"You know," Sophie continued thoughtfully, "all the time I watched you play, I never thought about you being a role model. That's really something special." She turned toward me and squeezed my shoulder. "It's something to be proud of. It's golden"

Proud, but still slightly embarrassed, I quickly changed the subject. "It's a beautiful neighborhood. But out of our league."

"For now," she admitted, as she placed her hand on my thigh. "But never say never."

A large Craftsman sat prominently on a corner. Painted dusty green with creamy yellow trim, it stood two stories tall with a huge deck in back. A picture window looked over a large, wrap-around front porch and a neat front yard. A riot of flowers and shrubs ran along the wrought-iron fence that ringed the property. The two-car garage was connected to the house by a short breezeway. *Perfect for winter or rainy days,* I thought.

"Does love at first sight happen twice?" Sophie asked.

"It just did." I touched her arm.

It became our dream house, whether or not we would ever be privileged to own it. We stopped, got out and leaned against the car, like two kids looking into the window of a candy store. I had never been so strongly drawn to any building.

"Can we help you?" A man and woman appeared on the front porch, catching us dreaming for the second time that afternoon.

"Just appreciating your lovely home." Sophie smiled. "It's beautiful."

"Thank you. We think so, too," the woman acknowledged.

"Looking for something in the neighborhood?" She asked curiously as she eyed my old car.

"Someday. Just dreaming right now." Sophie dug in her bag and pulled out a pen and a "Baxter, Cragen & Reed" business card from last summer. "In case you ever think about selling, please give me a call." She wrote her phone number on the back.

The man came down the steps, took her card and read the name of the firm. He raised his eyebrows. "All right, Ms. Barnes, it's a deal. When we decide to sell, I'll give you a call." He placed the card in his shirt pocket and patted it.

We said our goodbyes and got into the car.

"What?" Sophie did a double take when she found me staring at her.

"Another feeling?"

"I don't know what you mean." She looked at me feigning surprise.

"Sure, you do — 'If we want it, it will be ours?'" I paraphrased.

Sophie laughed. "Put it out to the universe and maybe ... just maybe ...."

◆

"It's been a wonderful day." I contentedly told Sophie as we sipped Margaritas and snacked on salsa and chips at Eduardo's, our favorite Mexican restaurant.

"Aside from running into Tracy." Again, a flash of distaste crossed her features. "It's hard for me to imagine the two of you together."

"Hard for me to imagine it, too," I mumbled. What Tracy might have said about Fitz still made me tingle with dread.

Sophie read my muttering as the need for a topic change. "Just think ... we added two items to our dream list today: the job at Washington Heights, and the Craftsman house."

I hummed a couple bars of "Beautiful Dreamer" for Sophie.

"For someone so practical and reality based, the dreamer in you never ceases to amaze me."

She considered my statement. "Maybe I'm a *practical* dreamer. I allow myself to dream about things that could happen someday." She leaned forward and pointed a chip at me. "That job description was written for you. How many people will have your exact qualifications? It's a logical assumption that you should have the inside track. Hence, a practical dream."

Sophie ate the chip, so lost in her thought she forgot to dip it in the salsa. "With the house … The couple's older and maybe in a few years they'll be looking to downsize. He didn't say 'if' they would sell, he said 'when.' I think by the time they're ready to sell, we may be ready to buy." She spread her hands and shrugged. "A practical dream."

I smiled, "Nice argument, Counselor."

Our burritos arrived along with our second Margaritas. Before I took my first bite I asked, "And was I a practical dream?"

Sophie took a long look at me. "You weren't '*a*' practical dream … you were '*the*' dream.

Two Margaritas and a burrito later, we headed home. But not before we made one last trip past the Craftsman house and Washington Heights High School.

Eleven

I stood two stories up on a scaffold and thought about possible Jensyventures to meet Sophie's request. For two summers I had painted houses with a crew of three guys, enjoying the physical labor and the loose camaraderie. Music wafted up through the humid air, and I turned to see Tony dancing in the yard.

"Hey, all-star! Come down and show me your moves!"

"Not on your life!" I called down to him.

"Doesn't this make you want to dance?"

"Not with you!" I teased.

"I'll give you lessons so you can impress your lawyer gal." He leered up at me and winked.

And just like that, it hit me. Dancing! Not just any dancing — ballroom dancing. Classy and sophisticated like Sophie. A Jensyventure that played to Sophie's grace and elegance. Not a dancer myself, I would just have to swallow my pride and make do.

"Thanks, Tony!" I blew him a kiss.

My gesture earned a puzzled, "For what?"

"For a new adventure."

✦

As I continued to paint, I thought about my high school friend, Joe, dancing with Fitz at Tolliver High School's Winter Fling Dance my junior year. My heart had been torn in two that evening, knowing how much I would have liked to dance with her. But even though jealous, I had to admit, they made a graceful twosome. Joe loved to dance, and at that point had taken ballroom dance lessons for several years. He enjoyed it so much that he now taught classes at a studio in the city. For several years he had urged me to give it a try. And now that I had the right partner, I would.

When I called Joe later that afternoon, we went through all the pleasantries of catching up, answered all the obligatory family questions and discussed any Tolliver gossip we were privy to. Growing up, Joe had been the only gay person I had known. He was the one who lovingly told me I was gay, long before I believed it myself. He had always sympathetically listened to me when I needed it and administered a verbal kick in the pants when I needed that, too. He was a confidante, keeper of secrets and a treasured friend — as dear to me as a brother.

Joe informed me that he was between boyfriends at the moment. "I'm taking a break from all that boy drama." And yes, he still taught dance lessons at a downtown studio. He was shocked when I told him I was interested in lessons.

"Wow! Just you?" Then hastened to add he would work with me individually if that was the case.

"No. I'll be bringing someone."

"Wait ... wait ... *wait*, girlfriend. Someone you're interested in? Not that Tracy-person, I hope." His tone snarky and hostile. He had disliked Tracy the first and only time he met her.

I laughed and assured him it wasn't Tracy. I also informed him that if I was going to take dance lessons, Joe should assume I was serious about the woman I was bringing.

"True enough," he agreed. "I couldn't imagine you wanting to dance unless you were totally smitten."

I mentioned I was surprising the person with the gift of lessons, so I didn't know how many to purchase. But Joe wasn't as interested in the number of lessons as he was in the woman I would be bringing with me.

"Does your darling have a name?"

"Sophie."

"Sophie — what a wonderful name. So, tell me about Sophie. I have all afternoon."

By 7 a.m. I was dressed and prowling the townhouse for my 10 a.m. interview.

"Well, I guess *someone* is ready." Sophie gently teased.

"Ready for it to be over." I paced the house, filled with nervous energy.

Fifteen minutes later, Sophie kissed me goodbye, and I was abandoned to my own devices. I took off my slacks, so I wouldn't wrinkle them, and aimlessly wandered through the house in my blouse and underwear. After a few minutes, I put my slacks back on and headed outside to the railing overlooking the river, where I stood nervously scanning for any activity.

I had researched the school district and Washington Heights. I read all the articles I could find on the girls' basketball team. Sophie prepped me by asking potential interview questions, and then took me shopping for new slacks, shoes, blouse, and belt. I had my hair cut and styled. I was as ready as I would ever be.

Minutes crawled by ... then, at last I was in the car, wrinkling my slacks, and heading to the interview. I was ushered into a conference room where an interview team of seven staff members awaited me.

From English curriculum to student discipline to developing a counseling program, the questions covered a wide range of topics. The underperforming basketball team was an important topic, and I spoke at length about the effort and timeline it might take to turn around the struggling program.

When it was over, I was confident I had done well. The English and counseling positions should have been full-time jobs, and the basketball program would take an inordinate amount of work and time. However, the staff impressed me with their commitment to the school and their students. It would be challenging and a tremendous amount of work, but I really wanted the job.

"Jensy." Dee Nelson, the guidance Counselor, stopped me as I reached the front doors. "Do you have a few minutes?"

"Of course." Curious, I followed her into her office. It was larger than I expected, with a desk, small round table, bookcase, and several chairs. Behind the desk was a large window that looked out on the football field. On her wall was a plaque that held a mounted baseball bat.

"I love baseball. That bat was personally autographed," Dee said when she saw me admiring it. When she mentioned the player, I whistled softly and moved in to take a closer look.

A pretty, petite, green-eyed blond with a disarming smile, I liked Dee Nelson immediately. She motioned for me to sit and positioned herself in the chair next to mine, as if we were already colleagues. "I'm sure this must be highly improper, but I wanted to give you some additional information and a heads up."

"All right." I nervously picked at my slacks, unsure if I should be hopeful or afraid.

"If the job sounds like a lot of work — it is. The last hire left at the end of the school year because the combination of teaching and counseling was just too overwhelming. It was too hard to do two completely different jobs during each day." Dee looked at me earnestly. "And *she* didn't have the added assignment of coaching a struggling program."

I leaned forward in my chair. "Are you warning me off?" *Should I be rethinking my desire to work here?* I wondered.

"No, I'm not. But I wanted to share the reality, before I give you good news." Dee leaned toward me. "Jensy, I've worked with part-time Counselors for the past four years. Full-time English or full-time counseling always looked much better to those folks by the end of the school year. I can't say I blamed them. I have fought the battle for a full-time Counselor every one of those four years, lobbying anyone and everyone to make the position full-time. And, finally, I've been successful. A year from now the half-time counseling position will become full-time."

Dee sighed. "The truth is, I really need someone who is willing to be here for a while so we can develop new programs for our students. There is so much that needs to be done. I love this school; but I've been stretched thin."

Dee's commitment to developing the program was good news, and so was the full-time counseling position. I nodded thoughtfully.

She paused, considering she wanted to say next. "If you're offered the job, I'd like you to commit yourself to more than one year. I know that's selfish, and I really can't ask it of you, but I'd like you to think about it. I thought knowing everything might help you make your decision. I'm telling you this because I want the Heights to hire you. I think we'd make a fantastic team."

Relief coursed through me. "Thank you. Thank you for the information. Knowing it does make a difference. I'd love to be here. To coach the team. To work with you. And the biggest bonus would be working with someone who loves baseball." I laughed.

She winked at me. "I was hoping the baseball bat would clinch it."

We stood up and moved to the door. Before I turned the knob, I turned to face Dee. "Just a question." Dee nodded. "If working here has been so difficult, why do you stay? There must be other jobs."

"Fair question." Dee thought for a moment. "I like the administration. I like and respect my colleagues. And I really love the kids. I want to do so much more for them." She shrugged. "Besides that, my family and I live close by. It's convenient. My boys love their preschool and their neighborhood, and I'm easily available if they need me. They also have the same school calendar and that's an added bonus." She looked at my hands, and I knew she noticed the absence of rings. "It'll be a really time-consuming job next year. It's none of my business, but are you single?"

It was a moment of truth. I looked into Dee's eyes and saw a potential friend. If I worked here in such close proximity to this woman, I didn't want to hide my life. "I have a partner. I'm a lesbian." I admitted. "I hope that doesn't matter."

She shook her head. "Not at all. In fact, our first venture together should be to develop a group for our gay and lesbian students."

Our eyes didn't break contact. My heart raced excitedly as I considered the opportunity. It was exactly what I wanted to do. "It's a deal." I grinned. "If I'm offered the job, I will commit to help you develop that group and many more."

Dee returned my grin.

"Dee Nelson is certainly in your corner," Sophie observed after I gave her the details of my morning. "You'll be offered the job, I know it. The question is, do you want your plate to be so full your first year of teaching? There will be other jobs."

I looked at Sophie and smiled slyly, "How much will be on your plate? How many billable hours will you have your first year?"

I could see her attempt to visualize what her first year might look like. She nodded her head and bestowed me with a small half-smile. "Touché."

Two days later Sophie's prediction became reality when I was offered the job. The principal told me he wanted to "snap me up" before another school got to me. I accepted immediately. My legs were weak, and I was almost dizzy with excitement as I lowered myself from the scaffolding.

I thought about calling Sophie, but I wanted to tell her face-to-face. I needed to see and feel her excitement. However, Thursday was Sophie's night to work late, and that would make it an unbearably long wait. But I had an idea —

I called Sophie and told her I would bring Chinese take-out to the office. Then I stopped at an Asian market for fortune cookies. At home, I cut two small strips of paper. The first strip contained a message on each side: "Thank you for believing" and "You were right. It's mine." The second strip had "Jensyventures" on one side and "Dance with me!" on the other.

I carefully slit two fortune cookie wrappers, put a steamer on the stove and steamed each cookie until it was soft. I gently pried it open, removed the original fortune, and replaced it with my own. Finally, I lightly pressed the cookie shut. When the two cookies had cooled, I replaced them in their wrappers and resealed using glue and a toothpick. Finally, I found an old calligraphy pen and styled a Jensyventure gift certificate for dance lessons.

I carried my backpack and a bag with several containers of Chinese take-out into the deserted law office. Sophie was working at her desk and didn't notice me at first. I stood for a moment watching her. Shoes off, blazer on the back of her chair, sleeves of her white blouse rolled up her forearms ... her cheek rested on her hand as she studied a document. I tiptoed behind her and kissed the top of her head.

"Umm ... I smell Chinese." Her hands stole up behind my neck. "My meal ticket is here."

"Well, that's romantic," I responded sarcastically. "But practical."

We laid out our feast in the empty break room. "I've been hungry ever since you called." Sophie savored her first bite, adeptly using her chopsticks. I adeptly used my fork. When she got up for napkins, she briefly touched my shoulder. In so many ways, Sophie was so easy to please. She seemed to melt with any of my thoughtful gestures, great or small.

"I can stay until you're ready to go," I offered. "I brought some work."

"I drove." She reminded me.

"Then I'll follow you home. Actually, I'd follow you anywhere."

Sophie raised her eyebrows. "I believe you would."

When we finished eating, I carefully removed the fortune cookies. "Now for the best part. Two for you; two for me." I watched as she unsuspectingly opened the first cookie.

Her expression was quizzical as she read both sides. After a moment, eyes shining, she looked up at me. "Dance with me?"

I handed the calligraphed card to her. Sophie reread the card several times, then raised her eyes to mine. For a moment I thought her eyes began to tear. "It's perfect," she whispered. "Just what I wanted. Thank you." She came around the table and kissed me.

"Hey, careful! No public affection at work." I reminded Sophie.

"Do I look like I care?"

"No, you certainly don't, you rule-breaker." I shook my head and held out the second fortune cookie. "One more."

Her fingers grazed my hand as she took it. Sophie read each side, then read aloud.

"'Thank you for believing.'" She sat down on my lap and turned the fortune over to read the other side. "'You were right. It's mine!'" Her eyes locked onto mine. "Really?"

I nodded. Her arms circled my neck, and she touched her forehead against mine. "I'm so happy for you! So proud. So ..." Her words ran out, and she kissed my cheeks, my eyes, and my lips. "Take me home."

"You drove," I reminded her.

"The car will be here tomorrow. Let's go home. Now."

Twelve

Apprehensive and fidgety, I surveyed the dance studio. The polished wooden floors reminded me of hardwood basketball courts. Square black speakers were suspended from the corners of the large, rectangular room. Unforgiving full-length mirrors lined one wall and promised to catch my every misstep. The huge windows on the other wall allowed the outside world to glimpse the interior proceedings. I was as nervous as I had been before any basketball game, and my right knee bounced uncontrollably while we waited for Joe.

I wasn't much of a dancer. I wasn't limber or graceful; my body didn't move that way. I was a rhythmically challenged former basketball player. But when I looked at Sophie, I couldn't imagine that dancing wouldn't come naturally to her, given her elegance and grace. We were a contradiction in terms. I walked like an ex-basketball jock, while Sophie glided. I was athletic, Sophie flowed. I felt totally out of my depth and that unnerved me.

Joe blew in like a whirlwind of positive energy, his presence filling the studio. I received a heartfelt hug, kiss, and an the admonition, "It's been far too long, Girlfriend."

He cast his eyes on Sophie. "Ah …" he intoned, "this must be the incomparable Sophie."

Joe gallantly kissed her hand. "It is truly my pleasure."

Sophie nodded and curtsied. "And mine." As they laughed

delightedly, I recognized a mutual attraction and admiration that would develop into friendship.

Joe led us into a smaller, adjoining studio, and we sat on three folding chairs. "It's just the three of us tonight. It's a special evening and I want us to get off on the right foot ... so to speak." The laughter helped calm my nerves. "I understand neither of you have ever had lessons. So, tonight we'll start with the very basics."

Joe winked at me. "Jensy, I know from personal experience you spent most of your time at high school dances standing against the wall. We're going to change that tonight."

I blushed and Sophie looked at me sympathetically.

"There are several types of dances under the ballroom umbrella: the waltz, foxtrot, tango, rumba, samba, quickstep and swing," Joe began. He went on to explain competitions — not only for male-female couples, but for same-sex couples as well. All information of which I was unaware.

He talked at length about the proper footwear. "Your feet bear the burden of all the exercise. Just like any sport, they'll get tired and hot. So, it's really important you get the right kind of shoes if you're going to pursue this." Joe looked pointedly at me. "It's just as important as having the right court shoes for basketball. You need arch support, breathability, and a suede or leather sole to provide grip while allowing you to glide."

He had us stand up and face each other. Joe took in our height differential. "Jensy, the heel of your shoe will add about half an inch to your height. Sophie, about two to three inches depending on the heel size you're comfortable with."

"You will need to decide who is going to be the lead. As you can probably guess, I have my ideas about that," he smiled.

"I'm willing to go with what you think, Joe," I told him.

"That's easy. I picture Jensy in a tux, as the lead." Joe looked from me to Sophie. "Sophie, I picture you in a breathtakingly sexy dress. So Jensy will be the lead and you, Sophie, will be the flash."

Joe paused, as if relishing it in his mind. "Yup, that's how I see it. You are free to do anything you want. It's up to you, but that's how I see it."

"A tux will work just fine for me," I agreed, before Joe or Sophie could suggest a dress.

"You'll look smashing in a tux, Girlfriend." Joe got down to business. "If you're both okay with Jensy leading, let's move on to the basics. The goal is for the two of you move as if you're one: seamless parts of a whole. Posture is important, as is breathing from your diaphragm — from your center. You need to control your breathing, and that will help dictate your posture. Everything flows together."

Joe had us "lift up" from our centers, rising slightly on our toes. He moved our arms into position. "Rest your palms against each other, like a gentle 'high five,'" Joe instructed us. "Just enough so you feel the pressure of each other's weight. Now, lean toward each other." With his hands on our back, he gently moved us into the correct stance.

"Share your energy." I was sure Joe had instructed these moves more times than I could count, but it was all new and anxiety-provoking for me.

I glanced at Sophie and saw her eyes were closed. She smiled slightly and nodded. Sophie was assimilating Joe's words, then sharing her energy with me. I swore I could feel it. My palm tingled with electricity, just like the first time we met.

We practiced several times ... rising up, palms meeting, transferring weight. Then Joe told us, "Good. Now let's put in some body movement. A bit of hip action. Side to side. Sway a little, Jensy. Sophie, let yourself sway with her."

Sweat broke out on my forehead. Everything was a difficult stretch for me. I couldn't seem to make my hips sway. Instead of swaying, they felt wooden and stiff, as if they were on rusty hinges. I didn't feel graceful or elegant by any stretch of the imagination.

"Here, let me show you." To demonstrate, Joe took Sophie in his arms.

A jolt of adrenaline shot through my body. For a moment, I pictured Joe dancing with Fitz at the Winter Fling Dance my junior year. Graceful and laughing, Sophie and Fitz could have been interchangeable. I shook my head, cleared my mind, and the moment passed. Fitz's intrusion left me momentarily off balance. I pushed Fitz back into my memory box and refocused on Joe's voice.

"You're trying too hard, Jensy. Relax. You were loose on the basketball court. You had great, fluid moves. You didn't overthink, you just performed naturally." He let go of Sophie. "You're not going to foul out of this game, girlfriend. I promise. Just let yourself go."

I knew my look of disbelief was evident. I was used to experiencing some initial success in my athletic endeavors, but this time I felt stilted and tight. I barked out a dry laugh, and Joe saw my discomfort. The more uncomfortable I became, the tighter my body knotted and the less able I was to relax. It was a vicious cycle.

"Sophie, why don't you take a five-minute break?" Joe suggested.

Joe watched Sophie wander to the hallway, then touched my arm. "Look, I know this is a stretch for you. I truly do. I remember you didn't dance at high school dances — by your choice, I might add. But I promise *this* will be fine; you might even enjoy it. Don't expect to be perfect. Just relax." He lightly patted my arm. "And remember, anyone watching you two will be looking at that pretty woman in your arms. A sexy dress on Sophie and no one will give you a second glance."

"That's encouraging," I muttered.

"Well, maybe a couple or three might notice ... after all, you are pretty cute." Joe held out his arms and I followed his lead, calmed by his banter. As we swayed, my hips and body started to relax.

"See, you're loosening up. Go with the flow. Think about Sophie in your arms and how wonderful she feels."

I smiled.

"Good. That's good, Jensy," Joe told me as we continued. "You're doing fine."

We took a break and waited for Sophie to return. "Not to sound unkind … but how did you end up with her, Jensy? I mean — well — thank God, she's no Tracy. Sophie's actually engaging and pleasant."

I laughed. "I ask myself the same question every day."

Suddenly, Sophie's hand was caressing the back of my neck. "Actually, I chased Jensy until she caught me." I tilted my head back against her hand and smiled at her touch.

"That's it!" Joe clapped loudly, and Sophie and I jumped. "Like that! When you dance, relax like you did just now when Sophie touched you."

I took Joe's words to heart and began to feel more at ease as the evening progressed. Joe's gentle prodding and the sensation of Sophie in my arms moved me along.

Sophie was a natural. Her movements were fluid and graceful. When Joe took her through some additional steps, I marveled at how easily she followed Joe and how quickly she mastered the steps. I would have to work hard to keep pace with Sophie.

On the way home, Sophie closed her eyes and leaned back against the headrest. I found myself gazing too long at the upturned nose, her slender neck, and the hollow of her throat. I had to swerve to get back in my lane.

"Watch the road, Tiger." Sophie opened one eye and squinted at me. "More driving — less watching." She teased but reached over and put her hand on my thigh. "Tonight was perfect, Jens. I had such a good time. I loved it. A Jensyventure unlike any other. Thank you."

"It was a great night." I agreed. "You were wonderful. As an English major, with an unmatched facility for words, may I say you were supple, graceful, lithe —"

"Jensy —"

"Elegant, classy and sexy," I finished.

"And you were charming and eager and —"

"Rhythmically challenged, but salvageable," I concluded.

"You're going to be good, Jensy. *We're* going to be good."

"We already are. But we'll be good dancers, too."

During the week after our first lesson, while Sophie studied for her bar exam, I would steal upstairs to practice. I worked at swaying gracefully to the music, in addition to practicing the first few steps Joe had taught us. I was determined to improve and took my solo practice sessions seriously.

I put on headphones and stood in front of the full-length mirror. I checked my posture, aligned my arms, and began to move my hips. I monitored my progress in the mirror while I imagined holding Sophie in my arms. Eventually, I closed my eyes and entered what I thought of as my "dance zone." No thought; just music, feeling and movement.

One evening, I jumped when I unexpectedly felt the pressure of Sophie's palm against mine. Her other arm slid around my neck. My eyes stayed closed, and I moved with Sophie to the music only I could hear. The steps slowed, the dance moves stopped, and we simply held each other.

Sophie took off my headphones and tossed them on the bed. She gripped the back of my shirt and held me tight. "Have I told you today how much I love you?"

"Tell me," I smiled.

Thirteen

That summer began a year that would be exciting and challenging for both of us. Sophie took the bar exam in July. It would be October before she got the results, but she was finally able to eliminate the relentless studying and devote her time solely to Baxter, Cragen and Reed. She slept better, ate healthier and even allowed herself to relax on weekends.

The preparation for my new job ramped up as soon as I signed the contract. I stopped painting houses and concentrated on the upcoming school year. I spent time at Washington Heights setting up my office, gathering supplies, developing curriculum, and watching three seasons of basketball games. I unpacked the books that had been stored in the townhouse and placed them on the bookshelf in my counseling office. Some were college textbooks, but there were also the copies of the books I would teach in my English class. Several were the same books Fitz had taught in her English class. I fervently hoped I would be a fraction of the teacher she was.

To make the office my own, I dusted off my camera and photographed certain areas of the school. I wanted to capture the Washington Heights environment, sans students, through a new perspective. I strove to find the unusual in the usual, to create a different point of view or to isolate a part of a whole. An empty hallway with sun streaks cutting through the doorway windows, highlighted by dust motes floating in the air. The all-weather track shot from ground level, only one lane number in focus. A lone custodian changing locker combinations, his fingers turning a blurred dial. All taken in black and white. I loved the stark contrast, softened by shades of grey. I hung the pictures on my office wall.

One afternoon, returning from scavenging supplies and looking through cupboards that had been unopened for years, I found Dee standing in my counseling office studying the photos.

"They're fantastic. Where did you get them?"

"I took them. Here. At Washington Heights."

Dee looked at me appraisingly. "They're very good ... unique."

"Thank you." I was pleased, but also slightly embarrassed. The photographs were the first serious shots I had taken in years, and I knew I could do better. "I have some other ideas, but for now, these will do." I had thought about rotating pictures throughout the year. "New photographs each semester of each school year," I explained.

Dee smiled at my allusion to years at Washington Heights. "Bob and I would like to have you and Sophie come to dinner on Saturday. Bob wants to meet both of you, and I want to meet Sophie. And, of course, I want you to meet the boys. Nothing fancy. Backyard grilling and comfort food. Please, please, please, don't bring anything but yourselves."

Their large Colonial-style home was only a few blocks from our designated dream house. Sophie and I took a lingering look at "our" house as we drove by. "Someday," she told me confidently.

Bob Nelson opened the front door. "Welcome, ladies." He was a tall, handsome man with a warm smile. With his green eyes and blond hair, he and Dee could have been mistaken for siblings.

"We're so glad you're here." Dee went directly to Sophie and gave her a hug. Then she embraced me.

"We're delighted you asked." I pulled a bottle of wine from behind my back. "And before you say anything, hostess gifts don't count as bringing something."

"Bob, take Sophie and Jensy to meet the boys." Dee headed off with the wine.

At the rear of the house a bright, colorful room with large windows overlooked a huge backyard. It was the perfect playroom for the two young boys who had littered the floor with blocks, LEGOS, and small trucks. When Bob introduced them, Mark and Richie shyly hid behind his legs.

"Don't worry," Dee chuckled as she entered the room. "Give them a few minutes and they'll treat you like they've known you their entire lives."

"Are they twins?" The boys looked to be the same age.

"Irish twins," Bob laughed.

When I looked confused, Sophie explained. "Siblings born less than a year apart to the same mother."

"Mark is four, in January, and Richie is three, in November. For so long, we tried to have a baby and then, within a year, we had two." Dee smiled.

Bob tousled both boys' hair. "So, Mark is slightly ahead, and Richie plays a bit of catch-up." Bob's love and pride was evident. "But they're best buddies. Right, guys?"

"Right!!" And the boys headed back to their scattered toys.

"May I?" Sophie asked Dee, indicating the floor where the boys were playing. When Dee nodded, Sophie sat down and watched silently. It didn't take long before Richie brought her a toy. Mark held one up to me, and I took a seat beside him. The ice was broken.

When nap time came, Dee herded the guys to their rooms. She quickly returned. "They're fussing for you. Could you tell them you'll be here when they wake up?"

I went to Mark's room to assure him, then stopped in Richie's doorway to wait for Sophie. I watched as she smoothed his hair and rubbed his arm. The gesture was so maternal it touched my heart. It occurred to me we had never had a conversation about children. Watching Sophie made me think we should.

Later that evening as the adults conversed, a sleepy Richie climbed on Sophie's lap and snuggled in. Sophie continued to talk, but her hand never stopped rubbing small circles on Richie's back.

"What a wonderful family," Sophie remarked when we returned home. She carried two wine glasses to the couch and handed one to me. Her arm circled around my neck, and she leaned against me.

"They are," I agreed.

We sat in comfortable silence, occasionally sipping our wine. The picture of Sophie, so maternal with Richie, kept running through my mind. I gently rubbed her leg.

"Would you like to have children?" I asked softly. My own thoughts about having children had always been ambivalent. I had never really pictured myself as a parent. It wasn't that I didn't like kids; I did. And I could do it — I would do it — if that's what Sophie wanted.

Sophie's hand rubbed my shoulder. "Why do you ask?"

"We've never talked about it. I guess it never occurred to me. But when I saw you today with those little guys —" I shrugged. "I thought we should have the conversation."

Sophie took a deep breath. "I don't know that I'm a full-time parent candidate. I think I'm good for a few hours, but probably not much more." She raised her shoulders, then let them fall.

"Maybe you're selling yourself short." There was a look in her eyes that I couldn't quite read. But there was much more beneath her comment, of that, I was sure. "If you don't want kids, that's fine. *I* don't *need* to have children. I've never really seen myself as a parent." I pushed blindly on. "But you —" I again pictured her with Richie. "Is it because of your relationship with your father?"

Silence.

I worried I had pushed too hard when discretion would have been a far better option. "I'm sorry. I overstepped." I pulled back to watch her closely.

"You're fine." She removed her hand from my shoulder and held her wine glass with both hands. "I used to think about it occasionally. I used to babysit when I was in high school. I loved it. The younger the kids, the better.

"Maybe my father's lack of parenting skill has something to do with it." She shrugged. "There's also the element of a lesbian couple bringing up a child in a world that still has so much hatred and fear. But it's also about being so career-driven. I don't know if I could give up that part of me. It's a lot of things. And it's about you, and how good it feels just to be with you." She smiled ruefully. "I don't know how good I'd be about sharing you."

I didn't know how to respond or if a response was even necessary. Everything Sophie said made sense. But it was her last admission that struck a deep chord in me. Because I knew that I really didn't want to share Sophie — with anyone.

The first month at the Heights was a difficult adjustment. I refused to complain or ask questions. I tried to wade through all the information on my own. I rushed from English classes to lunch supervision to counseling groups and individual appointments. I met with county social workers, probation officers and attended special education meetings. I worked late hours at home and arrived at school early in the morning. My time was consumed. And through it all, I was keenly aware that basketball season loomed large. I worried about failure. *Maybe*, I lamented, *I'm in over my head.*

"You're not taking your planning hour?" Dee asked me when I finally broke down and shared my fears. "You need to."

"Where do I fit it in?"

"Right after lunch," she suggested.

"Out of my counseling time?" My short laugh sounded more like a yelp. "I can't do that."

The next day Dee came to my office door and informed me that I no longer had lunch supervision.

I thanked her profusely, then asked, "How did you manage that?"

She waved her hand dismissively. "I can work magic, Jensy." She winked at me, "You have an extra half hour. Use those thirty minutes wisely."

Dee gave me the gift of time that helped assuage my raw nerves. It was a godsend. A few days later I noticed that she had taken on my assigned lunch supervision. I was speechless by her kindness. My eyes teared, and I brought her a dozen roses the next morning.

When October arrived, Sophie began to obsessively check the mail. For her, the wait for the bar exam results seemed to drag on forever. While she enjoyed what she was doing at the law firm, Sophie was ready to move to the associate level and all the new challenges that would entail.

As eager as Sophie was to get her bar results, I was equally eager to start the basketball season. I wanted to begin to erase the legacy of loss and dysfunction. I shared my initial observations with Sophie. "I've watched the tapes of every game for the last three years," I began. "The team was absolutely terrible."

"*Terrible* is a strong word."

"*Terrible*," I repeated. "They haven't won a game in three years, and over half those games they lost by more than thirty points." I shook my head. "Poor sportsmanship, flagrant fouls and no team-work. It's a wonder any of them still want to play."

Sophie reached across the table and took my hand. "How do you change that?"

I blew out a stream of air and squeezed her hand. "The school district has them playing a junior varsity schedule this season. They hope that way they'll experience some success."

"Can you turn this around?" Her voice was filled with concern and support.

"Watch me," I responded with more confidence than I felt.

When I did meet individually with returning players, they listened intently. Several of them had heard the same talk from three different coaches over the last three seasons. Their body language was wary and skeptical, showing the effects of those disastrous years. Still, they wanted to play, and I detected a small glimpse of hope in their eyes. *At least that's a victory of sorts*, I told myself.

The last person I talked to was Molly Cutler — the player who had decided not to play last season because of the team's awful performance.

"I don't know, Ms. Willett. I love basketball, but what's going to be different? It's mostly the same players. Girls who've had their butts kicked for years. What's different?"

"I am."

I waited in silence while Molly thought about that.

"You're different," I continued. "You didn't play last year. And several people have told me what a good basketball player you are." I folded my hands on the tabletop and sighed. "I'll be honest. I've watched tapes of every game for the past three years. A lot of it was painful: not much discipline, little stamina, poor decision-making all around. But I also saw potential. I know we can improve."

I tapped the table with my finger, emphasizing each point. "We can correct the lack of discipline. We can train and develop better stamina. We can improve our decision-making skills. And I will commit myself to coaching a better team." I waited until Molly made eye contact. "Come on, Molly. Get on board."

Molly was thoughtful for a long moment, then a faint smile appeared, "All right, Coach. I'll give it a year and see how it goes. I'm on board."

I was eager to relate my triumph to Sophie when she arrived home that afternoon. However, an official-looking envelope was waiting for her, and I knew it held the bar exam results. Though I was certain she had passed, my heart pounded with the thought of her opening that envelope. I propped the letter on our small dining table, pulled a bottle of warm champagne out of the cupboard, wedged it into the fridge then paced the floor waiting for her to get home.

When Sophie arrived a short time later, I dogged her every move. I followed her upstairs while she changed out of her work clothes. I literally bounced in anticipation.

"You must have had a great day," Sophie observed. "Lots of energy."

"I'll tell you later." Molly Cutler could wait.

"You can tell me now. My day wasn't nearly so exciting …"

"It will be."

The realization dawned when Sophie saw my smile. "It's here, isn't it?"

I grinned and Sophie took off downstairs, one shoe off and one on. When I got to her, she was already tearing open the envelope. I could see her hands shake. Sophie scanned the letter, sighed, and sank down onto a chair. "I passed," she whispered.

Then there was the dimpled smile and her sparkling laugh. "I passed!"

Finally, she jumped up and threw her arms around my neck. "I PASSED!" Her relief was palpable.

"Come on!" I grabbed the still-warm bottle of champagne with one hand and Sophie's wrist with the other. I led her to the center of our small, fenced backyard. I shook the bottle and worked at the cork.

"What are you doing?"

"Celebrating!"

The cork popped and champagne shot skyward. Laughing, we turned our heads up and caught champagne on our tongues, becoming drenched and sticky in the process.

When the spray dissipated, I took Sophie and the remaining champagne over to the side of the yard where we hunkered down with our backs to the fence. "We don't want to get the chairs sticky." I handed the bottle to her. "Drink up, Counselor."

Sophie took a swallow and coughed as the warm bubbles made their way down her throat. She wiped her mouth with the back of her hand and passed the bottle back to me. "Thanks. It's good."

I took a drink and laughed. "It's warm."

"That's okay. It's still good." Sophie took the bottle from me. Another swallow, this time without coughing. She leaned over and lightly ran her tongue over my arm. "You had champagne on your arm. Tastes good on you."

I licked her cheek. "Tastes good on you, too."

Our hair, our bodies and our clothing were wet and sticky, but it didn't matter. We were celebrating Sophie's accomplishment.

"Sophie Barnes, congratulations! You are now an attorney, with a new title and new job responsibilities." I toasted her with the bottle and took another drink. "You have moved into the world of adulthood," I told her wisely. The champagne was beginning to have a pleasant effect.

Sophie nodded as if these were the wisest words she had heard in some time and grasped the bottle for one last swallow. "Good to know."

I took the champagne bottle, tipped it over and pronounced it, "Done."

"Not quite." Sophie leaned toward me. "There's a bit more." She looked at my lips, then into my eyes. Her first kiss barely brushed my lips; the second was longer. Slower. "Now." Sophie told me as she pulled away. "Now … it's done."

Much later that night, I as drifted into the haze of sleep, Sophie's voice brought me back. She was on her side, looking at me in the semi-darkness. "Do you know what the best part of this afternoon was?"

"That you passed the exam?" My list of "bests" grew. "That you're now an associate at the most prestigious law firm in the city? That there will be a salary increase?"

Sophie placed a finger on my lips. "No," she paused. "It's that you shook up that bottle of warm champagne and drenched us. It's that we sat against the fence and shared what was left."

"Really?" I was surprised Sophie thought *that* was the "best."

"Really. I don't know anyone else who would make this day so uniquely special. Only you, Jens." She touched my cheek.

Twelve young women stood in front of me. They shifted nervously from foot to foot and looked everywhere but at me. I could feel skepticism radiating from them. Skeptical of their ability, skeptical of their power to turn things around, and skeptical of their new coach.

The future was unknown, and I couldn't guarantee that things would improve. They had no expectations for this season. All they had was the bitter taste of losing seasons, and a love of basketball that wouldn't let them quit. They looked weary and beaten before the season had even begun. I needed a positive way to begin the season.

That positive had been initiated by Sophie before the season began. "Let's get T-shirts for the team."

"Us?"

"Us." Sophie drummed her fingers on the dining room table. "I've been thinking about this. You want these girls to develop team pride and unity. Obviously, they haven't had much of that.

So, we get them practice T-shirts. You come up with a catchy slogan like 'Reaching for the Heights.' You give the shirts to the girls." Sophie looked over my shoulder as if visualizing her idea. "They don't even have to wear them to practice every day. They can wear them to school, or wherever — it doesn't matter. But you'll wear one to practice every day. It will be *your* practice uniform."

"We'll get the girls their own T-shirts," I repeated, mulling over the idea.

"Yes. The cost will be nothing compared to the goodwill it creates." Sophie reached across the table and touched my arm. "You come up with a design. I'll see if I can find a silk screen company. I have a friend who might be able to help."

"You're serious."

"Let's get this team off on the right foot." Sophie closed her eyes — more visualization. "This year, maroon with gold lettering. Next year gold with maroon lettering. Year three — white with maroon and gold —"

"Sounds like you're in it for the long haul."

"I'm right there with you." Sophie winked. "Partners. I'll contribute half."

"You're a champ." I told her. And just like that, Sophie and I were partners in the growth and development of the Washington Heights girls' basketball team.

The box of T-shirts now sat on the end line of the basketball court. I took off my sweatshirt and watched as the girls inspected my "Reaching for the Heights" T-shirt.

"Cool shirt, coach. Where'd you get it?" Hannah Giddings asked.

"Same place you're going to get yours. Right out of this box." I opened the flaps. "Hannah, you can hand them out."

"Can we wear them now?" Kara Perkins asked.

"Change right now, and then get back here ready to run." There was laughter and excitement as the girls ran to the locker room. It was my first step to put a dent in their skepticism.

Fitz was often on my mind over the next several weeks. I could hear her telling my high school team, "My goal is to help this team be successful." My initial practices were reminiscent of the paces Fitz put us through.

Fitz had told us, "We will out-practice, our-prepare and out-perform our opponents." My players were constantly reminded that these were the standards we were striving to meet. We worked diligently. I asked of the girls what Fitz had asked of us: to "make a commitment."

Finally, I stressed the importance of being a team. I told the players my goal was to put each player in the best position to contribute to team success. I quoted Fitz: "Make no mistake, I am a believer in the importance of TEAM."

Several players showed great potential. Molly Cutler was blessed with a natural shot and a sense for the game. Her positive attitude made her a natural leader. Hannah Giddings promised to be fierce in the lane, both on offense and defense. Kara Perkins was a freshman who had the ability and the desire to move into the starting lineup. I was confident that nucleus would put us in position to win games.

I was happy with the progress we made in the first two weeks. Each day showed improvement and a growing confidence. As a team we hadn't yet reached our top potential, but we were 100 percent ready to be competitive and begin the journey to respectability.

I couldn't sleep the night before our first game. I laid with my eyes wide open, running scenarios through my over-active mind. I worried about what I might have missed. I tormented myself about details I might have forgotten. What if we lost by huge numbers? What if —

"Go to sleep." Sophie rolled over and raised above me in the darkness. "They are prepared, they are ready, they want to do well.

You have done everything possible; now you have to let them play."

"I know," I grudgingly admitted.

"Then go to sleep." She nestled against me. "I love you," she whispered and kissed my ear lobe.

Her warmth began to calm me. Eventually, my eyes closed, and I drifted to sleep.

I paced the locker room, followed by the eyes of twelve nervous players. I was nervous and edgy but trying to marshal a look of confidence. I went over the specifics of our offense and defense. I discussed what we were likely to see from the other team; the junior varsity of one of the conference's perennial powers. This was our debut, and I was convinced it would set the tone for our season.

"We have prepared for this. We have practiced for this." I stopped pacing and drove home my point. "And *tonight* we will *perform*. We know what we have to do. We're ready! Let's go!"

And we did perform — like a team on a mission. The game was close, and when Molly Cutler scored with under a minute left, we were down by four points. At thirty seconds, I called a time out. We would throw the ball inbounds from under our own basket. I diagrammed the play, although we had practiced it so many times the girls could have run it in their sleep.

"Once we make the basket, we'll call another time out to set up our defense," I told the team just before they made their way back onto the court. The screen and the inbound pass were perfect. Hannah Giddings laid it in easily. Down by two.

Taking the second time out, I was so light-headed I thought I was going to faint. I gathered myself as best I could, and when I looked at the girls, I saw belief in their eyes. They would need to foul, hope the other team missed their shots, get the rebound and make the shot to tie the game. It was our only option.

I turned back to the bench, looked up at the stands and found

Sophie clapping, cheering and watching me. When we made eye contact, she placed her open hand on her heart and patted it twice. I did the same, squared my shoulders and refocused.

The girls did everything I told them to do. They immediately fouled and were set to get the rebound from the free-throws. But that never happened. Our opponents made both free throws and the final seconds of the game ticked away. A two-point margin of defeat.

In the somber locker room, I told the team how proud I was of them and how proud they should be of themselves. "Our first step was to be competitive." I reminded them. "We were." They sadly nodded. "Our second step was to put ourselves in position to win." I paused. "We did."

On the ride home, disappointment and letdown radiated from the back of the bus. I walked back to join them and tried again. "It's okay to be disappointed. But let's not forget the positives. Let's use those positives to our advantage in the next game. You had a taste of what playing well is like. You were close enough to a win to taste it. Next time, we will climb the next step. That step is to WIN!"

The group seemed to take my words to heart, and by the time we got back to the Heights the mood had lightened. When the last girl was gone, I locked the door behind me and headed to the parking lot. Sophie's car was parked next to mine. When she saw me, she hurried over and threw herself into my arms. She buried her face against my neck, her arms encircling me, her hands grabbing my coat's dense fabric.

"I wanted to be here when you got home," she whispered breathlessly. "I am so proud of you."

Our second game was a home game, and I was even edgier than at the first. While I appreciated the attendance of my co-workers and students, their presence made me doubly nervous.

Midway through the third quarter, Molly Cutler stole a pass

and lobbed a perfect throw to Kara Perkins. The basket brought the spectators to their feet. Two plays later, Hannah Giddings muscled her way to a basket in the lane, and the team never looked back. With every basket and every defensive move, their confidence grew. Their reward was a twelve-point win.

At the final buzzer, fans rushed from the bleachers to congratulate the team. Hannah Giddings cried and hugged me. Molly Cutler and I exchanged a thumbs-up. Kara Perkins shared an overly exuberant high-five. Parents sought me out to congratulate me. I was so proud and happy for the girls who finally believed that better things were on the way.

Through it all, Sophie was there with my camera, chronicling the events. She would go to every game she could — a constant presence. The girls began to seek her out after games to ask her if she had taken any good shots. A few of Sophie's pictures even appeared in the school newspaper, and later in the local paper.

As our skill level increased, personal and team confidence thrived. We lost some games, but we were competitive in each one. "Will it" became the team mantra, and banners appeared in the gym. More people started to attend our games. School cheerleaders showed up and the pep band played. The boys' basketball team claimed their cheering section right behind our bench. Students I didn't know greeted me as "Coach."

"Your team has become a school-wide phenomenon," Dee told me one morning as we watched a group of students congratulate Molly and Hannah on their latest victory. Dee patted my arm. "You're doing a fantastic job."

I juggled English classes, counseling duties and coaching; running back and forth, attempting to keep all my plates spinning. I tried to recall how Fitz had balanced the rigors of the job: remaining prepared and productive, exacting and flexible, academic and athletic, tough and sensitive. I thought of her often as I left the coach's office at the end of practice. But it was Sophie who was my rock. Always supportive and encouraging, her unfailing belief helped me through each day.

✦

As the basketball season rounded into its home stretch, and Sophie adjusted to life as a full-fledged attorney, we celebrated our first anniversary. Our chosen date was the day in February that we had committed to living together.

I got in touch with Jane Corman and Phil Blanchett a week before the date and received their commitments to be at the Ground Up at 7:30 that Friday night. I wanted to surprise Sophie by inviting the two people who helped bring us together.

I made one quick stop on the way home, and when I arrived Sophie was waiting for me. In my hand, carefully wrapped and bundled from the cold, I held one long-stemmed white rose.

"The first of many." I promised her.

The rose was immediately placed in a vase on the dining table. As Sophie moved the regular centerpiece to make room for the rose, she brought out a small box she had hidden behind it. "Happy first anniversary."

The box contained a silver cuff bracelet she had seen me eying in a jewelry store. Tears immediately stung my eyes. "Oh, Sophie, you shouldn't have ..."

"But I did." Sophie's eyes were sparkling with excitement. "Put it on."

I did and it was beautiful. "I'll always wear it. I love you." I touched her cheek and kissed her. "I didn't —" I began.

"That's okay." Sophie hurried to reassure me.

"— hide your present downstairs." I finished, while running upstairs and returning with a large, rectangular box. "Open it, Counselor."

Inside the box, a cloth bag protected its cargo. From that cloth bag Sophie removed a black, Italian leather briefcase. I had searched everywhere to find something worthy of Sophie. I had loved the briefcase the minute I saw it. The leather felt like butter when you ran your fingers over it: like Sophie — smooth, soft, and silky.

"Oh, Jensy ..." Sophie ran her hand over the leather. "It's beyond beautiful."

"A real attorney needs something more professional than an old, cloth briefcase."

"I love it. I love you."

Our anniversary dinner was at The Brew Pub, site of our first dinner. We sat in the same booth and ordered the same meals. We were setting our own traditions. I loved that feeling of commitment and promise, as we began to build our life together.

When Sophie returned from a short trip to the restroom, she crowded up against me on my side of the booth. She angled her body to block the view of any curious passersby. "This is what I wanted to do that first night we were here," she whispered and placed her hand on my inner thigh, moving it slowly upward.

"Jesus, Sophie ..." I breathed. My hands, resting on the tabletop, clenched into fists. I felt color rise from my chest to my throat to my face. "You are —"

"What?"

"So naughty." I couldn't look at her; not while her hand was moving up my thigh. I didn't know whether to smile or moan.

"What else?"

"A tease," I choked.

"Sexy?"

"Oh, God. That, too."

"I just want you to know what a hard time I had keeping my hands off you." She leaned in to deposit a quick, light kiss on my cheek.

Our waiter cleared his throat; he had arrived with our food.

"You can put my food on the other side," Sophie told him as

she looked over her shoulder. "I was just moving back."

The waiter raised his eyebrows, then made eye contact with me.

"What can I do?" I asked him as my color slowly returned to normal. "She just can't keep her hands off me." I shrugged.

"Lucky you." He sighed and winked.

After dinner, Sophie was delighted when I suggested we go to the Ground Up. The few blocks of snow-covered sidewalk reminded me of the previous winter when I had taken similar walks with her.

When we arrived, Phil and Jane were sitting at the table Phil and Sophie had occupied when I was first magnetically drawn across the room. Sophie had held me spellbound that evening, a fascination that left my knees wobbly and my thoughts disjointed. I had been lost in her eyes, her smile, and her touch. I still was. I couldn't imagine my life without Sophie — the love of my life.

"Surprise!" We all said in unison when we saw Phil and Jane sitting at the table; the situation dawning on us at the same time.

Jane and Phil laughed, "Happy anniversary." Hugs and kisses were exchanged. "Phil and I had to laugh. You two planned the same surprise. I swear, you're starting to think alike. That's frightening," Jane told us.

"Even down to telling us the exact time." Phil shook his head.

"Who better to celebrate with than the two who pushed us together — almost literally." Sophie reached out and took their hands. "Thank you."

The four of us sat back, sipped our lattes and reminisced.

"Jensy. Remember when I left you here with the specific instructions to 'get a cup of coffee and make your presence known'?"

I certainly did remember. That night Jane had forced me to wait for Sophie. Her instruction was followed by Phil's reminder of how special Sophie was. In retrospect, it was amazing Sophie and I had survived my hesitations and angst.

Jane continued, "I never would have believed chemistry like

that existed if I hadn't seen it with my own eyes."

I remembered Jane pointing out the young woman across the coffee shop. The current that drew me to Sophie had been so strong that it pulled me across the floor. Her large, captivating eyes and her arresting smile melted my heart then and now. I was in the right place at the right time: the beneficiary of Sophie's belief that dreams can come true. I would be forever grateful that all three at the table had pushed and pulled me through my insecurities.

I raised my latte to Jane, "Thank you, my friend."

I turned to Phil. "And thank you for being Sophie's best advocate. For letting me know how my behavior was affecting her." I raised my latte. "And for telling me that if Sophie hadn't been gay, you would have been working overtime to put a ring on her finger."

Sophie looked at Phil and blushed in surprise.

Phil nodded his "you're welcome," followed by a quick look at Sophie's left-hand ring finger. He smiled, "I see there's still some work to be done."

"Not for long." I looked at Jane, who reached in her pocket, pulled out a small box and handed it to me. I knelt in front of Sophie and opened the box. The ring was two interlocking bands: one white gold and the other yellow gold. Our initials were engraved on the inside of each band.

I took the ring and held it just millimeters from Sophie's finger. "This ring signifies the two of us ... our lives intertwined ... separate, yet one. If you'll have me, I'm yours forever."

"Yes. Oh, yes, I'll have you." Sophie whispered and, totally caught off-guard, wiped away her tears.

I gently slid the ring onto her finger. I got off my knee to the applause of several patrons and staff.

"But I didn't ... I wish ... I don't ..." Sophie stammered.

"But you do." Phil told her and took an identical box from his pocket. He pushed the box across the table to Sophie.

Sophie swallowed hard, and tears filled her eyes once again.

She thought for a moment, then took the ring, knelt in front of me and placed it on my finger. "Forever won't be long enough." Our impromptu ceremony, in front of our two greatest champions, was complete.

There was one last stop on our celebratory evening. Though the Cobblestone Bridge had not been part of our first meeting, it was imbued with special meaning. We walked to the center of the bridge. The night had become cold, and the top of the river was just starting to freeze. The city lights glinted off the ice and the partially frozen waterfall.

"I don't know where to start." I could hear the tenderness in Sophie's voice.

"Then let me." I took off my glove and placed my warm hand on her cold cheek. "For me, every day with you is like getting the best present ever. It's Christmas Eve — every night. Christmas Morning — every morning. Christmas Day — every day."

Sophie unzipped my jacket, slipped her arms around me, and tightly held the back of my shirt. "I love you," she whispered against my neck. I could have stood there forever.

Toward the end of the basketball season, I finally began to hit my stride. Basketball practices became more routine, and lesson plans came more easily. My guidance counseling role seemed to develop a rhythm as I became familiar with various resources. I developed a system, and my days had a pattern. I finally felt like I could take a breath.

Throughout that busy year Sophie and I always managed to make time for us. On most Saturday evenings we danced and, as Joe had predicted, I began to find it a pleasure. It was a new type of closeness that brought Sophie and me joy and satisfaction. Two nights a week we tried to schedule a sit-down dinner at home, working our way around late and busy schedules. Thursday evenings I joined Sophie at Baxter, Cragen & Reed on her self-imposed late night. I took my own projects and settled in the firm's law library until Sophie was ready to leave. We consciously and conscientiously made the most of our time together.

Our friendship with Dee, Bob and the boys blossomed that year. A typical get-together at the Nelson's often revolved around Mark and Richie, until the boys were finally tucked into bed and the adults were able to share time and conversation.

"The great thing about having you two here is that it's like having a date night right in our own home." Bob laughed, late that spring. "We feed you, and you watch our kids."

"We do have an ulterior motive for having you here tonight." Dee changed the conversational course. "But first. Jensy. The school board agreed to an additional half-time counseling position. You'll need to apply for that new half-time position, and that will bring you up to full-time counselor. It will just be the formality to get the paperwork done."

Sophie squeezed my hand. "I'm so relieved." She looked from Dee to me. "It's been a long year."

"I know." Dee commiserated.

"I'm relieved, too. Numb," I admitted. "I kept telling myself that it might not happen." I blew out a stream of air. "I'm just so glad it did. Thank you, Dee. I couldn't have made it through the year without you. You have been my life saver."

"There isn't anyone else I'd rather save — next to my own family, of course."

"Which brings us to our second agenda item." Bob cleared his throat, and I could tell that this was going to be important. "This is something Dee and I have discussed in the past, but we could never come up with anyone. But that changed when we met the two of you. We're asking if you'd be willing to be godparents to the boys. If anything happens to us, would you be willing to raise them?"

When Dee and Bob offered us the chance to discuss their request, we took the time right there. While they checked on the boys, Sophie and I walked out onto their deck and looked at the back yard filled with toys and structures for small children.

"I think we should say yes," Sophie said softly.

I raised my eyebrows and gave her a questioning look. I hadn't expected her answer.

"You think that's strange, given what I've said about having children."

"Confusing. *Especially* after our conversation." I put my arm around her shoulders. If Richie and Mark became ours, it would still entail bringing them up in what Sophie considered a challenging environment. It might require decisions on our jobs and how we would refocus our lives. It would no longer be just the two of us — comfortable in our safety net.

"Chances are it will never come to that. But if something did happen … we love those little boys. I would be willing to take them." Sophie's arm circled my waist and her fingers grasped onto my belt loop. "You said you're ambivalent about having children. What do you think?"

"I'd say 'yes.'" On the one hand it was so simple. On the other hand, it was potentially so complex. But I was humbled and touched by Dee and Bob's confidence in us, and Sophie was right, I did love those little guys.

She leaned her weight against me. "Good."

We stood for a few moments, thinking our own separate thoughts. Then we smiled at each other and returned to share our news with Dee and Bob.

✦

Three weeks later, Bob and Dee decided they needed a weekend away, and we willingly offered to take the boys. The Nelsons dropped off Mark and Richie very early Saturday morning, complete with clothes, toys, and a couple bags of favorite foods.

"Just go," I told them as I pushed them out the door. "They'll be fine. We have an entire weekend of kid things planned."

And just that quickly we were alone with two young children. We took our young charges to a park, then to the science museum. Home for a nap, then back to the park. On Saturday night we made individual pizzas. We ended the day on the floor, building with LEGOS and watching movies. Finally, baths were taken, jammies on, beds made up, and the boys tucked in. We were exhausted.

"My lord," Sophie sighed as she got into bed, "I thought I was in good shape."

I was ready to get in beside her but stopped myself. "Do you think we can close the bedroom door?"

Sophie wrinkled her nose. "Probably best to leave it open."

"Just think ... we get to do it all over again tomorrow," I reminded her as I threw off my clothes and sank onto the bed.

"Give us strength." We laughed.

"About having kids —" We looked at each other tiredly and shook our heads. "I think not." Sophie demurred with a sigh.

We lay on our backs looking up at the ceiling. I turned my head and looked at Sophie. It was Saturday night — "our" night.

"We probably shouldn't, should we?" I whispered.

Sophie smiled ruefully at me.

"We'd have to be very quiet."

She nodded. "No sex talk."

"No moaning or gasping."

"Certainly, no screaming."

I kicked her foot. "I do not scream."

Sophie scoffed. "We'd have to go under the covers."

"Most likely."

We both looked back up at the ceiling. "Nope." We agreed in unison.

In the early morning hours, I was awakened by Richie making his way onto our bed. He determinedly crawled up and wormed his way between us.

"What's the matter, sweetie?" Sophie whispered groggily.

"Wanna sleep with you." Richie was still half asleep.

"Okay." Sophie held up the sheet and Richie crawled under.

When I woke later that morning, Mark had wormed his way beside me. I swiveled my head to see Richie sitting up and staring at Sophie, the bedsheet had receded to her waist during the night.

Richie turned his head and smiled at me. I thought I heard him say, "Boobs."

I nodded, smiled back at him, and said quietly, "Sophe … Sophie … it's time to wake up."

There was a slight stirring as Sophie opened one eye. I moved my head to indicate the errant sheet. Richie watched as she reached down and pulled the sheet up around her neck. "Good morning, sweetheart," she said to Richie. Then, to me, "Could you get me a T-shirt?"

I looked at her wide-eyed and began to laugh. "I don't have anything on either. You get up."

"He's looking at me." Sophie whispered through closed lips.

"Looking," Richie echoed.

"He'll be looking at me if I get up. He's already seen you."

Sophie shot me an exasperated look that morphed into laughter at the absurdity of it all.

I poked Mark. "Hey, buddy, how about getting us some clothes? A couple shirts from the bottom drawer." Obediently, Mark sleepily got up, opened the drawer, and brought back two T-shirts. I distracted the boys while Sophie got dressed; then quickly dressed while she herded them to the stairs.

At the bedroom door, Sophie turned back to me and tapped her forehead. "Note to self: next time wear clothing to bed."

Early that evening, after another full day, Dee and Bob arrived to pick up the boys. Relaxed and rested, they told us they'd had a wonderful time. They chuckled when they saw our tired eyes, sagging shoulders and weary smiles. We looked haggard and a bit worse for wear. "Welcome to our world." Dee laughed and hugged her boys. "After a while, you learn to pace yourself," she chuckled.

Mark tugged at his father's sleeve until Bob bent over and listened to him. Bob's eyes lit up and he grinned. "Mark tells me you girls sleep naked."

"Boobs," Richie chimed in, looking at Sophie.

Sophie and I blushed furiously. "I never thought they'd show up to sleep with us. Live and learn." I offered helplessly.

"Tattletales," Dee playfully scolded the boys and winked at us.

We slumped against the door when it closed. "We're alone." Sophie said thoughtfully. "We can do whatever we want." She ran her eyes over my body and headed up the stairs.

"Can I scream?" I called after her, in hot pursuit.

Sophie called from the bedroom. "All you want!"

Fourteen

Dee and I hit the ground running my second year at the Heights. We began to do the work she had always wanted to do but had never had time for. We brought several support groups to fruition. Closest to my heart, was the program we developed to support our gay and lesbian students. To our relief and satisfaction, all our new groups were well-received and well-attended. In addition, I worked with an ever-growing number of individual students. I was challenged and fulfilled.

The basketball season saw Washington Heights' re-entry to varsity level play. True to Sophie's vision, we provided the team with gold practice T-shirts emblazoned with maroon lettering. The slogan the team adopted was the rallying cry: "Will-It, AGAIN." There was a new confidence and desire to improve. The girls believed that on-going success was likely and that they could create their own destiny. It was exciting to watch their transformation.

Taking a page from Fitz's playbook, I organized controlled scrimmages against the guys' team. It provided a chance to play against a more polished group and gave us another opportunity to develop and hone our skills. I adopted an offense Fitz had used in Tolliver. She was often there with me in spirit, responsible for many of the coaching decisions I made.

Sophie continued to come to games with my camera in tow. After some instruction from me, she came to a practice to take individual and group photos of the team. The pictures ranged from serious to fun, and highlighted the new uniforms that celebrated the team's return to varsity competition.

Most important, we began to win on a varsity level. The three-year drought was over. Like our junior varsity experience the previous year, we were competitive in almost every game. The lone exception was a twenty-one-point loss to the defending conference champions. I attempted to have a pep talk after our loss, but it was clear the girls were so bitterly disappointed they couldn't listen. The back of the bus was silent on the ride home. At one point I toyed with the idea of moving back and attempting the pep talk again. But I decided it might be better to let them sit.

I had closed my eyes and was reflecting on different coaching decisions I might have made when Molly Cutler's voice roused me.

"Come back here, everyone!"

I turned in my seat, leaned back against the window, and watched in the semi-darkness as the team squeezed into the last two rows. I could hear Molly's voice: the words indistinct, but the tone intense. The talk continued for several minutes. I could also make out Kara Perkins and Hannah Giddings' voices in the crowd. Then so loud it made me jump, their voices sounded as one.

"NEVER AGAIN!"

I smiled. I didn't think I would ever have to worry about leadership as long as Molly Cutler was playing. I closed my eyes again, and Fitz came to mind. As a coach, Fitz also demanded a lot from herself. Her planning and preparation skills were meticulous. She knew when to criticize and when to affirm. She knew how to be tough, and when she needed to soften and change course.

I aspired to be that kind of coach. I paid attention to detail and was analytical. I demanded that players be motivated and responsive to constructive criticism. I worked hard on my game preparation and did my best to prepare the team. I was learning when to be tough and when to be flexible. Like Fitz, I never forgot to emphasize our commitment to "we" — the team. On my best days I liked to think Fitz would have been proud of me.

After our sixth win, Dee remarked to me, "And just think, there were those naysayers who said it couldn't be done."

"What couldn't be done?"

"Turn this team into a winner at the varsity level."

"Ah ... well ... those naysayers were never very bright — were they?"

Dee raised her shoulders and shrugged. "Nope."

We finished our eighteen-game season with a record of twelve wins and six losses. We won the first game in district playoffs, only to lose the second game by three points. It had been a good season, but the close loss at the end was extremely bittersweet — bitter that we couldn't pull off a victory, but sweet that we had come so far.

I was in the coaching office stuffing my practice clothing and court shoes into a gym bag as the girls straggled out of the locker room. Several players, one last time, jumped up and touched the "Will-It, AGAIN" sign I had posted above the door. I was zipping my bag when Molly Cutler re-entered the locker room.

"Coach?"

"Molly?" I smiled at her.

She flashed a quick smile and entered the office. She stood alongside me like she had the year before when she made the commitment to continue for another year. Once again, she bumped her shoulder against mine. "We'll do it again next year."

"Yes, we will," I promised her for the second time.

We were at home on a Saturday night after dance lessons, when Sophie received a phone call from Clarisse. From Sophie's end of the conversation, I surmised that Clarisse and Henry were taking a short trip to the city. Though Henry wasn't in good health, he was insistent that he attend an important board meeting.

I was at the kitchen sink when the call ended. Sophie came up behind me, encircled my waist and put her cheek against my back.

"Should we call Viv and Mary to see if we can stay with them? Did Clarisse give you definite dates?" On other visits they had stayed at the townhouse, and Sophie and I had stayed with Viv and Mary.

Sophie didn't respond, except to hold me tighter. I slowly turned around in her arms and looked into her eyes. "What did Clarisse say?"

"They're not staying here. They're staying at a downtown hotel near the office." Her eyes drifted away from mine and over my shoulder.

"Why? We're fine going to Viv and Mary's —"

"Clarisse said Henry shouldn't be walking up stairs. It's too taxing for his heart."

"He's worse." There was no other explanation. I took Sophie by the hand and led her to a chair at the kitchen table.

She sank down weakly. "I'm so worried about him." I could hear the tears in her voice. "He's been like a father to me." She wiped her cheeks as tears began their slow descent.

"I know."

As Sophie's relationship with her own father deteriorated, her relationship with Henry had grown in importance. Not only was he her employer, but she had come to openly regard him as her surrogate father. I thought it had been good for her; after all, she deserved a father like Henry, someone who loved her and had her best interests at heart.

Sophie's anxiety tugged at my heart. "It's a good precaution. Henry and Clarisse just want to be careful." I suggested, making the tone positive and hopeful.

"Maybe ..." But we both realized that there was more to it than that. "I don't know what I'll do —" Sophie didn't take the unfinished sentence to its conclusion; she couldn't. She brushed away the rest of the sentence like she brushed away her tears.

I reached across the table and covered her hand. "Let's be positive." I tried to bring back Sophie's sense of optimism. But I felt her fear that she was going to lose Henry: not only the father-figure — but also the boss. The man who thought highly enough of Sophie to put her on the fast track to a partnership. Her champion.

Sophie was on edge the entire week as she awaited Henry and Clarisse's arrival. Though she said little, I knew Sophie was still bothered by what Clarisse's phone call had implied.

"Henry will be at the office today." Clarisse had called the night before to tell Sophie they had arrived. But Henry had been too tired to have visitors.

That morning, I noticed that Sophie seemed to be taking extra care with her appearance. She discarded a couple clothing choices before she settled on a navy-blue jacket and skirt with a sleeveless, scoop-neck, white satin blouse. White pearl stud earrings, a touch of lip gloss and blush completed her ensemble. She wanted to look perfect for Henry.

"You look delicious." I attempted to ease the moment.

"Thanks," Sophie raised her eyebrows. "But I just want to look professional."

To me, Sophie was always the ultimate in classy and impeccable. Tailored with a bit of almost-hidden sexuality thrown in. "You always look professional, Counselor. Professional to everyone else, but delicious to me. It's all a matter of perspective."

She graced me with a half-smile and shook her head. "Don't think for a minute I don't appreciate 'delicious.' I do." She touched my arm. "I just want to look professional for Henry."

"I know. And you do." I kissed the tip of her nose, afraid to disturb her lip gloss.

Sophie arrived home from a firm-wide dinner for Henry much earlier than I expected. She was shaken and pale; her mouth set in a straight line and her posture weary.

"Sophe?" I closed my book and placed it on the table.

She shook her head slowly, took off her jacket and slumped next to me. I put my arm around her and rubbed her shoulder. Placing her forehead against my temple, she murmured, "He's not well."

"We knew that," I replied gently.

"I mean, *really* not well." Once the words started coming, they didn't stop. "He's using a walker — not a cane — a walker." There was strained disbelief in her voice. "He's pale and fragile-looking. He was so fatigued at dinner I thought he was going to fall asleep. He couldn't even stay for dessert." Her eyes searched my face, looking for reassurance I couldn't give. "I left with Henry and Clarisse. When we got Henry situated in the taxi Clarisse told me it would probably be their last trip to the city. It was just too much for him."

My hand tightened around her shoulder, and I drew her against me. I nodded in sympathy. "Did you get much of a chance to talk to him?" I knew that was important to her.

"Not more than a few words." From the side I could see her eyes close, her lashes delicate against her cheeks. "He stopped by my cubicle for a moment to tell me the partners were extremely pleased with my work. He said I was right on track. That was it. He was at the end of his stamina." She put her hand on mine and looked at me. "Clarisse invited us to dinner tomorrow night. Just the four of us. I said we'd be there. You'll come, won't you?" Sophie asked with a tremor in her voice, sweeping her hand through her hair. "Please come."

"Of course." Nothing would keep me away.

✦

When we showed up at the hotel restaurant, Henry and Clarisse were already seated.

"Sorry, we're late," Sophie apologized, although we were on time.

"Actually, we're early." Henry chuckled softly.

I was shocked by his appearance. Once so vital, he now looked like a weak and fragile elderly man. His skin color was ashen, and he had lost weight. Only his blue eyes remained lively and interested. Henry seemed to energize when he saw Sophie; he even rose from his chair. The hugs and kisses were warm and heartfelt.

"How are both of you?" Henry inquired after we were seated. He and Clarisse had always been generous in their inclusion of me, making me feel like a member of their extended family. Normally I provided more information, but on this night I said my piece quickly so Sophie could have their attention.

"Sounds like your team is progressing." Henry nodded after my short summary, but his eyes were already shining on Sophie. I could see how much he adored her … and she, him. "And you, my dear, how is everything with you?"

"Fine. Things are wonderful at home." Under the table, Sophie touched my thigh. "I love the work I'm doing at the firm. It's perfect: challenging and interesting. I think it suits me."

"It certainly does," Henry nodded in agreement.

There was a short silence that Clarisse filled. "Henry and I have something we want to share with you, Sophie, before it becomes common knowledge at the office."

Henry cleared his throat and looked into Sophie's eyes. "My time at the firm is coming to an end. There's no other way to say this, Sophie, dear. I do not have the stamina to continue — even in a limited role. And to be honest, my desire to participate is flagging." He reached across the table and covered Sophie's hand with his. "I had hoped to work for many more years, but my heart had other plans."

"Henry —" I could see tears in Sophie's eyes.

"These things happen." He patted her hand. "It's the natural course of life, as I am sure you understand. I won't be able to tolerate another trip north." He reached into the upper pocket of his suit coat and handed Sophie his monogrammed handkerchief. Sophie blotted her eyes. "You are in a good place at work and in your personal life. I'm so happy for you, my dear. As long as I am able, I will be here for you."

Clarisse reached across the table and held my hand. "Come see us," she offered. I squeezed her hand.

"I will remain on the board in an emeritus capacity. No duties whatsoever — just a title. I will be excellent in that role, I promise." Henry laughed a little, then looked closely at Sophie. She returned his look, but had to turn away, blinking her eyes and fighting to hold back tears. "This is how things need to be." He told her gently.

Sophie bowed her head and nodded in agreement. Henry placed a finger under her chin and lifted her head. "Clarisse and I were never blessed with children. But we were blessed to have you come into our lives. You have been our breath of fresh air. Our daughter by choice. You have made us proud. We love you."

I looked away. I couldn't bear to look at the two of them: the childless father-figure and the young woman who longed for a father. My heart ached for both of them.

After dinner, we all stood in the lobby by the elevator. Clarisse led me aside to give Henry and Sophie a private goodbye. "She's taking this hard," Clarisse observed.

"She loves you both." My voice was choked with emotion.

"And we love her very much," she said. "Take care of her, Jensy. She's more fragile than you think." Clarisse kissed my cheek and followed Henry into the elevator.

We walked slowly to Sophie's car. Wordlessly, I held out my hand and Sophie gave me her keys. On the way home, she silently processed the evening; her only recognition of my presence was her hand resting on my leg. I parked on the street, put my arm around Sophie and held her against me while we walked. Instead of turning up the stairs, we crossed the street to the bench overlooking the river.

"He was saying goodbye." Her voice was quiet and subdued.

I had felt that, as well. The lights above the walking path highlighted the tears glistening in Sophie's eyes. Neither of us had ever lost anyone close. It was a difficult 'first', and I tightened my hold on her.

"This shouldn't be happening," Sophie insisted. "Henry should have many years left. It's not right." She was sad and incensed at the same time.

"It's not right," I agreed. I thought for a moment, searching for something consoling to say. "But it is right that you were able to meet such a kind and caring man. It's right that he thinks of you as a daughter. It's right that you love him. And it's right that you feel a sense of loss."

Sophie put her head against my shoulder ... and we sat.

My third season of basketball had just begun when Sophie received a call from Clarisse Baxter. My life was now moving at the speed of light, and the first couple days of practice were exhausting. I was half-asleep on the couch when Sophie answered her phone.

I didn't pay attention until I heard a startled Sophie say, "Oh, Clarisse."

I sat up and listened to the one-sided conversation.

"When? ... Where? ... How long? ... What can I do? ... Tell Henry I love him."

Silence. I got up and found her standing in the kitchen, with the phone still clutched tightly in her hand. Her head was bowed, and her shoulders heaved once. I gently removed the phone and enfolded her in my arms.

"He's in ICU. Clarisse says it's bad." Her hands grabbed the back of my shirt and held tight. "Oh, Jens ..."

"Go there, Sophie. Now. Tonight."

I was going to offer to go with her, when she told me, "I know it's a bad time for you. You need to be here for the team. I'll be okay. Clarisse will be there."

"You're sure?"

"Yes."

"Then call Clarisse back. Go pack." I took out my phone. "I'll get you a flight."

Sophie and Clarisse were at Henry's side when he passed three days later. Sophie was able to tell him she loved him before he slipped into a coma. She stayed with Clarisse for a week before returning to the city late Sunday evening.

Sophie was quiet when I picked her up from the airport. Unless I asked pointed questions, she shared little about Henry, Clarisse, or the funeral. Even then her answers were short and held little or no elaboration. She was exhausted, sad, and easily teary. I knew Henry's death weighed heavily on her. I tried not to press too hard and give Sophie the space she needed to work through her feelings. I didn't force or pry; I just watched and waited.

Our lives were further complicated by the fact that my own schedule was running full tilt. The week Sophie returned I was engaged in late practices. I left early for work and returned late. I assumed we had returned to our normal, busy routines. It wasn't until the second week after Sophie's return that I began to notice things that concerned me. One evening when Sophie was standing at the bathroom sink, I noticed she had lost weight. Her clothing seemed to hang on her already-slender frame. I racked my brain trying to remember the last time we had eaten together. I was upset I couldn't remember.

I looked again to make sure I was correct about her weight loss. "I can start making you a lunch." I offered.

"That's nice, but not necessary." She swept away my suggestion.

I went shopping anyway and picked up things I knew she would like and packed her lunches. I woke early in the morning to the sound of the shower, Sophie's side of the bed already cold. By the time I made my way downstairs, I was greeted by a quick kiss goodbye or a posted "thank you" note for the lunch I had made. This was new for us. Typically, I was the earlier riser. Often, we had morning coffee together. I missed that.

Sophie's work hours began to spill into the evening. "Let's go back to our evening eating routine," I suggested to entice her to come home earlier. We had always reserved at least two nights a week for us. But my suggestion went unheard. So, I stopped waiting. I was just too hungry to wait past 7 p.m. If I made something for the two of us, I would leave it for Sophie to reheat. She was good about letting me know that she was "hung up" at the office and would be late, but the increasing frequency of those nights bothered me.

"Are things okay at work?" I asked. "You're working longer hours than normal. Do you have new clients? Has your workload increased?'

She sighed. "No. I'm just trying to do my best work." She didn't offer anything more than that.

"Are *we* okay?"

"Why would you ask?"

"You're distant. You're gone a lot. I miss you." I ticked off the items and knew my voice sounded plaintive.

"Times like these come and go. You know that, Jensy." She dismissed my concerns.

Around mid-evening she would disappear to the bedroom to

sit in bed and do paperwork or read legal tomes. She had done this on occasion ever since we had been together, but it had become more frequent. I often found her asleep, sitting up in bed, with papers and books scattered around her. I would remove the items, gently help her down under the sheets and climb in beside her.

"Do you know how much I love you?" I asked Sophie one night as she snuggled sleepily against me.

"Not as much as I love you." She kissed a spot beneath my ear.

I gently moved a stray hair from her forehead. Henry's death seemed to have touched somewhere so deep inside her that neither of us were able to reach it.

"Are you all right, Sophie?" I whispered into the darkness.

She let out a trembling breath.

"Sophe?"

"I don't know," she responded quietly.

Her answer was both expected and unexpected; it tugged at my heart, nevertheless. Over the two and a half years I had known Sophie, she had always been so solid: together, logical, and insightful about herself and others. Sophie had been the problem solver — not the problem. Now she seemed lost. I waited, but she didn't say anything.

"How can I help?" I moved my hand to the back of her head. "What can I do?"

Sophie took a deep breath. "I don't know what anyone else can do. *I* don't even know what to do."

Sophie had always known who she was and what she wanted. She had always been the one who helped me out, calmed me down and reasoned me through. She always had a plan. Simply put, she had always been my rock. Now when the situation warranted it and she might need me, I wasn't sure what to do. I felt helpless.

I struggled to find something meaningful to say. Something that would make a difference and change the course of events for Sophie. I wanted so badly to help her; but my old feelings of inadequacy resurfaced. If I couldn't help Sophie, what did I really have to offer her? I finally responded with what I knew was an imperfect suggestion, "Just continue to make Henry proud of you."

At first, Sophie stiffened in my arms, and I feared my suggestion had been found wanting. I believed I had failed her. Then her hand moved to my chest and rested there. I ran my hand up and down her back until her deep breathing indicated sleep.

For a while our weekends remained the same, but gradually they began to change. One Sunday we were invited to Dee and Bob's for an afternoon of football, young boys, and hot dogs. I reminded Sophie of the invitation the Friday evening before.

"I'm so sorry, Jensy, I forgot. I promised Randy Myers I would go in Sunday afternoon to give him some help."

"Reschedule." I urged her. It wasn't like Sophie to forget or not honor a commitment. "We haven't seen the Nelson's in over a month."

But Sophie was adamant. "I'll tell Dee I can't make it. But you go, please. You'll have fun."

I was annoyed, then felt guilty that I was annoyed. But for the first time, I went to the Nelson's house without Sophie. Richie was heartbroken, and even though Dee had already told him that Sophie wouldn't be there, he still asked where she was. He couldn't believe that 'at work' was more important than he was.

Dee sent home some leftovers. "Tell Sophie how much we missed her today. Especially Richie."

When I got home at seven, Sophie wasn't there. Finally, at eight she arrived. "You've been gone more hours than a regular workday," I remarked. "Randy must have really needed your help." I couldn't help the slight twinge of sarcasm that entered my tone.

Sophie kicked off her shoes and slumped onto the sofa. Sitting sideways, her back against the armrest, she stretched out her legs and closed her eyes. When I offered to get the leftovers, Sophie shook her head.

"Massage?" I asked, trying to make up for my sarcasm.

Sophie sighed and put her feet in my lap. As I began the massage, I could see her begin to relax.

"What's going on with Randy now?" I asked about the new hire who had become Sophie's mentoring project.

Sophie shook her head and her eyes remained closed, but her tone was defensive. "Nothing a couple hours couldn't straighten out." She let out a long breath as I kneaded her arch.

"And what about all the other hours you were there? What's going on?" My voice rose slightly.

"Just work and more work."

"Work and more work." I repeated, my annoyance level rising with a tone that I couldn't keep in check. In the last few days, she had become increasingly withdrawn.

"It's been busy, Jensy. There's a lot to do." That part of the conversation was abruptly finished. Frustration, guilt, and tension filled Sophie's voice. Her mouth was set in a straight line and her eyes seemed to focus on something in the distance. She removed her feet and sat upright, her posture tight and protective. Then, she seemed to literally shake herself and move on. She waved her hand and changed the subject. "I would much rather hear about your time at the Nelson's."

I didn't press her, but my voice mirrored her tension. "Everyone missed you. Richie especially. He doesn't understand about 'working' when you were supposed to be there with him."

"Next time."

But 'next time' was the same as the last time, as the next invitation to the Nelsons met with the same fate. I was disappointed, hurt and concerned. It felt like I was being shut out of Sophie's life. We had always talked about everything, always done things together. The pattern of our lives had changed, and it left me confused and afraid.

That evening we watched television in silence. I didn't ask

about work or question why Sophie had declined the invitation. By the time I crawled into bed, Sophie was already on her side, turned away from me. I was lonely for her; I missed her. As I spooned her, I ran my hand up her leg to her breast. I lightly tongued the back of her neck. Sophie took my hand and moved it away.

"I can't. I'm just too tired."

I rolled over on my back and looked at the ceiling.

"I'm sorry." Sophie's voice was detached, as if it came from far away.

"I am, too." I could feel myself withdrawing, building my wall of self-protection.

It was a month after Henry's death when Dee took me aside. "Is everything okay at your house?"

"You mean aside from the fact that Sophie's working thirteen-hour days and weekends?" I shrugged, knowing I sounded petulant. "Everything's wonderful."

"And you've talked with Sophie about why she's working so hard?"

"Whenever I ask her something about work, she answers in one or two words or redirects the conversation. I thought the firm was getting new clients, or that they put Sophie on a new project. I don't know. She hasn't mentioned anything about anything. Right now she's not inclined to discuss her work or our lives — or anything, really."

"I'm sure it will sort itself out. Just be patient and give it time."

"How much time do I give it?" I wanted Dee to have a concrete answer.

"I wish I knew." She looked at me sympathetically and put her hand on my shoulder. Patience was a stretch for me, and Dee knew it.

✦

Sophie's changes seeped into the basketball season. Though Sophie still cheered for the team and took photos, her attendance at our games became sporadic. The girls had always loved having her there, and they missed her constant presence and support. But I was the one who hurt the most when she failed to show.

We talked less, and silences that had once been companionable were now filled with uneasy tension. I was tired of asking unanswered questions, and tired of trying to explain Sophie's absences. I continued to withdraw. Sophie had already withdrawn.

Every aspect of our life together became a casualty when Sophie's absence finally extended to dancing. We had danced almost every Saturday night for over a year. We had progressed to the point where we entered contests and did reasonably well. It had become a joy-filled experience for both of us. As with everything else, Sophie's attendance initially became irregular; then she was either too busy or too tired.

One Saturday when I called to cancel, Joe offered a proposal. "I have a student who broke up with her partner a while ago, and now she'd like to finish her lessons. How about coming in this afternoon and being her dance partner? It would help me out and give you something to do."

I was interested. Aside from work, I hadn't done much of anything for a while. My time at home was often unproductive, with my mind spinning on our lack of communication or yearning for our former level of camaraderie and intimacy. Though I really had no desire to dance with anyone but Sophie, I needed to get out and do something. I needed to give my mind something else to think about. I looked around the empty townhouse and reluctantly agreed.

I left a note for Sophie and headed to the studio. When Joe saw me his relief was visible. It was a large class, and everyone was coupled up, but for one.

"Jensy!" Joe called to me and hurried across the floor with a woman in tow. "Anna Thomas, this is Jensy Willett ... your partner for tonight."

Anna Thomas was probably a few years older than I. She was pretty and petite: raven haired with warm brown eyes, a disarming smile and infectious laugh. We laughed when she stepped on my toes or when she turned one way while I was leading the other. Despite everything, it was good to laugh and wonderful to dance.

"I was never that good to begin with," Anna confessed. "But I know I've regressed since Jill and I broke up."

Making polite conversation, I asked, "How long ago was that?"

"Six months."

"I'm sorry. That's hard."

"It's one of those things. We're still friendly. I'm doing fine." She shrugged a "moving on" kind of shrug. "How long have you been working with Joe?"

"My partner and I have been working with him for a year and a half. But I've known Joe all my life."

"Where is your partner, if you don't mind my asking?" Anna glanced around the room.

I hesitated. For an instant I had the desire to share everything with Anna, a neutral party who just might be sympathetic. Instead, I answered, "Working."

But she had picked up on my hesitation. "I'm sorry. That was intrusive of me." She switched the focus. "I bet you make a good dance team."

"If we are, it has certainly taken me a long time to get there." I laughed, thinking of myself practicing in front of the mirror.

I left the studio in a good mood; it had been an enjoyable evening. It felt good to get out, see Joe, and have a good laugh. It wasn't optimal; it wasn't with Sophie ... but still, it was something.

The following Saturday Sophie came home from the office and

immediately stretched out on the couch. Joe had phoned earlier and asked if I would be willing to help with Anna's last lesson.

"I wish you'd come," I told Sophie wistfully. "I miss the feeling of dancing with you in my arms."

She opened her eyes, and I thought I saw a flash of interest cross her features. Then, she shook her head, "That's sweet, but I'm just tired. All I want to do is relax."

"I think I'll go anyway."

"But I'm home tonight. I thought ..." Sophie's voice drifted away, and she looked upset.

"I'm doing Joe a favor, Sophie. I promised him. There's a singleton student, and Joe volunteered me to help her."

"Lesbian?"

"Yup." I kissed Sophie on the forehead and moved to the door. "See you later."

"Is she pretty?" The tone in Sophie's voice had taken on an edge.

"Yes. But she's not you." If Sophie really wanted to know, she could come with me.

For a second week I danced with Anna Thomas and enjoyed her energy and ready smile. But she wasn't the one I wanted, and I desperately wished Sophie had come along. Joe would have needed to come to some arrangement with Anna, but he could have figured that out.

At the end of the evening Anna and I walked out into the winter night. Our cars were parked next to each other, and we stopped between them.

"Tonight was the last of my lessons. I have to decide if I want to sign up for more." Anna looked at me pointedly.

She reached out and grasped my arm tightly enough so I couldn't easily pull away. "I didn't get the impression that things are going all that well at home. I thought we might go out for a drink. You could talk about it, and we could get to know each other."

Again, I thought of how nice it might be to talk to a neutral party. How good it would be to just let everything out. But underneath Anna's offer there was a suggestive quality in her voice and a hooded look in her eyes.

"No. Thank you." I was tempted, but also leery. I disengaged my arm.

"Because you're taken ..."

"Because I'm taken." *And because I'm not interested in what you might be interested in*, I told myself. "Look, Anna ... you're fun ... attractive —"

"But it would have to be in a different lifetime, in a different universe." Anna finished for me and smiled ruefully. She looked me up and down. "That's such a shame." She searched in her purse, pulled out a business card and placed it in my palm, curling my fingers over it. "In case you change your mind."

I looked at her card, thinking about the "offer" she had just made. I was watching her car pull away when Joe came out. "That was Anna's last lesson. She said she'd call about taking more."

"I wouldn't count on it."

Joe regard me curiously, "I thought not. Well," he sighed, "she's a nice lady."

"She is."

"Attractive."

"She is that."

"Did she try to hit on you?"

"She did." I showed Joe her business card. "She gave me her card."

"I thought she might — the way she looked at you. But it would be hard to be tempted when you have someone like Sophie to go home to."

I smiled and chuckled wearily. I wanted to tell Joe that I was tempted, just not the way he thought. Tempted by the allure of a neutral, listening ear. I patted Joe on the chest and slipped Anna's card in his pocket.

He kissed my cheek. "Tell Sophie I miss her."

When I arrived at the townhouse, Sophie was waiting for me, ready to confront. She was already standing as I entered; her mouth set and her eyes flashing a steel grey. I could tell things weren't going to go well.

"Was she there tonight?" They were the first words out of her mouth. "That pretty woman you went dancing with." I could tell she had been working herself into this since I left home.

"I didn't go dancing with her. I was helping Joe give her lessons."

"Semantics," Sophie spat out. The top note in her voice was frustration; the bottom note — jealousy. Fueled in between by her anger. I didn't like her tone and certainly didn't like her unspoken accusation. Sophie was tired and fuming; I was upset and offended. It was a bad combination — we were both angry and defensive.

"Anna Thomas," I said. "That's her name."

Saying her name stoked Sophie's ire. "Are you interested in her?" The jealous, possessive edge in her voice raised a notch.

"How can you even ask?"

"Then why aren't you answering my question?" Sophie's challenging stare cut like a dagger. "You were certainly in a hurry tonight. You couldn't wait to leave. And I was home —"

"So? So, I could stay home and watch you read legal case books or write briefs?" I shot back. "You could have come dancing with me. I asked you to come. That's what I wanted. I am not interested in Anna Thomas. I — am — interested — in — you. *You.*" I emphasized each word and spread my arms wide. "But tonight's just part of it. You won't go dancing — something we loved. You don't go to Dee and Bob's. Basketball is hit and miss. You're gone more than several nights a week, and I can't even remember the last time we ate together. And intimacy ..." I dropped my arms to my sides. My voice had risen steadily. I was breathing hard, like I had just run wind sprints.

"You're not home every night," Sophie countered, exasperated. "You have late games and late practices."

"That's a scheduled, contracted part of my job. That's different. You're choosing your extra hours." I rubbed my hand over my face. "Haven't you heard what I just said? You're not here — physically or emotionally. You're unraveling."

"I am so far from that. I am totally *raveled.*" Her words were harsh. "Maybe you're just feeling sorry for yourself." She deftly switched the conversation from herself to me.

We were so far outside our norm: staring at each other and gulping huge breaths of air. Sophie's eyes were wide, as if she was stunned by our negative emotions. And I — I was shocked. I had never known Sophie to be mean or nasty; she was the kindest, gentlest person I had ever met. I looked more closely as we stood there watching one another. Makeup couldn't totally conceal the dark circles under Sophie's eyes. She had continued to lose weight. Even her hair seemed to have lost its normal shine. She looked weary.

I was going to disagree but stopped myself. "You're right. I *am* feeling sorry for myself." My tone was matter of fact, and I exhaled a frustrated breath. "I miss you. I miss us. I need you to be an active participant in our lives, not a missing piece. I'm not sure I know this person who slips in and out of my bed morning and night."

"I'm doing this for us." Her frustrated words slipped out and caught us both by surprise.

"*THIS?* What's the '*this*' that you're doing for us?" I was confused. "I don't see you except in passing. Is that for us? You don't share. You're working all the time. Is that for us?"

Then, suddenly, I knew. What I had known all along but had never put together. *This* was about Henry's death. *This* was about making him proud. *This* was about losing a father figure. But there was more to it than all of that. When Henry had been alive, Sophie believed that her work ethic and Henry's support would make a partnership in the firm a certainty. *This* was about a partnership at Baxter, Cragen and Reed.

I shook my head. "You're worried about not making partner if Henry's not there for you. You're working so hard because you feel like you're on your own." My throat tightened. "You're afraid that on your own you're not enough."

We looked at each other in astonishment; my words provided a stark look at the truth.

"This *is* for *us*," she repeated tight-lipped and walked away.

"But you are enough, Sophie. You have always been enough." I said to her retreating back.

Tired, discouraged and at wit's end, I sought out Dee Nelson on Monday morning. When I told her I wanted to talk about issues at home, she immediately informed me, "I'm not going to take sides, Jensy. I think too highly of both of you to do that."

I agreed and related my story from my point of view.

"Communication, Jensy." Dee sighed. "Maybe you need to establish a protocol for weekly check-ins. Discussions where you both agree to honestly share any issues that may be surfacing. This may also help address any future problems. Tell her how much this means to you. You not only need to communicate but you need to find an effective way to communicate. Because I can guarantee that future issues will come up."

I thought I *had* really tried to communicate. I had asked Sophie what was wrong. I had given Sophie space, hoping she would seek me out and share with me. For the most part I had held my frustration in check and hadn't been visibly angry until the other night. But obviously, I was missing some tools in my relationship toolbox.

Dee folded her hands on her desk. "I just wonder what's been going on with her."

"Henry's death." I shook my head, knowing how heartbroken she was when she lost him. I shook my head and took it one step further. "Her wanting a partnership in the firm."

"Is she afraid that with Henry's death she may not get that partnership?" Dee ventured.

"I think so." I turned the idea over in my mind.

"She believes she's doing this for both of you." Dee restated what I had told her earlier. She looked away, but when she looked back her eyes pinned me to my chair. "But what happens if she doesn't make partner? Will she feel she let you down? Is she afraid she will look "less than" to you? So, she works harder and harder to make the partnership a reality and loses focus of everything else. Then finds herself on a never-ending treadmill."

Dee came around her desk and sat down beside me. "I'm guessing, Jensy. Sophie has always seemed so grounded, but maybe she's lost her footing. Maybe it's your mission to help her find her balance again."

What Dee said made sense. Sophie *had* always been able to keep herself balanced and grounded. I had always admired her confidence regarding her career goals. At least, up to now, that had been the image Sophie projected. But what neither of us had reckoned on was Henry's death and how that might affect Sophie's concept of herself and her job. Dee's words rang true.

Dee patted my hand. "There's no relationship that I know of that doesn't go through some rough patches. Work to find a way to talk about these things. Lay the ground rules for your discussions and use them. That way you're more likely to avoid these issues."

◆

Joe called me at work that day. "Hate to bother you, girlfriend. It'll be the last time, I swear. But Sam is out of town, and tonight's my biggest class. If you have time —"

"Joe." Visions of the Anna Thomas fiasco surfaced in my mind.

"No singletons, I promise. It's just to help me monitor everyone's progress. If you can make it, that would be great!"

I sighed, "I'm going to start charging a fee." I heard him laughing as he hung up.

When 6:30 arrived and Sophie wasn't home, I left a note on the refrigerator door: *"Helping Joe. Not Anna."*

It was a huge class, and Joe did need the help. "Thank God," he said when he saw me. "Sam signed up too many people and now he's out of town. Count your blessings, it's the waltz. At least that's simple and straightforward."

We reached the halfway point and took a break. I was standing in line at the water cooler when there was a tap on my shoulder. I thought it was Joe coming to give me further instructions. I turned around to look into the most startlingly beautiful eyes I had ever seen. Her hand briefly touched my cheek, and I thought my knees would buckle.

"I miss the feeling of dancing in your arms." Sophie said simply.

We talked for hours when we got home. Dee had called Sophie and asked her to stop by after work. When Sophie asked if everything was okay, Dee had told her cryptically, "I *think* everything will be fine." Then Dee sat Sophie down and they had a long, heart-to-heart talk.

Sophie unburdened herself to Dee. She shared how terrified she had become after Henry's death; terrified she would be unable to attain her dream of a partnership at Baxter, Cragen & Reed without Henry's help and support. For the first time in her life, she felt totally lost. She knew that I had always considered her to be my "rock," and that caused her to ask herself what I might feel if she failed. Would I find *her* a failure? Would I feel let down? So, she battled her fears alone trying to keep up a confident front.

"I *did* feel like I was unraveling." Sophie admitted when she finally looked at me. "And then with Anna Thomas — I was so jealous — so worried I was going to lose you." It was the first time Sophie had ever considered she might lose me. Suddenly it wasn't just about self-perceived inadequacy at work and not getting a partnership; she thought her life with me was in jeopardy.

"You were never going to lose me." The fear and sadness in Sophie's admission was heartbreaking for me to hear.

"But something did happen with her, didn't it?" She sighed. "I thought something happened because you blushed so furiously when I confronted you. It's your '*tell*.'"

What happened was not what Sophie feared but, rather, the fact that I had thought about confiding in Anna. I felt the heat creep up my face. "She wanted to go out for drinks. I turned her down, but I thought about going. Thought about telling her about our difficulties. She gave me her business card and told me if I changed my mind … I gave the card to Joe." I waved my hands and lifted my shoulders in a helpless gesture.

Sophie nodded, and I knew Anna Thomas was finished as a topic of conversation. "Dee told me I need to open up to you. That I need to allow myself to share my vulnerabilities with you. I'll work on that, Jensy"

Then I shared my feelings of frustration and abandonment as I watched Sophie's career eat up more and more of her time. I told her how much it hurt that she didn't feel she could share her fears with me, and how much I missed the everyday conversation and sharing. "Dee told me we need to set aside time to discuss things, including our issues. I think she's right. It would encourage us to talk, even when it's difficult."

Sophie nodded. "She must think we're quite a pair."

"I think she's protecting her godparent investment," I joked, and we exchanged tired smiles.

"I want so much for us," Sophie told me as she moved across the couch and leaned against me. "I want this law partnership for all the things and opportunities it will give us."

"I love that you want that for us." I put my arm around her shoulders and pulled her close. "But I want *our* partnership, the two of us, for all the things it gives us. Without *our* partnership, your partnership at Baxter, Cragen & Reed is meaningless to me. There is only one thing I want or need. You. Period. End of story."

"I love you, Jens." She kissed my cheek.

I took a deep, jagged breath. "And I love you, Sophie Barnes. So very much."

We were exhausted after weeks of running on empty. We undressed each other slowly and carefully. Starved for Sophie's gentle, loving touch, I drank it in. "Oh, God, Sophie." I whispered, taking her in my arms.

In bed, Sophie put her head on my shoulder, and I wrapped my legs with hers. It felt so good to be close, to be talking, to feel there was an "us" again. Exhausted, physically and emotionally, my eyes began to close.

"Do you mind if we just sleep tonight?" Sophie whispered.

My hand moved slowly up and down her back. "I'm already asleep," I whispered back.

Fifteen

Sophie and I worked to restructure and rebalance our lives and recommitted to the things that had initially defined us. We danced every Saturday evening. Thursday evenings, I arrived at Baxter, Cragen & Reed and worked on school projects until Sophie was ready to go home. All household chores were done in one frantic frenzy on Sunday mornings, which freed us for time together in the afternoon. The structure worked well for us and kept us connected.

We instituted a weekly check-in that had no time limit or dedicated structure beyond open and honest sharing. I worked on tempering my tendency to use sarcasm or flippancy to mask my deeper emotions, and Sophie worked on sharing her fears and letting herself be vulnerable. When Sophie first started to share some of her deeper feelings and fears it was as though a dam had burst, spilling everything.

The only feelings that Sophie continued to keep close to her heart concerned her father. Her outward display regarding William remained thoughtful and composed. Occasionally she mentioned her desire to please him and her confusion about his attitude toward her, but that was as much as she shared. My only real glimpse into Sophie's need for a father-figure was what I had seen with Henry Baxter. Henry had nurtured and affirmed her and had given her the father-daughter relationship she had never had.

However, one early autumn day as we made an infrequent pilgrimage to the "Barnes Family Farm and Creamery," Sophie surprised me. We were a few miles from the farm when Sophie shared, "I'm about at the end. I'm not sure I can keep doing this."

I knew immediately she was talking about her father. I didn't respond right away, but I had been at the "end" with William Barnes since the first time I met him. His treatment of Sophie was demeaning and despicable and made me furious. I wanted to say something affirming, but I wasn't sure I could guarantee a neutral tone. I simply touched Sophie's arm, hoping she would continue.

"I've been doing a lot of thinking about this visit. Things just seem to get worse with my father." She looked over at me, and I nodded my silent affirmation. "Dad and I never really talked all that much in the first place, but now we don't talk at all. For more years than I can count it's been a case of diminishing returns." Sophie sighed. "Every time we visit, my stomach's in knots for days before and after. I'm caught in that definition of insanity — doing the same thing over and over, expecting different results."

"The rest of your family always seems glad when you visit. *They* certainly love you." My eyes opened wide as I realized my verbal gaffe, and I hastily tried to cover my mistake. "I didn't mean that your father doesn't love you."

"Jensy, it's okay." Sophie looked out the window as the farm-land rolled by. "You know, I used to think I had just disappointed him as I grew older: my sexual orientation, career choice, not coming back here to live ..." She gestured at the land. "But when I think back to my early childhood, I'm not sure he ever really loved me. Then, when Henry came into my life, it made me realize what having a father could feel like. I felt loved, valued, and respected. Accepted. All the things I so wished I could have had from my own father. Things I'll never have no matter how much I want them or how hard I try." The rush of words trailed away.

"I know it's been hard, Sophe. It's a lot to accept. A lot of disappointment." I floundered to find meaningful words.

She nodded. "I am disappointed and hurt and confused. But I've lived with that for years. I know I can't make him love me or accept me. And now, I'm just tired. Tired of fighting the battle. And sad that I've had to fight any battle with him."

I could hear the resignation in her voice, mingled with grief and an edge of animosity. I recognized that Sophie was admitting defeat. I wondered how many more times she would make this trip.

Sophie's family was waiting when we got to the house. Kevin was at the front door, ready to share the latest from his baseball season. Steven and Rick were cordial and welcoming, and Christine seemed to take pleasure in having her daughter home. The lone absence was Sophie's father, who was still out in the barn. The peaceful exterior of the creamery along with Sophie's waiting family hid the dysfunction that was William Barnes.

"Go get your father, please," Christine directed Kevin.

"I'll get him," Sophie offered before Kevin could start for the door.

Kevin looked from his sister to me and back again. "I'll go with you," he volunteered.

"No. I'll get him." Sophie's face was set and determined. The unwavering resolution was something I had witnessed before when Sophie tackled a problem or overcame an obstacle. She would follow through on this, no matter the outcome.

Sophie returned alone several minutes later; her face stripped of emotion. "He said he'd be in as soon as lunch was on the table — no sooner." Her eyes locked on mine. Sophie had never shown any overt affection to me in front of her family, but she came to me now and put her arm around my waist. With that simple gesture, Sophie showed all those present that *I* was her family. I pulled her close and protectively put my arm around her shoulders.

When her father did come in, he didn't offer a word of greeting or acknowledgment. He took no part in the stilted conversation swirling around him. William Barnes seemed to enjoy the stifling effect of his presence. Declining dessert and a cup of coffee, his back ramrod straight, he returned to the barn.

All conversation stopped with his exit, and we sat in oppressive silence. No one knew what to say, but everyone knew that we couldn't change things or make things right. I turned down my dessert as well; my stomach couldn't handle the thought. We were all embarrassed, though the embarrassment shouldn't have been ours. Kevin looked at me and hurriedly looked away. Sophie quietly excused herself from the table and headed in the direction of the bathroom.

I angrily considered following Sophie's father; instead, I sat in place and attempted to muster a modicum of self-control, though my emotions were festering and raw. I could feel my impulse control waning and my fury rising to the surface. Sophie didn't need to state her opinion or make a scene. I would gladly do that for her. This was *my* Sophie. William Barnes was no longer going to treat Sophie with disdain or lack of respect. We were finished with him, and I was going to start by making that clear to the rest of the family.

I started before Sophie returned. "I know this is uncomfortable for all of you, and it certainly is for me." My voice low and barely under control. "I don't have an issue with anyone in this room." I made eye contact with everyone at the table, stopping last at Christine. I noticed her eyes shift to look over my shoulder. Sophie had returned.

I plunged ahead anyway; I was not going to back down. "I do have a huge issue with the way William treats Sophie. I realize you're not my family, and I may be out of line … but Sophie *is* my family." Then Sophie's hands were on my shoulders, her fingertips resting lightly on my collar bones.

I swallowed hard and continued. "We won't be coming back

here." I reached up and touched Sophie's fingers. "Sophie has tried with William, and nothing ever changes. We all know that. And that's not fair to Sophie." Out of the corner of my eye I saw Kevin's slight nod.

"You are all welcome at our home any time. Our door is always open to any of you — but not to William." Sophie kissed the top of my head.

I stood up, circled behind my chair, and put my arm protectively around Sophie. "I love Sophie too much to allow him to continue to treat her this way." Once again my eye contact, once again, stopped with Christine. Her face was a conflicted study of a mother's sadness and a wife's loyalty.

Before we left, Christine stopped me. "I'm sorry, Jensy." After those three words and a quick hug, she let me go. At the car Sophie placed her keys in my outstretched hand. I was moving toward the driver's side when I saw her father watching from the barn's open doorway.

Without allowing myself to lose my courage, I strode across the driveway, stopping a few feet from where he stood. The look on his face was smug and self-satisfied, a man who was pleased with the toll his behavior had exacted on his daughter.

I put my hands on my hips and stared at him until he broke eye contact. "We are done with you. *You* are done kicking Sophie around. I won't allow it, you son-of-a-bitch." My voice was threatening, filled with venom, and loud enough for him to hear. "Strike three." I waited and watched until his smug look disappeared, then I wheeled around and marched back to the car.

"What did you say?" Sophie asked when I got into the car.

"I thanked him for his hospitality," I responded through clenched teeth.

Sophie didn't press me for more; instead, she rested her cheek against my arm. "You are my champion," she whispered.

✦

We accepted Clarisse Baxter's invitation to spend Christmas in Florida. She was thrilled to have company, and it was a wonderful break for us. Sophie and I made a pact that neither Baxter, Cragen & Reed nor Washington Heights would make the trip with us. A true vacation with no work sounded delicious. I packed a couple novels that had been actively gathering dust, and Sophie loaded up on magazines.

"It's vacation," she told me. "I only want pictures and captions."

It was a wonderful week of perfect weather and a fabulous hostess. During the unseasonably warm days we explored the area. We found a couple seashells we would rehome in the city. Sophie bought a big, blousy white shirt dress, and I splurged on a couple of T-shirts.

In the evenings we strolled the beach in front of Clarisse's bungalow. At sunset we often sat on the beach and shared a bottle of wine as we watched the orange-red sun sink into the Gulf. Several evenings, Clarisse joined us in passing the bottle back and forth. We delighted in her lively and charming company.

We tried swimming in the Gulf one warm day, but most often we swam in Clarisse's pool. Sophie tanned to an elegant golden brown, whereas I tended to burn to a lobster red. In the lobster stage, I opined about life's unfairness while I lathered on sunscreen or hid under the big, floppy-brimmed hat Clarisse insisted I wear.

One afternoon I sat under the large umbrella by the pool watching Sophie swim. Like so many things Sophie did, she moved with an elegant, effortless grace. My breath caught as I watched her long, lean form in the water — she was beautiful to watch.

Sophie surfaced at the edge of the pool, pushed her hair back from her face and motioned to me to join her. Leaving the shelter of the umbrella, I ventured into the sun and over to the side of the pool. I wore a T-shirt to give my hot, pink back and shoulders a break and shorts to protect my burned thighs.

"Help me get out." Sophie held out her hand.

I took the offered hand, and in one quick tug, she pulled me in. I went completely under and came up sputtering. Sophie's hands brushed back my hair. She draped her arms lightly over my burned shoulders; one hand in the wet hair at the nape of my neck and her other hand grazing against my back. She laughed delightedly.

She kissed me a long, hard lingering kiss that I didn't want to end. But when she broke off, I quickly scanned our surroundings, hoping none of the elderly residents had seen us.

"Who's watching?" she asked.

"No one I can see."

"Then let's try again." Another long, lingering kiss that left me limp and wanting so much more.

That afternoon when Clarisse informed us she was going out to play cards, her eyes were bright with mischief. "We call it bridge, but it's really poker. And we play for money. Gambling. Pretty exciting, all-in-all." Clarisse looked from Sophie to me. "Unfortunately, I must drive, so the two of you will be on your own all afternoon. But then, what's a vacation without some time to do whatever you want? Heavens, my dears, I imagine you'll find something to keep yourselves occupied." Clarisse raised her eyebrows and shrugged.

I glanced over the top of Clarisse's grey head and caught the first of a light blush moving across Sophie's face. Clarisse caught my eye, and when she winked, I was certain I knew exactly what she had suggested.

I started to laugh, "I swear, Clarisse, you are one naughty lady. What would Henry have said?"

"Who do you think taught me all the virtues of naughtiness?" She wriggled her fingers in a hurried wave and left us to our own devices.

When Sophie and I opened the guest bedroom's veranda

doors, sunlight streamed in and played across the bed. A light breeze gently moved the gauzy curtains.

"I was ready to make love to you in the pool." Sophie ran her cool tongue across my burned shoulders. "Ummm ..." she exhaled lazily. She ran her fingertips down the inside of my arm to my palm, and her mouth explored the side of my neck and the hollow of my throat. I pulled her to me. Sophie pressed against me, grinding her hips against mine. I knew she could feel the heat of my desire.

I groaned. From the throbbing between my legs to the fullness of my breasts, I was ready for us to make love. I cupped the back of her head in my hand and brought her lips to mine. She ran her hands underneath my tank top and lifted it over my head. When her fingertips grazed my nipples, they hardened immediately.

Sophie laughed a deep, throaty laugh, "I'm going to have my way with you, Tiger."

"Jesus ... please do," I gasped as her hand slipped beneath my shorts and slowly stroked and rubbed me. My knees went weak, and I curled my fingers onto her shoulders. Her hands deftly stripped off my running shorts then pushed me back onto the bed.

I held her by the waist as she straddled me and stripped off her top. "You're gorgeous," I breathed.

My hands cupped her perfect breasts, and I ran my thumb over her erect nipples. Sophie leaned back and thrust herself against my hands. I took her into my mouth and rolled my tongue over her nipple until she gasped. As I suckled her, I watched the reddish flush of excitement creep from her breasts to her neck and face.

Sophie arched her back and reached behind her until she found me wide-open and ready for her. "Now," I groaned.

Her fingers entered me slowly with long strokes that became quick and insistent. My hands gripped the sheets in a stranglehold, and I pushed my head back into the pillow. I felt Sophie moving inside of me. Blood thundered through my veins as I built to an explosion. I closed my eyes and with an uncontrollable rush, I came. I was limp, sweating and sated.

Sophie laid herself on top of me, her head nestled along my neck. Her lips kissed her way to my ear lobe and gently pulled it. One of her hands stroked my cheek and her other hand ran gently up and down the inside of my leg. I sighed contentedly.

"Consider yourself taken, Tiger," she breathed into my ear.

I did.

"You girls are welcome to make this an annual holiday tradition." It was our last evening, and we had joined Clarisse on the patio for a glass of wine and a gulf sunset. "I know Henry would have been thrilled to have you here. It's an offer made from my heart and Henry's." In a sweet and simple gesture, Sophie took Clarisse's hand and kissed it.

Sophie raised her glass. "To Henry." We repeated the toast and took a sip of wine.

Clarisse raised her glass. "To the laughter that has once again filled this house." Again, we drank. "It's been selfish of me." Clarisse laughed heartily. "But I haven't had such a good time in ages!" Clarisse clapped her hands. "And if that isn't enough, I have some big news to share."

We both sat forward expectantly.

"I made a killing at the poker table this afternoon! I won it all! Ten dollars! My lucky day! I bet you can't say you got that lucky this afternoon." She smiled slyly.

"Probably not," I sighed. I winked at Sophie who had the decency to blush crimson.

"I thought not." Clarisse nodded wisely and winked at both of us.

Six months later, when the school year came to an end, I happily headed into summer. Instead of painting houses, I was going to put all my effort into a series of black and white photographs highlighting landmarks in the city. A friend of mine owned a gallery and after seeing my school photographs, she and I discussed the possibility of an exhibit. I was intrigued and excited.

I began with the Cobblestone Bridge, primarily because of the personal significance it held for Sophie and me. I spent several days there with my camera, trying to capture the magic Sophie and I felt every time we walked across the bridge.

My list of places to photograph was long and ambitious. I shot every day, rain or shine, sunrise to sunset. I searched for unusual angles, captured different elements of light, and looked to create mood and tone. It stretched me as a person and as an artist; it felt good.

"I haven't seen you this excited in a while," Sophie remarked as I shyly handed her my first shots. I so wanted her to truly love them. She went through one by one, taking time to thoughtfully study each. "They're truly wonderful, Jens," she enthused when she had looked at each photograph.

I began to ask if she really meant it, but she anticipated me. "Yes, I do mean it. They're strikingly beautiful — eye-catching. I really like the unusual perspectives and your use of black and white. They're amazing." She pulled out two I had taken of the Cobblestone Bridge. "When you exhibit, I want to pay the gallery price for these. One for your office at school and the other in our office at home."

"You don't have to pay for them." I insisted.

"Jensy, an exceptional artist should be paid for everything she produces."

✦

Two evenings later, Clarisse called to say was coming to town and would like to stay with us at the townhouse. Clarisse's intent was to take five days to see some old friends, spend time with us, and attend a meeting at Baxter, Cragen & Reed. Sophie and I were delighted to have her company.

I picked up Clarisse at the airport on a Wednesday afternoon. As always, she was interested to hear about what was transpiring in my life. But she was most interested in quizzing me about Sophie's life at the firm.

"Things seem to be going well. I know Sophie's really happy there." Though Clarisse hadn't asked, I added, "We've been working hard to keep an 'us' in the center of our busy careers. I think, and I believe Sophie would agree, that we've found a good balance."

"I'm so glad to hear that. I always tried to make sure Henry's life had balance, and that the balance was tipped toward me, of course." She patted my arm. "And you, my dear, you're happy with Sophie." Her remark was both statement and question.

I smiled and nodded. "I still can't believe my good fortune. Every day I feel like the luckiest person on earth. She means the world to me, Clarisse."

When Sophie arrived home that night, we talked for hours over a take-out Chinese dinner. We laughed, drank wine, and Clarisse entertained us for hours with stories about her life with Henry. It was late when Sophie admitted she needed sleep if she was going to be able to function the next day and headed off to bed.

Clarisse and I continued the conversation well past midnight. She shared that she finally felt like she was beginning to get her life together; that the periods of grief had begun to turn into memories of pleasant times. She spent time swimming, golfing, gardening, and playing cards. There were also several gentlemen who wanted to "see" her. Clarisse found it flattering, but thought it was too soon; although she was sure the time would come. "Henry never wanted me to be alone."

I dropped Clarisse at the firm late the next morning as I headed out for my photo shoot. When I pulled over, she put a wad of cash in my hand. "Get a couple bottles of champagne — the good stuff. We're celebrating tonight." I took the money, knowing better than to ask what we would be celebrating.

That night after we had eaten and cleared the table, Clarisse instructed us, "Sit down, dears, we have some business to discuss." Clarisse indicated one of the champagne bottles. "Jensy, would you be so kind as to do the honors?"

I worked a soft pop and filled the three champagne flutes. Before Clarisse raised her glass, she looked at Sophie and asked, "How old are you now, Sophie?"

Sophie, a bit perplexed by the question, shrugged and laughed. "Twenty-eight." She raised her eyebrows and looked over at me. I opened my eyes wide and shook my head; I had no idea why Clarisse had asked that question.

Clarisse noticed our exchange. "Oh, believe me, my dears, this *is* going somewhere." She put her flute forward and touched my glass, then held her glass to Sophie's for a prolonged moment as she said, "To the youngest partner in the history of Baxter, Cragen & Reed. Congratulations, my dear."

Sophie's flute remained suspended in mid-air. Her huge, luminous, eyes searched Clarisse's face, as if she needed further affirmation that it was true. It was so unexpected that Sophie appeared to be in shock. The moment seemed frozen in time.

"To you, Sophe," I finally found my voice.

Sophie's mouth opened and closed several times as she searched for words. She shook her head, trying to take it all in.

"Have some champagne," Clarisse teased. "It'll loosen your tongue."

All of Sophie's hard work, all the fortitude it had taken to stand up to her father and pursue the career and the life she wanted, all that and more had contributed to this moment. I kissed her cheek. "Congratulations, Counselor. Or should I say, congratulations, *partner?*"

"I ... but how ..." Sophie was still trying to find her voice, even after the swallow of champagne.

"I attended the board meeting today," Clarisse explained. "I have Henry's proxy vote. So, my dear, Henry did vote for you today — although his vote wasn't needed. The decision was unanimous. That's why I came up here, to vote Henry's vote, as he would have wanted. I asked the partners if I could share the news with you tonight. The firm will officially make the offer tomorrow."

"Thank you." Sophie's lips quivered and the champagne flute trembled in her hands.

"I didn't do a thing, my dear. You did. Your hard work, the quality of your work, your knowledge, your PR skills, willingness to help others, bringing in new clients and, of course," Clarisse winked, "all those billable hours ... brought you this." Clarisse laughed, "But, you're welcome."

Sophie took my hand and kissed my cheek. "Thank you," she told me softly. Tears made her eyes look liquid. I put my forehead against hers. I was proud beyond words.

"Ahem ... before you two get all lovey-dovey on me, there is one more item on the agenda."

Surprised, we turned back to Clarisse.

"It's something Henry and I discussed and finalized just before his death. To make this happen, two conditions had to be met. Sophie, either you had to become a partner or turn thirty, which-ever came first. So, you've met that first condition."

"The second condition was to be a judgment call on my part. Jensy, this includes you as well. I needed to be as convinced as I could be — and in life that's difficult because anything can hap-pen at any time, for any reason —" Clarisse stopped for a moment, and I knew she was thinking of Henry. She sighed and contin-ued, "I needed to be convinced that you two are committed to a long-term relationship. Of course, no one can see into the future, but I do believe that's the case. With the two conditions being met," Clarisse reached into her large tote and pulled out a folder, "here is the deed to the townhouse. You are listed as Joint Tenants in Common with the Right of Survivorship. When everything has been signed, it's yours."

"You can't —" Sophie began.

"Ah, but we did." Clarisse interrupted. "It's what Henry wanted. It's what I want. Henry and I love you both. I only ask that I am invited to stay here from time to time when I travel back this way." Clarisse threw her arms wide open. "Come here, my children." We held each other and laughed and cried.

"Isn't this grand?" Clarisse asked rhetorically.

That night as I lay awake waiting for sleep to find me, I couldn't imagine anything more wonderful than the life Sophie and I shared. Our world was perfect. I glanced at Sophie beside me, and my heart swelled with love. I had found my perfect match, and she had found me. My future was with Sophie. I knew the world was ours.

Part Two

Sixteen

Viv and Mary once asked me if Sophie and I had discovered the "fountain of love." I told them I was certain we had. In our own words, we were still "certifiably, undeniably, crazy in love." Still, we worked hard to maintain the magic of our relationship.

Into our thirties, our careers were satisfying and appeared to be set — though I often told Sophie that she wouldn't be satisfied until her name was on the company letterhead: Baxter, Cragen, Reed & Barnes. Her reply to my needling was always the same: a slight shrug of her shoulders and an enigmatic, "Maybe."

As for myself, my confidence had grown over the years. I no longer feared the failure of our relationship. I no longer felt I was unworthy. Although I sometimes thought about Fitz, it was through the long lens of history. I was comfortable and relaxed with Sophie's love and our commitment to each other. However, there were occasions when our good fortune made me pause. Everything was so good that I sometimes wondered if it could last.

At Washington Heights, Dee and I had both been honored, in consecutive years, with the State Department of Education's Guidance Counselor of the Year Award. I believed the foundation of my award was the work I had done with our gay and lesbian student population. The program had grown from school groups to community outreach and service. The award was a satisfying and humbling recognition that the work I was doing was important.

As entered my seventh season, the girls' basketball program continued to build a tradition of success. Two trips to the state tournament had doubled the number of girls who wanted to participate. After my sixth season I had been honored with the conference's Coach of the Year award, which I proudly shared with the team. "You made this happen," I told them. "Without your effort and hard work, this award wasn't possible."

But my proudest moment was when Molly Cutler found her way back to Washington Heights as a teacher and my assistant basketball coach. Before our first practice, Molly sidled next to me in the coach's office. "We'll do it together this year," she told me as she bumped her shoulder against mine, in homage to years past.

"Indeed, we will," I smiled.

Sophie arrived home early one summer afternoon. She rushed upstairs without a hello and returned downstairs, less than thirty-seconds later, still in her work clothes.

"Come on." She grabbed me by the hand, dragged me out of my chair and toward the front door.

"Hi, how are you? Fine, and you? Doing well. I'm glad you're home." I carried on a make-believe conversation between us. When that went nowhere, I asked, "Where are we going?"

"Don't ask questions," Sophie scolded. She opened the passenger door of her car and pushed me inside. Once behind the wheel she handed me an old bandana. "Put this on."

I put it on like a bank robber and waggled my eyebrows.

"Not like that. Over your eyes." Sophie snatched the bandana from my hand, folded it over several times, placed it over my eyes and knotted it behind my head. "Now tilt your seat all the way back."

"I guess I'm not supposed to look," I snickered.

"No, you're not. All the way back. *Do it.*" I couldn't quite place her tone. It was somewhere between impatient and excited.

I complied. "This has all the earmarks of a 'Sophieventure.' Is that what this is?"

"Maybe."

With the circuitous route we were taking it was obvious she didn't want me to know where we were going. At first, I tried to keep up and figure it out, but there were so many turns that I soon abandoned the effort. "I haven't had this much fun in ages," I wise-cracked.

"Just wait."

There was an elation in her voice that was rare for Sophie. Her excitement was palpable, and I could feel her enthusiasm filling the car. By the time she slowed to a stop, I was on fire with questions.

"Don't move." Sophie instructed me, and I could hear her rummaging in her tote bag. After a moment she uncurled my fingers and placed keys on my palm. She closed my fingers over the keys, leaned over and kissed my hand. "Happy Birthday. Happy Anniversary. Happy lifetime. Happy everything," she giggled.

I took off the blindfold and looked at the set of keys nestled in my hand. Not car keys — house keys. I looked up and her twinkling eyes were watching me excitedly. Returning the seat upright, I looked out my side window and directly at our dream house. Its "For Sale" sign was covered by a diagonal "Sold" sticker.

I looked from the house to the keys to Sophie. "Ours? It's really ours?" I couldn't get the words out fast enough.

"I told you — someday." Sophie's laugh sparkled.

"My God!" I was out of the car in a flash. I vaulted over the three-foot-high front gate and pounded up the steps. Then I remembered Sophie was still in the car. I retraced my steps, opened her door, and extended my hand. Racing up the steps, I opened the front door, scooped Sophie into my arms and carried her over the threshold. Once inside, I twirled in a full circle, before setting her down.

To the right of the front door was a large formal living room with a gas-insert fireplace. To the left, a front sitting room was next to a formal dining room. The modern kitchen at the end of the hallway included a breakfast nook. There was a door at each end: one leading to the breezeway that connected to the two-car garage, the other leading onto the deck. Upstairs we found a master bedroom with its own bathroom and walk-in closet, two guest bedrooms and a study. A finished walkout basement completed our tour.

"My God, Sophie, it's wonderful. It's gorgeous." Though I was not normally attached to things, this house had spoken to me for years. It was charming, alluring, and compelling. In a way that was inexplicable to me, the house seemed to know us. It was a representation of who we were; and because of that, it truly touched my heart.

"How did you keep this a secret?" I gestured around the house. "How did you manage it? Can we afford it? Are we mortgaged to eternity?" My questions rolled forth.

Sophie laughed at me. "To answer your questions … I did my best to keep my mouth closed, although a couple times I was sure I had blown it. There was a month of clandestine planning and meetings. Yes, we can afford it. No, we are not mortgaged to eternity."

Sophie was our financial wizard, the manager of all things money. For seven years we had banked my salary and some of hers, waiting for this moment. An investment counselor had helped us invest wisely. Considering the gift of the townhouse, we had wherewithal that most young couples didn't have. Sophie knew our money, and if she said everything was fine — everything was fine.

"Let's stay here tonight." I suggested.

"There's no furniture or electricity, in case you hadn't noticed."

"There's carpet in the living room, and we have candles and flashlights at the townhouse. It's ours. Let's stay."

We hurried to the townhouse and back again.

When the house began to darken, we brought out candles and a bottle of wine. It was a quiet celebration. We sat upright against the living room wall and poured the wine. We listened to the unfamiliar creaks and groans that were part of our new house.

"To our new adventure." We toasted the house.

"To Henry and Clarisse." We toasted our benefactors who, through their generosity, had helped make our dream come true.

We toasted our journey and our good fortune. We drank to my career and the accolades I had received, and to Sophie's rise to partnership and prestige at the firm. We toasted all the people and circumstances that had made us who we were, individually and as a couple. And finally, we toasted each other and all our "ventures" to come.

The night deepened, and when I looked at Sophie her head nodded, and her eyes were closed. She breathed deeply as she hugged her knees to her chest. Her presence filled my heart; Sophie, my cherished gift.

Eyes still closed; Sophie leaned against me. "I know you're looking at me."

"How do you know that?"

"I always know."

I put my arm around her. "Have I told you today how much I love you?"

Her lovely, wide eyes opened and gleamed at me in the candle-light. "Tell me."

"I love you." I kissed her forehead. "I love you." I gently kissed her eyes. "I love you." I slowly and lingeringly kissed her lips.

That began the first night in our new home.

✦

The two houses became my summer job. Instead of selling the townhouse we decided to keep it as a furnished rental property. As soon as we moved, I would begin to paint, clean and get it ready to rent. Sophie and I were nostalgic as we packed our belongings. We sat on the sofa that last day and reminisced about our years in the townhouse: our first night together, Sophie's proposal that we move in together, the champagne in the backyard when Sophie passed the bar exam, the parties we had thrown, the love we had made. It was an immeasurable and loving gift that Henry and Clarisse had bestowed on us. Our moment of leaving was bittersweet.

When everything was packed, we gravitated, as if by mutual agreement, to the bench overlooking the river. We had claimed it as "our" bench when we first moved in, a place of quiet conversations and spirited discussions.

Sophie took hold of my hand. "I'm so excited. But I'll miss the townhouse."

I nodded. "So will I." One chapter in our life together was ending; giving way to the beginning of another.

Our first visitors were Dee, Bob, and the boys. We sat on the deck as the sun peeked through the leaves of our red maple tree. Mark was flipping through some football cards he had purchased with his weekly allowance. Richie sat on the glider next to Sophie; too old to want to be obviously close, yet too young not to.

"This isn't just a house. It's a home," Dee enthused. "It's so perfectly you. It's just lovely."

Seventeen

After two summers of labor, the house remodeling was finished. It had been transformed into our house — the house we had envisioned. I had enjoyed the process: refinishing hardwood floors, laying tile, and installing ceiling fans. I stained both the porch and the back deck and painted every room with two coats of paint. Amazingly, I became adept at things I never imagined. When I surveyed my results, I was proud of my handiwork.

In the summer I was the primary remodeler, though Sophie helped when she could. I was weary, I ached, and I always felt sweaty and dirty. It seemed I drank or showered at least half of our water bill. Several evenings I fell into a deep sleep while Sophie gave my aching muscles a massage. More often than not, I fell into bed already half-asleep after an exhausting day. But it was worth it; my satisfaction far outweighed any inconvenience.

Most weekends Sophie and I reserved for ourselves. We continued to dance and entered contests frequently. We walked along the river and did things with friends. Jensy and Sophie ventures were put on hold; the house was our "venture."

When the work on the house was finished there was only one more ingredient we needed to make our lives complete.

I clandestinely researched dog breeds and breeders, and even stopped at the Humane Society before introducing the subject to Sophie. I intuitively knew she might not be as enthusiastic as I, but I was still willing to try. Finally, one evening as we relaxed on the giant swing on our front porch, I broached the subject.

"You know how much I love our house. And you know how much I love you —"

"And you'd love a dog." Sophie moved away from me to the end of the swing and regarded me closely. "You want one, don't you?"

"How did you know?"

"Oh, Jensy," she scoffed, "how transparent can you be? All the research you've been doing?"

Apparently, I hadn't been as clandestine as I thought. "All our friends have dogs."

"Not all —"

"Most." I gave my best, disarming smile. "It would make us a family."

"We are a family."

"Oh, come on, Sophe. You know you would love one."

Surprisingly, she nodded. "I would love one. We always had dogs on the farm." But her nod turned into a head shake. "But Jensy, we lead busy lives, and it's such an obligation. Like having a toddler for twelve to fourteen years."

"I'll do the bulk of the work," I promised earnestly. "I'll let it out in the morning, feed it, take it for walks, pick up poop. Of course, I would allow you to take part in any or all of the previously mentioned chores. If you want to." I offered another heart-melting smile.

Sophie sighed. "Why do I think that sounds more promising than it will actually be?" For a few seconds neither of us said anything. Then Sophie broke the silence. "I suppose you have already picked out the breed."

"As a matter of fact, I have."

Sophie coughed; she had expected as much.

"A Pembroke Welsh Corgi. Joe's family had one when I was growing up. I loved that little dog."

"The little dogs with the short legs? The breed the Queen of England has?"

I could sense that Sophie was intrigued. "Yes. A big dog attitude in a little dog's body. They're protective, good watch dogs, loyal, smart ..."

"Do they shed?"

I was a bit uncomfortable about that aspect. "They do. Twice a year for six months each time." I mumbled through that sentence.

Sophie raised an eyebrow. "Add 'frequent brushing' to your chore list."

"Done."

She reached over and put her hand on my knee. "Oh, Jensy, I don't know ..."

But I knew. I had already found a breeder who had four pups available. The breeder also mentioned a fifth pup that had been sick but had fully recovered.

"So, you knew how this conversation would turn out?" Sophie questioned.

"I knew how much you really wanted one."

"You knew how much *YOU* really wanted one."

"You just don't know how much you want one." I used my endearing tone.

"Go. Bring it home." Sophie shook her head and acquiesced.

Sophie didn't make the trip with me; she had a deposition that day. However, as I got in the car to make the three-hour pilgrimage, she gave me one parting instruction. "Do not bring home the sick one."

The drive through rolling farm fields and small towns was much like the fields and towns where I grew up. Dairy cows grazed contentedly, and crops were getting tall. The breeder, a middle-aged woman in jeans and a T-shirt, lived on a large farm, with a huge kennel behind the house.

"You must be Jensy." She opened my car door and extended a callused hand. "Edy Franklin."

Just then two Corgis came racing around the back corner of the kennel: a female full of milk and a handsome male. After an initial interested sniff, they turned around and headed back to the kennel. "They're eager to show you their creations," Edy laughed and guided me to the kennel's entrance.

Inside, I saw four Corgi pups scrambling in their hay-covered pen. They jostled for position so I could pet them. Two were reddish with white ruffs. The other two were tricolor: black, white, and tan. "They're ready to go," Edy told me. I picked them up one by one. "Take them outside if you like. They're too little to run far."

When returning one pup, I noticed a lonely-looking tricolor all by himself in a large pen. He didn't rush forward like the others; instead, he hung back, shy and unsure of himself. "Who's that?"

Edy smiled, "That's Gunther. He was a pretty sick little guy, but he's fine now. It's just that whenever I put him back with his litter mates, they pick on him."

"He's gorgeous." I went to the edge of his pen. He was by far the most handsome puppy of the litter with his white half-ruff and the white line up his nose.

"He'll probably ignore you," Edy warned me. "He's very timid."

I knelt outside the pen and extended my hand for him to sniff. I lowered my voice and told him what a good and handsome boy he was. Slowly he came to me, hesitantly sniffed, then licked my hand. His timidity, the feel of his soft tongue on my hand, and the cool, wet nose against my arm won my heart. I scooped him up and he nestled his muzzle against my neck, a little fur ball with puppy breath.

"I'll take him."

Edy was wide-eyed as she looked at the two of us. "Well, I'll be." She smiled. "I can have him ready to go on Tuesday."

"I'd like to take him today." *No more time all alone in that pen, little guy,* I silently told him.

As soon as we were out of the driveway, Gunther was re-christened Tobie. It was the name Sophie chose; fitting for either male or female. I thought that naming the Corgi would help facilitate Sophie's bonding with him and overcome her initial reluctance. I suggested the "ie" on the end of the name to mirror the "ie" on Sophie.

In the three-hour drive back to the city, I never put Tobie in his crate. He nestled happily against my neck. We stopped several times along the way, and Tobie would sniff and frolic in the grass, running in his waddling, awkward puppy gait. After he pottied, we would be on our way; the little Corgi once again snuggled against my neck, snoring while he slept.

When we arrived home, I immediately let Tobie into the backyard. Sophie greeted me, and we stood arm-in-arm watching as Tobie explored his new territory. He chased among the plants, then popped out from under them and barked. He snapped at a falling leaf and fell over on his back, rolling and groaning and bicycling his short little legs in the air. We laughed at his puppy antics.

"You got the sick one, didn't you?" Sophie pinched my arm.

"He's not sick anymore." I glanced sideways at her. "How'd you know?" She always knew.

Sophie kissed my shoulder. "I know *you.*" She let go of my arm, bent over and clapped her hands, "Come on, Tobie! Come over and say hello!"

At first Sophie seemed rather overwhelmed by our tiny addition. She'd come home from work and there was Tobie — a bundle of energy surrounding short naps. Tobie loved me by day, but when Sophie came home, everything changed. He followed Sophie everywhere, begging for her attention. She would scratch his ears and tell him he was a good boy, but Tobie *always* wanted more. Sophie liked him, but I was worried that she wasn't enthusiastically bonding.

Because I wasn't working during the summer, I potty-trained and leash-trained him. I took him to puppy obedience classes and worked on simple commands. I slept with Tobie's crate by my side of the bed, my fingers through the wire, and shushed him when he cried. When necessary, I took him out in the middle of the night, and I got up early in the morning to take him out again.

One morning I woke with a start, realizing that his early morning restlessness hadn't awakened me. I put my fingers into the crate, but no wet nose touched them. I was immediately wide awake and panicked. My breathing returned to normal when I saw the crate was open, and Sophie's side of the bed was empty. I got up and padded quietly downstairs.

In the kitchen, Sophie was sitting on the floor with her legs bent. She was leaning over our little bundle of fur; Tobie on his back, resting on Sophie's thighs. I could hear her singing "You are My Sunshine" as she ran her hands up and down Tobie's chest and belly. Unaware of my presence, Sophie finished her song and kissed his muzzle between his eyes. I turned and headed quietly back upstairs … smiling.

We began to walk Tobie together, we attended puppy socialization classes and worked on his training. Eventually, he began every night at the foot of our bed, until he got too warm and found a cooler place on the floor. Or until we made love, at which point he would disgustedly huff and puff off the bed and sleep in the hallway outside our door.

I was his "you got me from the breeder" mama and took care of most of his basic needs. But with Sophie it was different. Sophie was Tobie's soulmate. He followed her every move and always had to know what she was doing. During the summer when she wore shorts, Tobie would sit by Sophie and lick her leg. In the midst of his licking, he would look up at Sophie with such naked love in his eyes, it would leave me speechless — and, perhaps, a little jealous.

When Sophie laughed at Tobie's licking, he would simply lick harder and faster, his eyes lovingly fixed on her. I shared my observation about his devotion with Sophie, and she smiled. "He comes by it honestly, its the same way *you* look at me. You just don't lick my legs as often." Sophie had bonded and my goal had been achieved. We were family.

Eighteen

For years Sophie had worked late on Thursday evenings so she wouldn't feel compelled to work on weekends. Typically, on Thursday evenings, I would pick her up, often arriving early with my own work. During the winter we would juggle late basketball practice and Tobie's needs to preserve our Thursday tradition.

A few weeks before one of those Thursday nights, Sophie gave the most important presentation of her career to a large, multi-national corporation. Her charge was to secure their commitment to Baxter, Cragen & Reed's representation. She worked for months developing a presentation, compiling facts and figures, and putting together a portfolio of all the things her firm could offer. An acceptance would be a huge achievement for Sophie, as well as the firm. The entire process had driven Sophie's normally high level of motivation and determination into overdrive. At home she was uncharacteristically absent-minded and unfocused, edgy and nervous — tired but wired. I knew the outcome of this deal meant more than she could put into words.

With all the pressure, there had been more than a few fitful, restless nights. On Wednesday night, before the corporation's decision was revealed, Sophie's tossing and turning awakened me.

I got up. "Roll onto your stomach," I quietly directed her. I massaged her legs, back, arms, hands, shoulders, and neck. Sophie's shoulder muscles were knotted, and I spent extra time working on them. When I was finished with the stubborn knots, I gently ran my hands over her body. I settled back down and watched her wide-awake eyes watch me.

"My mind won't turn off. I'm sorry," she whispered. "I should just go to the guest bedroom."

"There is one more thing we could try," I told her suggestively.

She laughed and rolled onto her back. "Have at me, Tiger." She opened her arms wide.

I whipped off the sheet. Sophie had one leg bent and her knee raised. I placed one hand on her thigh and my other hand on her lower leg. I started by kissing her knee.

Later, she put her arms around my neck and drew me down for a kiss. "Thank you," she said drowsily.

I ran my hand through her hair. When Sophie turned on her side, I spooned her, waiting for her deep breathing to indicate sleep. Even then, her hand was curled into a tight fist. I tenderly uncurled her fingers and wove them with mine.

The next day I ran a couple errands, then hurried home after school. In quick succession I took care of Tobie chores: food, potty and walk. Once home from our walk, I ran a couple miles on the treadmill. After my run, I took a quick shower and put on clean jeans and a flannel shirt. I fixed a sandwich, arranged what I had purchased on my errands, and plopped down on the couch with a novel to await Sophie's call.

I had been busily putting my positive thoughts out to the universe; willing the outcome Sophie deserved. Sophie had always believed that if circumstances were right, whatever we wanted would be ours — I so wanted this to be hers. I was impatient and wanted an immediate call with the results. I opened a book, but it seemed I was reading and re-reading every paragraph.

I had looked at four pages when Sophie called. I glanced at the clock. Only half past six — earlier than I had expected. "Hey, Counselor," I began tentatively, my throat dry with nerves.

"We got it, Jens. The firm was awarded the contract!" Her voice was jubilant, relieved, and tired — all emotions mixed into one.

"Good for you!" I grinned with relief. "I'm so happy for you! I know how much it means to you." The contract was so important that there was even the possibility of the firm opening a branch in New York City. I was ecstatic for Sophie, and so proud of her. She had worked hard and put so much effort and research into crafting the proposal — hours upon hours to make it perfect.

"I'm coming to get you."

"You read my mind," she laughed.

I couldn't get to the law office fast enough. I raced through the lobby and was met at the elevator door by the evening security guard. Over the years, Howard and I had developed our own routine. He opened the door and ushered me in with a grand sweep of his arm.

"If you're here, it must be Thursday," Howard greeted me. "Should I ring Ms. Barnes and let her know you're on your way?" He always asked the same question, and I always gave the same answer.

"No thanks, Howard. Tonight, I'll just surprise her."

He always winked and smiled knowingly. "I'm sure Ms. Barnes loves a good surprise."

Typically, when I arrived around nine p.m., the lights were dimmed, and the only visible light came from Sophie's open office door. But on this particular evening the lights were on, and I could hear the offbeat clatter of computer keys. The entire office was still buzzing with excitement and activity.

I was headed toward Sophie's office when a woman came striding down the hall toward me. There was an air of negative, aggressive energy about her that I had never noticed before at Sophie's firm. I had never seen this woman. She was a tall, large-boned woman several inches taller than I. Her black hair was cut in a severe bob, framing a chiseled, but not unattractive, face. She cut an imposing figure.

I stood still and watched her approach. Within an arm's length of me she stopped mid-stride, and I had the unnerving sensation that we had just been playing a game of "chicken." She gave me the once over, her eyes traveling slowly up and down. When she stared into my eyes, both her pupils and irises looked black. I was unsettled by her scrutiny.

"You *have* to be Jensy." Her voice accented the word "have" in a way that was neither pleasant nor a compliment. Her inflection was flat, distant, and emotionless; a tone that immediately made me wonder why she disliked me. Her black eyes traveled again to my Washington Heights windbreaker, flannel shirt, jeans, and hiking boots. I knew I had just been examined, and found wanting. I could sense a competitive nature as well as anyone, and I swore that was what was happening here. I had just been summarily dismissed.

Before I could comment or move on, I heard Sophie call from down the hall. "Jens!" I breathed a sigh of relief that she was coming to rescue me from this intimidating woman. Sophie slipped her arm around my waist and my heart quickened as it always did. Her presence was like stepping from winter into a warm, summer day. I needed that feeling right now.

"I see you two have already met."

"More or less," the woman told Sophie.

"Less," I pointedly responded. I didn't like this woman — her tone, her dismissive look, her aggressive posture — or the lack of the human niceties and common courtesies I normally found at Sophie's office.

Seemingly oblivious, Sophie went on, "Jensy, this is Carol Novak, our newest partner."

"Carol ..." I acknowledged, but she was already done with me. While Sophie was looking at me, Carol's eyes were scanning Sophie up and down.

"You're Sophie's partner." Carol's voice was flat. Her eyes flicked to me, then back to Sophie.

"Happily, so," I acknowledged as I put my arm around Sophie's shoulders and possessively pulled her closer to me.

"... came from Chicago a month ago." Sophie was in the midst of explaining. "Carol wanted a less hectic life."

I watched Carol closely.

"I wanted a more 'rural' feel. Some place smaller than Chicago, and I thought this might fill the bill. The pace of the largest law firm in Chicago was getting old. I thought this would be a nice break."

Again, the tone. An attempt to dominate — to be "better than." There was a disdainful note in her voice as she referred to our "ruralness" and wanting a "nice break." It made me wonder what her story really was. But what bothered me most was the look in her eyes as she watched Sophie: an open interest that went beyond that of a colleague. It made me wary and watchful.

"Let's go home and celebrate." I said, reminding myself there was a bigger event than Carol Novak. As we walked toward the door, I looked over my shoulder to find Carol Novak watching as we exited the office.

On the way home Sophie excitedly shared the events of her day. There was the conference call, the jubilation as the news spread through the office, a hastily conceived buffet, and her congratulatory meeting with Daniel Cragen and Alex Reed. Sophie's batteries were recharged, and she seemed to be floating above the car seat for the entire ride home.

"Worth all your sleepless nights and worry?" I asked as I rubbed her shoulder.

"Absolutely."

We arrived home to a dark house, except for a dim light I had left on in the dining room. I hurriedly lit the candles as Sophie and Tobie exchanged greetings. There was a bottle of "our" champagne

— Billecourt-Salmon Brut Rose — waiting in an ice bucket. The table was set with our best linen, two candles, two plates, two Champagne flutes, a box of French pastries, and a card that read in part, "Congratulations, Counselor!"

"I'll turn on the light." Sophie said, and I heard her move to the switch.

I met her just as her hand touched it. "Leave it." I covered her hand with mine and guided her down the hallway to the dining room. "Congratulations." I kissed her cheek.

In bed, filled with pastry, Champagne and love, I returned to what had been on my mind since I had first seen Carol Novak. "Who hired her?"

"Who?" Sophie sounded genuinely perplexed.

"Carol Novak." She seemed to have forgotten all about Carol; I had not.

"Dan Cragen. Why?"

I rolled onto my side and looked at Sophie's profile. I wasn't sure where I wanted to go from there. Sophie admired and respected Dan Cragen, and I didn't want to make it sound like I was casting aspersions on him.

Sophie turned her head to look at me. "Why?" she asked again.

"I was just hoping it wasn't you." She wrinkled her nose at me, but I continued. "It would have been awful if you had been the one to hire a person who disliked me so intensely at first sight."

She shook her head and laughed. "Carol didn't dislike you."

"Then you weren't at the same conversation I was."

She shook her head as if she couldn't believe the turn our conversation had taken. "Really, Jensy — that's absurd."

"Can you say 'predator'?" I asked.

"Jensy ..." Sophie laughingly looked away ... then looked quickly back at me as she realized I was serious. "What on earth —"

"Carol Novak has no boundaries, Sophie. She only wants what

she wants. And she'll probably do anything to get it."

Sophie looked at me closely and narrowed her eyes. "This isn't like you, Jensy, to be so ungracious about someone you don't even know."

"Oh, but I do know her. Not personally, of course, but I know her type." I put my arm protectively around her. "Be careful, Sophie. She has designs on you." Sophie never assumed the negative about anyone and automatically dismissed that notion. But I *knew*. I *knew* Carol had designs on Sophie. I was as certain of that as I was certain of Sophie's love. It made me uncomfortable and nervous for Sophie. My guard was up, and I would keep a vigilant watch.

Sophie put her hand on the back of my neck and pressed her lips against mine. "Not a chance," she breathed into me.

But I knew with Carol Novak it wasn't about chance. It was about opportunity.

Nineteen

Every year around Valentine's Day, the "Lesbian Business and Professional Association" held a gala event. It was an expensive, glitz-filled affair, punctuated with beautiful cocktail dresses, gowns and tuxedos. A live orchestra played the first part of the evening and was replaced by a deejay for the last two hours, making sure everyone's musical and dance tastes were met. The hot and cold buffet was elaborate and extravagant. There was also a large cash bar that offered the possibility of any alcohol-soaked concoction. Tables, four deep, ringed the large dance floor. Despite the expense, the evening attracted hundreds of lesbians from all over the state. It was the "Who's Who" of the lesbian community: a night to see and be seen. Sophie and I loved it.

The gala was also special to us because of its proximity to our anniversary date. We regarded the gala as our own special anniversary celebration. That night Sophie and I were celebrating thirteen magnificent years. She continued to make my heart race and my pulse pound, filling my life with unimaginable joy.

We had changed some over those years. There were a few more laugh lines around the corners of our eyes. Both of us wore reading glasses more frequently. The route we jogged around the lakes took a bit longer. But in other ways we remained much the same. We still enjoyed good books, good wine, and an occasional beer or margarita. We delighted in each other's company and laughed easily and often. Our desire for physical contact, whether simple touch or passionate intimacy, continued unabated. And we still deeply believed we were better together than we would be on our own.

The Saturday night of the ball, I dressed carefully. My tuxedo had been recently dry-cleaned, and its slacks were pressed to razor sharp. Even my black patent leather shoes had been spit-polished, buffed and shined. Only my black bow tie remained to be tied, and that required Sophie's nimble fingers. I headed to the kitchen and let Tobie into the backyard. I was doing my best to avoid his thick white undercoat that wanted to attach itself to my black slacks: Tobie's constant shedding was unavoidable. I checked my watch repeatedly and wandered the first floor while I waited for Sophie to appear.

She had consigned me to dress in the guest bedroom. That had never happened in all the years we had attended the gala. Normally, I sat and watched as Sophie got dressed, helping as needed. It was the only formal event we attended, and I always sat and watched in awe as Sophie transformed herself. She was always unfailingly classy and stylish; however, on gala evenings, she became resplendent and elegant. But this year Sophie was secretive about her dress. She wanted it to be a surprise.

At 6:30 sharp the bedroom door opened, and I rushed to the bottom of the stairs. I looked up and caught my breath. After thirteen years, Sophie could still make my head spin and my mouth go dry. My heart raced. Sophie — my walking alliteration: seductive, sensuous, sultry, and sexy. Sophie was stunning. She dazzled. I was transfixed.

This year, for the first time, Sophie had chosen a long gown. A dark purple halter, made of a sparkly, lamé fabric that flashed and glittered when she moved. She stood at the top of the stairs — a special entrance, only for me. She smiled into my eyes and began her slow descent. The gown shimmered with each unhurried step. A slit ran high up one side, exposing her leg and thigh as she moved toward me: a flash of cream in a sea of purple. Stiletto heels, the same color as the gown, were visible just below the hem. Her only jewelry was a pair of deep purple stud earrings and the ring I had put on her finger thirteen years before.

I held out my hand to her and touched the tip of her fingers. The jolt of electricity between us was so intense it almost dropped me to my knees. Sophie's eyes widened in surprise, and she laced her fingers through mine, pulling me to her lips. I smelled the scent of her shampoo, a mixture of rosemary and mint. I kissed her neck and tasted perfume on her pulse point. One of my arms circled around her, and I laid my palm under the thin straps that crisscrossed between her shoulder blades. I traced the back edge of her gown, my fingertips just under the fabric. I gently moved my hand over her silky skin, all the way down her side and around to the small of her back. My other hand moved up her thigh in a lingering caress.

"Dear God, Sophie," I breathed as she ran her hands over my back. "You are lovely."

I kissed low on her neck, up to her jaw line and then to her lips, her tongue cool against mine. Sophie's fingers curled into my shoulders. I leaned back, lost in the depths of her eyes. "Why do I feel like I'm seeing you for the first time?" I whispered.

Sophie laughed, the laugh of summer and sunshine. "You've seen *all* of me for years."

"But not like this."

"Ssshhh ..." she breathed into my mouth and kissed me again. Her fingertips touched my cheeks and glided gently over the sides of my face. My hands were still on her skin — moving lower, under the fabric on her back — moving higher to the crease of her thigh. She drew a shuddering breath.

If Tobie hadn't barked at that moment, we might not have made it to the gala. I rested my forehead on her bare shoulder and took a few trembling breaths. Sophie threw her head back and took a deep swallow of air. We reluctantly pulled away from each other.

"Another minute and we would have been past the point of no return." Sophie let out a shaky laugh. "I'll let him in."

I walked on wobbly legs to wait at the end of the breezeway as Sophie closed and locked the kitchen door. I silently showed her the lint roller I had taken so we could rid ourselves of Tobie's fur once we arrived at the dance. She smiled and took my hand as I helped her down the steps.

As I opened the door, I touched her cheek with my forefinger and gently kissed her. "How is it possible that just when I think my heart is full of loving you, I find myself loving you more?" I ran my finger over her lips. "I love you, Sophie Barnes."

Sophie softly kissed my fingertip. "And I love you, Jensy Willett."

All the trappings were there for a wonderful evening. We held hands as we crossed the dance floor, making our way to the table we'd share with Viv and Mary. I was vaguely aware of heads turning in our direction, but I was so caught up in Sophie, I hardly noticed. Several people stopped us along the way to say "hello" or to ogle Sophie's gown.

"Happy anniversary!" Viv and Mary called when we finally arrived at the table.

"You two make a splendid couple tonight!" Viv enthused. "The most attractive couple in the room. I just don't know how you do it. The rest of us age. But every year that goes by, the two of you just get better." Viv turned to Mary. "Remember that day at the ice fishing house, when these two were just a 'novice' couple?" Air quotes from Viv. "And we interrupted them? Remember how cute they were ... all flustered and embarrassed and so in love."

Mary laughed. "Putting themselves back together ... Jensy

couldn't even get her shirt buttoned straight, and Sophie was all blush and befuddlement trying to hide Jensy's bra."

We all laughed. "And Sophie's still blushing!" Viv astutely pointed out.

"And then you waved my bra out your truck window, handing it back to me in front of a car full of guys." I picked up the thread of their story. "'You forgot something, Jensy Willett,'" I mimicked Viv. "The end of the story was that it hung from my rearview mirror all the way home. Put there by little miss blushing violet." I pointed at Sophie.

We sat and happily reminisced. Other friends and acquaintances made frequent stops at our table. Several asked if Sophie and I were going to show off any ballroom dance steps this year. Last year we had been doing the Foxtrot and having such a good time we hadn't even realized that most of the dancers had stopped and cleared the floor. When we finished there had been applause and some scattered whistles. We had been persuaded to dance another. But this year, I gestured to Sophie's stiletto heels and told them it depended on her comfort level, since stilettos were not part of her typical dance ensemble.

Sophie smiled, "We'll see, but I'm guessing there'll be nothing fancy."

Before the band started, the four of us took turns at the buffet table. First Sophie and Viv went up, leaving Mary and I to watch their belongings. When they returned their plates were piled high.

Mary made her way to the hot entrees, while I took a place in the cold buffet line. I put a little of almost everything on my plate and created my sample platter. I was almost at the end of the line when someone bumped me from behind. "Hey! Careful! Full plate here!" I laughed and turned around.

Carol Novak offered no apology. She simply stared right through me as if I didn't exist. After several seconds she redirected her focus to me, and her look said it all. The animosity I had experienced during our first meeting had not been a mistake — either in my interpretation or her intent.

"Oh, yes. Jensy. Right?" Disingenuous and dismissive. "Sophie's ..."

I waited her out as the silence lengthened. Finally, I could stand it no longer and filled the empty space. "Partner. *Significant* other." I emphasized "significant."

Well over six feet in heels, Carol Novak towered above me. She must have had at least four inches on my five-foot-nine frame. From the look in her eyes, I knew it was an advantage she enjoyed using.

"Yes, of course. I saw the two of you make your grand entrance across the dance floor." As if she suddenly remembered. "Even heard your friends wishing you a happy anniversary." There were no congratulations from her. "How many years?"

"Thirteen." I answered before I could stop myself.

"Hmmm ... unlucky thirteen." She shrugged and started to move off. But before she had gone more than a few steps, she returned to take another verbal swipe. Stopping just inside my personal space, she looked at me as if she was confused. "I didn't know teachers were considered professional people." In a sarcastic and demeaning tone, she was questioning my right to attend the gala.

I had to stop myself from emptying my plate down the front of her dress. But Carol Novak seemed to read my mind, and she reached over and brushed my lapel as if there was a speck on it. "Be very careful, Jensy ... you wouldn't want to do anything to make a scene." She waved a hand intended to dismiss me and turned her back.

But I wasn't done. "What's your problem, Carol? What is your issue with me?"

Very slowly, with great effect, she turned around to face me. "You're mistaken, Jensy. I don't have an issue with you. I don't even think about you."

Stunned, I rocked back on my heels. When I recovered, I leaned forward into her space. "Really? Well, then, let me help you out. You *do* think about me. I know you think about me because you have an issue with Sophie and me. I have something you want, and you're jealous. Not that you want her for the long term — you just want her for the now. You *do* think about Sophie."

Carol smiled coldly. "Oh, that I do. Often." She didn't bother to negate a single word I said.

I seethed as I watched her coldly calculate her odds with Sophie. I had never met anyone like her. "Piece of work" as my father used to say, but she was even worse than that. Carol Novak knew only one way to deal with someone who stood between her and what she wanted. She would simply walk over me if she could. I wondered how she presented herself to Sophie at work. Sophie rarely mentioned Carol, but I wasn't sure if it was because she, herself, had no time for her or because she knew how I felt about Carol.

"Who is that?" Viv leaned close when I returned to the table. Sophie was out of earshot, busily chatting with Mary.

"Carol Novak. A work colleague of Sophie's." I didn't bother to hide the distaste in my voice.

"She's hard to miss." Viv attempted humor, but I didn't laugh. "What does she have against you? It's obvious you're not her favorite."

"That's an understatement."

"But there's something else about her ..." Viv's voice trailed off as if she was unsure how much she should say. Viv tended to be blunt in her assessments of people, sometimes to the point of being crude and cruel. I raised my eyebrows, giving her my nonverbal permission to continue. She lowered her voice even more. "There's the scent of a woman in heat coming from her. The scent of a woman who will stop at nothing and crush anyone who gets in her way. That's how I see it, Jensy." Viv told me unapologetically. She glanced at Sophie and then returned her eyes to me. "And Sophie's too nice to realize it."

"I agree." My agreement was verbally mild, but when I looked over at Carol, I felt a loathing so intense it caught me off-guard. She made my blood boil and run cold at the same time.

"I can't begin to tell you how angry she makes me," I admitted. "And livid and hateful: anything and everything negative. I don't think I've ever felt this way about anyone." Viv nodded sympathetically.

In addition to what Viv said about Carol, I also agreed on her assessment of Sophie. Sophie always tried to see the best in people. Usually, I saw it as Sophie's strength — but with Carol Novak, I saw it as a weakness.

Later that evening, I was dancing with Mary, and Sophie was across the floor dancing a slow dance with our friend, Erin. I was talking to Mary when suddenly, her focus on our conversation abruptly ended.

"Wow," Mary breathed, her eyes were razor-focused and her eyebrows raised.

I followed her stare to where Sophie was now dancing with Carol. I watched as Carol's hand moved lower and lower down Sophie's bare back, until it rested on the fabric covering her buttocks. I was incensed. Enraged, I started to pull away from Mary, but she held on to my arm.

"Wait for it." Mary had noticed something else.

Several things happened almost simultaneously. Puzzled and surprised, Sophie looked up at Carol, disengaged and took two quick steps back. At the same moment, Viv, who had been moving across the floor, slipped neatly between the two. Viv danced Sophie into her arms and left Carol standing alone in the middle of the dance floor.

"See?" Mary said simply.

I gave Viv a nod of thanks when I returned to the table. Viv nodded back triumphantly, "No one takes advantage of Sophie."

I searched the ballroom and when I finally found Carol Novak, she was putting on her coat and heading out the door. I followed her into the hallway, grabbed her by the arm and spun her around. "*You. Stay. Away. From. Sophie.*" I punctuated each word with venomous hatred.

Carol's eyebrows lifted at the vehemence I displayed. Then she pointedly looked at my hand and slowly pulled away. She appraised me up and down. "When the time comes and Sophie tires of whatever charms she thinks you possess, I'll be waiting."

"That'll be a cold day in hell." Out of the corner of my eye I saw Sophie coming toward us. With a withering glance at Carol, I turned abruptly and went to meet Sophie.

"I'm sorry she's been such a problem. I don't understand; she's not like that at work." Sophie was apologetic and embarrassed. "Tonight was supposed to belong to us."

"It still does." I assured her.

"Jens, no one touches me that way but you. No one."

"I know," I assured her again. I had originally told Sophie that Carol wanted her, but now wasn't the time or place to bring that up again.

As we walked back into the ballroom, Sophie posed a final question about Carol Novak. "What did she say to you?"

"She told me if you got tired of me, she'd be waiting."

Sophie's eyes widened in surprise. She shook her head in bewilderment. "That would be a cold day —"

"That's exactly what I told her." I put the issue to rest and banished Carol Novak from my mind. The remainder of the evening we ate dessert, listened to music, danced, and journeyed from table to table to mingle with friends.

"Come on, gorgeous ... dance with me." I held Sophie's fingers and led her to the dance floor. It was an old standard that

Sophie adored: "The Way You Look Tonight." I pulled her close. No ballroom dance for this one, just swaying close together. I softly sang in her ear. Sophie had one hand on my back and the other draped on my shoulder, her fingers brushing the hair on the nape of my neck. Everything drifted away and it was just the two of us. I closed my eyes and smiled.

She kissed my cheek. "I love you," she whispered. They were the best four minutes of the evening.

Sometime later, I found Sophie standing alone by the bar, an empty martini glass in one hand and the bar railing in the other. I guessed her two martinis had started to take effect. I took her glass and set it on a nearby table, then came up behind her. Putting my arms around her waist, I rested my chin lightly on her bare shoulder. The small orchestra was switching out to make room for the deejay.

"Did you get enough to eat?" I asked.

"Too much."

"Have you seen everyone you wanted to see?" Sophie had been hobnobbing with people all evening.

"Uh huh." She leaned back, resting in my arms; her hands covering mine.

"Have we danced enough?"

"Ummmm …"

"Do you think you've had enough to drink?" I teased. Hard liquor tended to have an erotic effect on Sophie. After two cosmos or martinis she became a little loose and easy; not really drunk, but a few steps away from sober. It didn't happen often, but when it did, our life was unrestrained and much less predictable.

"Oh, I'm sure I have." Sophie laughed her two-martini laugh. She put her head back until her lips were close to my ear. "Take me home and …" My eyes widened, and I gulped as she finished her sentence.

"That'll be my pleasure," I assured her. It promised to be a wonderful continuation of the ten or fifteen minutes before we left for the gala.

Sophie took my arm, and we made our way toward the door. We stopped briefly at a few tables to say goodnight. Viv smiled knowingly and winked. I raised my eyebrows and winked back. Mary gave us both a hug and a kiss and told us "Happy Anniversary" one more time.

As soon as we entered the parking structure Sophie took my lapels in her hands and pulled me to her for a long, slow kiss. Her hands slipped between the buttons of my shirt, and she sighed when she touched my breast.

I gently pulled away. "Let's go home, Sophe."

"It takes so long to get there." A tipsy laugh.

"I'll hurry," I promised.

When we got to the car Sophie fumbled around in her small clutch until she finally found her keys. I suppressed a smile as she put the keys in my outstretched hand. "You drive," she told me, stating the obvious.

"You're right, I'll drive." I chuckled as I closed the passenger door and made my way around to the driver's side. By the time I slid into the driver's seat, Sophie had reclined her seat and had wriggled her gown up around her hips.

I felt a rush of heat rise from my chest to my face. I was glad I was sitting: my legs were immediately weak, and my body was hot. "Really?"

Sophie's hooded eyes seemed to undress me, and her smile was seductive and knowing. "Really. Multi-task, Tiger."

So, multi-task I did. The fifteen-minute ride home seemed like an eternity. I drove as fast as possible while scanning for police and performing my other "task." In the meantime, Sophie worked her hand inside my shirt, fondling my breasts, while I touched her. I was flushed, sweaty and horny as hell. Finally, we were at the house — in the garage — at the back door — inside the house —

Tobie barked and raced around our ankles. "Not now," I told him. Nothing was going to break the spell of this moment. I'd been waiting all evening. I hurried to turn on the lights to the stairway, but Sophie's voice stopped me mid-stride.

"Here. In front of the fireplace."

I changed course, grabbed at the coffee table to move it, miscalculated, and banged my shin. "Dammit," I muttered though clenched teeth. I tried again ... grasped the table and pushed it out of our way, seized the pillows and a throw blanket from the sofa and threw them on the floor, pushed the starter button on the gas fireplace. All the while whisking off my tie, jacket and unbuttoning my shirt. When I turned, Sophie was gliding toward me — naked except for her purple stilettos.

My head reeled. Sophie was lovely, so breathtakingly beautiful in the golden firelight. My eyes roamed over her body. From her shoulders to her breasts, from her abdomen to the slight bump of her lower belly, I savored her. The silken thighs and her delicate, slender legs ... every inch of her was perfect.

Taking my hand, Sophie began to lead me to the pillows. "Just a sec," I gasped as I frantically started to undo my pants.

"Now, Jensy."

I lowered myself above her. Her body was beautiful in the flickering light, shades of golden browns and creams. My lips brushed hers in a kiss that deepened in intensity. The taste of martinis still lingered on her tongue, and I groaned.

"You're so beautiful," Sophie whispered as she parted my shirt and ran her fingers over my chest, circling my nipples until they were hard. Her hands glided around me, barely touching me until her palms rested flat on my back, pulling me down to her. My body was on fire wherever Sophie touched me. My desire rose in waves.

I started with her lips and slowly kissed my way down her body. Her head pushed back into the pillows, exposing her neck.

She moaned and arched her back when my lips closed over her nipple; licking and sucking it erect. My lips continued their way over her stomach, and down between her legs.

"Touch me," Sophie whispered as she took my hand and guided me to her. She inhaled sharply, as I circled her entrance. Her hips moved against my hand. I slowly entered her, thrusting in a long, slow rhythm that made her gasp in sharp, jagged breaths. Strokes that made her writhe against me, as if she was trying to draw me further inside. I watched her in the firelight: back arching, neck stretched taut, eyes closed. Small sounds escaped from the back of her throat, then a deep inhale — frozen in time, until she came.

I placed my cheek against her neck and felt her pulse pounding against me. I felt the velvety smoothness of her skin. Sophie put her arms around me and gripped the fabric of my shirt.

I looked up and saw Tobie, on the couch, spreading his thick, white undercoat on my tuxedo jacket. I felt guilty he was still waiting to go outside, but when I started to rise, I was stopped by Sophie's fingers on my wrist. "Not so fast." Tobie turned his head away, either bored or disgusted, but continued to watch me out of the corner of his eye. *You can wait a little longer,* I silently told him.

Sophie raised her head and brought her lips back to mine. In an instant, her hands were under my unbuttoned shirt and her nails were raking lightly over my back. Her hands moved to the front and cupped my breasts. I unzipped my pants, and Sophie pushed them over my hips as her kisses moved lower. Her fingers found me. "God, Sophie," I moaned. I rode her fingers until I came.

When I finally got up, Sophie was dozing. I leaned down and carefully took off her heels, tenderly kissing the top of each foot. I scooped Tobie off the sofa, grabbed my dog-fur-covered tuxedo jacket and let him outside. While waiting for Tobie, I rescued a comforter from upstairs and spread it over Sophie. I picked up her gown, still on the floor where she had stepped out of it, and draped it over a chair.

Sophie had turned onto her side, facing the fireplace. I stood in the shadows and watched the firelight dance on her bare shoulder and arm. Tobie trotted over to Sophie, turned several circles in front of her, and laid down where Sophie would spoon him. I watched them breathe in rhythm, her hand on his haunch. I slipped out of my clothes and laid down behind Sophie. I traced her arm with my fingers until they finally came to rest on Sophie's hand. I kissed the back of her neck.

"Did I embarrass you tonight?" she asked sleepily.

"You could never embarrass me."

"Maybe I should stop drinking martinis."

"What, and deprive me of such pleasure and excitement? I'm hoping we'll still be doing this when we're seventy-five."

"You think? Seventy-five?" Sophie chuckled lazily.

I laced my fingers through hers. "I can't imagine a time when I wouldn't want you." I ran the tip of my tongue across the nape of her neck, just below her hairline. She tasted like a spring day, combined with the taste of Sophie after making love.

With a contented sigh, Sophie squeezed my fingers and easily fell back to sleep. I smiled at her sleeping form. I adored her beyond words. The last things I remembered before I fell asleep were the sound of Tobie's small mini-snores and the rhythm of Sophie's breathing, matching mine.

Twenty

For the third time in four years the Washington Heights basketball team was playing in the region finals, and the girls were eager to have another opportunity to advance to the state tournament. Between classes they walked through the halls sharing high-fives and radiating excitement. Sometimes they stopped by my office to share their enthusiasm, as well as the all the supportive things people were saying about the team. They shared positive notes that had been taped to their lockers and mentioned teachers who took a moment to seek them out and wish them good luck.

I took home the only game video of the Lincoln City Raiders my athletic director had been able to find. The quality was grainy, shot from the top of the bleachers and sometimes so out-of-focus that it was difficult to read the numbers on the players' jerseys. Lincoln City was the smallest school in the region, and I knew very little about the team, except what the tape showed and that their win/loss record was not as good as ours.

Sophie sat down next to me as the images unfolded. "I'd certainly get my money back for this movie," she laughed. "Even buttered popcorn won't help." It wasn't too long before she wandered away in search of better ways to spend her time.

The following day Molly and I watched the video during her planning period. Despite the poor quality, we worked our way through and developed our strategy. Over the last several years Molly and I had become an effective coaching team. She was knowledgeable and blessed with a great coaching aptitude. I trusted her opinions and instincts.

After we had developed our game plan, Molly and I had the team watch a few select minutes. I was afraid the poor quality of the video would become its own distraction if the girls watched too much, and I needed them to focus. The Lincoln City offense was very similar to one I had adapted several years ago from my high school days, and though I no longer used it, I knew all its strengths and weaknesses.

"Pay attention," I told the girls. "Notice how they go to their right at least ninety percent of the time. Probably not very comfortable going to their left. We're going to overplay them and force them to go to their left."

I ran through various snippets of the game tape, adding my commentary. "They played zone defense the entire game. Playing zone defense got them to regionals, so I'm guessing they will continue to use it. As you all know, zone defenses have holes, and it's our job to expose them." I outlined what I wanted from the offense, and Molly gave the defensive strategy. From there it was on to the practice court.

A couple days before the game, Sophie came home frustrated and upset. "Dan and Alex called a mandatory partner meeting for late afternoon on Friday. I won't be able to make it to the game."

She had been to every game during our season, and I knew she was emotionally invested in the girls and the success of the team. However, I also knew that when a meeting of the partners was called, she needed to attend. I was disappointed, but for Sophie's sake I understood.

"Obviously I want you in the stands. I always feel better when you're there. But if things go our way, you'll be able to see us play in the state tournament. On the other hand, if things don't go our way, you'll have me home early every night." I attempted to add some levity to balance Sophie's disappointment.

"A win either way," she smiled wanly.

"The team might disagree."

"Win." Sophie told me. "I really want to see the girls play at state."

The girls seemed loose and relaxed as they sat in the back of the bus. There was bantering back and forth, some players sang, and Cassie Duncan and Andie Stevens led cheers. They exuded the confidence of a team that was ready to play.

Molly and I discussed the upcoming game. "I think if our girls play their own game and execute what we worked on, we should win."

"All things being equal, we probably should." I agreed with her assessment. "But did you notice the way Lincoln City played? They played their own style and forced their opponents into mistakes. They never got too upset or flustered. I think they're well-coached; the kind of team that could sneak up on you." I thought about what I had seen on the tape. "Remember, the tape we saw was mid-season. They've had a lot of time to make improvements. And they do have two or three good players. I don't know, Molly, I'm just feeling a bit apprehensive."

"How about this? I'll be confident and you can be a bit apprehensive. That way we'll cover all our bases." She bumped her shoulder against mine.

Through the locker room door we could hear the muffled sounds of the Washington Heights band as Molly and I gave our pregame instructions. I was so proud of the girls: they epitomized the word "team." With their chemistry and work ethic, they were the easiest group I had ever coached, and I so wanted them to be able to experience the state tournament. Excited, nervous, enthusiastic, and eager to play, they exited to the gym.

As soon as I walked onto the court, Andie Stevens trotted over. "The tape's too loose, Coach." She immediately sat down on the bench and took off her shoe and sock.

I inspected the tape job our student trainer had done. Andie was right; there was too much "play" for the tweaked ankle we were trying to protect. I got scissors, tape, and went to work. I was fully engaged, trying to get Andie back on the court as soon as possible. The team needed her warmed up and ready to go.

I was almost finished when I felt a hand on my back, and Molly's voice in my ear. "The Lincoln City coach would like a word with you."

"Almost done." I completed the job and handed Andie her shoe. "That should work. Let me know right away if it doesn't feel right." I patted Andie on the shoulder.

I put on the "happy to meet you; happy to beat you" smile I reserved for opposing coaches and turned around.

My smile immediately dropped away, replaced, I was sure, by a look of dumbfounded surprise and disbelief. Her slender frame was slenderer than I remembered. The dark brown hair was longer, and more lines emanated from the corners of those liquid, amber eyes. My knees went weak from the shock and my heart thudded.

"Jensy." Fitz crossed the distance and hugged me. As if on their own, I felt my arms hesitantly go around her. I closed my eyes for a fleeting second, then pulled away.

"Fitz." I shook my head to clear it. I was dimly aware of Molly standing alongside me, watching my reaction. "Molly, this is Lisa Fitzhugh." The introduction gave me a moment to recover. "Lisa was my high school coach."

I struggled to find an appropriate remark, while my mind slogged along in slow-motion. Finally, "So, how long have you been at Lincoln City?" I sounded like I was speaking from a deep hole, my voice echoed inside my head.

I didn't know what else to say to the woman who had broken my heart so many years ago. I didn't know what to feel about the unsolicited hug from the woman who had never wanted to touch me. I wondered if she even remembered my feelings or my declarations of love.

"Three years." Fitz peered at me as I shook myself back to the present. "You look wonderful, Jensy. How long has it been?" Fitz hesitated as she thought about the answer to her own question.

"Fifteen years." I replied, having unthinkingly done the math. I searched for an appropriate comment and finally settled on, "It's good to see you, Fitz." I cut off any further conversation by turning to watch the girls as they warmed up. I couldn't do this game of "normal."

I was hot and cold at the same time: the unexpected heat of seeing her again, mixed with the cold of her past rejection. Emotions roared through me. Love, longing, hurt, and confusion threatened to explode to the surface. I swallowed over the lump in my throat and inhaled deeply to catch my breath. My wall of protection rose as quickly as I could cement each brick.

"You, too." Fitz was appraising me thoughtfully when I glanced back at her, much as she had done the first time we met in the Tolliver High School gymnasium. She nodded and returned to her bench.

Molly was still standing next to me. "I had no idea you knew each other." She looked at me curiously. "So, you didn't keep in touch?"

"No. She's just someone I used to know." I answered softly. I had never tried to find Fitz. I was never certain if that was because I had emotionally moved on or because I didn't know how I would act if I saw her again. Would I welcome seeing her or would I revisit old feelings that were better left buried? I still didn't really know, but I suspected it would have been better to let Fitz stay a memory. I stuffed my feelings into the back of my mind and turned to pick up the clipboard I had set on the bench.

Every move I made; Fitz countered. It was like a chess match — each move producing a carefully planned countermove. It seemed as though we were standing in each other's huddle listening to game strategy.

I paced the sideline. I cajoled and pleaded with the refs for foul calls. Part way through the first quarter I took off my blazer and symbolically rolled up my sleeves. By the middle of the second quarter my voice was hoarse and raspy. By the end of the third quarter, I was sweating profusely. It was that kind of game.

I tried not to turn my head toward the opposing bench. I already knew what I would see. Fitz encouraging and willing her team to play better. Using every strategy she could employ to help her team achieve their goal. I knew how she worked. I knew because I had been there. I had lived it.

Midway through the fourth quarter we began to create some distance. A steal by Andie Stevens gave us a ten-point lead with four minutes remaining. We began to wear down the Lincoln City team. In the end, our starters were stronger, and our bench was deeper. When it was over, we had earned our eight-point victory.

Our crowd went wild, and fans mobbed the floor. I was pummeled and hugged and high-fived until I ached all over. I scanned the crowd for Sophie, then sadly remembered she wasn't there.

Fitz walked over and put her hand on my shoulder. "Former player surpasses coach. Well done, Jensy. Good luck at State." Fitz hesitated, then asked, "Is there any chance we could get together sometime?"

I didn't know what to say, and finally settled on, "Thanks for asking, but things are really busy for me. I'm not even sure when that would be." I shrugged my shoulders. "I just don't know." I turned toward my players but took a brief glance back as I walked away. There was a look on her face that I couldn't interpret.

For part of the ride home Molly and I sat in the back of the bus, celebrating with the team. When we returned to the front, Molly observed, "You were right, they were well-coached."

"It won't get any easier." I nodded and deflected any further questions about Fitz. Everything about the game left me tired and exhausted. I rested my head against the window glass and closed my eyes. Memories washed over me — things I had compartmentalized for years. A well of feelings were dredged back up to the surface. My emotions collided: love, hurt, excitement, confusion, abandonment, anger, and sadness. I relived them all during that bus ride home.

Sophie was elated that we won. She would get her opportunity to see another game. "I thought you'd be so excited that I'd be pulling you down from the ceiling." We sat in front of the fireplace and shared Sophie's glass of wine. "Instead, you just seem tired."

"I am." I was weary. "The game was too close to ever get comfortable. It was a difficult game — start to finish." I took a sip of wine.

"Let's hope next week is easier."

What Sophie couldn't know was that next week would be easier, regardless of the outcome. True to the vow I had made years ago, I hadn't ever mentioned Fitz. I could have, but I didn't. As time passed, and Fitz became a distant memory, I decided there was no need to dredge up the past. Fitz had become a moot point: a memory during basketball season or in an occasional random thought. And, of course, I had no intention of seeing Fitz again.

Twenty-one

Though a second-place finish at the State Basketball Tournament was not what we had hoped for, the girls were proud of their accomplishment. They were giddy when they hoisted the trophy in front of their peers at our all-school celebration. I pushed Fitz back into the box of my memories and enjoyed the festivities.

Two months after our state tournament appearance, my office phone rang. I was about to leave for a meeting and debated if I should answer. I didn't recognize the caller ID number and hoped if I answered I could keep the call short and avoid having to return a voicemail.

"Good afternoon. This is Jensy Willett."

The silence went on so long I thought the caller might have hung up. Then: "Jensy."

Fitz. Heat and color immediately flooded my neck and face. It was the same reaction I had at the game — the lump in my throat, the roiling stomach, followed by the feeling of surprise and disbelief. I hadn't wanted this to happen. I swallowed with some difficulty.

"I hope I'm not bothering you." That voice, still with the same hint of accent; the melodious cadence. "I wasn't going to call. But

I really do want to see you." There was another pause. "I'm in the city tomorrow for an appointment. Is there any possibility you could get away for the afternoon? Lunch, maybe? I know that's hard to do at the last minute."

I rubbed my forehead with my free hand. I was not looking to establish anything with her. I didn't want it. Didn't need it. I needed the contact to end; but I had been taught to deal with difficult things face-to-face, and this was *one* of those difficult things I needed to deal with in person. I looked at my calendar and found nothing scheduled.

"Jensy?"

"I don't have anything on my calendar." I didn't want to do it; I didn't want to face her — but it had to be done.

My thoughts were interrupted by the sound of Dee clearing her throat. I looked up and she was making "hurry up" motions and pointing to her watch. "I'm late for a meeting. Where and what time?" I jotted the information on a scrap of paper. "I'll be there tomorrow."

Dee looked at me curiously. "Tomorrow?"

"Old friend in town. I'll take half a personal day."

"Nice way to start the weekend." Dee patted me on the shoulder, and we headed to the meeting.

I was distracted through the entire meeting; unnerved by Fitz's phone call. After seeing her at the basketball game, I had finally managed to put Fitz back into a compartment in my memories and return my life to normal. I had believed my cool response to Fitz would be enough to show her that I had no desire to see her again. So, I was totally caught off guard when, despite my chilly reception, she had chosen to persist.

I also had Sophie to consider. Cognitively I realized it wouldn't destroy our relationship if I told Sophie about Fitz now. But keeping that part of my life a secret had become a habit I couldn't break. If I didn't tell Sophie, it would be no different than it had been for years. Yet, I knew that not telling Sophie was a lie of omission. I felt guilty; boxed in by my loyalty to a promise I had made myself years ago and my loyalty to Sophie. My mind kept spinning.

The next afternoon I was in the lobby of an upscale downtown hotel, waiting for Fitz to arrive. I watched her enter the lobby, scanning to find me. She seemed thinner than at the basketball game. Thinner — and pale. As she got closer, I could see lines etched across her forehead. However, her smile and the light in her eyes was the same as it had been all those years ago.

Fitz quickly crossed the lobby and engulfed me in her arms. Once again, I wasn't sure what to do. Finally, I tentatively hugged her. She drew back and held me at arm's length. "Now that I have a better chance to look at you, you *do* look fantastic."

Uncomfortable with her compliment, I simply nodded.

We sat at a small table at the back of the bar. Fitz ordered a Manhattan, and I ordered a beer, although it wasn't yet noon. "What kind of appointment brings you to the city on a Friday morning?" I asked, searching for a neutral opening.

Fitz shrugged; her tone dismissive. "Some medical problems." She waved it off and changed the subject. "By the way, congratulations on your success at the state tournament. Well deserved. I'd like to hear about that, and your coaching, and your teaching career at Washington Heights."

My earlier resolve to simply tell Fitz I wanted no more contact and then leave for home, thawed as I began to talk about my work at Washington Heights. Fitz fed me questions and listened intently to my answers. I talked about my coaching career, the strategies I used, and how I had developed the program. When I shared that I had taught some English my first year, she seemed pleased. Finally, I mentioned my counseling position and the program Dee and I had developed for our gay and lesbian students. Fitz seemed to hang on my every word.

Then, she shared the tragic loss of her parents in a plane crash, and the year and a half she spent pursuing wrongful death litigation. After her parents' deaths she had sold the family's substantial acreage to a real estate developer. "It was the ultimate awful trade-off — being paid off for losing your family." She told me ruefully.

"After that was finished, I discovered I had the means to do whatever I wanted, but had no idea what that might be. I came back here, bought a cabin on a huge lake up north and planned to live there full time. I was comfortable being alone, perhaps more comfortable than being with people.

"But I did miss teaching and coaching. When I took the job in Lincoln City, I rented a small apartment during the week and went back to the cabin on weekends. It was ideal — I was doing what I loved yet had the privacy I craved."

Fitz had never shared much about herself when she was in Tolliver, and I was surprised that she was sharing so much now. Despite her willingness to talk about herself, I didn't ask her what she had done immediately after she had left Tolliver. Nor did I mention seeing her in the stands at a couple of my college basketball games. That information was no longer important to me. The important questions, regarding whether or not she had ever had any feelings for me, I also left unasked.

As business in the bar had increased, so had the noise level, and we raised our voices to be heard. "Why don't you come up to my room? It's a suite. We can order lunch and talk in a normal tone," Fitz suggested.

I agreed to the meal but was reluctant about the suite. However, I had nervously consumed three beers and the resulting buzz signaled my need for food. In addition, I still needed to tell Fitz that any communication between us needed to end. I was adamant about that.

"Just a minute," Fitz said, walking into the suite's bedroom and sitting on the side of the bed. "I really need to get out of these shoes."

I followed her into the bedroom carrying her raincoat. "Where do you want me to put this?" I asked.

Fitz pointed absently to a chair. "I followed your career, Jensy. I know the awards you've won as a player and coach. I've been proud of you every step of the way. You outdid my expectations — and they were high."

I was touched and surprised.

She sat on the side of the bed rubbing her hands vigorously, her brows knitted in a frown. I walked unsteadily toward where she was sitting. "Are you okay?"

"Lately it seems that my hands are always freezing."

"Something to do with your medical issue?" I asked.

She nodded, reached out with one hand and closed her icy fingers around my wrist.

I hadn't seen it coming. But as soon as she touched me, I knew what was happening. I started to back away, but Fitz's other hand rose to the back of my neck and pulled my head to her upturned lips. Her mouth was hard against mine, forcing my lips to part for her. I was seventeen again. Seventeen — and in love for the very first time. No thought, just physical sensation. Nothing else existed. Nothing else mattered. Nothing else entered my mind.

Fitz unbuttoned my shirt, and I could see her fingers trembling with impatience as she fumbled with the buttons. She unclasped my bra, sucking in breath as she struggled with it. It was as if I was watching myself in a movie. I couldn't think. I couldn't move away from her. Fitz's lips moved from my mouth to my neck to my breasts.

"Jesus, Fitz." I licked my dry lips and took a shaky breath. My head pounded.

Her hand unzipped my slacks and slipped inside. I gasped and dug my fingers into her thin shoulders. She pushed me back onto the bed and pulled off the rest of my clothes. Her eyes seemed to devour me as she hurriedly stripped off her clothes. Her lips and tongue glided down the length of my body and back again. I brought her face back to mine and kissed her as I had wanted to all those years ago.

Everything I did, every move, every response, took on a life of its own. Time raced. Seconds compressed. I was a frantic tangle of unthinking actions and reactions. I rolled on top of her; my hands and lips were everywhere. My heart beat furiously and my breathing was hoarse and jagged. I didn't think. I couldn't slow down. I didn't want to slow down.

Eventually, I closed my eyes and tried to calm my racing heart. Fitz's head was on my shoulder. She ran her foot slowly up and down my leg, and the tip of her finger traced a circle on my breast.

For a moment my breathing became normal, until my mind returned to the present. My thought process returned at the same time Fitz noticed the interwoven bands on my finger.

Sophie.

"You're involved with someone." Her voice was flat and emotionless.

Panic. Fear. Dread. My mouth went dry, and my heartbeat became erratic. I was sweaty and hot, cold and clammy at the same time. Bile rose in my throat, and I feared I might be sick. I was overwhelmed, scared, and frightened to death. I knew I had just jeopardized everything I held dear, and I was petrified. Filled with terror.

I abruptly disengaged from Fitz, swung my legs over the side of the bed and began to put on my clothes.

"Jensy?"

"I need to go. Now." I threw on my underwear, slacks, and shirt. Sitting back down on the edge of the bed, I pulled on my shoes. My hands shook so violently it took me three tries to tie the laces.

"Jensy, I didn't know that you're involved with someone." Fitz said softly.

"No. You didn't. But I did." When Fitz touched my back, I stiffened and jerked away. "I'm more than just involved. I've been with Sophie for thirteen years."

"You didn't tell me."

"You didn't ask. You didn't ask me anything about my personal life." I blamed Fitz, when really the blame was mine. It wasn't fair, but I didn't care.

"You didn't want to tell me." She countered defensively.

"You didn't want to know." Harsh, bitter.

We were at a stalemate. Neither of us really wanted to take the ownership or responsibility. I stood and faced Fitz. "I love Sophie more than anything." I bit my lip and tasted blood. My declaration of love for Sophie sounded outlandish after what I had just done.

I rubbed my forehead. "I don't know what happened ... I don't know ..." I was trying to understand what I had done, but I couldn't think. Everything in my mind was jumbled. My world was askew with panic and confusion. I wheeled and took long strides to the door. My hand was on the doorknob when Fitz's voice stopped me.

"I didn't mean ..."

The sound that issued from deep in my throat was a half-strangled sob. I walked out the door and closed it softly behind me.

I drove to the Cobblestone Bridge, my mind so muddled I didn't remember the drive. I ran the bridge end-to-end five times, before I finally stopped in the middle, gasping and panting. My lungs heaved, and I bent over and grabbed at my knees. My head throbbed and my heart continued to beat in a frantic, irregular pattern.

I berated myself, blistering myself with derision and blame. In Fitz's presence I had lost all perspective and the ability to control my emotions. My grasp on the present had been replaced by times past. I could blame it on my seventeen-year-old emotions, but that meant nothing. I had misplaced who I had become, what was important and what I had to lose. I didn't understand myself or why I had let it happen.

I stood on the bridge and looked down into the grey water, a scene as bleak and desolate as I felt. I held the railing and leaned over as far as I could and watched the water from the falls churn toward the bridge. I followed the current as it broke against the concrete. Directly below me dead tree branches were caught against the piling; suspended in time with nowhere to go — like me. At that moment only one thing seemed to make sense: I leaned farther over the railing.

"Miss? Are you all right?" A kind voice made me turn my eyes from the grey water below. "Can I help you?" the stranger asked, obviously concerned.

"No, thank you. There's nothing you can do," I managed, and headed back to my car. I turned around at the end of the bridge and noticed that he continued to watch my sad, slow progress.

When I arrived home, Sophie was kneeling on the kitchen floor cleaning up a mess Tobie had made. I stood rooted in guilt, quietly watching her. Guilt for not calling to tell her I'd be late. Guilt about the mess she was cleaning up. Most of all, guilt about what had happened with Fitz.

Unsuspecting, Sophie looked up at me and smiled. "Why don't you take off your jacket and stay a while?" When she rose and kissed me on the lips, I pulled back.

"It's okay. Things come up. I was late, too. Because I stopped at the grocery store, the poor little guy just couldn't hold it." She leaned over and patted his head. "I waited to eat. Thought you might be hungry."

Sophie placed her hand on the side of my face. Normally, I would have kissed her palm, but tonight I couldn't. Nothing was normal. Sophie waited a couple seconds longer, and when she finally realized no kiss was forthcoming, she slowly pulled her hand away.

Her eyes searched mine. I was certain if Sophie just looked hard enough, she would read the entire story written in the sound of my voice, the look in my eyes, and the set of my mouth. I wanted to fall on my knees and beg forgiveness.

"I'm not feeling well." Both a lie and the truth. "I think I'll just go to bed."

There was concern in Sophie's eyes, a concern I knew was misplaced. I was a liar several times over. The first lie was not telling Sophie about Fitz at the outset of our relationship. The second lie was neglecting to tell Sophie about meeting Fitz after the regional basketball game. The third lie was not immediately owning up to what had happened that afternoon.

Sophie reached up and felt my forehead. "I don't think you have a fever."

I ended up in the guest bedroom. I couldn't bear the thought of being in our bed. Not tonight. Hurriedly, I removed my clothes; they felt dirty by their association with my deceit-filled afternoon. I took a shower and harshly scrubbed every inch of my body. I sprawled naked on top of the bed, staring at nothing. How long would it take before I felt normal again? Should I tell Sophie? *How* could I tell Sophie? How could I explain to her why things had happened the way they did, when I couldn't explain them myself? Could we, as a couple, survive what I had done?

My thoughts raced and whirled. I peppered myself with questions for which I had no answer. Why had I gone to the hotel to meet Fitz? What did I think was so noble about a face-to-face meeting? How could I have let things happen? How could I have misread the situation? How could I have lost all control? I had no explanation. There was no rationalization or justification for what I had done. None. I had destroyed, in three hours, everything Sophie and I had built for thirteen years — every promise we made. Everything rested solely on my shoulders.

I must have slept, because the next thing I knew, Sophie was covering me with a blanket. The room was dark except for light filtering from the hallway.

She sat down beside me and indicated a glass on the night-stand. "I went to the store and got you some Ginger Ale." She gently moved a strand of hair off my forehead. "My mom used to give it to me when I wasn't feeling well."

"Thanks." Her act of kindness threatened to tear my heart in two.

"Why don't you come to bed with me? I think you're just exhausted. It was a long basketball season, and the final loss was tough. You've been working overtime meeting with incoming freshmen and their parents. It's all been emotionally draining." She laced her fingers through mine. "Come on, Tiger."

I squeezed her hand, striving for any sense of normalcy. "I think — just in case — I'll spend the night here." I closed my eyes and lied yet again. "In case I do have something, I don't want you to catch it."

Sophie kissed my forehead. I smelled the familiar scent of her light cologne and felt the warmth of her fingers entwined with mine. When she lightly touched my cheek, I turned my head and closed my eyes.

The next morning, I found Sophie eating breakfast and avidly reading the newspaper. She was a news junkie, reading both the city paper and the New York Times. Our morning ritual included Sophie turning over the sports and entertainment sections to my pedestrian tastes, while she devoured the hard news. My sections, and a glass of orange juice, were waiting for me when I sat down.

"Better this morning?" Sophie asked, taking off the glasses she wore only when she needed to see.

"Think so." A cautious reply, testing the words … testing my voice.

Sophie got up and moved behind me, resting her hands on my shoulders. Her lips brushed the top of my head. "I'll make you breakfast. Anything you want."

I stood so abruptly that a startled Sophie retreated a couple steps. The thought of her doing *anything* for me was almost too much. "Sorry," I mumbled. "I think I'll just have some cereal."

"Okay." Sophie returned to her chair and picked up the paper. "Still out of sorts, I think," she speculated while glancing at me. I could almost feel her trying to figure out what was wrong.

"Yeah, I guess I am."

Saturday was not our usual chore day, but I changed that. I needed to be busy. The beds were stripped, the laundry was done, work clothes were ironed, and the hardware store visited to get a washer for a leaky bathroom faucet. Sophie took my hint and did chores herself; never reminding me that Saturdays were our time. That night I put on an old movie and watched uncomprehendingly. It was all just empty movement and sound.

When I finally made my way to bed, Sophie was sitting up reading a book. I knew immediately that she had been waiting for me. As soon as I entered the bedroom, Sophie closed the book and regarded me curiously.

"Should we talk?"

"About what?" I feigned surprise.

She took a deep breath. "Something's off. Something feels wrong." Sophie shook her head. "I know you, Jensy." Her eyes locked on mine. "What is it? What's going on?"

Instead of answering I crossed quickly to the bed and forcefully kissed her. I undressed quickly. It was as if my inner demons were unleashed. There was no tenderness — no gentleness. This sex was hard and edgy, a world away from my usual romantic lovemaking. Sophie's eyes widened in surprise. When I was finished, she turned away from me and silently moved farther onto her side of the bed.

Twenty-two

I raised on one elbow and watched Sophie as she woke. I started to reach out to her, thought better of it and drew back my hand. I didn't know how to describe what had happened last night, except that I had been angry with myself and had taken it out on her. My emotions had been raw, and I'd been harsh in a way that was uncharacteristic of me. It had been sex, not love. I had simply taken what I wanted, and Sophie didn't deserve that.

Sometime during the night, through a haze of sleep, I had become aware of Sophie's arm draped over my waist and her body pressed against mine. That simple gesture added to the overwhelming guilt that engulfed my entire being. "I don't know what to say," I told her when she opened her eyes. "I'm sorry. I don't know what got into me."

"It's okay, Jens. I was just surprised. You've never …" Sophie shook her head and gave her shoulder a slight shrug. She had already forgiven my behavior. "You've always treated me like porcelain. Maybe you just decided I wouldn't break." As she tried to explain the inexplicable, Sophie took the hand I had just withdrawn and guided it down her body. "Touch me," she whispered, and gave me an undeserved chance.

One day stretched to two days, and two days to three, then more, as I attempted to find a way to deal with what I had done. Some days it seemed like I had selective amnesia. On those days it was as if I had erased the incident or packed it safely away in its own compartment. Most days, however, thoughts of that afternoon would come to me unbidden and fill my hours with panic and dread. Mine was now a fear-filled world, where everything was in constant danger of coming apart. I didn't know what to do. I endlessly debated whether to tell Sophie. I was distraught over what that would do to our relationship. I was sick at heart.

Late spring was a busy time of year at Washington Heights, filled with countless events and preparations for the next year. That busyness should have offered an opportunity for some emotional respite — but that didn't happen. I had difficulty maintaining concentration and focus. It was almost impossible to listen to students' issues when I was so busy beating myself up about my own. I hypothesized that I was the one who should be sitting on the other side of the desk, spilling my soul. Some days I couldn't imagine how I was going to survive. The rainy, grey, spring weather was a perfect match for my mood.

Sophie was busy as well, working to bring several new clients to the firm. We were like two planets orbiting Tobie and our home. Dinners were rushed, Tobie's walks were short, and our rare conversations were hurried. I was not diligent about preserving "our time." I had purposely forgotten our rules about discussions. Sophie seemed to sense this, and after several aborted attempts, stepped back to give me space.

I begged the universe for time and distance, just enough so I could get my emotions under control. But I couldn't turn off my thoughts: thoughts about what I had done, thoughts about my guilt and complicity, and thoughts about my best course of action. My life was a chaotic, tangled mess. The only thing I knew for sure was that Sophie was as important to me as breathing. Whatever my future held, I desperately needed her to be part of it.

✦

I had finished my last Friday afternoon appointment and was staring absently out the window when my phone rang. I swiveled in my chair and looked at the vaguely familiar Caller ID number. Suddenly, it came to me — Fitz.

I briefly considered letting the phone go to voicemail and ignore her attempt to communicate. But I needed to deal with at least one aspect of my indiscretion. Apparently, my exit from her hotel room hadn't been enough, and I needed to tell Fitz there would be no further communication. It couldn't — wouldn't — happen again. That afternoon had been the biggest mistake and the worst lapse of judgment of my life. It would not happen twice.

I picked up the phone. "Jensy Willett." My usual greeting pared down to two terse words.

"Jensy, it's Fitz."

They were only three short words, but I knew something was terribly wrong. "Fitz?" There was a drawn-out silence, and I thought she might have hung up. "Fitz?"

Her silence was followed by heavy, deep breaths. "Just a minute." I told her. "I'm going to close my office door." I needed to buy myself a few seconds to try to calm my nerves. I remembered Fitz's cold hands. Her doctor appointment at the renowned medical center. Her thin, gaunt look and her reticence to say anything. An aura of dread enveloped me.

By the time I returned to the phone, I thought I knew. "I'm here."

"Jensy ... I know you would rather not hear from me. But I needed to let someone know. I'm sorry, but I needed to share ..." Her voice faded.

"Share what?"

"It's not good, Jensy." Her voice was just a trace; so soft I had to strain to hear. "I'm sick."

My hand on the receiver became clammy. My face turned hot. "What's wrong?" I blurted into the silence.

"I'm out of remission. The cancer has spread. It's everywhere." I heard a choking sob. "I found out this afternoon."

My mind reeled. "I'm sorry." My heart thudded against my ribs, and my hands tingled. For a brief second my vision blurred as tears swam in my eyes. My voice was halting and slow, each word weighed on my tongue. "What happens now? What'll you do?"

I heard her sharp intake of breath. Fitz tried to sound normal, although normal was no longer possible. "I'm going to pack up my apartment and move to the cabin. It's about two hours north of the city on a beautiful lake. What time I have, I want to spend there."

"But what's the treatment plan? Where will you get treatment? Will there be surgery?" There were many treatment options here, but I wasn't sure what was available in the northern part of the state.

"There won't be any surgery; there's no point. And there won't be any more treatment, Jensy. A new treatment might buy a little time, but it won't assure quality of life." Fitz's voice was resigned. "I know I don't have a lot of time, Jensy. So, I want my time to be at the cabin."

My heart stuttered. "When are you going?"

"Next week." Again, a long pause and the sensation the phone connection might have been lost. After a few moments, Fitz resumed. "I'm not asking you for anything, Jensy. Not for help, not for kind words, not for sympathy. I just wanted you to know there will be things ... some papers ... a few things ... after ..."

"Fitz —"

Fitz sighed. "Don't say a word, Jensy. I probably shouldn't have called. But there will be some documents, and I wanted you to be aware. I know I'm not making much sense, but eventually it will. I'm not trying to make your life more difficult than I already have. I'm sorry I put you in such a terrible situation."

She broke the connection. I thought about redialing the number but knew she didn't want that. I felt a powerful sense of loss before the loss had even happened. I was stunned. I envisioned how hard the road was going to be for her, and it tore at my heart.

Then my thoughts turned to Sophie. I thought about how much I loved her, and the magnitude of what I was hiding from her. I thought about what it would feel like to lose her, and I felt my world crumble before my eyes. My world would be a desolate place, an existence where I had no one to blame but myself. Life had been one miserable disaster after another. When I turned back to the window, the rain had become a downpour.

The afternoon my world collapsed, I wasn't prepared. I was sitting in my study when Sophie suddenly appeared by the side of my desk with a small piece of paper in her hand.

"I ran into Dee at the dry cleaner. She asked me about the afternoon you took off to meet your 'old friend.' Dee said you had both been so busy she'd forgotten to ask." Sophie's tone was curious. "I don't think I knew you were meeting someone. Who is she?"

Sophie placed the piece of paper on the desk in front of me. But it wasn't just a piece of paper: It was Fitz's business card. My face flamed while the rest of me went cold and numb. Sophie let the card rest in front of me for several seconds, then casually turned it over. A note from Fitz was clearly visible: *"Jensy, I really want to see you. Please call me. Fitz."*

"Is Lisa Fitzhugh your old friend? The card was in the blazer I took to the dry cleaner." Again, Sophie's tone sounded curious — nothing more.

But *I* was dumbstruck. I had never seen that card. Fitz must have put it there the night of the region finals. I stared — trapped, cornered — and my heart raced so frantically I thought it might explode. My mouth opened wordlessly, but I wouldn't have known what to say even if I had been able to speak. I knew I looked flustered and guilty; I couldn't help it — I was. All the emotions I had been pushing down were rising to the surface faster than I could control them.

"Yes ... yes ..." I finally stammered, then cleared my throat. "I ... yes ... an old friend." My face grew more heated with every word.

I briefly looked up into Sophie's eyes but couldn't meet her stare. My hands closed into white-knuckled fists, and my right knee bounced uncontrollably. I could feel my entire body trembling with fear. I wanted to run from her scrutiny, at least until I had a chance to pull myself together. The oppressive silence seemed to suck all the air out of the study: Sophie waited for an explanation, while I tried to avoid giving one.

Things might have been different if I had just been able to control my actions and reactions. But Sophie had always been able to read me like a book. She knew all my quirks and nuances — every look and every tone of voice. "The old friend you met, and then came home distant and aggressive? That *old friend*?" When Sophie took a step back, her tone was still curious, but now it was laced with an added undercurrent of disbelief and distrust.

"My old ... my old high school coach ..." I told her lamely, still unable to meet her eyes.

"Don't lie to me, Jensy. Don't you dare lie to me." Her voice now a low whisper.

"It's true. It is." And I knew right away that this partial admission sounded like a lie. "Lisa Fitzhugh. Fitz."

"That's all?" Sophie was incredulous. "Then why are you so nervous and upset? Is this part of what's been going on with you lately?" She shook her head, and I could hear in her voice the awareness that my words didn't ring true. "The truth, Jensy. What else?"

I gulped, "Well ... I ..." I couldn't lose the damning tremor in my voice. "I ... I had ... I had a crush on her." I shrugged.

Sophie folded her arms over her chest and waited. I looked into her eyes, and they bore right through me, pinning me to the back of my chair. "I think it was more than that." She enunciated each word slowly and clearly.

As much as I wanted to deny it, I couldn't. "Okay, yes. It was more than that. I was in love with her. At least as close to being in love as I ever imagined being." I began to ramble — spilling information that was meaningless in the larger scheme of things. "I was a seventeen-year-old high school junior in love with my coach. She left at the end of that school year.

"She was at a couple of my college basketball games. We didn't even talk. I didn't see her for years. Didn't want to. I had you. I love *you*." My words poured out faster and faster. "Then, there she was, the opposing coach at the region finals. She must have put the card in my blazer after the game." Even that sounded like a lie. I was consumed by panic.

"So, you went to meet her." Her voice was ice.

"Yes. Yes. She called me." I could feel the sweat gather under my arms and begin its descent down my sides. I squirmed in my seat.

"You slept with her." A statement, not a question, as the truth dawned on Sophie.

What did I expect? My behavior during past few weeks had been distant and edgy. I had stubbornly refused to adhere to our rules of discussion, though Sophie had reminded me of the process we had promised to uphold. I had withdrawn and built a wall to protect myself. And now Sophie was tearing down that wall, making it impossible for me to lie, though she might not want to know the truth.

I couldn't respond — couldn't answer her statement. Finally, I looked into the blue eyes that stared unfocused into the distance. I watched in hopeless sorrow as Sophie realized what my silence meant.

"I see." Her two words hung in the charged air, and she moved to the doorway.

I stood. "Sophie —"

She stopped, turned, and raised her teary eyes to mine. "Us, Jensy. You betrayed us."

"I didn't plan this. It wasn't what I wanted. I was going to tell her I never wanted to hear from her again. It just happened." My voice, loud and strident, was finally unleashed. "I can explain —"

"Don't." She held out her hand to silence me.

I watched her closing down, emotionally retreating from me. Except for the tears threatening to spill, Sophie's face was a cold mask, devoid of feeling. She wrapped her arms around herself as protection from me.

"She's dying, Sophie." The words came out before I could stop them.

"What? And that makes everything fine?" She was incredulous. "It's all right to sleep with the person you were in love with because ... oh, by the way, she's dying?" Bitter and angry.

I wasn't sure she believed me or if she even cared, but I plunged on. "She's packing up to move to some godforsaken cabin in the woods, to wait to die."

I was angry and frustrated, mired in a situation I made worse by the second. I loathed myself for what I had done and for using Fitz's illness to try to garner sympathy. I couldn't imagine how to repair the damage I had caused, but I knew I was causing more harm as each minute passed.

Unable to stop myself, I blundered again. "It's true. Can't you at least have some compassion?" My comment was impulsively and cruelly tossed in Sophie's direction.

Sophie bit her lip and searched my face. I could see the emotions rolling over her: anger, hurt, distrust, confusion.

"Compassion? That's what this is about, Jensy? *My* lack of compassion?" Her voice was raised in incredulous frustration.

She slowly shook her head. "No. It's all about what you just admitted. It's about what happened between you and that woman. It's about whether *you* still love *me*." I watched Sophie back out of the study. One step back, then two, as she backed over the threshold. "I don't know what to believe." She drew in a shaky breath. "I can't talk about this right now. I can't."

Sophie's eyes filled with hurt, but her voice trembled with anger. "Maybe you should just go help her move." In a sudden movement she whirled and ran up the stairs. I heard the bedroom door quietly shut, followed by the click of the lock.

Sophie withdrew from me, not by inches, but by miles. She cut off my attempts at discussion with a stare that lined up somewhere between fury and indifference. Her mouth perpetually set in a cold, hard line. On those few brief instances when her eyes met mine, there was the distinct look of wariness and suspicion.

The week after Sophie found out felt like a lifetime. Time slowed to an excruciating crawl. I moved into the guest bedroom, and we lived separate lives under the same roof. Even something as simple as the kitchen seemed to personify our barren existence: no tandem cooking adventures, no eating together, no shared newspaper — nothing. The refrigerator was perilously close to empty, and there were no dishes waiting to be washed after the morning rush. Without Sophie, my life was desolate.

I sank down on the kitchen floor next to Tobie and idly ran my hand over this thick coat. He was long over-due to be brushed. For a millisecond he paused and gave me a quizzical look, then returned to his food. That's where I was sitting when Sophie walked in. It was Thursday afternoon, normally her late night, but this Thursday she was home well before dinner.

Sophie smiled when she saw Tobie, but that smile vanished when she noticed me sitting next to him. Her face swiftly became a mask as she crossed her arms over her chest and leaned against the door frame.

"I'm going to a law conference in Atlanta this weekend. With Carol. We're leaving tonight."

No hello. Just that statement: terse, unemotional and to the point. I was up off the floor so quickly that Tobie gave a startled yelp.

"To Atlanta? With Carol? *Tonight?*" I repeated, as I attempted to process the information. The news came from out of nowhere, and I felt like I had been bludgeoned with a heavy hammer. I was stunned. In my heart I knew that Carol's purpose at the conference would be to take advantage of Sophie and turn her against me. But I no longer knew what was in Sophie's heart. Was this simply about attending the conference or something more? Was it revenge? A way to make me hurt like she had been hurt? Or even worse, was she sending a signal that she was done with us? I couldn't let myself believe that we were done. I needed to believe that we could survive this.

"You can't leave before we talk about this." I desperately wanted Sophie to stay.

Her look said more than any words. Her steely eyes focused on mine; this wasn't open for discussion.

Frightened and angry, I tried again. "You know, don't you, that Carol wants to have you just so she can say you've been had … another notch on her headboard."

Sophie looked away and shook her head, "That's low, Jensy. Is that all the credit you give me? That's what you think? That I'm just a notch on someone's headboard?"

"Not someone — her." We stood warily watching each other across the length of the kitchen. "Certainly, you know that from the dance."

Sophie opened her mouth to say something but thought better of it.

"You felt it at the dance. You know you did," I insisted again. "Are you that naïve?"

"Carol and I have a working relationship."

Panic rose as I felt another step closer to losing Sophie. "That's what you think. But what does Carol think? How close does Carol want your working relationship to be?" I crossed the kitchen floor, closing our distance to about a foot. "This close?" I detested Carol and her motives, even though my own behavior had been abominable.

I shouldn't have pushed, but my anger and jealousy escalated quickly. I couldn't help myself. Sophie's eyes were guarded as my next step put me inches from her.

"How about this? This close?" I breathed. We were so close I could feel Sophie's breath on my lips. "How close do you want your working relationship to be?"

Sophie stared at me as if my words had struck her. Her eyes never left my face — never blinked. She didn't flinch and her voice was acerbic. "How dare you? *You,* of all people. After what *you* did. To suggest that about me?" Her voice cut through me like a knife.

"After what I did and what you're planning to do?" I called after her retreating back.

Sophie whirled around. "I don't make plans like you do."

I heard the closet door open as Sophie removed a suitcase, the sound of her footsteps traveling up the stairs, drawers being opened and shut. I rubbed my forehead. My anger was gone; replaced by despair at not being able to control my emotions ... my propensity to say things without thought or foresight.

I trudged upstairs listening to the sounds of drawers and zippers. The suitcase was open on the bed, and Sophie was at the closet door.

"I'm sorry. I didn't mean to —"

"Right now, I don't want to hear what you meant or didn't mean."

"I wish you wouldn't go," I said meekly, praying it would resonate with her.

Sophie held up two hangers and examined the dresses. "I don't think you really have any say in the matter." Scrutinizing the dresses, she all but ignored me.

I didn't want her to take that black dress, the one I found so attractive on her. Sophie knew how I felt about that dress. Maybe she'd listen to that request. "Take the blue one," I suggested.

Sophie hung the blue dress back in the closet and packed the black one. It was pointless. I was defeated.

"I don't have time right now, Jensy. Carol will be here in a few minutes." Tobie bounced onto the bed and into the open suitcase. "Oh, no, Tobie. You'll shed all over everything." Sophie scooted him out of the luggage and off the bed.

I turned to the dresser and picked up the lint roller we always kept handy. When I handed it to Sophie our fingers touched, and it seemed that we stood there frozen. I burned where her fingers touched mine. Sophie took a deep breath, gently took hold of the roller, and placed it in the suitcase.

"Come on, Tobie," I told the little Corgi. "Let's go out." He looked from Sophie to me, trying to assess our tension. He wanted to go out, but he didn't know if he should. He didn't want to let Sophie get away. After a moment's hesitation he followed me down the stairs.

Sophie came down with her suitcase a few minutes later. She left it at the front door and went to say goodbye to Tobie. I had the irrational desire to hide the suitcase, so Sophie couldn't leave. Then, maybe, our lives together wouldn't evaporate. She returned quickly and stood at the front window with her back to me; pointedly shutting off any avenue for conversation.

"Please, Sophie." I begged; my voice laced with tears. "Please, don't do this. Don't go. Stay here and let's work this out." I sobbed — loud, hiccoughing sobs.

I saw her shoulders heave and I knew she was crying, too. When Carol's car pulled up, Sophie quickly opened the door and started outside. The house was now silent except for the sound of her rolling suitcase being pulled over the threshold.

"Please call me," I begged.

Sophie stopped for a moment and bowed her head. Still facing away from me, she took a deep breath and squared her shoulders. "Don't count on it." But I heard the tears in her voice as she continued on her way. I stood unmoving, my hand on the doorknob, watching her leave.

Twenty-three

As I watched Carol whisk Sophie away, my sadness changed to anger. I was furious. I moved onto the front porch and looked down the empty street where Carol's car had just disappeared. I punched a wooden beam as I thought of the snide, knowing look Carol had thrown me after bestowing a welcoming smile on Sophie. Carol's black, dead eyes signaled to me that she was moving in on Sophie. The shark was circling, and the prey was Sophie.

I prowled the house. I paced the downstairs thinking about Sophie with Carol. I pounded up the stairs and stood outside the bedroom door. Tobie jumped on the bed, sniffed where Sophie's suitcase had been and watched me closely. I slammed shut a drawer that had been left open and went back downstairs. Tobie followed me onto the deck. The late afternoon sun sparkled through the leaves of our maple tree, a sight that in normal times would fill me with peace and contentment. Today, however, I sat on a deck chair, hitting my fists on its arms. Sophie with Carol. I couldn't calm myself — I couldn't stop thinking or imagining.

After another minute, buoyed by negative energy, I rose. Tobie rose with me and cocked his head expectantly. "Do you want to go for a walk?" I asked.

Of course, he did. He raced inside and we picked up his leash. Once on the sidewalk Tobie tugged to go our usual route, but I had a different idea. Unlike the rest of my life, at least on this walk, I knew where I was going. I just wasn't certain what I would decide when I got there.

Six blocks later we arrived at our destination: Washington Heights. Far down the hall I could see Ben Cutler bent over a locker. I let Tobie off the leash and he took off at a fast trot to share a "meet and greet" with Ben.

"Tobie!" Ben knelt and greeted the Corgi. "How are you, you old devil?" He asked as Tobie squeaked and groaned. Ben looked down the hall to where I stood waiting outside the counseling office. "Jensy! The school day's over! Go home!"

"I need to find something, Ben. I won't be long."

"No problem. Just lock up the office door when you leave."

I entered my office and sat down at my desk. A recent photo of Sophie and me, taken during Christmas break on our last trip to Florida, was facing my chair. We had been the picture of the quintessential happy couple. I picked it up and studied the "us" we had been. As I gently returned it to its place, I stared across the room at my photograph of the Cobblestone Bridge. That photo, striking in its simplicity, had been featured in my first photography exhibit. The black and white print was beautifully framed, signed (by me) and numbered: a gift from Sophie. My first sale as a professional photographer. My life was so inextricably bound to Sophie.

I swiveled in my chair to look out the window. When Tobie saw I was looking outside he wanted up on my lap. I held him tightly and together we surveyed the trees, the playing fields, and the lush, green landscape punctuated with colorful flowers.

"What should I do?" I asked him and kissed the top of his head.

Finally, after several long minutes, I put Tobie on the floor and turned to my desk phone. I scrolled through the list of past calls until I found what I was looking for. From my desk, I pulled out a pen and jotted down the number.

I was unsure about anything and everything. I was a mess. I was stuck … spinning the same thoughts over and over. Whatever route I chose seemed linked to irrevocable damage and disaster. I wanted to go to Atlanta and bring Sophie home by whatever means necessary to make her work things out. But forcing her home wasn't the answer.

In addition, there was also the part of me that kept thinking about Fitz, and the cruel turn life had handed her. Sophie's voice, cold and distant, echoed in my mind. "Maybe you should just go help her move … Maybe you should just go help her … Maybe you should just go … ."

I took out my cell phone and dialed the number.

Early Saturday morning I placed Tobie, his necessities, and my small duffle into the back of the SUV. When we arrived at Fitz's apartment the door was open, and she was waiting. I was startled by the deterioration in her physical appearance in the last two months. Fitz was thin and frail. Her hair was lackluster and uncut, and her liquid amber eyes were tired and dull. She moved slowly, and though still under her own power, it took Herculean effort.

"No furniture." She told me as I eyed the apartment. "I rented it furnished. It's just the boxes and a few other mementos. The cabin is fully furnished, and I'll be having people come in to care for me."

I indicated the boxes. "They won't be a problem." I quickly mentioned Tobie. "I had to bring my dog. He couldn't be alone for the weekend, and it was too late to find a sitter."

"Sophie's gone?"

"She went to a conference." I took a deep breath and let it out. "She's gone, figuratively and literally. She found the business card you must have put in my blazer the night of the game. She knows everything."

I knew my tone was harsh and accusatory. I needed to blame Fitz, or at least have her share the blame and responsibility with me. Perhaps that was the underlying reason I was at her apartment, to assign blame. But when I looked at Fitz again, my mind wouldn't go there — not now — not under these circumstances.

"About the business card —"

I waved her off. "Look, Fitz, I'm here to help you move and get settled at your cabin." I sighed tiredly. "Anything more emotionally complicated than that, I can't do. I'm just trying to do one good thing in the sea of mistakes that has been my life lately." I raised my shoulders. "I don't want to talk about what happened between us. I won't discuss the year you were in Tolliver. It's all too much. Too hard." I pinched the bridge of my nose. "All I want to do is help you move."

Fitz nodded. "Fair enough." She abruptly switched the subject. "Why don't you get your dog and bring him in to meet me."

First, Tobie sniffed and explored the apartment. When he finished his inspection he trotted over to Fitz and gave her his canine once-over sniff test. Test passed — Tobie vaulted onto the sofa and placed his muzzle on Fitz's leg. Fitz closed her eyes and stroked Tobie's head and ears. She smiled as she felt the silky fur of his muzzle. "It's been such a long time since I've petted a dog." Her voice held simple joy.

"Tobie," I told her.

"Tobie," she repeated, and he looked up at her with his large, serious brown eyes. "You are such a beautiful boy," she whispered.

Between my trips to the car, Fitz told me that most of her clothing had been donated to a thrift store. "Oh, how I hated to part with my suits," she sighed. I thought of Sophie and her suits, and I knew she would have understood Fitz's regrets.

Fitz's belongings were few. There was a box that contained some photos and awards. Another two boxes held books. The last box included odds and ends of clothing: underwear, T-shirts, and sweatpants. There was a small, three-legged stool that had belonged to Fitz's grandmother. I packed an abstract canvas and a small sculpture; both of which I remembered from her apartment in Tolliver. When the car was loaded, Fitz paused as she closed the apartment door for the last time.

"Everything packed? Everything okay?" I indicated the apartment behind us.

Fitz gave a brief nod. "It's just the finality of so many things," she said softly. Then she visibly set her shoulders and moved on.

I placed the written directions Fitz had given me on the center console. "It's likely I won't be able to stay awake," she told me, embarrassed by needing to make that concession.

It didn't take long for sleep to overtake her. She initially asked me to tell her Tobie's story. Sometime early in the storytelling, when I glanced over at her, she had fallen asleep. Fitz slept a hard, restless sleep that made me wonder if she was in pain. My eyes teared, and my throat had the raw feeling I always had when I was trying not to cry.

Fitz was still sleeping when her directions led me down a long, gravel driveway. The trees opened into a clearing that was dominated by a large log home with its own detached garage. I could see the lake through the space between the two buildings. I checked the directions again to make sure I was in the right place, because this was no cabin — it was a huge lakefront home.

"Fitz? Fitz." I reached over and gently shook her awake. "I think we're here." I knew my tone sounded dubious.

She opened her eyes and squinted through the bug splattered windshield. "Yes ... this is it."

"This is no cabin, Fitz. It's —"

"Home," she finished. "It's home."

I walked Fitz up the stairs and into the "cabin." I could see her eyes shine when she entered. It was the most alive I had seen her that morning. The inside was large, open, and filled with light. The furnishings were an interesting combination of rustic and modern: a combination that accurately reflected Fitz. Sliding doors flanked either side of a massive fireplace and opened onto a deck overlooking an enormous lake — every bit as inviting as the house.

"Go ahead and open the sliders. I'm sure Tobie has something he has to do," Fitz suggested.

Tobie navigated down the steps from the deck to the ground. I crossed to the railing and watched as he sniffed, snorted, rolled, and occasionally marked his territory. He waded hesitantly into the water and snapped his mouth in the water — fishing for minnows. Then he was back in the grass, rolling and grunting with happiness. Fitz moved alongside me, and we leaned against the railing, breathing in the scent of the lake and the pines.

"It's beautiful, Fitz."

"I'm happy to share it." She paused for a moment. "It's been a lovely oasis. Renewing and refreshing."

I rested my chin on my hands. I couldn't bring myself to look at the gaunt form standing next to me. It was heartbreaking. "I'm so sorry you have to go through this."

Fitz's hand briefly touched my arm. "I tell myself that life is what it is. Sometimes it's just messy and not what you want or hope for. It doesn't really matter what's right or fair. So, let's just enjoy the lake and the day and the sunshine. That's why I'm here."

That afternoon Fitz asked me to take her into town. She wanted to get a haircut, and she needed to go to the grocery store. I looked at her, considered her lack of strength, and felt certain she had already depleted her energy reserve for the day. As if reading my mind, she told me, "Look in the study."

The study, or more accurately, the "museum" to Fitz's accomplishments, was filled with memorabilia. The wall cabinet was filled with trophies, medals, and framed certificates. Prominently displayed in the middle of everything was "our picture." I was lifting Fitz, my coach, off the floor after the biggest win in Tolliver basketball history. Toward the top of the photo Fitz's arms were thrown wide open, and toward the bottom her feet were bare after kicking off her high heels. My face was shining up at her.

In the corner of the room, I saw the wheelchair.

"Did you find my chariot?" Her tone was light, but as I wheeled it out, her eyes were sad. "I decided I needed to be prepared for the inevitable." She gave a slight, miserable shrug of her shoulders.

While Fitz got her hair cut, Tobie and I walked through the small town. It consisted of the beauty shop, a tiny post office, a grocery store/gas station, and a Dairy Queen: for anything else you needed to travel twenty miles. Tobie and I headed down to the boat landing, and when I squinted across the lake, I thought I could barely make out Fitz's cabin.

Twenty minutes later, Tobie was in the car, and I was back at the beauty shop. The stylist met me at the door. "She's asleep in the wheelchair. In fact, I didn't even have her get out when I heard what she wanted me to do. It didn't take but a few minutes."

I approached the wheelchair and touched Fitz's arm. When Fitz opened her eyes, she saw the surprise in mine. "Oh, Jensy, it's only hair."

It was gone — or rather — most of it was gone. Only a crew-cut remained. My throat constricted around the lump I felt there. Fitz's hair had always been beautiful: perfectly styled, neatly cut. It had been one of her most distinguishing features.

"Well, thank God your head is perfectly shaped," I imperfectly attempted to add some support to her decision.

Fitz smiled ruefully. "Charmer." She pulled out a baseball hat that she had stuffed against the side of the chair. "But I am a bit self-conscious," she admitted, shrugged, and pulled the brim down low.

When I suggested taking her back to the cabin while I did

the grocery shopping, an exhausted Fitz readily agreed. When I returned, I stocked the groceries and made myself a mug of instant coffee. While Fitz slept, I was at loose ends. I headed to the deck, followed by Tobie. I surveyed the huge lake and the combination of pine and birch trees that dotted the landscape. Eventually, I turned to look at the cabin and garage. No wonder Fitz loved it.

I pictured Sophie at the lake. Then I simply pictured Sophie. I missed us. I wanted her back. I knew I needed a next step, a plan about how to move forward. But right now, I couldn't figure out what that plan should be — I simply wanted her back. I wanted her to want to come back to me. When I returned to the cabin, Fitz was sitting up in her bed, resting against the headboard. I stood in the doorway, a mug of coffee in my hand.

"You looked deep in thought." Fitz indicated the dock, clearly visible from her bedroom windows. I shrugged, not willing to discuss where my thoughts had been. Fitz ran her hand through what was left of her hair and emitted a sudden, surprised laugh. It was the light-hearted laugh I remembered from her days in Tolliver. "We used to say that a crew-cut felt like velvet theater seats. I'd forgotten, but it's true."

"We said the same thing." I laughed briefly with her, then raised my mug. "Instant coffee?"

"I don't think I could drink a full cup. But I'll try a sip, if that's okay." Fitz took a small sip of my coffee, grimaced and returned the mug. "I guess I've lost my taste for coffee. Oh, how I used to love coffee ... any kind of coffee, even instant."

Another indication of her changing world. I hurt for her.

"Please, Jensy." Fitz resettled herself against the headboard. "Sit down."

I sank into the large chair in front of the huge windows.

"I know you don't want to talk about things. I respect that. I do. But I do need to say something. If you could just find it in your heart to bear with me. Call it the prerogative of a dying woman."

Our eyes locked. Fitz looked so tiny and pathetic sitting there, that I nodded for her to go on. "I appreciate that you came here to help me. I know it's probably cost you more than I will ever know."

I looked away and rapidly blinked several times.

"This was never how I wanted things to be for you. I tried to avoid hurting you, but I *always* did. When I left Tolliver, I thought one big hurt would be easier than all the many hurts there would have been if I had stayed. But when I saw you at the regional basketball game ..." Fitz shrugged and looked down at her hands. "Forgive me ... I wanted what I wanted ... and what I wanted was you. I already knew I was sick, knew that things didn't look good, and I wasn't going to be denied that one thing I wanted."

My jaw muscles were grinding so hard my mouth hurt. I looked over at Fitz and tried to open my mouth to stop her, but she continued before I could say anything.

"At the hotel, I planned everything that happened."

"Enough. Stop." Anger and frustration rose to the surface. "If you're trying to make things easier for me so I can justify and rationalize — It won't work. You don't owe me an 'out.' You don't owe me an explanation. You don't owe me an apology. You don't owe me a thing. Not one ... damn ... thing."

My pent-up words tumbled out, one of top of the other. "I let things happen. I was an active participant. That's my responsibility. I beat myself up every minute of every day, for what I did." I tried to take a sip of coffee, but my hands were shaking so badly I couldn't bring the mug to my lips.

"I'll unpack your things and put them wherever you want. I'll stay until tomorrow when you meet with the caregivers and get them settled in. Then I'm going home to see if there is any way I can save my relationship." My voice took on the tone I used when I needed to protect myself — distant, aloof, and rigid.

We settled into an uneasy truce for the rest of my stay. We sorted through boxes, and Fitz directed the placement of the items.

Books were placed in alphabetical order on two vacant book-shelves. The awards and framed certificates were arranged in her trophy case and clothing was folded or hung. Fitz's painting and sculpture were placed in her bedroom in her direct line of sight. That night I made supper of scrambled eggs, bacon, toast, with orange sherbet for dessert — all at Fitz's request. She ate little, but at least she ate.

I started the night in the guest bedroom. After much tossing, I finally fell into a dream-filled sleep. I dreamed about Sophie. *We were making love ... an erotic, sensual tango. It was warm, and we were both slick with sweat. It was so real I could inhale her scent, taste the salt on her skin and feel the smooth silkiness of her damp body. I felt her hard nipples as they rubbed against mine, and her slick wetness when I entered her. I heard her as she moaned with pleasure, her breath hot on my skin. I saw her taut muscles and watched her look of wild passion as she came.*

After, I gazed at her. Sophie was naked. Arms over her head, She stretched ... arching her back, raising her breasts. My desire stirred again.

Her eyes were closed. "I know you're watching."

"You do?"

"Of course," she smiled. "I'm doing this for you." She ran her hand over her breasts and between her legs. I reached for her. Then she was gone and left me grasping at air.

I awoke with a start, and found myself sitting up in bed, reaching into the darkness. I was drenched with sweat. Shaken by the reality of the dream, I got out of bed and made my way to the living room and sprawled out on the sofa's cool leather. For the rest of the night, the images of the dream haunted me — hot and vivid and real.

Early Sunday afternoon I met Margaret, Terry, and Katherine, the three local women who would be taking care of Fitz. I imme-diately liked them and was confident they would take good care of her. They would also work with the local hospice agency. Fitz seemed at ease with them and the care plan.

"Will you be coming back?" Margaret asked as she settled in for her shift.

"No. I don't think so," I told her as I packed my duffle and put Tobie's necessities in his travel box.

Margaret studied me closely with eyes that probably saw too much. "That's a shame. I can tell that Lisa is quite attached to you."

"I've known her for quite a long time." I offered no further explanation.

When Tobie and I entered the bedroom for the last time, I put him on the bed, and Fitz petted him while he licked her face. "He liked you right away," I told her.

"The feeling was mutual."

I finally set Tobie back down on the floor. "I don't know how to do this, Fitz." It was awkward and uncomfortable. A forever goodbye.

"I don't either." Fitz looked at me and smiled sadly. "Didn't I say that life is messy?"

I nodded. "You did." I was close to tears. I wanted to say something that would mean something. I struggled to say something meaningful, and even as I said it, I knew it was inadequate. "I became a teacher and coach because of you. Everything good about what I do with kids, came from you. I carry you to work with me every single day. That means more to me than you can know." My feelings for her, my "I loved you," remained unspoken.

She put her arms out, and I sat on the edge of the bed and hugged her for what seemed like both an eternity and mere seconds. Finally, Fitz patted my back and let me go. We looked at each other for a long time, neither of us moving. In the end, she simply said, "Jensy."

"Godspeed, Fitz."

I made it to the door of my car just as my tears started to fall.

The long drive home was filled with tears and grieving. I was relieved that Fitz had sensitive and competent women to take care of her. I grieved for her journey, but I couldn't be a part of it. I had gone as far as I could go. The road of my journey was the road back to Sophie. I had to look to my future, and I needed that future to be with Sophie. She was the most important person in my life. I couldn't even begin to imagine who I would be without her. I headed home to win her back.

I had been home less than an hour when I heard a door slam, followed immediately by the sound of the car pulling hurriedly away. When I opened the front door, Sophie was walking up the sidewalk.

"I'm glad you're home."

"So am I." She briefly glanced at me. Sophie's eyes, deep in their sockets, were tired and dark. Her mouth was set in a thin, straight line. There was a remoteness that seemed even more distant than when she had left. My stomach roiled and I tasted bile in my throat. I was panicked that Carol had turned Sophie against me.

I backed up to let Sophie pass. She left her suitcase at the bottom of the stairs and headed for the kitchen with Tobie at her heels. I took the suitcase upstairs, then followed her.

Sophie was kneeling on the floor scratching and petting a delighted Tobie. "Were you a good man this weekend? Did you miss me?" His entire rear end wagged at Sophie's attention.

I wanted to tell Sophie where Tobie and I had been. I wanted to tell her that, despite where I had been, she was the one who dominated my thoughts and dreams. I was so tired of lies, hidden truths and deceptions. I wanted to discuss our future, but I should have known, given Sophie's demeanor, that asking her anything was not a good course of action. But I was so determined, I bulled ahead anyway.

"How was the conference?"

Sophie's eyes searched my face, as if trying to assess the meaning behind my question.

"Did you and Carol have a good time?" I pressed, trying not to sound bitter.

That question made her eyes flash. When she finally spoke, her voice was tight and controlled. "I am not taking part in your fishing expedition."

I almost said, "I'm not fishing" — except that I was. *I* needed to know. But I also wanted *her* to know that I was terrified by what was happening, and that I would do anything to win her back. I wanted to start that conversation now. But it wasn't going to happen tonight — maybe not in the foreseeable future — or maybe it would never happen. The weekend with Fitz had wrenched my gut; but being home with Sophie tore at my heart and soul.

I nodded and broke eye contact. Without another word I climbed the stairs to the guest bedroom and quietly closed the door.

Twenty-four

It was Monday evening, the day after I had returned from Fitz's cabin: The day after Sophie had come home from the conference. The Sophie who had returned from Atlanta remained edgy and distant — sometimes bordering on openly hostile. Even Tobie was treated with half-hearted indifference, creating a confused, furry little bystander. The hurt she had taken with her seemed to have changed to a palpable, underlying fury.

I was hesitant to bring up the dancing exhibition but it was important. "We made a commitment, " I insisted. "This is Joe we're talking about. We told him we'd do this. I know it slipped our minds, but —"

Sophie shook her head. "Joe will be fine."

We had committed to this evening of dance demonstration two months ago. Sophie and I had done these demonstrations for Joe's beginner classes several times over the years. His goal was to showcase what two ordinary people with no previous dance experience were capable of doing. He'd talk about my struggles, as well as the development of Sophie's natural grace and ability. He'd mention the contests we'd entered and the awards we'd won.

Then, Joe would have us perform the waltz in full costume, while he gave a running commentary on things his students should notice. Demonstrations of the waltz were often followed by the foxtrot, samba or tango. Sometimes we would even make a costume change during the evening. Sophie and I enjoyed sharing our love of ballroom dance, but for Joe, this evening was important to him and his growing clientele.

"You're right. Joe will be fine." I held out stubbornly. "But this is also about who we are. We honor our commitments. We follow through." As soon as I said the words "honor our commitments" I wanted to reach out and pull them back. I certainly hadn't honored my greatest commitment, my commitment to Sophie. Telling her how we should act triggered my guilt and shame.

But Sophie appeared not to notice. After a long silence, she took a deep breath and nodded. "Okay."

"If you get home in time, we can ride —"

Sophie cut me off. "I'll meet you there."

The exchange of words — I couldn't even call it a conversation — was over. Sophie walked down the hallway to the stairs, with Tobie trundling after her. Sometime later she appeared carrying a garment bag containing her dance dress; letting me see that she was, indeed, going to honor our commitment.

I arrived alone at Joe's dance studio Tuesday night.

"Where's your lovely better half?" He questioned me.

"Working late," I mumbled, "She'll be here."

Something in my tone caused Joe to look at me again. "You okay, girlfriend?"

"Sure," I nodded and attempted to add a lightness to my voice. I entered the small studio, stretched out and changed into my tuxedo and dance shoes. The waltz would be first, and we always dressed formally for it. I looked at my watch — Sophie would be cutting it close.

Then, there she was. Already dressed, she had changed her clothes elsewhere. Her midi-length gown was white silk with white lace. The skirt slits, the sleeves and the deep V bodice were all made of lace. The back was bare to just below the shoulder blades. My heart rate accelerated. Sophie was lovely, and I stared.

"Don't look at me like that," she told me quietly.

"Like what?"

"Like you want me." She turned away and left the room.

Sophie was right; I did want her. But I wanted her in more ways than the one she was referring to. I wanted everything — all of Sophie. The closeness, the companionship, the laughter, the communication — all those things I had lost. I sank down onto one of the folding chairs.

Fifteen minutes later Joe re-entered the room with Sophie. Realization seemed to be dawning as he looked back and forth between us. He chose not to say anything and led us onto the dance floor.

Joe waited until we were in place, then began his short description. He talked about the original waltz, ending with, "It is the most romantic of all the waltzes, and during the dance the couples may even seem to establish an emotional connection." His definition made me nervous as I glanced at an impassive Sophie.

Sophie placed one hand on my bicep, and my hand rested on her shoulder blade. The palms of our free hands touched, and we lightly held each other's fingers. Our bodies pressed together as we moved across the floor. I hoped our tension wasn't as visible as it felt.

Next, Joe had us demonstrate the foxtrot. The foxtrot was a more complex dance, but still required that Sophie and I have close physical contact. When the dance was over, Sophie, almost imperceptibly, pushed me away. It wouldn't have been noticeable to anyone else but me.

I thought our part of the evening was over, but Joe threw in a surprise. "Wait a minute, you two." He caught us by the arms and turned to the prospective dancers still seated in their chairs. "How about an encore?" The class applauded. "Over the past several months Jensy, Sophie and I have been choreographing a new routine. I think they should share it with you."

God no, I thought. Sophie stiffened. The routine was a combination of all the dances we had worked on. It had a variety of steps, twirls, lifts, and dips. Joe had choreographed it to be sexy and sensual. There were times when Sophie's hands ran up my arms, across my shoulders, and rested on my neck, and my hands ran down her sides and rested on her hips. I cradled her head in my hand when we dipped; my lips inches from hers.

We had chosen Michael Franks' "Every Time She Whispers" for the Latin beat as well as its lyrics. We had often talked about how the song seemed to have been written for us; "us" set to music.

"We haven't finished it yet," I protested.

"Close enough," Joe contradicted. "We'll do as much as we have."

I was sure I saw Sophie open her mouth to object. Then she closed it, sighed, and gave a slight shrug of her shoulders.

The dance began with us in an embrace: Sophie's forehead rested on my shoulder, one hand behind my neck. Michael Franks' lyrics about passion, sighs and whispers filled the studio. I looked at her, and she looked away; but not before I saw the tears in her eyes. Our dance finished in our initial pose. The music ended and Sophie quickly let go of my hand, removed her fingers from the back of my neck, and was gone.

I had changed my clothes and was tying my shoelaces when Joe appeared in the doorway.

"What's going on?" he questioned.

I turned away and began to put my tux in the garment bag, my eyes stinging from holding back unshed tears.

"Something's wrong with you and Sophie, isn't it?" Joe was suddenly behind me, his hand consolingly on my shoulder.

I nodded.

He turned me around. "Ah, shit, Jensy." We sat down on the folding chairs.

"We almost didn't make it here tonight, but I insisted. I hoped it would go well … But really, I knew it wouldn't." I was working hard to keep my emotions under control. "It just keeps getting worse and worse. Sophie was at a law conference over the weekend and when she got back things were terrible. I guess she had too much time to concentrate on everything that's wrong. There doesn't seem to be anything I can do to make it better. My world is falling apart …" My voice trailed off.

"What happened?" I could hear the surprise in Joe's voice.

I wasn't exactly sure what Joe would think when I told him, but I knew his appraisal would be honest. I needed to tell someone. So, I forged ahead. I told him about seeing Fitz at the regional game. Told him how she had called me and wanted to see me.

Joe's eyes narrowed. He had never liked the situation with Fitz and had repeatedly told me that nothing good would come from my feelings for her. He had been concerned that I was the one who would be hurt. He had been right all those years ago, and he was right now.

I looked at him and owned up. "I went to see her at the hotel."

Joe's eyes widened as disbelief spread across his face. "Jesus H. Christ, Jensy … you slept with her." Joe had told me once that he could read me like a cheap paperback novel: easily, and without too much thought.

I nodded my head miserably.

"What on God's earth were you thinking?"

"It just happened."

"Nothing *just happens*, Jensy." Joe shook his head. "Do you really believe it *just happened?*"

"Yes … no … I don't know …"

He rolled his eyes, exasperated and upset. "I can't believe it. I simply can't." At first, he seemed at a loss for words, then found them again. "You cheated on Sophie? On *Sophie?*"

"I'd change it if —"

"You can't." He exhaled a long stream of air. "You and Sophie were the most perfect couple I had ever seen. I was always so envious. You were so solid. You were a given. Anything else in the world might happen, but you two were a constant."

He stood up and looked down at me. "You know I love you, Jensy. You've always been like a sister to me." Joe shook his head again. "But I told you years ago that your infatuation with Fitz would lead to nothing but trouble. That there would be nothing but hurt." Joe turned and walked tiredly to the door. "I am so disappointed." Before he left, he shook his head and issued one exasperated final thought. "I wouldn't be surprised if Sophie leaves you."

I was totally alone. I picked up my garment bag and made my lonely journey home. The house was dark except for the light above the kitchen sink. I sat on the floor and took Tobie in my arms. I cried, gut wrenching, heartbreaking sobs that I tried to stifle — but couldn't. Tobie frantically tried to comfort me by licking the tears from my cheeks.

Twenty-five

T he Thursday night after Sophie's return from Atlanta — after the fiasco at the dance studio and the next two nights of unendurable silence — I drove to her office to pick her up. I was on a mission to begin the process to make amends. Whatever it would take, I would do. I would fight to save our relationship.

I entered the building and breathed a sigh of relief when Howard, the night watchman, was nowhere in sight. I wasn't in the mood to exchange pleasantries. When the elevator doors opened onto the lobby of Baxter, Cragen, and Reed, I took a deep, shuddering breath and marshalled my courage.

I walked slowly down the darkened hallway toward the pool of light that I knew was coming from Sophie's office. Cubicles lined the interior, with conference rooms and individual offices on the outside. Halfway to Sophie's office I saw an office door with Carol Novak's name plate. The thought of Carol Novak inhabiting the same floor space with Sophie made my blood boil. I didn't know what Carol had said to Sophie to make her turn completely away from me — but I hated her for that.

My tennis shoes made no sound on the carpet as I moved down the hall. I could make out Sophie and Carol's voices coming from Sophie's office. I slowed my pace, coming to a halt a few feet from her door. Carol's raised voice sounded frustrated and harsh.

I sensed that this conversation had been in progress for some time.

"*She* cheated on *you*, Sophie. Is that what you're worth?"

Sophie's voice was tired, and I could hear her sigh. "That seems like an unfair statement after what I did in Atlanta last weekend."

"That was different." Carol's voice was dismissive of Sophie's comment.

"Was it? Really?" A pause … then … "How?"

I couldn't get my breath and leaned weakly against the wall. Sophie and Carol. I felt sick to my stomach as I tried to push the mental picture out of my mind. The reality of knowing was worse than anything I had imagined. I never thought that Sophie … I was hurt and angry, furious and shocked. My head pounded and I felt like my legs might give way. It briefly crossed my mind that his was how Sophie must have felt when she learned about Fitz and me.

Carol never attempted to answer Sophie's question. I knew the answer wasn't important to Carol. What she had "accomplished" in Atlanta was what mattered to her. The silence was finally broken by Carol telling Sophie, "It's time for you to get out and trade up, Sophie. Way past time."

My hands closed into fists.

"We've already discussed this, Carol. I won't discuss it again." Sophie's voice was low and pinched; always a giveaway that she was becoming angry. I debated leaving, but I couldn't. I was paralyzed by hurt, regret and anger.

"I think we should discuss this as often as it takes," Carol responded. She laughed without humor. "Jensy certainly seems to cast a spell on you, doesn't she?"

"That's enough." Sophie's voice had gained volume and strength. "Browbeating me isn't going to force a decision. I can't have these discussions with you, Carol."

"That certainly wasn't your 'position' in Atlanta." Carol emphasized the word "position."

"That was a mistake."

"A mistake? Really? You didn't act like it was a mistake. Not at all."

I heard fabric rustling, and a briefcase snapping shut. Then Carol was out the door almost running into me as she turned the corner. Her eyes widened in surprise, before they gave way to open dislike. She circled around me, and I turned with her: face to face.

"Well, well, well," she whispered contemptuously. "Just look what the cat dragged in. Eavesdropping. You probably heard it all." The whisper was harsh. "Well, let me tell you something, sweetheart. Your Sophie was quite the gal in Atlanta. Yes, she's a great time with a couple drinks in her … if you know what I mean." Her voice dripped with sarcasm, and she sneered at me triumphantly.

Before I could stop, my hand shot out and slapped Carol hard across the face. She didn't flinch, didn't even raise her hand to her cheek, though red marks instantly appeared.

"If you ever touch me again, I will have your ass for assault," she hissed, and her black eyes flashed. "Sophie!" Carol called out. "Guess who's been skulking outside your office? Listening to our private conversation! She didn't even have the decency to leave." All the while, Carol looked into my eyes, taunting me. "Add that to Jensy's list of *talents*."

My arm started its arc to strike her again. But just as it did, it was forcefully pushed back down against my side.

"Jensy." Sophie's voice was stern, and her grip was like a vice. She continued to hold my arm and didn't let go while Carol and I stared at each other.

I felt fleeting pleasure when Carol was the first to break the stare. She looked both of us up and down, finally letting her gaze rest on Sophie's hand gripping my arm. "On second thought, maybe you two deserve each other." She winked at Sophie, spun around, and strode down the long hallway. The last we heard was the door to the office lobby slamming shut.

Without another word, Sophie started down the hall. I raced after her, caught up and then matched her stride for stride, into the elevator and out into the night. Once on the sidewalk Sophie turned and started to walk toward the bus stop.

"Sophie, I came to take you home."

"I'll take the bus." The words were coolly tossed over her shoulder as she continued to walk.

"Sophie —" I watched her stride away.

I got in the car and drove to within half a block of the bus stop. I parked and gripped the steering wheel as hard as I could to keep my hands from shaking. Occasionally, I would loosen my grip and work back some feeling, but my hold tightened again as soon my hands returned to the wheel. My sight blurred through my tears. I was angry and frustrated with Carol and Sophie, but mostly with myself. I had caused this: I had driven Sophie to Carol.

I couldn't stop picturing Sophie with Carol. My stomach lurched, and I quickly got out of the car. I made it to the grass by the curb and vomited until there was nothing left. Then I heaved some more. A light rain was falling as I knelt in the grass, shaking and wretched. When I finally was able, I unsteadily climbed back into the car. I peered through the rain on the windshield and saw Sophie still standing in a patch of light half a block away.

Fifteen minutes later, Sophie got on the bus. I followed behind until she exited about four blocks from our house. As I pulled alongside her, the rain began to fall harder. I noticed that she had forgotten to change out of her dress shoes. I lowered the window.

"Please, Sophie. It's raining and you're still in heels."

She slowed her pace.

"Get in. I promise I won't talk. I won't say anything."

Sophie stopped, squared her shoulders, and before she changed her mind got into the car. We rode in silence. When I pulled into the garage neither one of us made a move to get out. Two minutes later the light timed-out and we were left in total darkness.

Sophie's tired voice cut through the darkness. "It was sex. I didn't make love."

"Oh, and that makes everything fine?" Parroting her words back to her. "And what happened to the Sophie who didn't believe in sex without love?" My anger rose to the surface, my tone greased with scorn. This wasn't the Sophie I knew.

Neither of us moved. I looked forward into the darkness, afraid to turn my head. Inside the house, Tobie barked, wondering where we were and what we were doing. Finally, Sophie opened her door and went in to Tobie.

I continued to sit until the light timed out for the second time. I thought about what Sophie had said. She had always been so definite about the difference between love and sex, and she had just told me that what happened in Atlanta wasn't about love. *Then what happened to me with Fitz?* I asked myself. *What had I been feeling?*

What happened to me didn't seem as simple as Sophie's definition. With Fitz, it had been sex tangled with complex pieces of my past. There were feelings for Fitz, but after all this time I would no longer call those feelings "love." Fitz was a monochrome of my past, shades of grey against the stark background of my youth. Sophie was my life's source of color. *Then why did I let it happen?* I asked myself for the umpteenth time.

I let myself into the house to the sound of Tobie's welcoming bark. A light was on over the kitchen sink; everything else was dark. I let Tobie into the backyard, gave him fresh water, and did something I rarely did — poured two fingers of bourbon and downed it while waiting for Tobie to finish his business. I poured another and sat in my study, slowly nursing the drink. I was in no hurry to pass by our closed bedroom door.

Tobie raced ahead when I ascended the stairs. He paused at the master bedroom door, cocked his head and listened intently. Whining softly, he pawed insistently at the wood. Again, he listened, pawed, and whined.

"Sophie?"

No response.

"Sophe? Are you all right?"

I heard it for the second time that night. The sound of vomiting. I tried the doorknob and found it unlocked. Sophie was sitting in her bra and slip, propped up against the bathroom door. Her knees were drawn up to her chest, her arms holding them tight.

I crossed the room and knelt beside her, but she paid no attention to me. Even Tobie hung back.

"What can I do to help?" I asked.

"That's rich ... asking me if you can help." Her voice cracked, and she silently began to cry. She turned her head to look at me ... tired ... sad ...

I stood up and offered my hand to help her up, but Sophie ignored it, "Please, close the door on your way out."

I nodded, walked to the door, and began to close it behind me.

"I'm sorry, Jensy." It was so soft I wasn't sure I had even heard her say it.

I stopped ... not knowing what to do. After several seconds, I turned and went back to her. "I'm sorry, too." Again, I knelt. "We need to talk, Sophie."

She shrugged, not yet willing or ready to concede anything to me.

But when I offered my hand again, she took it. I turned back the covers while she got undressed. Setting Tobie on the bed, I waited at the door until I heard Sophie slide between the sheets. Then, I turned out the overhead light and began to close the door.

"You can leave it open."

For the first time in what seemed like forever, the bedroom door stood open. I headed to the guest bedroom, where I let that door stand open as well.

Twenty-six

There were a few days I took Tobie to the Heights with me. With the stress at home, as well as the lack of walks and attention, I thought it might be a good change of scenery for the little guy. He would stand by my office door, cock his head, listen intently to the voices that drifted in from the outer office, and wait for students to enter. He offered his own brand of canine therapy, giving unconditional acceptance to all who entered. It amazed me how open and relaxed students were when their hands were busy petting Tobie.

In fact, Tobie seemed to provide more counseling than I did. The continuing tension at home made it difficult for me to focus. It was a constant struggle to compartmentalize work and home. I felt like a fraud, pretending an interest in the problems of others when all I could think of were my own.

I restlessly paced my office, stopping only after repeated reminders to myself. I was tired to the core of my being, and when I thought about how long it had taken Sophie to talk to me when Henry died; I sighed in frustration. I sat at my desk and picked up the photo of us and ran my fingers over it. My old insecurities surfaced. *Maybe I should just give up,* I told myself more than once, *and chalk this up to another relationship I managed to destroy.* But this wasn't just another relationship, I scolded myself. This was Sophie.

One afternoon I took Tobie and stopped in the doorway to Dee Nelson's office. I knocked lightly on her door. Dee had always been there when I needed her. For years she had been the person I had turned to and now I needed to turn to her again.

"Hey." I said softly when Dee looked up from her computer. "May we come visit?" I indicated Tobie and myself.

"Sure." Dee shut down her computer and gave me her full attention. "I haven't seen much of you lately. To what do I owe the pleasure of this visit?"

I shut the door and sat heavily in the chair in front of her desk. Dee was right. I had been avoiding her because she had always managed to see right through me, and I'd been feeling too fragile to handle her scrutiny.

"Keeping Tobie in?" Dee motioned at the closed door.

"And everything else out," I muttered. I rested my elbow on the chair's arm and tiredly rubbed my eyes.

"What's up?" Dee's words were light, but her tone betrayed her concern.

"I need to talk. I need some advice." I took my hand from my face. "Do you have time?"

"All the time you need."

Now that I had asked for her time, I didn't know where to start — or if I wanted to start. I was desperate ... and desperately embarrassed. I wanted Dee to know everything without having to tell her. I felt panic and discomfort rise in me; my stomach started to roil, and heat rose to my face. I couldn't seem to put the words together. I felt paralyzed.

"The beginning is usually a good place to start." Dee prompted gently.

I took a deep breath. "When I was a junior in high school, I fell in love with my basketball coach." Unleashed, my words tumbled out and I told Dee about the startling intensity of my feelings when Fitz had touched my injured ankle, my growing romantic and sexual feelings, the evenings I spent parked down the street from her apartment waiting for something — *anything* — to happen. My mistakes and misguided attempts to win her over. My pleading, my declaration of love, her rejection. My taking matters into my own hands and kissing her. Her subsequent departure at the end of the school year. My devastation.

I plunged on to my two relationships that had failed because of the torch I had continued to carry for Fitz. Dee looked at me sympathetically. "Jensy, I'm sure there were other reasons those relationships didn't work out."

"Maybe. But Fitz came up so often they told me they felt like there were three of us in the relationship. It was their main complaint when they broke up with me."

"You weren't ready to leave Fitz behind."

I shrugged. "You're probably right. But I thought my relationships were cursed because of what I felt for Fitz. I vowed that I would never talk about her in any future relationship. No matter what."

Then I explained how Sophie entered my life. The immediate chemistry between us that was so much stronger than anything I had ever experienced before. The feeling of Kismet — that we were meant to be. For the most part, my relationship with Sophie had relegated Fitz to a back compartment in my memory.

"And then?" Dee pulled me out of my reverie, waiting for my backstory to lead into the present.

I took another deep breath. "And then, Fitz reappeared in my life." The basketball game. The phone call. The hotel room. The seduction.

"Why do you think it happened?" Dee's voice took on a clinical edge, but there was an underlying stunned bewilderment in her tone. It was as if I had hurt her — and then I realized I had; she was so invested in both Sophie and me.

"I don't know." I was miserable. I didn't know; at least, I didn't think I did. That afternoon was a blank. I remembered it, but I didn't want to remember it.

"I think you know." Her comment was gentle, yet firm. "I think you wanted what you could never have, all those years ago. Maybe it was all subconscious ... but somewhere, inside of you, you wanted it." Dee's statement was matter of fact and her expression guarded. "When Fitz seduced *you,* it was easier to rationalize what happened."

"I don't know, Dee. I'm not sure what the truth is." Her insight threw me off-balance. It also hurt that Dee would put the responsibility back on me. I didn't want to believe that I had been an equal part. It was easier not to know why I had let things happen. It was easier to play the part of the wronged, injured party.

"That's just my assessment, Jensy. And you know that I'll always give you my honest assessment."

I knew that, and I wanted that from Dee — yet I didn't. I wanted to feel like someone understood, like I had one small island of support. It was hard to have Dee dissect my behavior when all I really wanted was her support. Instead, my shortcomings became even more damning.

"I thought I owed it to Fitz to tell her in person that I couldn't —" I swiped my hand at the words I had just spoken.

"I don't think you owed her anything." Another statement stripping away my rationalizations.

I plunged on. "I was afraid to tell Sophie and afraid not to. But she knew something was off. Something was different ..." I related the phone call and Fitz's illness. I rose and leaned against Dee's bookshelf. Tobie looked back and forth between us, then put his head on his paws. I let out a deep, broken sigh. "Then she found out."

"I'm not surprised."

Then. Sophie's trip to Atlanta with Carol, and my helping Fitz move to the cabin that same weekend. I had been at loose ends, and Sophie seemed to be finished with me; my rationalizations continued. Finally, I shared the conversation I overhead between Carol and Sophie. Then I was finished ... out of words ... depleted of emotion. I felt like a shell; everything inside me leached out and gone.

Dee sadly shook her head. "Oh, Jensy, I'm afraid this is way beyond my level of expertise." She intently studied the pen she was turning over and over. "I think you need professional counseling ... maybe individual, certainly couples."

I returned to my chair.

"It's just been one bad decision after another." I confessed. "Error upon error upon error ..."

Dee nodded. "And the hardest part may be yet to come. Whether or not the two of you can save your relationship. Or if you even want to."

Dee sat down beside me and placed her hand on my arm. "One mistake compounded by other mistakes. As if neither of you could stop. Neither you nor Sophie could distance yourselves enough to begin to sort through and rationally figure things out. That's understandable in the immediacy of the moment, but now you need to figure things out before you reach the point of no return. That means you'll need to get to the point where you both can discuss things."

"How will this end?" I put my head in my hands. It was a rhetorical question, but I wished someone had an answer.

"I don't know, Jensy." Dee's voice sounded tired. "I love you both. To me, the greatest shame would be if you lost each other. There is so much to love and admire in you and Sophie as a couple. It's something rare. But how will everything work out? I don't pretend to know."

I sat back in the chair and took a breath to steady myself. "Thank you for listening, Dee. I appreciate you and your honesty. I just selfishly wish you had a crystal ball that could give me the answer I want to hear."

"Jensy, I do have one more thought. Whether it's helpful or not — I don't know —"

"Any thoughts —"

"Sophie may not be consciously aware of it," Dee shared hesitantly, thinking aloud, "but she may have leveled the playing field and given you both a place to start."

"What do you mean?"

"The physical act — the sex — you with Fitz and Sophie with Carol. No matter how you got there, it's sex. It might allow you to start back at zero. Maybe this is an equalizer, and perhaps that gives you a way to move forward. I don't know, it's just a thought."

Maybe ... perhaps ... I wasn't sure ... I didn't know anything anymore.

"Have you and Sophie discussed this? Used your discussion guidelines that you put together after Henry Baxter died?"

"No. We've barely managed to be civil. She knows we need to talk but doesn't seem willing."

"I can't give you a timeline on when Sophie will be ready. But I'm not sure it's as much *unwilling* as *unable*. I remember her emotional upheaval about Henry Baxter. Knowing Sophie, she is processing her own behavior and culpability, in addition to yours. It seems that she needs significant time to process big emotional upheavals. Withdrawal is her way of self-preservation." Dee came to me and put her arm around my shoulders. "You may need to be willing to bend and be patient if you want your relationship to survive.

"Remember, Jensy, you *both* have to want to talk. You can't force Sophie. She may not be ready. But hopefully, sooner rather than later, you both can sit down. Then you can discover if you can still find your home in each other."

✦

I sometimes saw glimpses of hope. The temperature between us had been downgraded from frigid to chilly. We could enter the same room without the other one immediately leaving. The tone of any short, daily conversation was civil. But there was still no meaningful discussion; just words tossed back and forth … empty and lonely.

Late one night, after falling asleep in my study, I headed up to the guest bedroom. The door to the master bedroom remained open; a small crack in the ice that had frozen our lives. When I glanced inside, Sophie was sitting against the headboard; eyes closed, glasses sliding down her nose, book open on her lap. In spite of myself, I smiled.

I tiptoed into the bedroom. Sophie was breathing deeply, head bobbing just perceptibly: asleep. I gently removed her glasses, folded them, and put them on the nightstand. I slipped the thick book from her hands and marked the page. Then, as I had so many times before, I placed my hands lightly on her hips and whispered, "Slide down, Sophe."

As had become our routine over the years, Sophie complied and slid down on her side, facing away from me. In her sleep her hand found mine and pulled it across her body, tucking it against her stomach.

I stood frozen — unsure what to do. Nothing had been resolved, and I didn't believe that getting in bed with Sophie would make things better. I feared what her reaction would be if she woke and found me there. Her heart might be ready, but I was certain her mind wasn't there yet. Sophie was still trying to exist in the kitchen with me … let alone the bedroom. I waited until Sophie had settled, then little by little I removed my hand from hers.

"Goin' somewhere?" she mumbled in her sleep, her voice

drowsy and her words slurred.

"Not far," I whispered.

"Good." She sighed and shifted her body.

My vision blurred as my eyes teared; I knew that in her heart, Sophie still loved me. I leaned over and softly kissed her forehead. I turned off the light and headed back to the guest bedroom. I wanted to be hopeful — but dared not.

Twenty-seven

After Sophie agreed that we needed to talk about our issues — I waited. After Dee told me that I needed to give Sophie time to process — I waited. After trying to gauge where Sophie was emotionally — I waited. Every day that I waited seemed like forever. I was frustrated, bordering on angry. I remembered years ago when Sophie told me to "move forward or she would move on." I had moved forward then, and I needed Sophie to move forward now. Our situation had reversed, and I didn't like the feeling.

We continued to circle warily around any meaningful discussion. Despair, longing, and sadness became the words that defined my life. I was starving for love, warmth, companionship, and Sophie's touch. I lost my appetite, and when I did eat, I couldn't keep anything down. I cinched my belt another notch tighter. Dee took over the bulk of the work to wind down our groups for the school year. I plodded along, registering students for next year and entering their data on my computer; projects that I usually completed quickly and efficiently. I was glad there were only a few school days left.

My thoughts were set on continuous replay. I pictured Fitz at the cabin, waiting to die. I worried about her pain and wondered if all her needs were being met. I wondered constantly how much time Sophie would need before we could discuss our future. I was cautious about Sophie's need for time to process and, per Dee's instructions, I did not push too hard. I obsessed on whether or not Sophie and I could survive this.

It was a Sunday afternoon, and we both happened to be in the kitchen. Tobie and I had just returned from a late morning walk. Sophie rubbed the top of Tobie's head while she listened to him squeak about all the smells and sights, then returned to making her lunch. She was barefoot, standing at the counter in shorts with a long-sleeved shirt rolled up to her elbows — so heartbreakingly beautiful she took my breath away. I ached to have an "us" again.

We didn't acknowledge each other; instead, I filled a fresh bowl of water for Tobie. The sandwich-in-making had Sophie's full attention. When I heard Sophie slap her hand on the counter, I turned around to see what was wrong. She was struggling to open a jar of pickles. Without thinking, I went to her, put my hand on her arm and said, "Let me try."

Sophie jerked her arm away as if she had been burned. "I'll manage," she said tightly.

I felt like the truce we had established had been undone. I stepped away. The tears that filled my eyes contained frustration and anger. It was just too hard. Waiting for Sophie to be ready to talk had depleted my limited reserve of patience. I was worn out with waiting. Worn out with frustration. Worn out with sadness. Worn out .... .

"I can't do this anymore," I addressed Sophie's back.

I grabbed my set of keys and left. Tobie whined as I closed the door. I got in the car started to drive, hoping to get my emotions under control. I needed to be out of the house and away from Sophie. I needed to think about what I was going to do. When I started the car, I wasn't sure where I was headed, but my subconscious seemed to have a plan.

I drove to Eduardo's Restaurant and pulled into the parking lot. I sat in the car with my eyes closed. I visualized the good times we had there. I lowered my head to the steering wheel and felt immense loneliness and sadness. Tears ran unchecked down my cheeks.

I moved on, tears blurring my vision as I passed Dee and Bob's house. A retrospective of our times with them and their boys played through my mind. I remembered Richie finding Sophie on the couch, climbing on her lap and nestling in. The weekends the boys — our godsons — had spent with us. I yearned for those times of laughter and family.

I swung the car in the direction of Washington Heights and, once there, parked in the teacher's parking lot. This time I turned off the engine, got out and made my way to the football bleachers. As near as I could remember, I found the same spot where Sophie and I sat thirteen years before. I remembered her certainty and confidence that the Washington Heights job was mine if I wanted it. Sophie had always been prophetic and supportive, with an unfailing belief in what I could accomplish. I missed her so much my heart was breaking in half. I cradled my head in my hands and rocked slowly back and forth.

I stopped at the Ground Up, but I was in no shape to go inside. I clearly remembered the first time we met. I remembered how everything in my world had gone to shades of grey — except for Sophie. The sound of her voice, the touch of her hand, the large blue-grey eyes, and dimpled smile. It had been love at first sight.

The dance studio, now owned by Joe and his partner, Sam, was closed when I drove by. Ballroom dance had been my idea, but it was Sophie who had given it life. It was such a satisfying departure from our everyday existence. Each time we danced we became one. It was thrilling and sensual — I could never get enough. A jagged sigh escaped my soul.

My final stop was the townhouse. We still owned it and rented it out as a furnished unit. At the moment we were between renters, ready to start interviewing for new tenants that summer.

I took my key and unlocked the front door, stepping into the empty hallway and then crossing into the kitchen. I wandered over to the sink and looked out the window at the small yard. I could almost hear the champagne cork popping, could almost feel the sticky wetness as the liquid cascaded over us, could almost taste the bubbles as we passed the warm bottle back and forth. Our celebration when Sophie passed the bar exam. There were so many good memories from our time at the townhouse.

I trudged slowly to the second floor. I stood in the bedroom doorway; my hands fisted into my pockets. I remembered our first night in that bed, an experience unlike any I had ever had. It was in the townhouse I came to recognize the signs of Sophie's desire. Her fingertips curled into my shoulders, her breathing deeper, her eyes bluer. Her kisses became longer, slower, and more seductive. There was a way Sophie's body pressed against mine; I shook my head to clear away the memories. Every part of my life held a piece of Sophie. It hurt my heart just to remember.

I went downstairs, closed the front door behind me, and headed across the street to the bench overlooking the river. I sat at the far end. Dad and I had more than one deep conversation while sitting on that bench; how I longed for his steady shoulder and sage advice. I believed he would tell me to clear my mind of the past and concentrate on my present and future — with or without Sophie. I needed to do that. I had hoped that together we would find a solution. But that wasn't happening. We were stalled — spinning in place, going nowhere. I turned my face up into the sun and closed my eyes.

Taking deep, slow breaths, I imagined myself on the basketball court shooting free throws. I became lost in the repetition: the bounces, the breathing, the feel of the basketball. My pulse rate dropped and my breathing deepened. Clothing rustled and I could feel a presence at the other end of the bench. The last thing I needed was to have someone watch as I wiped away any errant tears or to hear the random sob that escaped from my broken heart. I willed myself to ignore and hoped the person would just get up and leave.

Finally, exasperated by the intrusion, I squinted at the opposite end of the bench.

Sophie.

I blinked and refocused my eyes to make sure I wasn't imagining her. I was shocked that she had bothered to find me. She was sitting sideways on the bench, her knees drawn up to her chest and her arms wrapped around them. Her red-rimmed eyes regarded me sadly. I looked away, then looked back to make sure it was really her.

"Hey," she said softly.

At first, I couldn't respond around the huge lump in my throat; I merely nodded. The calm I had worked to build dissipated to a weary dread. Finally, I managed to reply in kind, "Hey."

Boats filled with passengers passed by, celebrating the warm afternoon and an early summer river ride. A young couple stopped just beyond us and shared a long, passionate kiss. I looked away. I couldn't watch someone else's happiness while we were encased in our own misery.

I hadn't planned to say anything, but when I cleared my throat, the words burst forth on their own. "I'll move into the townhouse — at least until we get new renters." I glanced at Sophie and saw her eyes widen in surprise. "Or I can make an offer to buy out your half."

Sophie rearranged her surprise into an expressionless mask. "If that's what you want." Her tone was unreadable.

"No. That's not what I want." My voice radiated all the frustrations and turbulent emotions that I had been bottling up inside. "I want to change everything that happened. I wish I could erase it. I want to change things back to the way they were. But as you've told me before — wishing won't make it so. Right now, I don't know what else to do." My voice rose a notch. "We *could* try counseling. We *could* just sit and talk. I love you more than anything, Sophe. But I need to move forward."

I finally turned to face her.

"Thirteen years. In all those years, I never so much as looked at anyone else. Never wondered what it might be like to touch someone else, kiss someone else, have someone else — I had *everything* I needed and wanted in you." My voice was raw. I shook my head and sighed. "Three hours out of those thirteen years. And I ruined it all. *Three hours.*"

My voice cracked. "I'm not trying to downplay or minimize what happened. What I did was wrong. I betrayed us. You were right about that. Did I want it to happen? God help me, I didn't.

"Did I stop it? No. For that and everything that followed, I take full responsibility. I have no excuse. There's nothing I can explain to you. Anything I say will sound like a meaningless rationalization. I can only own up to what I did."

I twisted my hands together so tightly my knuckles were white. "I don't know how many ways there are to say I'm sorry. If I could say it one hundred ways, each one would be heartfelt and true. But it only matters if you believe me."

I stood up and headed to the railing near the river. I hadn't expected Sophie to follow me, but she did. I looked out at the river and continued to talk. I wanted it all out. It no longer made any difference if Sophie wasn't ready to talk — I was.

"That afternoon, after it happened, I went to the Cobblestone Bridge and stood there. I thought of all the times we had gone there to watch the city's reflection on the water as it ran over the falls. But that afternoon, I leaned out as far as I could and looked straight down. It was such a long way down and the water was so black. I leaned out as far as I could and thought about how death would be better than the guilt I was feeling."

My voice was dispassionate. "I wondered what it would be like to just go over the side — to have the water close over me, so I wouldn't have to feel anymore. Then a man stopped and asked if I was okay. That stopped me. But that would have been so much easier than facing you. Easier than going through this." I whispered and gestured back and forth between us.

Sophie took a step closer. "Oh, Jensy, nothing is worth that."

"My heart said you were." It was a simple statement that came from the depths of my battered soul.

"But then I thought that wouldn't be fair to you. You would have gone to work in the morning thinking everything was fine. And when you found out you would have wondered what had happened. You might even have thought it was your fault. I didn't want that to happen." I shuddered.

"So, I went home. It wasn't until I got there that I realized nothing — not one thing about what happened would be fair to you. It wasn't fair that I had never said a word about Fitz. What I did that afternoon wasn't fair to you. It wouldn't be fair if you never found out the truth about what happened with Fitz. Just as it wouldn't be fair to you if you did. Nothing would be fair. Period. I destroyed everything that meant anything to me. I don't think I can ever forgive myself." My hands grasped the railing until my fingers ached. My body leaned forward, mimicking my posture at the Cobblestone Bridge.

My words rasped their way out of my throat. "As for your time with ..." I couldn't even bring myself to say Carol's name. "If I hadn't done what I did, nothing would have happened with her. So, part of that's on me. And I live with that every minute of every day."

I took a long look at Sophie's profile, then looked away. "But you know what happens when you have a couple drinks of hard liquor. *You* are well aware of the effect it has on you." My mouth was dry. "You knew she wanted you. You knew what would happen, and you let it happen anyway. *That* is on you."

When I glanced back at her, tears brimmed in Sophie's eyes. She was watching me, not looking away. "We've had to face a lot of truths. And sometimes the truth hurts ... doesn't it?" I asked, not unkindly.

Sophie bowed her head and nodded.

"For me, there are other truths." I sucked in another breath of air and turned directly to Sophie. "The truth is: I will never love anyone the way I love you; from the first time I saw you, to this moment and into forever. The truth is — you fill my heart. The truth is — nothing you have ever done could change my love for you. I would forgive you anything, Sophie. Anything."

I was done. There was nothing left for me to say. I walked wearily toward the townhouse, stopping just short of the bicycle path. I turned toward Sophie one last time. "The end of the school year is always hectic, but I'll try to have my things out of the house by the end of the week. As for Tobie — I'll take him. Or we can split time with him. You decide."

Inside, I sat on the stairs, exhausted. I wanted to cry, but I had no tears left. After what seemed like forever, I got up and looked out the window. Sophie still stood at the railing. While I watched her, neither of us moved. I wasn't even sure I was breathing. I finally went to get a drink of water and make a list of groceries I might need. When I returned to the window fifteen minutes later, Sophie was gone.

Twenty-eight

Thursday was an early release day at school, and I took the opportunity to "release" myself at noon. I needed to pack for my move to the townhouse, and I didn't want Sophie at home while that happened. It would be difficult enough without her being present.

When I opened the front door, I knew something was wrong. There was no Tobie racing excitedly to greet me. My heart thumped. I looked everywhere and called his name repeatedly. I checked inside the closets to make sure he hadn't been trapped inside. I went onto the deck and called him again.

I was about to call Sophie when I noticed the yellow note posted on the refrigerator. "Tobie's with me. Back by mid-afternoon." Cryptic — but at least there was a note. At least I knew Tobie was safe.

Within an hour all my camera equipment had been moved to a space by the front door. Eventually, two large duffle bags of clothes took their place next to the gear. My backpack, filled with laptop and writing supplies, was over my shoulder for my first trip to the car. My hand was on the front doorknob when I heard the back door open. Tobie raced down the hall to see me, squeaking his hello.

Our reunion was short-lived when he heard Sophie filling his food dish. When Sophie came down the hall, she didn't turn away from me to go upstairs. Instead, she stopped a couple yards from me and stared at the bags on the floor. Her hand went to her eyes, and she stood frozen for several moments. Her shoulders rose and fell as she tried to stifle a sob. When she took her hand away, her eye lashes were wet.

"Before you ..." Sophie cleared her throat and began again. "Before you go, could we talk?"

Sophie headed for the couch, our usual venue for serious discussions. My heart rate accelerated, and my hopes started to rise; maybe this was the start of our new beginning. My mouth was dry, and my hands tingled. I had prayed for this moment and didn't want the opportunity to slip away.

Sophie closed her eyes, and I knew she was deciding how best to approach whatever she wanted to say. As the silence lengthened, I began to get restless. My stomach was queasy, and a tension headache began to form behind my eyes. Maybe I had been wrong, and this was the end of us: Sophie was deciding how to tell me. If that was the case, I needed to leave before I lost my nerve. I put both feet on the floor and started to push myself up. I had gone from hopeful to devastated in a matter of seconds.

"I'm sorry. I'm just trying to get things straight in my mind." Sophie opened her eyes and stared into mine. "I went to the cabin."

Initially, her statement didn't register. "Cabin?" I asked. "What cabin?"

"To see Lisa Fitzhugh." Sophie's voice was low and intense.

Emotions rolled over me: confusion, surprise, bewilderment and even a fleeting sense of admiration. "Why?" The first and only word out of my mouth.

Sophie shook her head and bit her lip.

"I had to see her. I needed to find out why she was so important to you — this other woman you loved. I had to see ..." Her voice trailed off. Sophie shrugged and looked up at the ceiling. "I wanted to go there and hate her. I wanted to scream at her for ruining my perfect life. I was so angry and hurt and scared." She pulled a Kleenex out of her pocket and wiped her eyes.

"I thought it was odd," she continued. "Tobie seemed to know his way around. He headed to the back, up the deck stairs and pawed on the deck door — like he had been there before." Sophie stared at me. "A woman named Katherine let me in when I said that I was your friend. I didn't even have to mention Lisa." Sophie sighed sadly. "You helped her move."

I nodded. "I wanted to tell you when you got back from Atlanta, but it was clear to me that night that you weren't interested in anything I had to say." Any hope I had for our getting back together, died right there. I feared that Sophie would view it as just another lie; something I had purposefully hidden from her. I glanced at my belongings lined up by the front door and thought I should just get up and begin loading the car. "I'm so tired of lies and deception ... of suspecting everything and knowing nothing. Of being afraid to say or do anything."

Sophie reached out and put her hand, palm down, near the center of the couch. "No more lies," she whispered.

"No more lies." I repeated, and moved my hand just inches from hers.

Sophie slowly pulled back her hand and began the story of her visit to Fitz:

After Katherine let them in, Sophie heard a cry of surprise coming from another room. "Tobie!" Fitz had sounded delighted to see him. Then Fitz called louder, "Jensy?"

Without replying, Sophie made her way to the bedroom door. Fitz's initial smile, the expectation of seeing Jensy, was replaced by confusion and eventually, recognition. "Sophie," Fitz's voice was apprehensive and tentative. "I wondered if you'd come ... to tell me off or yell profanities or ..." Fitz loosely waved her hand. "I'm sure I deserve all that, and more."

The self-deprecating tone and the conciliatory words caught Sophie off guard. She wasn't sure how to respond. To buy time she picked up an insistent Tobie and placed him on the bed. It gave her a few moments to observe the skeletal woman with skin stretched tightly over her bones. But Sophie also noted her beautifully expressive brown eyes: eyes that were the only "alive" part of a woman who appeared to be shrinking in on herself.

Fitz delightedly petted Tobie as he squeaked and squirmed to get close to her. But Sophie could tell that even that effort tired her, and she returned Tobie to the floor. Seeing Fitz like that had stolen the venom from Sophie's heart. Confrontation and hatred seemed pointless. "Lisa …"

"Please, call me, Fitz. It's much more 'me' than Lisa." Fitz pointed at to chair across the room. "Move it over. It's easier for me to talk when I don't have to expend much energy." Sophie moved the chair and sat down. "It's okay if you don't know what to say. I'm not sure I do, either." Fitz's eyes closed, and Sophie wondered if she had fallen asleep.

When Fitz finally spoke again her voice was so small that Sophie had to lean forward to hear. "I told Jensy that life is messy … things aren't always right or fair … or turn out the way we expect."

"No, they don't," Sophie agreed as she looked at Fitz's diminished frame.

"I had such strong feelings for her," Fitz said simply. "All those years ago, I never told her. I had to let her go. I was her coach … it was wrong to have feelings for her. When I left it was the right thing to do." Fitz closed her eyes. "All those years ago, Jensy told me she loved me. She was seventeen years old and in love for the first time. It was a love I knew would probably flame and burn out." Fitz focused on Sophie.

When Fitz had seen Jensy at the basketball game, it had opened a floodgate of emotions that she had buried for years. She set up everything at the hotel. Fitz knew she was sick, was likely out of remission, and decided she was going to have what she had denied herself years ago. When Fitz met Jensy that afternoon she had deliberately guided the conversation away from any questions about Jensy's personal life — she didn't want to know. Fitz didn't know about Sophie until later.

Fitz's voice became weaker, and she drifted off to sleep. While Sophie waited for Fitz to wake, she and Tobie explored. She sat at the end of the dock and dipped her feet in the deep, blue water. The beauty of the setting helped calm her thoughts. She couldn't hate Lisa Fitzhugh, although she had wanted to. Sophie was too tired to be hateful or vengeful. She carried too much guilt about what she, herself, had done, to pass judgment on Lisa Fitzhugh. Her anger was replaced by sadness for all three of them, and for the next steps they each would have to face.

Sophie returned to the chair in the bedroom and she also began to doze. When she opened her eyes, she found Fitz watching her closely.

"There's something you need to know." Fitz sighed softly. "Jensy loves you, Sophie. She does. At one time she may have loved me ... but that time isn't now ... and her love for me was never as strong as it is for you. And for my feelings ... if the timing had been different ..." Fitz stopped speaking and effectively dismissed the rest of the unfinished sentence. "It may sound strange, given what has happened, but Jensy loves only you . Please, think about that."

Fitz hesitantly reached a hand toward Sophie, and without thinking, Sophie took it. "Would you do me a favor?"

"What can I do?"

"Tell me about you and Jensy."

And Sophie did.

The story, or at least as much as Sophie was willing to share, ended. Whatever else they had talked about would remain between Sophie and Fitz.

Sophie looked past me, into the distance. "I thought you and I were perfect — the gold standard. I believed in us — not just you — not just me — us." Her voice was barely above a whisper. She closed her eyes and let out a sigh. "I want to believe Fitz about the strength of your love. But I just don't know what to believe. I'm no longer sure how well I know you. I'm not even sure how well I know myself. And I really don't know who *we* are. Not anymore."

She got up and stood in front of me. I hesitantly raised my eyes to meet hers. "But I do know that Lisa Fitzhugh is very sick, and I don't think she has much time. She's without anyone she holds dear. I don't know what could be worse than that."

Sophie looked tense, scared, defiant and sad. I dreaded what might come next — whatever that pronouncement might be. But I wasn't prepared for her next words. "I think you need to go to her. For her *and* you. Go ... until it's over."

I stood up and took a step toward her, but Sophie held up her hand and stopped me. My stomach churned. What was happening? Was Sophie making a personal sacrifice by telling me to go? Or was she sacrificing us?

"Why are you telling me to go?" I was confused; I felt hollow inside.

"I'm encouraging you. I'm suggesting you go. I have no right to tell you what to do." Her eyes burned intently into mine. "But I think there are several reasons you should go. Regardless of what you want to believe, you're attached to her, and she's attached to you. It's the end of her life, and I think you'll feel guilty if you don't go." Sophie acknowledged, "And there's the guilt I'll feel if I keep you from going. I simply can't shoulder any more guilt than I have right now."

"What about the guilt I'll feel if I *do* go?"

"Life is messy. Isn't that what Fitz told both of us?"

I nodded. "What about us?" I asked hesitantly.

Sophie took time before she responded. "I don't know. I need time to decide what I'm going to do." She walked to the end table and looked down at a picture of the two of us. She reached toward it, then pulled her hand back. "For all these years I only thought of the two of us. I didn't need anyone else; I had you. It was always us: Jensy and Sophie. I never imagined anything different. I have no idea who I may be on my own. I need to figure out who I am without you."

Sophie kept her face devoid of emotion. "I need to think about our years together and come to terms with the fact that you deliberately chose not to tell me about Lisa Fitzhugh. You could have come to me, Jensy. You could have told me. I would have understood. You could have shared, and maybe all this," she waved her hand, "wouldn't have happened. You didn't trust me — us — enough to share that part of you."

I knew Sophie was right. "I wanted to tell you, but I couldn't," I tried to explain. "I promised myself I would never say a word to you about Fitz. I couldn't risk losing you. My feelings for Fitz had destroyed two other relationships." I said the things I should have said years ago. "But I've always loved you more than anyone else. Always." I was heartsick. "I know now that our love would have survived my telling you." My hands clenched so tight that my nails dug painfully into my palms. I knew my explanation was far too late.

Sophie shook her head and tears filled her eyes. "I still need to understand the infidelity, yours and mine. I need to decide how to live with that."

"I love you, Sophie." My heart was torn in two. I wanted to throw myself at her feet and beg her not to leave me. I wanted to grab onto to her hand and never let go.

"I know. And I'll always love you. I would never deny that."

My heart plummeted to my knees. Everything was over. "Sounds like a closing statement, Counselor." I was numb.

Wordlessly, I climbed the stairs carrying a small duffle. I sorted through what was left of my clothes. Jeans, shirts, and underwear were haphazardly tossed into the open bag. I was startled when I turned around and saw Sophie standing in the doorway.

"Why don't you take your old Tolliver sweatshirt? She might

like that." When I looked at her in surprise, she raised her shoulders slightly. "That sweatshirt is warm and soft."

I nodded, dug through my dresser drawer and put it in my bag.

"And a pair of your thick, wool socks."

"Sophie —" I wanted to tell her how grateful I was for her kindness and compassion, but she didn't give me the chance.

"She told me she's always cold."

I put my duffle and backpack by the front door, and quickly placed my other bags in the front closet. Sophie was not in the living room when I was ready to leave. I heard the back door bang shut and Tobie roared into the room where he suspiciously sniffed my duffle. I found Sophie in the kitchen, looking out the window, hands holding the edge of the counter on either side of the sink. She gave no indication she knew I was there, but she did know. Sophie always knew when I was watching her.

"I'm leaving."

"Call me when it's over." Her voice was sad, and she continued to look out the window. "Please."

It was Tobie who followed me to the front door. I knelt and scratched his ears. "Take care of your mom." I kissed his muzzle. "Love you, big guy."

I went to my car and put the duffle in the back and my backpack on the front passenger seat. Hands in pockets, I leaned against the car door and stared at our home. *Our home.* The big Craftsman we had so ecstatically purchased and lovingly restored. The huge front porch, the beautiful hardwood front door we had painstakingly found, the hanging swing where we had spent many summer evenings, and our large bedroom window that caught the morning sun.

Our home, into which we had poured so much of ourselves. Our home, where we had spent so many happy hours, days, months, and years. Our home, where we had planned to live forever. Together. I wondered what would happen to it … and us.

I thought I saw movement in the front window. I wanted it to be Sophie. But in the end, only Tobie stood in the window and watched me leave.

Twenty-nine

The journey to Fitz's cabin was long and lonely, with grief and dread my only companions. I was driving away from a woman who I was certain would leave me and driving to a woman who was going to die. The changing landscape was my only respite as I left the city and headed north. The rolling farmland that eventually gave way to forest and lakes was a visual comfort to me. After a while, I lowered my window and breathed in the fresh, clean scent of pine. My grip on the steering wheel loosened, my shoulders dropped, and my breathing became deeper.

I directed all my attention to driving, and the miles flew under the wheels. Gradually, the late afternoon changed to dusk and then to early evening. Darkness had nearly descended when I turned onto the gravel driveway.

I climbed the porch steps and rapped lightly on the front door. Inside the cabin I could see the glow of lights giving the interior a cozy, golden look. I knocked again, a bit harder. "Margaret, it's Jensy."

The porch light went on and the door opened slowly. I put my hand up to shield my eyes from the light's glare. Margaret peered out at me.

"Jensy?" The screen door was unlocked, and Margaret ushered me in. She held both my arms in a firm grip. "Jensy, I'm so glad you're here."

"Is she —"

"Sleeping. Right now, she's sleeping." Margaret's whispered. "Come in and sit down. Coffee?" She asked as she picked up her cup. When I shook my head, she sat down across from me in an armchair. "Things aren't good, Jensy. She's no longer mobile. Very little energy. She sleeps most of the time. We just got a hospital bed yesterday. Hospice has provided morphine, and I think we'll need that soon." Margaret struggled to be matter of fact.

I rubbed my palms back and forth on the arms of my chair. "How long?"

"The hospice nurse said maybe a week — probably less."

I got up and walked quietly to the bedroom door. The room was dimly lit by a table lamp, and I could just make out the slight rise and fall of Fitz's breathing beneath the blanket. She was a very small form, even in the twin-size hospital bed. I tiptoed back, sank into the chair, and closed my eyes.

"How long can you stay?" Margaret asked.

"To the end."

"And that's all right with Sophie?"

I looked at Margaret in surprise. "Sophie told me to come," I answered simply.

"I met Sophie." Margaret bobbed her head thoughtfully. "Earlier today. I didn't know that our other caretaker, Katherine, got a call and had to leave a few hours early. When I arrived, Sophie was in the bedroom with Lisa. She was sitting in the chair next to the bed, holding Lisa's hand. I couldn't hear what she was saying, but she seemed to be telling Lisa a story of some sort. I honestly thought Sophie was a substitute caregiver, she was so kind and gentle with Lisa. Then I saw Tobie and wondered about her connection to you."

Margaret continued. "She introduced herself as Sophie and told me that she knew you. She asked me to tell Lisa that she would think about everything Lisa had said. I promised I would, and she left.

"When Lisa woke, I shared Sophie's message and Lisa told me the story. I hope you aren't upset. I think she needed to unburden herself to someone. She feels responsible for what is happening to you and Sophie."

"Fitz told you everything?"

"I think I know the basics. I know about you and Lisa — all those years ago." Margaret thought for a moment. "I know Sophie's your partner, and I know why she was here."

I should have been embarrassed or angry that Margaret had been made privy to my private life, but it really didn't matter anymore. I was too tired and weary to know how to feel about anything, much less what Margaret did or didn't know. It was just another thing to process in a world full of things to process. "I don't think Sophie's going to be my partner much longer," I said ruefully.

"Lisa seems to believe that she will." Margaret contradicted.

I took a jagged breath and stood up. "I'd like to be with Fitz when she wakes up," I told Margaret as I headed for the bedroom. I moved the large chair into position as close to her bed as I could. I held onto the rail of the hospital bed and looked at Fitz. Her skin was stretched tight over her face — all sharp lines, and angles. Her rapid decline in less than a month was startling. I had to watch her chest to make sure she was still breathing. She was so thin that looking at her me feel ill. I physically hurt for her. She was a shadow of the Fitz I had known.

"Oh, Fitz," I whispered. No matter what had happened, no matter all the negative thoughts had I harbored — this was unimaginable. I rested my forehead on the bed railing.

"Jensy?"

I raised my head when I heard the soft voice. Fitz's brown eyes were open wide. She stared at me and blinked once — twice —

"Hey, there."

"Jensy?"

I stood up and leaned over the railing so she could see me better. "In the flesh."

"I thought I was dreaming."

"No such luck. You can even ask Margaret; I'm really here." I took the rail down, reached over and held one of her hands in both of mine. Cold and limp, her hand was light as a feather and papery soft. *This was the hand that shot basketballs with ease*, I thought and bit back a bitter laugh at the incongruity of the two.

Fitz sighed. "I didn't think I would have the chance to see you." She refocused. "How long can you stay?"

"For as long as you need me."

"To the end?"

"To the end. If that's what you want."

Fitz's eyes searched my face as if to verify what I said. Finally, she nodded and closed her eyes. "On loan from Sophie," she said.

"More like given to you, I think."

Her eyes opened and she studied me again. There was a slight shake of her head. "No. On loan. I feel certain of that."

I hoped with everything in me that Fitz was right. I wondered what Sophie hadn't told me about her conversation with Fitz. Was there something that would give me a new sense of hope? There had been small, occasional glimpses of hope; but they had been so brief I didn't know how much they meant or if I could believe them. Margaret said Sophie was thinking about things Fitz had said. I wondered if I could allow myself to believe things might work out.

Think about that later, I instructed myself. *You have other things to think about right now.* "I'll be right back," I told Fitz. "I brought you something."

I raced to my car and brought my belongings into the cabin. I put the duffle on the sofa and rummaged through the loose clothing until I found the items I was looking for. "For you," I said when I re-entered in her room. I held up the thick, wool socks and the old Tolliver sweatshirt.

Fitz's smile went from her eyes to her lips. "My God, how wonderful."

I pulled up the covers from the foot of the bed, blew into my hands to warm them, then rubbed each cold foot. I put on the socks and tucked the covers back into the foot of the bed. Then I helped her into the old, worn, soft sweatshirt.

"It feels like heaven." Fitz smiled. "That was so thoughtful."

"Sophie's idea. She thought you might like it."

"She was right." Fitz nodded and immediately slept.

Night had closed in, and I sank down on the sofa to attempt to get some sleep. However, my good intention didn't translate into a good result. My exhausted mind was still spinning in overdrive. Seeing Fitz like this was one of the most difficult things I had ever witnessed. It was heartbreaking. I wanted to do my best for her, to take good care of her for whatever time she had left. But, the fear of doing the wrong thing played on my already frayed nerves. I had never done anything like this — didn't know if I could.

I needed to talk to Sophie. I sat up, turned on the light and took a picture of Sophie out of my wallet. She was my rock and my strength: the glue that held my life together. She had always helped me through difficult times, and I needed her to help me get through this. I dialed the first three numbers of Sophie's cell phone, hesitated, and then disconnected the call. In the back of my mind, I heard Sophie instructing me to "call when it's over."

After a couple restless, sleepless hours, I went back into Fitz's room, sat down and placed my hand on top of hers.

Fitz stirred. "Jensy?"

"I'm here." My presence seemed to comfort her, and she fell back to sleep.

The next day, the hospice nurse pulled me aside and told me she thought we should begin to give Fitz the morphine because she was becoming more agitated and uncomfortable. I watched as the nurse demonstrated how to fill the syringe and how I should administer the dose. It was an enormous, frightening responsibility. I was overwhelmed.

The nurse read my panic and spoke kindly, "This is end of life. You won't make a mistake. Margaret has been through this before; she'll help you." Margaret rubbed my arm in a comforting gesture. "You need to remember that our goal is to keep Lisa pain free and comfortable." That eased my mind, at least a little.

When the nurse mentioned the morphine to Fitz, I thought I detected a flicker of alarm in Fitz's eyes. I was sure she saw it as another indication of her mortality. Slowly, Fitz nodded. "Okay." She looked directly into my eyes. "There are things I need to say to you before the drug takes that away from me. After I'm done, I'll start the morphine."

Over the course of the late morning and early afternoon Fitz said what she needed to say. She tired so quickly that our conversation had to be divided into short increments. At times she fidgeted, her discomfort visible. At times she seemed to struggle for words or to remember what she wanted to say. Yet she persevered because it was so important to her.

"I'm sorry about what's happening between you and Sophie. But I'm not sorry about what happened that afternoon." Fitz closed her eyes, as if picturing that day in April.

I swallowed hard. I couldn't grasp how Fitz could be sorry about what was happening to my relationship, but not sorry about what had happened that afternoon in her hotel room. I didn't understand.

As if she had read my thoughts, she whispered to me, "I don't expect you to understand." Fitz closed her eyes, as if gathering her words. "Years ago, you shared your feelings with me. Now, I need to share mine with you."

"You were right about that day at practice when I touched your ankle. There was something that happened between us. I felt it, too." Fitz sighed, then continued. "I was attracted to you."

I nodded. I had always believed that was true.

"I thought about you so often, and I didn't know what to do about it. I couldn't admit what I felt, that would have been too dangerous for both of us. There were so many times I wanted to tell you. I knew you were suffering and confused. I wanted to tell you that I was suffering and confused, too. I wanted to tell you that I was afraid of how strong my feelings were for you." Her words were rushed, and when she was done, she sagged further into the pillows.

I felt the tears roll down my cheeks. For years, all I had ever wanted was confirmation I hadn't been wrong.

"I couldn't tell you, Jensy. When you kissed me and I responded, it tore me apart. I didn't know if I could remain in Tolliver without something more happening between us. I *knew* I would cross the line if I stayed. I had to leave … I left *because* of my feelings for you. I hope you can understand." Her breathing had become more labored as her emotions took a toll.

I wiped the tears away and answered shakily, "I do understand." After all these years, from my adult perspective, I understood. As a seventeen-year-old, I had been devastated.

"Some feelings never completely go away." Her gaze held mine, until her eyes began to slowly close. Her breathing evened out and became shallow. Fitz slept.

I wandered out onto the deck and stood looking at the lake. I understood why Fitz had done what she had done all those years ago. And I understood the ramifications there would have been if Fitz had allowed our feelings to be realized. I understood that now. For so long, I had wondered about Fitz's feelings. Now that I knew, I wasn't sure I needed to know as much as she had needed to tell me.

What I did know was that Fitz had been a part of every relationship struggle I had ever been through. Not because of what she'd done or hadn't done; but because of me — because of how I acted and reacted and hadn't been able to let go. I now understood that there would always be a part of my heart that belonged to Fitz. Regardless of anything that had happened, Fitz would always be my wonderful, terrible first love. Maybe now I would find closure to that long chapter of my life. I just hoped and prayed that the closure wouldn't come at the cost of losing Sophie.

"I would like you to be the executor of my will," Fitz told me when she next awakened. "There's an envelope for you on the desk in the study. It has a copy of my will, my attorney's name, all the information about the cabin. Everything."

"I'll make sure it's taken care of."

Fitz seemed to hesitate for a moment, took a breath and went on, "I need you to accept what I am going to tell you, Jensy. No argument ... please." Her eyes implored me.

"Okay."

"I'm leaving everything to you."

I remembered what she had told me at the hotel, about losing her family ... the money from the settlement and sale of property that had left her able to do anything. "You can't. There must be someone —" I was overwhelmed at the thought: It was simply too much.

She waved her fingers to silence me. "I've thought and rethought. There are charities I would like you to donate to. Scholarship funds that can be started. But the rest is yours. When I saw you at the basketball game, I knew what I wanted to do." She paused and I helped her take a sip of water.

"I want to do this, Jensy. I know you'll be a good steward. I have no partner, no family, no one. I have my memories of you. THey mean everything to me. Tell me you accept." Her eyes held mine.

I wasn't sure what to say. It was unexpected, overwhelming, and heartbreakingly sad. Finally, I touched her cheek and nodded, "I accept."

Fitz slept again. Half an hour later, she woke and told me, "Morphine ... after this." Her hands moved restlessly, picking at the sheet that covered her. In just a few hours, her eyes had become almost glassy and seemed to have sunk deeper into her head. Her skin was stretched to translucent. It had become increasingly difficult for her to focus. The spaces between her words lengthened.

"When Sophie came here ... I thought ... she wanted to tell me ... she hated me. She never did ..." Fitz closed her eyes. "She's hurt ... defensive ... sad ..." I could see her eyes moving under her closed lids, searching for the right word. "Fragile."

"She told me you're ... smart ... tender ... funny. Told me stories about your lives." Fitz was silent and I thought she was asleep. I started to get up, but she spoke again. "Sophie ... loves ... you."

She lapsed into silence, but when she spoke again, her words were stronger; more like the Fitz I remembered. "I wish I ... had someone who loves me ... as much ... as Sophie loves you. Someone ... who loves me ... as much as you love her."

The effort to talk had drained her, and Fitz sank back against the pillow. Her eyes were hollow and pain-filled, and her hands clutched at sheets.

"Jensy — "

"Do you want the morphine now?" I already knew the answer by looking at her. Fitz had spent every ounce she had to tell me her story.

"Yes," she whispered.

"I heard what Lisa said to you," Margaret said as we sat side by side after administering the morphine. We watched as the morphine overtook Fitz and sent her into a deep sleep. "I know it's none of my business, but have you and Sophie had a chance to talk about all of this? About your future?"

"No." I shook my head, bit my lip, and sucked in a lungful of air. "We've each said things. We've talked around things. But we haven't really discussed. I don't know. I'm not sure I know what a discussion feels like anymore." My sigh was ladened with regret. "But my actions spoke loudly and led to terrible things. Maybe there are no words to make things right."

"Don't underestimate the power of words, Jensy. You, in your profession, should know that. Sophie should know it as well. She's a lawyer — words are her currency. Words are important." Margaret continued, "You've both been hurt by actions. Maybe it's time to see what a meaningful discussion can do. You both need to take that step, no matter how difficult. No matter the outcome."

Margaret and I continued to sit side by side, lost in our own thoughts. Time passed and I dozed while sitting on the sofa. Suddenly I was roused by a noise coming from the bedroom; Fitz was awake and agitated. When I got to the room, she was trying to push herself up and out of bed.

"What do you want, honey?" Margaret asked.

"Need — need — to get — UP. HELP ME." Fitz's voice was frantic.

"You can't get up, sweetie. You're too weak," Margaret patiently explained.

"Then I'll do it myself." Clear, succinct, unreasonable. At that moment, Fitz was determined to get her way.

"Fitz?" I touched her arm. "Why do you want to get up?"

"To see ... the lake ... have to ..." Fitz's eyes wildly roamed everywhere.

"Let's just turn your head," Margaret suggested.

"Straight on ... *straight on* ..." Fitz insisted; she would not be denied.

I looked at Margaret and our eyes locked. "I think we can make this happen," I told Fitz.

I told Margaret what I had in mind. Through our efforts to maneuver her, we finally managed to get Fitz where she wanted to be. Fitz and I were on the side of the bed with my legs on either side of her. My arms held her securely around the waist. I pulled her frail body against me: her back rested against my chest and her head against my shoulder.

"There you go. Your lake."

The shimmering sun that dappled the leaves on the trees and the deep blue water created a picture just for Fitz. A hummingbird sat on a branch just outside Fitz's window, looking in at us, his bib an iridescent glow. I had noticed him several times, perching for upwards of fifteen minutes, looking in the bedroom window.

"The hummer," Fitz stated.

"He's there a lot. Looking in."

I felt Fitz nod against me. Her whisper was barely discernible. "My guide ... waiting ..."

A chill went through me. I knew the end was very near and so did Fitz.

"So beautiful," Fitz whispered.

"Yes," I whispered, my lips against her ear.

"You ... you are beautiful." Her breathless whisper. "You loved me?"

"Yes."

"Still?"

"Always." I kissed the hair at her temple, and she leaned heavily against me.

✦

Fitz never woke after that. I remained on the bed next to her after Margaret and I laid her back down. I stretched out on my side, my head next to hers, and spoke about the things I remembered: English class, her belief in my writing ability, the kiss I had initiated in the parking lot. I told her how important she had been to my career. I thanked her for all she had taught me about teamwork, commitment, and leadership. And I told her I loved her. When I was finished, Margaret and I moved her back to the center of the bed.

I staggered out to the couch. I desperately needed to talk to Sophie. I needed to hear her voice and know that she was there. I picked up my phone and once again punched in the first three numbers, then hurriedly disconnected. I couldn't ask Sophie to help me. Not now. My phone clattered onto the table.

Margaret stood across the room watching me.

"I just wanted to hear her voice." Plaintive, weary.

Margaret handed her cell phone to me. "If you just want to hear her voice, she won't know this number."

I stared at Margaret's phone as it rested on my palm. I was so nervous just thinking about calling the familiar number, that my stomach was queasy. Taking a deep breath, I dialed. It was ten p.m., and that late at night Sophie would usually let a call roll to her voicemail. At least I would be able to hear her voice in the recorded message.

The phone rang a couple times, then the sound of dead air, followed by, "Hello?" That familiar, soft tone. "Hello? Who is this?"

I was silent.

"Jensy?"

I covered my mouth and stifled a sob. Margaret took the phone from my hand. "I'm so sorry," she told Sophie. "I must have dialed the wrong number."

When the call ended, I took my hand from my mouth and began to sob. Everything in my life seemed to press down on top of me. It was all too much: Sophie, Fitz, my own emotions and guilt. Margaret sat down next to me and put a protective arm around my shoulders. With that act of kindness, I turned into her arms, and she held me while I cried.

For two days we administered morphine and watched Fitz decline. It was still early in the evening when Margaret roused me from a fitful sleep. Fitz needed another dose of morphine to help ease her pain and calm her agitation. I had not been back on the couch for more than twenty minutes when Margaret called me again. I ran into the bedroom. Fitz's breathing was labored and gasping.

"She's shutting down," Margaret told me. "Talk to her, Jensy. She can still hear you."

"It's okay Fitz. You can let go." I told her, while I rubbed her shoulder. "I love you, Fitz. It's okay to let go." Over and over and over.

Then she was gone.

Thirty

Margaret stayed with me until the hearse had come and gone. She hugged me before she left, and while holding me close, told me, "Call if you need anything. Anything at all." I nodded into her shoulder. "She was a wonderful person."

It was late when I finally closed the door and turned off the porch light. I faced the empty cabin alone, exhausted, and numb. I needed a shower, a change of clothes and something to eat; but most of all I needed sleep. I slumped down on the couch, leaned my head on my trembling hand, and let the tears come once again. Not for myself, I was done crying for myself. I cried for Fitz and a life cut far too short. And I cried for Sophie and the happiness I had stolen from her. When my tears were finally spent, I slept.

Five hours later I awoke to sunshine and birds singing. I showered, put on clean clothes, and made myself eggs, toast, and coffee. I stripped the sheets, picked up towels and dirty clothes and did the laundry. I washed dishes and straightened up the cabin. When everything was clean and in place, I went into the study and picked up the packet with my name on it. Back on the sofa, I repeatedly turned the manila envelope in my hands before I finally unclasped the metal prongs.

Inside there was a copy of Fitz's will, as well as the property deed and all the other papers regarding the cabin. There were statements from a brokerage account, checking account and several savings accounts. Everything had my name on it, transferrable on Fitz's death.

When I had finished reading, I stared through the deck doors at the sun-sparkled water. Though Fitz had briefly talked about her parents' deaths and the litigation and property sale that followed, I had no idea that her estate would be so large. I was overwhelmed.

After several minutes I picked up the last item in the packet; an envelope addressed to me, written in her familiar green, felt-tip pen. I ran my finger over her recognizable script. I opened it carefully and pulled out the thick, cream-colored papers folded neatly in thirds. The writing was shaky, but it was Fitz's.

Dear Jensy,

When you read this note you will know that I have passed. It would be nice for me to think you are reading this at the cabin and that we have seen each other again. I hope so. If not, there are things I want you to know.

First, I am leaving all that I have to you. Please accept this, Jensy, in the spirit in which it is given … with love and gratitude that you have been part of my life … not only once, but twice. I have given my decision a great deal of thought. This is what I want.

Second and most important, I loved you that year in Tolliver. That is the answer to the question you asked, and I would never answer. There was too much to lose … career, community …. You were much too young, and I was much too old; it would have only led to heartache. But know that you filled my heart.

I wanted to tell you these things in Tolliver but talking about it would have made it too real. I just couldn't face my feelings. The night in Tolliver when you kissed me, my world was turned upside down. When I responded to that kiss, I knew I couldn't control my emotions. I tried to distance myself, but it was impossible in that small school. Neither of us could have gone through another year like that — you, pushing for an answer and me, pushing you away. I had to leave.

And then to see you again this spring. My only regret about that afternoon is the pain that it has caused you and Sophie. Sophie is an extraordinary woman, Jensy. But you already know that. She is all the things you said: intelligent, kind, insightful and compassionate with a generous spirit.

What you don't know are the things she said about you. She believes you make her a better person. You make her feel treasured and cherished. Just as she treasures and cherishes you. She feels you make her complete. And I know, that through it all, she still believes these things.

With all my heart, I believe you and Sophie will be able to work through this. You've both told me that's what you want. Work for it Jensy ... harder than you've ever worked for anything. Sophie's worth it ... and so are you.

Fitz

The last three paragraphs were added between Sophie's visit and my arrival later that evening. The writing was scrawling and difficult to read. I couldn't imagine the effort it had taken Fitz to write it. I refolded the letter and put it back in its envelope. Like our last conversation, it was all the things Fitz had never been able to say before. In her last few days, Fitz had shared her greatest gift with me — the gift of her feelings for me. I took that knowledge and put it with the piece of my heart that was reserved for Fitz.

Thirty-one

I reread the packet of papers, had a bite to eat and then, once again, wandered through the cabin. I stood in front of the glass case that contained Fitz's awards: the oldest was an "All-Conference" high school basketball award; the most recent, last year's Teacher of the Year award in the Lincoln City School District.

I spent a long time studying the picture in the center of Fitz's trophy case: "our" photo. My face a picture of unabashed joy as I gazed up at Fitz. That candid shot revealed so much more than the excitement of winning the big game. It was a depiction of the entirety of my feelings for Fitz. My junior year at Tolliver wrapped up in one iconic moment.

As I wandered through the cabin, a voice in the back of my head kept urging me to call Sophie. I found it ironic that when I couldn't call, I wanted to; but now that I needed to call, I was hesitant.

I finally sat on the deck and took out my phone. I let out a long breath. I was reluctant to call because I was terrified of what the final verdict might be. But my purpose had never changed. My purpose was to get Sophie back. Period. But I had no idea what Sophie wanted.

Before I engaged the number, I envisioned the call going through on my personal ring tone: the first bars of "The Look of Love." Sophie had once told me she often waited to hear all the ringtone before she picked up, building her anticipation to hear my voice. My ringtone for Sophie's calls was Gershwin's "The Way You Look Tonight." The song we had danced to at the gala. It was *her* song: classy, elegant, smooth.

Memories washed over me. Sometimes when we were home, but in different rooms, I would phone Sophie and chuckle while I listened to the faint sound of my ring tone combined with her laughter. She was apt to hear from me anywhere, anytime. I would call her while I shoveled snow in the driveway and she did the front walk, or even while she soaked in a bath. My personal favorite was when Sophie stood at the kitchen sink. I would stand five or six feet behind her and complete the call — creeping stealthily forward to put my arms around her while the ringtone was still playing. She would laugh and lean back into my arms. I shook my head and wondered if these things would ever happen again.

Sophie picked up on the first ring. "Jensy." Though it was just my name, her voice was laced with sympathy. She already knew the nature of my call.

At first, I couldn't get the words out. There was a long pause, then I managed: "She's gone."

"I'm sorry, Jensy." The sincere compassion in her voice offered me some comfort.

I could only nod. I cleared my throat and attempted to find my voice. "There are a few things I need to do here. I'll be back on Tuesday or Wednesday." I didn't sound like me. My voice was hoarse and raspy, on the verge of tears. "I need to meet with the attorney, the funeral home and anyone else who might be on her list."

"I understand. Jensy, I really am sorry."

"I know." There was nothing more to say. Nothing I could trust myself to say at that moment. I ended our conversation.

I whiled away time during the afternoon. I found the garage door opener and raised it to see Fitz's SUV parked alongside a beautiful pontoon boat. The boat looked pristine, as if it had been recently cleaned and detailed. Her SUV was shiny and clean as well. A kayak and a canoe were suspended from the rafters. A mountain bike hung on a side wall. Life vests and fishing equipment were in storage containers under a workbench along the back wall. Above the workbench tools were hung and neatly arranged. The interior of the garage spoke of an active, athletic life. Tears stung my eyes. I lowered the door.

I left the deck door open to let fresh air into the cabin and moved to the deck's railing to look out at the lake. The water winked and sparkled in the afternoon sun; a magnificent canopy of trees gave shade to the area of the deck where I was standing. The smell of pine enveloped me. I took a deep breath, held it, and exhaled slowly; my attempt to match the peacefulness of the setting. I felt like I could stand there forever and let the tranquility of the scene wash over me.

But my swirling thoughts intruded on the tranquil setting. There were the thoughts about Fitz; her death, her legacy, and her place in my life. I was still trying to work through her place in my life. But mostly there were my thoughts about Sophie and where we were headed. There was the grim reality that I might have to plan a life without her. Yet, I couldn't seem to move beyond the fact that I knew I needed a plan. Too many emotions still compromised my ability to think.

Out of the corner of my eye I saw sudden movement: a small, black shape darted from tree to tree. Tobie: in glorious pursuit of everything and anything. He ran in circles, barked, sniffed the air, and scouted the shoreline. He rolled in the grass and scurried around the trees.

"Tobie!" I called softly. He stopped immediately and scanned upward. When he finally located me, he headed up the stairs and bounded onto the deck. He squeaked with unbridled happiness, wagged his backside where a tail should have been, and licked my face. After a few moments he wriggled out of my arms, then looked up at me to ask permission to continue his explorations.

"Go ahead," I told him and waved him to the stairs. Off he scampered. As I watched him negotiate the stairs, I heard the car door shut.

I turned back to face the lake. My hands grasped the railing so tightly that the muscles in my arms ached. My stomach heaved and my legs were weak. As much as I wanted to see Sophie, I didn't know if I could face any more bad news. Not today. Not right now. My entire world teetered on the brink of collapse. I gripped the railing tighter to keep my legs from folding underneath me.

"Hey." Sophie's voice floated across the afternoon breeze.

I closed my eyes and whispered. "I want you back, Sophie." I willed her to return that sentiment to me.

Slowly, I turned around. Sophie was leaning against the frame of the sliding door. Her arms were crossed over her chest. The whites of her eyes were red, and her cheeks were blotched: she'd been crying. Looking at Sophie, with her dark-circled eyes, sunken cheeks and belt clinched another notch tighter, was like looking at myself in the mirror. She was so frail, so thin. My arms fell to my sides. My right leg shook uncontrollably.

"I didn't know what to do. I didn't know if I should come or just stay home and wait for you. But I can't do this anymore — neither the silence nor the conversations that don't really solve anything. Those things just hurt both of us. I didn't want to wait." Sophie moved forward until she stood little more than an arm's length away. Her eyes seemed to look everywhere, except at mine. I had no idea what she was thinking or where this was going.

She took a deep, shuddering breath. "There are things I need to say to you." She finally looked at me, and her eyes searched my face. "Please, let me say them. Let me say everything I need to say."

My heart sank.

Another deep breath. "I don't think I've slept since you've been gone. I've thought about truth and our relationship. I've wondered how many other lies or omissions there have been. I've asked myself hundreds of times why you didn't trust me enough to tell me about Lisa Fitzhugh at the beginning of our relationship. And I asked myself at least a hundred more times, why you didn't tell me everything when you saw her again. I've wondered what honesty and truth look like for both of us from now on. I've tried to understand and come to terms with my own actions, and how that affects us. I've thought and worried about whether or not we can go on together." Her hushed tone contradicted the nervousness in her eyes.

"Sophie —" I couldn't help myself, but she held up her hand and stopped me.

"The first time I came up here, I just wanted to confront Lisa Fitzhugh. Instead, she told me how much you loved me. She told me the things you said about me. I just didn't know if I could believe her after what you had done."

Sophie reached up and pinched the bridge of her nose in an effort to stifle any tears. This time I didn't say anything — I didn't even breathe. I simply waited for her to go on.

"I went to see Dee. We sat on the back deck at her house, and I watched her boys, our godchildren, playing catch in the yard while she told me that she and Bob had been headed toward divorce a few years back and how hard they worked to stay together. She told me that some things are worth the effort it takes to save them. She asked me if our relationship was worth that effort."

She looked away from me toward the lake where Tobie was wading on the shore, snapping at minnows. "Then there was Tobie … whining by a different door each night, waiting for you to come home. I'd pick him up and carry him to the couch, but he'd jump down and head right back to the door." Tears brimmed over and her slender fingers wiped them away. "One night I followed him out to the kitchen and laid down next to him. The two of us …

waiting for you to come home."

With that image, my heart broke, and my eyes filled with tears.

Sophie returned her gaze to me and wiped under her eyes one more time. "I'm sorry I haven't been able to talk to you when we so desperately needed to talk. I felt so shattered. It was all I could do to pick up *my* million pieces.

"And I'm so very sorry about what happened with Carol. That was something I never thought I would do. Because of that, I don't know if I can ever trust myself again, let alone forgive myself. I don't know if *you* can really trust me again. I've been so ashamed and disappointed in myself."

Sophie took another step forward, now within easy reach.

"But I *am* able to get up every morning. I go to work, and I actually function. I can even carry out tasks for fifteen minutes without thinking about you." She smiled ruefully and drew a deep breath. "I used to believe that I couldn't live without you. I've come to the realization that I can — if I have to live without you, I can."

Defeated, discouraged, desolate. My head felt fuzzy and light, like I was going to pass out. My heart beat erratically against my rib cage and the pulse in my neck throbbed. I fought back the tears that threatened to burst.

She came within inches of me.

Her voiced trembled and tears glistened in her eyes. "But the truth is … I don't want to live without you. I've been trying to be rational and thoughtful when all I really want to do is think with my heart. I don't want to lose *you*, and I don't want to lose *us*."

Her voice washed over me like a touch: From deep inside me, a gut-wrenching sob broke to the surface. I held out my arms and Sophie moved into my embrace. My left arm circled her; my right hand rested in its familiar place on the nape of her neck. Sophie's arms reached around my back, clutching my T-shirt — holding me tight. Everything I held dear, I held at that moment.

Time seemed to stop as we held each other. Tears clouded my vision. Our breathing gradually relaxed, and then we were breathing as one. Sophie took a deep breath and took in my scent, as she always did whenever we had been apart for several days. "Yup, it's you," she softly breathed against my neck, her tears moistening my skin.

I kissed her temple. "Yup, it's me."

We turned toward the lake and watched as sunshine glimmered low on the water. I put my arm around Sophie's shoulders; her hand held on to my belt loop. "We'll find our way," I told her. She put her cheek against my shoulder and nodded.

We turned slowly and headed into the cabin. I knew there would be many hours spent piecing our lives back together. Many difficult conversations were yet to come. I didn't know if we would be able to survive as a couple, as much as I wanted it. But now I had hope. The one thing I did know was that my entire adult life had been about "home"— and, beyond any doubt, Sophie was my home.

I had no sooner closed the deck door than I heard a whining and scratching from outside. Tobie. As soon as I opened the door, he cannonballed inside.

The three of us.

Together.

18642142R00179